A DIFFERENT LIFE—WHAT IF?

A MARTINIERE MULTIVERSE NOVEL—A DIFFERENT LIFE
BOOK ONE

JOYCE REYNOLDS-WARD

CONTENTS

PARTIAL MARTINIERE FAMILY TREE
(US/NORTH AMERICA)
(HIGH-LEVEL HEIRS ONLY)

LOUIS—DONNA***

SAUL   PHILIP
 RENATE   ANGELICA
  (via IVF, wife of Philip)   (via IVF, wife of Saul)
  Joseph (Joey)*   Gabriel (Gabe, Gabie)*
 ANGELICA   RENATE
  (natural, spouse)   (natural, spouse)
  Louisa (Weeza)   Justine (Tine)**

*Joseph and Gabriel were raised by their mothers' husbands until they were sixteen, per negotiation between Saul, Philip, and Donna regarding who would become the Martiniere after the death of Louis. Gabriel lived with Philip for two years; Joseph lived with Saul for two months.

**Gabriel brought his half-sister Justine to live with Saul and Angelica when he was eighteen and Justine was twelve.

***Other children of Louis and Donna include French residents Gerard (Gerry), Madeline, and Jeannette; British resident Peter; and Canadian resident Melusine.

OTHER MARTINIERES OF IMPORTANCE

David Martiniere—Gerard's son, married to Therese. (France)
Arthur (Artie) Martiniere—Louis's cousin. (France)
Charles Martiniere—Arthur's son. (France)
Christopher (Chris) Martiniere—Peter's son. (Britain)
Mark Martiniere—Peter's son. (Britain)
Fiona Martiniere—daughter of Mark, sister of Kendra. (Britain)
Kendra Martiniere—daughter of Mark, sister of Fiona, married to Scott. (Britain)
Piotr Vygotsky—married to Arthur's sister Katrine. (Canada, formerly Russia)
Sergei (Serg) Vygotsky—son of Piotr and Katrine. (Canada)

CHAPTER 1

THAT EXCELLENT GRANT CANDIDATE
APRIL, 2029

GABE

Gabriel Martiniere sprawled on the living room couch in the Corvallis condo belonging to his half-sisters, studying the four files projected in front of him. Oregon State University was the last stop in his assigned series of interviews to determine the finalists for the Martiniere Grant. This scheduling was due in part to a desire to spend the weekend with Louisa and Justine afterward. But it was also because Dr. Asa Green's agricultural robotics program was one of the finest in the United States.

Saving the best for last.

Meanwhile, his cousins were surveying elsewhere in the world. But as a high-level Martiniere male heir born in the United States—North America was Gabe's assigned interview area.

And the competition to become the Martiniere-in-waiting, second in charge of both the privately-held Martiniere Group and the far-flung, enormous Martiniere Family, came down to this year's Grant recipients. The quality of the prospects that Gabe and his cousins discovered—and hopefully recruited—to advance the

Martiniere Group's famous agricultural technology programs, would make that final determination.

Gabe scratched his freshly-shaven chin as he considered his line of questions. He was *oh-so-close* to becoming the Martiniere-in-waiting. The right Grant candidate could put him over the top—yes, Jeff Swait was good, but if he had a second, equally good if not better candidate—*two* candidates capable of winning Grants would clinch the position.

"Deep thoughts, Gabie?" Justine, the sister he shared a father with, entered the kitchen, still in her pajamas and robe.

"Just reviewing today's interview candidates."

"Ooh. Let me look." Justine poured herself a cup of coffee and picked up the carafe to top off Gabe's cup. "Unless this is super-secret Martiniere boy business."

Gabe snorted. He didn't approve of the Group and Family structures that adhered to the old French Salic Law, excluding women from major leadership positions. Thankfully, most of his cousins who would eventually become Group and Family leaders agreed with him. And the ones who didn't—

"As if the Martiniere Grant candidates are super-secret from Family, especially my sisters," he said. "Besides, I figure you and Weeza know some of these people. I'd appreciate your insights."

"Hmm." Justine returned the carafe to the coffeemaker and sidled in beside Gabe. "Let me see. Oliver Reed, ag economics." Her major, bolstered by a minor in accounting. "Smart, but soft-spoken. Tends toward the Chicago school of economic thought, so a conservative; politically leans toward the Honest Republicans. Not an innovator."

"Noted." He wanted innovators.

"And he's a bit of an ass."

"*Definitely* noted." He didn't need anyone who might prove to be difficult.

"Linda Coates. Ag robotics," Justine mused. "Under other

circumstances, she'd be an excellent candidate. How many can you choose, Gabie?"

"I've already selected an ag robotics guy, Jeff Swait, from the University of Arkansas. He's developing a biobot targeting moisture retention in a particular strain of dryland rice. Agronomy and robotics combined. Any candidate from either category needs to be stellar."

"Linda's not your woman, then." Justine chewed her lip. "Perrin Buhler is agronomy and he's not that stellar. Nice guy. But." She pointed to the last file. "Ruby Barkley. You want stellar, Gabie, she's your woman. She's the *under other circumstances* I meant. Linda is good. Ruby's better. And they're good friends. If you could take them both—"

"Unfortunately, I can't. Tell me more." Gabe leaned back and sipped his coffee.

He had already fingered Ruby Barkley as his first choice—not just his own opinion. When the cousins had reviewed potential finalist candidates in Paris last week, with Cousin Arthur and Uncle Gerard, heads of the French Martiniere subsidiaries that dominated the Martiniere Group, Arthur and Gerard had prioritized Ruby Barkley. She showed a pattern of innovative bot design in various competitions that intrigued Arthur, and her background in the arid plateau country of Northeastern Oregon might translate well to the Southwest Asian markets the Group sought to develop, especially in the area of Ukraine post-war recovery. That interested Gerard.

Besides, Dr. Green had highlighted Barkley as one of his *special* candidates.

There was one huge problem, however. Barkley was older than the others, and she wasn't a junior yet. Normally, unless the recommending department supervisor designated a candidate as *special*, they needed to be juniors, with the Grant financing a senior project.

Ruby Barkley was twenty-three and still a sophomore, four years younger than Gabe. She had a history of irregular college attendance, though that could also be explained by her family circumstances.

Orphan, raised by grandparents with failing health. High grades except for two terms, when she dropped out.

"Weeza and I know Ruby," Justine said. "She works at Lora Smith's barn."

"I saw that in her bio." Another point that caught his attention. Gabe and his sisters had ridden with Smith when she was based in Los Angeles—former Olympic medalist in eventing. Additionally, Lora had bailed Gabe out of a very dark time in his life. A positive factor for Ruby Barkley, because Lora Smith didn't hire idiots, even if all Barkley did for her was muck stalls and feed horses. Unlikely, given Barkley's background.

"What does she do for Lora?" he continued.

"She's pretty damn good, Gabie. First one up on Lora's greenies. Lora doesn't ride them herself anymore—that's what Ruby does."

Gabe raised his brows at that. "Thoroughbreds or warmbloods?"
"Both."

"Hmm." A talented horsewoman, capable of managing both the sensitive and the powerful horses in Lora's training program.

Well, Barkley *was* a rodeo queen, and impressive in that arena as well.

First runner-up Miss Rodeo America. Miss Rodeo Oregon. A fistful of other rodeo crowns, as well as a competitor in barrel racing and breakaway roping. Ruby Barkley was part of a world that intrigued Gabe—most of his equestrian experience involved riding jumpers and eventers—but he was curious about rodeo.

"She's also concerned about Weeza and her horse," Justine continued.

"Oh?"

"Yeah." Justine rolled her eyes. "Ruby's doing most of the lessons with Weeza, and she's a good instructor."

"What's her concern?" Though Gabe thought he knew, from Weeza's history with horses.

"You know Weeza and her attraction to difficult horses. At least Midnight adores her when she handles him on the ground. Not a mean bone in his body, but he's an aggressive jumper with a lot of scope, more than Weeza should be handling, and she's gonna get hurt. Ruby tried to talk her out of buying Midnight, and spends time schooling him before Weeza gets on."

"All right," Gabe sighed. Just as he thought. Weeza was being ambitious and overestimating her ability again. "Good thing you told me to bring my boots, so I can warm him up for her tomorrow, hmm?"

"I didn't want to make a big deal about our riding there, especially since I knew Ruby is a Martiniere Grant candidate—wasn't sure if she was a finalist." Justine raised her brows. "Good morning, Weeza."

"What's up with Ruby?" His other half-sister, Louisa, the one with whom he shared a mother, joined them. She was already dressed for the day.

"Martiniere Grant finalists. She's one of Gabie's interviewees," Justine said.

"Oh, goody!" Louisa grinned as she poured herself a cup of coffee. Then she leaned against the kitchen counter, her expression becoming more solemn. "Before that. Gabriel, I have urgent news best heard from me rather than other Family members—or the media."

There were several things this could be, and none of them good since his sister called him *Gabriel*, not *Gabie*, the nickname both sisters used for him.

Gabe tensed. "I'm assuming it's not that great."

Louisa frowned into her coffee cup before looking back up. "It's Mindy."

Gabe winced at the mention of Miranda Cathcart-Rogers, his ex-girlfriend. Mindy had dropped him for cousin Joey, the other half-brother of his sisters.

"Has she discovered the dark side of Mr. Sexually Exciting and Innovative?" It was all Gabe could do to keep his tone even and not bitter.

"It seems that perhaps Joey is a bit *too* exciting and innovative for Mindy's tastes."

"I wouldn't know. I blocked her from every damn piece of social media I could think of." That was *after* Gabe caught Mindy screwing Joey in *their* apartment, in *their* bed, six months ago. Followed by the epic argument, the dramatic breakup, the gossip media. "What happened?"

"Mindy walked in on one of Joey's orgies. Just last night."

Justine flinched. "How bad?"

"The worst."

Gabe and Justine's eyes met, their lips tightening, shared memories immediately coming to mind.

"I suppose Daddy-fucking-dearest was also part of it," Justine snapped, giving voice to Gabe's thoughts.

Louisa nodded. "And, unfortunately, your father went after Mindy."

"I hope to hell she filed assault charges," Gabe growled.

"It's Mindy. What do you think? Of course not. She messaged me begging to have you call her, Gabie. She wants you back."

"Nope," Gabe said, popping the p. "How long before she decides once more that I work too hard, travel too much, and care more about the Family and the Group than her? All she's interested in is the prestige of dating *Gabriel Martiniere.* Not about me. Gabe. The real person. She chose Joey. I warned her about him when she started showing an interest in Joey last summer, but she chose him."

The last words Mindy had said to Gabe before he left her for good had been *you're boring and never here, Gabie. How do you expect me to stay entertained when you're always working?*

Unfaithful as a girlfriend—unfaithful as a spouse. No. He'd seen enough of that lifestyle in the two years he spent in his sperm donor Philip's house. And after sixteen years of growing up under the guidance of Philip's older twin Saul, who passionately loved his wife Angelica, Gabe's mother, the casual infidelity exhibited by Philip and his late wife Renate wasn't something Gabe accepted. He wanted *love* and *respect* in a relationship, not *transactional* and *what can you do for me this week?*

No more, Gabe vowed, as he had ever since he left Mindy. He would *not* replicate the life of his damned sperm donor.

If it took him forever, he'd find someone who loved *him* as much as his mother loved Saul. Someone he could love as deeply as Saul loved Angelica.

"Gabie." Louisa's voice held a concerned note. "You okay? You zoned out there for a moment."

Gabe shivered. "Just—remembering."

The sad thing was that he *had* entertained the possibility that Mindy was *the one.* He had spent several nights drinking with Saul and pouring out his heart after this last breakup. Saul, though actually his uncle and Philip's older twin, was more his father than Philip could ever be.

Forget about Mindy right now.

She was a distraction and a liability to his campaign to become Martiniere-in-waiting.

Though—Gabe supposed he'd better do something about Philip. His biofather facing potential criminal charges could pose a problem for his future goals. Philip had been defanged from any real power in the Family and the Group, but he was still capable of poisoning his biological son's prospects. Especially since he was going into politics with that damned Real Truthers political party. Rumor had him planning a Presidential campaign.

That was a subject to take up with Justine later, since Philip *was* their father. *Much* later. Maybe tomorrow.

"Sorry to be the bearer of bad news." Genuine regret filled Louisa's voice.

"I appreciate finding out from you rather than someone else. Thanks."

"You're welcome." Louisa crossed the room to look over Gabe's shoulder. Her tone changed. "So. The Grant prospects—and you said Ruby's on the list? Excellent."

"What do *you* think about her?" He was happy to change the subject. Louisa's field of study was ag media. Her input would give him an idea about who might be most media-friendly. Promotion was an important part of the Martiniere Grant.

"Well, she *was* the Miss Rodeo America first runner-up the year she competed," Louisa said. "I've not seen her videos, but given that Ruby's financials are pretty damn tight, I'd say she had *something* going for her above and beyond horsemanship and appearance in her competition for rodeo crowns. Level-headed. When she wants, she can project a presence. Pretty dedicated to anything she chooses to do. And she's a damn good instructor."

Gabe hesitated. Was it a good time to ask about Louisa's latest horse? *Probably not.* "Cousin Artie and Uncle Gerry like some of her bot design competition work."

"So is the decision today?" Louisa asked.

Gabe nodded. "I'm bringing the winner or winners and their significant others to dinner at the Belvedere, along with Dr. Green and—I hope both of you."

"Wouldn't miss it," Justine said.

"Same here," Louisa echoed.

"Bringing someone?"

"Donald, of course," Justine said, a smile sneaking onto her lips at the mention of her fiancé Donald Atwood. "He's flying in this afternoon."

"And Ginny for me," Louisa said.

Gabe raised his brows. "Are you and Ginny getting serious, Weeza?"

Virginia Westley had been frequently escorting Louisa to Martiniere functions over the past year. Gabe wasn't sure how he felt about Ginny. Too focused on society for his taste, but on the other hand, she made his sister smile. Weeza needed that in her life. Too many of her relationships had gone bad—just like his, but for different reasons. Weeza didn't have the shadows hanging over her that he and Justine shared. Thank God.

"Maybe," Louisa said. "And what about *you*, Gabie?"

He laughed, hollowly. "My job is to pay for the whole thing. Dr. Green's my date, if anyone is."

"Poor Gabie," Louisa sighed. She kissed his brow. "And I have to rush off. Early class. But don't you worry. Tine and I will find you someone."

Another hollow laugh. "Don't waste your time, Weeza. I work too hard and travel too much for any woman's interest. At least according to Mindy."

Louisa shook her head and left.

Justine glanced at him, her lips pursed, brown eyes hard and glittering. "Damn, that bitch really did do a number on your head, didn't she, Gabie?"

He shifted uneasily. Justine in this mood was too reminiscent of Philip.

"I was a fool. Expected too much. I don't know that any person can put up with what I'll have to do should I become the Martiniere-in-waiting."

Justine exhaled through her teeth. "That's bullshit, Gabie. You don't work any harder than either me or Donald. Not every woman demands every second of your attention."

"Yeah, but—"

"No *yeah buts*, Gabie." She pressed her lips together, shaking her head. "My best brother deserves to have someone who cares about him. Who loves you for who you really are. And that person is *definitely* not Miranda Catherine Cathcart-Rogers."

"No, but she was a reasonable compromise. I thought."

"A reasonable compromise like my mother Renate was, when our fucking father couldn't have Angelica? No, Gabie. You saw where that led, for both of them. You deserve someone who loves you."

"Eh, I don't have time for it right now." He rubbed his face. "Maybe once this Martiniere-in-waiting piece is settled."

"Maybe," Justine echoed.

But something in her voice made him suspicious.

It was one thing for his sister Louisa to entertain the concept of matchmaking for him.

However, if his sister Justine took up the campaign...he was in trouble.

Maybe.

CHAPTER 2

A CRUCIAL INTERVIEW

RUBY

Ruby Barkley made one last stop in the bathroom before going to her interview with Gabriel Martiniere. The remaining step before she became a Martiniere Grant finalist—and, by God, she *was* going to win this award.

The quick look at the ranch financials during Spring Break, before Gramps switched the screen—that told Ruby she had no alternative *but* to win.

Damn it, Gramps. I could have postponed college for another year. Especially given how secretive he had been about the debt.

Ruby bit her lip.

Focus. Prepare. This is like a queen competition interview.

She began the routine of checking her clothing, makeup, and hair. Martiniere was allegedly a sharp dresser, so she needed to make a good first impression.

Check.

A second review.

Turn to look over your shoulder, make sure your skirt isn't askew and there's no mud or hair hanging anywhere.

Check.

Face forward, look from toes to chin, chin to toes.

Dark blue shoes to match her suit, no dust or mud from the barn smearing them. Cheap copies of expensive shoes, the best she could afford, even though her best friend Linda had offered to loan her a pair. No bulge or gap from skirt pockets. Blouse lay smooth under her jacket, no straining at any buttons. Lucky silver locket containing the picture of Gramps and Granma Ryder gleaming on her chest—she had polished the locket and its chain last night. Granma's pearl studs in her ears.

Check.

Hair and makeup.

Long dark auburn hair pulled back and restrained in a silver clasp that had been donated to her during rodeo queen days, carefully-curled tendrils around her face. Makeup smooth, enough to mask freckles. Ruby bared her teeth—no lipstick on them.

Check.

She exhaled.

Showtime.

This was no worse than competing for a queen title. She needed to keep telling herself that, not think about the money at stake.

Five hundred thousand dollars if she became a Grant winner. Enough to pay off the loans against her grandparents' Double R Ranch. Maybe enough to develop a rudimentary biobot lab at the ranch, so she could work on the senior project the Grant was supposed to fund. Half that amount if she became a finalist, but didn't make it into the top five in this year's competition. Still enough to pay off Gramps's debt, and in that case, no senior project obligation.

Damn it, Gramps. You didn't need to risk losing the ranch!

Granma's cancer was finally in remission, but—for how long? Remission had happened before. And then the cancer came back.

Forget it for now, Ruby. You don't dare come off as desperate. Especially with that privileged ass Ollie as your competition.

Focus on her vision, instead. The potential senior project, two years off. Nanobiobots capable of monitoring and reporting micro-conditions within a field while deploying trace elements of supplements, cultivated in growboxes that any farmer or rancher could manage and transport without the need for specialized lab equipment. Nanobiobots that degraded into field nutrients during the fallow season. Over the course of multiple years, the nanobiobots would enrich soil, improve moisture retention, and reduce water and supplement usage while increasing carbon capture.

Complex, but doable, according to Dr. Green. It might take her years to fulfill her vision, but still within probability, if she had enough financing to do it.

Wouldn't prototyping this idea be worthy of a Martiniere Grant?

Believe in it.

Ruby headed toward the ag robotics department offices where Martiniere was holding his interviews. No one sat in the waiting area, and Nan, the receptionist, was out—so what did that mean? Ruby stepped up to the retina display security access. Once inside the office complex, she went to the suite where Martiniere was at work.

If you're chosen, Martiniere will take you out to dinner to discuss the next steps in the process, Dr. Green had told them yesterday. *He could choose one, two, or none of you.*

Could it be that Perry and Ollie *hadn't* made the cut? Or had one or both of them stepped out for fresh air before going to dinner with Martiniere? Ruby checked her phone for the time. The interview order had been Ollie, Perry, Linda—then her.

Linda was interviewing now.

Breathe. Breathe. What was the best approach to pitch Martiniere on her concept?

Creativity, innovation, efficiency, and applicant financial need are the primary selection criteria. Stated up front in the Martiniere Grant application.

Her research into the Martiniere Group's projections showed expansion into dryland grain cultivation markets in Europe, Asia, and Africa as a potential five-year goal. Well, her experience growing up in the arid grain lands of Northeastern Oregon meant she knew something about that type of climate, right?

Homestead field. Talk about the mapping work you've done on Homestead, if you get a chance.

After all, even though there had been no money for her to attend college during Granma's struggles with cancer, she'd used the time to survey the microclimates of the most difficult field on the Double R, in preparation for developing her biobot.

Wouldn't that count?

The door to the inner office opened. Her best friend and classmate Linda Coates came out.

"Whew," she sighed. "He's tough."

Ruby's gut tightened.

Stop it!

"How did you do?"

Linda shook her head. "No invite, just a thank you and a request to keep the Martiniere Group in mind when I'm sending out job applications next year."

"Damn. I'm sorry, Linda."

"Eh, well, I got put off my stride from the beginning." Linda crossed the room and leaned in close to Ruby, fanning herself with one hand. "He's *hot*, Ruby. That distracted me," she whispered. "Hotter than his pictures. Oh. My. Lanta."

"What about the others? Do you know how they did?"

As for looks—forewarned was forearmed—not that Martiniere's appearance would make an impression on *her*. He was way, *way* out of Ruby's league. Fantasy, perhaps, but nothing more than that.

Linda had money—banker's daughter. She might have a chance with someone like Gabriel Martiniere. And her brother-in-law, Clyde Newsome, was rising in the Real Truthers party. Linda was much more likely to snag herself a rich husband—not like Ruby, tied down to the Double R and elders who needed her.

Linda snickered. "Perry told me he didn't make it—and that Ollie stormed out without saying anything to him."

The door opened again.

"Ms. Barkley?" Gabriel Martiniere stood in the doorway.

"Yes." Ruby inhaled sharply.

"Good luck," Linda whispered. "Looks like you're the only one who has a chance at the Martiniere Grant this year."

"I don't have it yet," Ruby murmured, before facing Martiniere.

"You will," Linda said.

"Come on in," Martiniere said, stepping aside, gesturing.

"Thank you," Ruby said. She walked past him, quickly glancing to get an impression of the man.

Gabriel Martiniere *was* attractive, and well-dressed. Neatly-fitted double-breasted blue suit just a shade darker than hers, that accented his lean, athletic frame. Perfectly adjusted gray tie with matching pocket square. Carefully-styled dark hair, and smoldering dark brown eyes. Either tan or naturally brown-skinned—she thought the latter, probably Hispanic. He looked like a couple of her favorite streaming stars who were Hispanic.

He bowed to Ruby and she reciprocated—then noticed his footwear as she straightened up.

Well-polished Western boots, with pointed toes.

Noconas, I'll bet.

Almost identical to the pair one of the judges for Miss Rodeo America had worn.

All right. She could handle this. Think of Gabriel Martiniere as a wealthy rodeo patron, perhaps even a bronc rider.

Martiniere sat in one of the chairs and crossed his legs. She eased herself into the other, crossing her ankles and resting her hands on the chair's arms as she sat up straight, like she would on horseback.

"So. Ms. Ruby Barkley." Martiniere's voice was a pleasant tenor. "You have an *interesting* resume."

"Which part?" she parried. "My rodeo history? My bot competitions? Or something else, Mr. Martiniere?"

Keep your little bit of sass going, Ruby's queen advisor and neighbor Vickie Chandler had recommended when Ruby consulted with her about this interview. *You dulled it down for Miss Rodeo America, and that may have made the difference between the title and being first runner-up. Martiniere is Corporate. They want a little bit of an edge, will prefer to see you as a go-getter. Keep it polite, but don't be afraid to show some spark.*

That earned her a quick smile. "Call me Gabe, please. And yes—all of it." He interlaced his fingers. "I have a couple of concerns that I want to address right away. One is your college attendance history. The other is your age. You are older than the other candidates, and still a sophomore. How do I know that you'll be able to fulfill the terms of the Grant?"

"Both are due to my financial and family circumstances," Ruby said.

"Dr. Green mentioned that you had a special situation."

"My grandmother developed cancer in the spring of my freshman year of college—that's why that term's grades are problematic. I had to leave school partway through fall term of my sophomore year to help my grandfather at home. I tried to come back in the spring a year later but—things happened." She took a deep breath. "I had to repeat my sophomore year when I was finally able to return. That's why I'm an older sophomore."

"Um-hmm. You were orphaned at six and raised by your grandparents?"

She was *not* going to tell him how that happened.

Talk about doing Miss Rodeo Oregon while Granma had cancer instead.

"Yes. I almost resigned my title as Miss Rodeo Oregon when my grandmother got sick, but she insisted that I continue, including competing to become Miss Rodeo America. She wanted to contend for Miss Rodeo Oregon when she was younger. Circumstances kept her from doing that. My winning that title fulfilled one of her dreams for me. However, the combination of my competition and her medical expenses meant I needed to stay home, in order to save more money to continue my education. I spent that time micromapping soil analysis techniques to a difficult field on the family ranch, as well as taking in bookkeeping clients. Which I still do."

That earned her an eyebrow raise. "You work for Lora Smith, manage bookkeeping clients, and carry a heavy academic load?"

"Yes. Whatever it takes to keep myself out of debt." *Or at least anything above what Gramps has already taken on.* "Within reason, of course—not into dealing drugs or selling my body. But I *am* aggressively pursuing any option that will defray my educational costs, including the Martiniere Grant."

A shallow nod in acknowledgement. "You're not afraid to work."

She let a brief smile touch her lips. "I'm ranch-raised, and my family would be best characterized as land-poor for well over a hundred years." *At least the Ryders. The Barkleys are—something else.* "That means long hours and hard work in lieu of money. We look better on paper than we really are."

Martiniere rested his chin on his clasped hands. Those smoldering dark brown eyes studied Ruby further, sending a curious warmth through her.

"What are your long-term goals?"

"Graduation." She would *not* bring up paying off the ranch loan. Not unless it became necessary. "Prototyping and eventually selling my integrated nanobiobot and growbox systems. Taking over the ranch when my grandparents die."

He tapped his chin with his forefingers. "Nothing more ambitious than that?"

"Even with the Martiniere Grant, I won't have money to burn." Ruby allowed a tart edge to slide into her voice. "By the time my responsibilities to my grandparents are done, I'm likely to be too old and out of touch with research developments to aspire to anything greater. You said it yourself, Mr. Martiniere. I'm an older candidate for the Grant. That will work against me once my obligations no longer exist."

How dare he imply I'm limiting my horizons? I don't have a lot of options, Mr. Fucking Martiniere. I don't have your billions.

He winced. "Call me Gabe and—point taken. Your dedication to your family is commendable."

"My grandparents didn't have to take me in!" she snapped. "My father's family had younger relatives who were willing, and my life would have been much worse with them." Her voice turned bitter, almost too much of an edge, but *damn it*. This was her reality. "I owe quite a bit to my grandparents. It's *my* responsibility to ensure that they are cared for. My mother was their only surviving child. My uncles were in the army, and died in Afghanistan. They left no heirs. So it's just me."

"I understand." His voice softened. "But if your grandparents were provided for and you could do anything you wanted—what would be your dream?"

She exhaled. "I don't dare let myself dream, Mr. Martiniere."

Dreaming hurt. And five hundred thousand dollars just provided the seed for a new life based at the Double R.

Gramps and Granma needed her. And she wasn't a fucking billionaire.

"*Call me Gabe*, damn it!" Then he sighed and pinched the bridge of his nose, leaning back in his chair and slumping. "Look. I'm sorry. I'm being nosey and intimidating, and you're reflecting that back at me. What I'm trying to get at is—all right. Look," he repeated. "My situation is very different from yours in some respects, and not so much in others. I'm locked into competing to become the Martiniere-in-waiting because—well—my parents and the Family expect it of me. But if I could do whatever I wanted—I'd be doing carbon capture field research. Pursue a doctorate. However. The Family has the resources to hire people to do that work, and not so many candidates who would be useful and effective serving as the Martiniere, the head of the Group and the Family. Especially in this era."

Three mentions of *the family* in that speech, and Ruby could swear she heard a capital "F" in *family* each time. All right. Perhaps he understood her situation after all. Sort of. He didn't need to think about providing for frail elders. But following a path set forth by family obligations, perhaps—

Gabe dropped his hand. "I'm sorry. What I'm trying to get at is this—if you were free to do as you pleased, and the Group made you an employment or consulting offer—would you be at all interested? Would you pursue further education, especially if it were part of your compensation?"

"If I did not have obligations—then hell yes." The vehemence in her voice startled Ruby.

"And, in your current situation, if an employment or consulting offer included not just further education, but care support for your dependent family members, so that you could work away from the ranch without worry?"

"Yes, but—that's unlikely to happen."

No. She had to be dreaming. She wasn't hearing this. The prospect that Gabriel Martiniere held out to her was just a fantasy, a dream, and shortly she'd be waking back up to the reality of her confined life.

"Possibilities exist," Gabe said. "And your integrated nanobiobot and growbox concept is exactly the sort of possibility that could open those doors for you. Especially if you design it to be effective for low-tech farmers to use in extreme conditions in less-wealthy countries."

She stared at him. "But Mr. Mar—*Gabe*—surely I'm not the only one with such ideas."

"Ms. Barkley—Ruby—the combination of your vision and your experience in Northeastern Oregon dryland farming is a skill set which is going to be critical in this next decade," Gabe said. "And if I become the Martiniere-in-waiting, I intend to recruit women and men like you to face the climate change challenges ahead. Even if that means I fund care services for dependent family members so that my recruits can work without concerns."

Ruby shook her head. "That's expensive."

"I'm a fucking billionaire. There's no way in hell that I'm ever going to be able to spend it all. Why not do something positive with my money?" Gabe rubbed his face. "We're facing a climate crisis. If getting the right people in place means I pay for their peace of mind about dependent relatives, then so be it." He leaned forward and rested his elbows on his knees. "Since *that's* out of the way, let's talk about your ideas. Tell me more about your design concepts. They're quite ambitious."

A smile lit up his face, and her stomach flopped. Damn. Linda was right. Gabriel Martiniere—*Gabe*—was hot. Especially when his expression softened and he gazed at her with *those brown eyes.*

Ruby drew a deep breath, and began to describe design challenges.

She lost track of time as she described her bot ideas, parrying Gabe's inquiries. No doubt in her mind as they spoke—he *could* do quite a bit in the field should he go into research. Talking to him was like brainstorming with Dr. Green. Ruby snapped up a projection and started taking research refinement notes about the nanobiobot as they spoke—oh *God*, it would be wonderful to work with someone like this man.

If that were even the faintest of possibilities.

A rap on the door startled both of them.

Dr. Green opened the door. "Gabe? It's time to leave." He glanced at Ruby. "So—is she?"

That big grin that Ruby was growing to like spread across Gabe's face.

"Yes, Asa." His smile expanded further as he looked at her. "If you've not already figured it out, Ruby—you are a Martiniere Grant finalist. Will you be able to join us for dinner, along with my sisters? And do you have a significant other that we should invite?"

Wow. Now that this was a reality, she didn't know what to say.

"I can join you for dinner," she said. "And there's not a significant other."

"Marvelous." Oh, *that smile.* He rose and offered her his arm. "Asa, you and I have a lovely companion tonight. Along with my sisters and their significant others."

Dr. Green smiled. "Always entertaining to have dinner with Justine and Louisa."

"Wait, what?" She knew that Justine and Louisa were Martinieres, but— "I thought they were cousins. They ride with Lora."

"I know," Gabe said. "They told me that this morning. Justine and Louisa are cousins to each other—but Justine and I share a father, while Louisa and I share a mother." He waved a hand. "Complicated. You'll learn more about the Family later."

There it was again. Family with a capital F.

Ruby took Gabe's arm, her head whirling.

Had her world really changed this much?

Martiniere Grant finalist. She just had to hope that Gramps kept things together until June, when the funds were distributed. The sooner she could get the obligation to Zingter off of the Double R's books, the better.

Ruby excused herself and ducked into the bathroom as Gabe and Dr. Green paused outside of Dr. Green's office, while Dr. Green went in to get something for Gabe.

She texted Linda.

—*Made it.*

—*I knew you could,* Linda sent back. *Congratulations.*

Ruby exhaled, looking into the mirror.

First step accomplished. Now to win the full Grant.

She set her lips firmly together.

She was *not* going to think about how hot Gabriel Martiniere was. Even if she won the full Grant, no matter what, she wasn't in his league.

Martiniere was simply a very nice, polite, *brilliant* man with excellent manners and ambitious goals. He had just given her an opportunity to move beyond the Double R someday.

If only he wasn't—

No, Ruby. He's out of your league, and that is that.

CHAPTER 3
FAMILY COMPLICATIONS
APRIL, 2029

GABE

There was *something* about Ruby Barkley, all right. Once Gabe got her talking about research—oh yes, he could definitely see her working in the Group's labs. She had relaxed and even allowed a real grin to break through.

But damn it. Her refusal to consider other options early in the interview irritated him. That outright resignation to fate, to family demands—maybe he had gone too far in revealing his own ambivalence about the Family. And yet that sharing of his situation seemed to have broken her resistance to thinking about options. He had to look into her updated family financials, not just hers, because that would be a key to hiring *this* candidate.

And Ruby—*Ruby* now, not *Barkley*—walked demurely to the SUV between Gabe and Asa Green, holding his arm. Oh, he could just see presenting her at the Grant announcement dinner in June. Could imagine her as *the* first-place winner.

If he could secure a commitment from her to work for the Group upon her graduation, then the Martiniere-in-waiting title was his.

Definitely so. He didn't dare let any competitor get their hands on Ruby Barkley, especially Zingter Enterprises. Oh, what she could do once she was in the Martiniere Group labs…he might be lucky enough to work with her.

His pleasant contemplation of the future abruptly halted as they approached the two waiting SUVs. His security held several paparazzi at bay, and he spotted the faint haze of a Martiniere dronecam blocker field.

"Mr. Martiniere!" someone called as they approached the SUV. "Is it true that your father Philip Martiniere attacked Miranda Cath-cart-Rogers?"

"No comment," Gabe snapped, even as his gut tightened.

Mindy's gone public. Damn it, damn it, damn it!

Asa moved slightly ahead of Ruby, blocking one dronecam shot.

"Is this your new girlfriend?" another reporter hollered.

"*No comment,*" Gabe growled as security clustered around them.

"I'm driving," said Lance Helgessen, the head of his security team.

"Understood," Gabe said. Standard procedure when paparazzi were involved—normally, he drove himself.

Asa entered the SUV's second row of seats. Gabe helped Ruby inside, then sat next to her.

"Sorry," he said as they drove off. "Ex-girlfriend drama."

Maybe he needed to have that talk with Justine about their father *sooner* rather than *later*. Like tonight, after dinner. But Saul would need to be involved as well, and that could blow up every damn plan he had for this weekend. The pleasant time he had planned with his sisters, and checking out Louisa's latest folly of a horse purchase—

What a damned mess.

Gabe sighed and slumped against the back of his seat, pinching the bridge of his nose again, feeling the beginning twinges of a headache coming on.

"I'm sorry," Ruby said.

He shook his head. "It's not your problem. Just mine."

"How late are we going to be?" Ruby asked. "I'd like to tell my grandparents—if there isn't an embargo. They go to bed pretty early."

"The official announcement will go out on Sunday from Paris, but yes. Go ahead and call them right now, especially with these leeches lurking about. Let them know you haven't suddenly acquired a billionaire boyfriend," he said.

Ruby gave him a sideways glance. "I don't think they'd jump to that assumption very quickly."

"Good," Gabe said. And that suggested something else about Ruby Barkley—was she coming off of a problematic breakup, like him, or was she more interested in women, like Louisa?

Gabriel, it doesn't matter. She is a potential employee, not a date. Remember that.

Not that he was ready to date anyone, not after the shred job Mindy had done on him.

Besides, he needed Ruby in the labs more than he needed another girlfriend to blow up in his face.

He closed his eyes as Ruby spoke to her grandparents—and then remembered. His other weekend obligation. Damn, this business with Mindy really *did* have him rattled. Normally, he wouldn't forget about this aspect of managing a Grant finalist.

"Ruby?"

"Just a minute, Gramps," she said. "Yes?"

"We need to meet with your grandparents as soon as possible," he said. "Once the announcement's made, they'll need further security support. Maybe even before then. They need to be briefed about what happens from this point on."

"I have lessons tomorrow and it's an eight-hour drive—"

"We can fly out and back in a day."

"But there's no commercial flights to Lakeside—"

"Private jet. We'll have several hours at the ranch. That should be enough. Does Sunday work?"

"Gramps? Gabriel Martiniere wants to meet with us on Sunday, to discuss security issues." A pause. "No. He's flying us out." Ruby raised her brows and glanced at him. "Gabe. We would be coming into Thunder State Airport?"

"Yes." It was small but doable—he had already checked the ability for his corporate jet to fly into the closest airstrip, just like he had with the other candidates' families. No possibility for an electric charging station, but maybe the solar cells on the plane could do the job. He'd burned far too much fuel this week already. "Security will drive us. They are already en route to Lakeside. Standard procedure."

"All right. Gramps, we'll have a ride to the house." Another pause. "Gabe, it works. About what time?"

"Ten o'clock."

She nodded. "I'll tell Lora after I finish with Gramps."

"Good." He had already messaged his cousin Serg Vygotsky, second-in-command of Martiniere security, with the details. Might as well check on the progress of setting up more security for Ruby's family.

—Team will be in place for remote monitoring by tomorrow morning, Serg answered. *Handling the family briefing yourself?*

—Yes. Fly out with me on Sunday? Want you to handle this assignment in person.

—I'll be there.

—Thanks.

Ruby exhaled as she hung up. That brittle tension radiated from her again.

"Everything all right?" he asked.

"Yes. They're excited." But her voice was flat and she pressed her lips tightly together.

"What's wrong?"

Another deep sigh. "I may as well tell you. I didn't know until two weeks ago that my grandfather is on the hook for a *huge* loan. From Zingter Enterprises. Apparently they're calling it in next week, unless he accepts some pretty reprehensible and outrageous interest and conditions."

Oh shit.

He *had* to move fast on this one.

"Zingter's heard rumors about you and the Martiniere Grant?"

"I don't know—but Gramps just got a notice, a half-hour ago."

"I'll take care of it," he said.

"But—"

"*I'll take care of it,*" he repeated. "They see an opening to take advantage of vulnerable family members of a Grant candidate. This is *not* the first time that Zingter has done this."

"I—see," she said. Quieter, she continued. "Thank you. I had a fit when I discovered the amount of the loan over Spring Break. Gramps is usually wiser about these things—"

"But when it comes to his beloved granddaughter's future, he'll take a risk." Gabe patted her hand. "Relax."

"Ruby, you've just been identified as a valuable property for companies like Zingter to acquire," Asa Green added. "I've seen this situation before, and it's why I recommend the Martiniere Group's programs."

Ruby pursed her lips, a thoughtful expression crossing her face. "I never thought of myself as a property before, even when contending for Miss Rodeo America."

"Just being a finalist for the Grant means that we see you as a potential employee or contractor," Gabe said. "On the positive side, that makes you more appealing to other future employers. On the other—it makes you a target for anyone with a grudge against the Martinieres. Are there others besides your grandparents who need to be considered for protection?"

Ruby's face hardened for a moment. "No blood kin. But the barn —Lora and the horses—would they be targets?"

"Lora is already under Martiniere security," Gabe said.

"Oh." She nodded. "That's right. Your sisters. That—explains a lot."

He left it at that—she didn't need to know about his past. "No one else?"

"No one else," she said, reaching up to twist a tendril of hair, the first nervous mannerism she had exhibited around him. "And oh. I'd better call Lora about Sunday."

While she talked to Lora, Gabe quickly reran the financial records check for Ruby's grandparents, going into the deeper level that would reveal the details of the Zingter loan. He winced at the amount. More than Ruby's schooling—that was right, her grandmother had been sick with cancer. Medical expenses on top of college.

But it had all been under control until three weeks ago, when Zingter bought out and consolidated those smaller loans into one huge one—and demanded higher interest plus a balloon payment. Just barely within the bounds of the law, damn it.

Ron Ryder, Ruby's grandfather, wouldn't have been able to meet the balloon payment. He had the choice of higher collateral or—loan default.

None of that debt had been included in Ruby's filing for the Grant, of course. It wasn't her debt but her grandparents'. But it *was* part of a Zingter pattern that exploited the vulnerable connections of a Martiniere Grant candidate.

Next would come an offer posed as a pleasant alternative to losing the ranch. If Ruby declined the Martiniere Grant, and signed an employment contract with Zingter, then the loan default would be deferred. That contract would lock her into restrictive terms that she couldn't escape, unless she catered to old Walter Braun, Zingter's perv of a CEO.

Braun often targeted ambitious young women like Ruby. Had signed off on this loan himself. Ruby had caught Braun's notice. An attractive woman who would advance Zingter's research and—end up as unwilling eye candy on Braun's arm.

Damn it.

While he wouldn't let Braun get his fingers on *any* woman, Gabe was especially going to keep *this woman* from him. She was too damned *good.*

Ruby inhaled sharply. "Does that mean what I think it does?" She peered at the projection in front of Gabe.

"Yes. It looks like your grandfather has been borrowing against the Double R for several years."

Right. She took in bookkeeping. She understood financial spreadsheets.

"Since Granma's diagnosis." Her voice was flat. "But why Zingter—" She paused, then nodded. "Oh. You said they try to take advantage of Grant candidates' vulnerable family members."

"Your grandfather was doing the right thing, until Zingter bought up and consolidated his small loans. That's how they get their fingers on prime farm and ranch properties. Well—not this time."

He calculated current interest through Monday at that fucking outrageous percentage rate. Grift. He hated like hell to reward Walter Braun for his behavior, but—

Gabe added an extra twenty-five thousand dollars to the total to cover any sneaky charges that might bounce back on Ron Ryder. Then he sent the entire amount to Zingter Enterprises' real estate loan payment portal, with the proper routing and reference numbers so that it would be processed correctly. He added the urgent coding he'd learned from Justine's fiancé Donald, who worked in banking, so it would slip through easily. The code included immediate notification when the payment processed.

"Wow," Ruby said. "You really—damn it, I need to pay you back."

"You can pay me back by winning the Grant," Gabe said.

"Why? Does this have to do with that title—Martiniere-in-waiting?"

Very perceptive on her part. Oh, he *needed* this woman to be part of the Martiniere Group future he planned to build.

"Yes," he said. "But—more than that. It's personal. Walter Braun, the CEO of Zingter Enterprises, is a total ass. Even if I were already the Martiniere-in-waiting, I'd get your family out from under obligation to him. He has a—history of exploiting young women in debt. The price for the young women to escape that debt is—well—" he sighed. "Where do you think all those pretty women around Braun come from? Not by choice, I assure you. He holds power over them, usually their relatives."

"*Shit.*" Ruby inhaled sharply, blanching more than he might expect. "Damn. I dodged a bullet."

"Definitely."

"Does that mean you're trying to be a knight in shining armor?"

He snorted, choking back a laugh. "Oh, Ruby. Mindy Cathcart-Rogers would *so* disagree with you. But yes. A small notion on my part. I'm not the only one, however. My sister's fiancé, Donald Atwood, is another. He works in banking and his mother runs an organization called Real Lives for Women. I'm telling Don about this."

"I've heard of Real Lives for Women."

"Braun has been one of Barbie Atwood's targets for years. Never been able to prove anything solid about this little gambit of his. If I thought this information would help Barbie's work—" he gestured toward the screen. "I'd send it to her for evidence. But it's too vague. Too many layers, too many unspoken expectations buried under non-disclosure agreements. I learned a lot about this whole damn predatory process from Don, before I started doing these recruitment interviews for the Martiniere Grant."

"That's commendable—for both of you."

His lips tightened. "Ever since I learned that my biological father was Philip Martiniere and not Saul, I've been doing my best to be the absolute opposite of that man. My fucking sperm donor is utter slime. But Braun's worse."

Ruby's lips tightened and she nodded. "I've heard about both Philip and—Joseph? His son?"

"Adopted, just as I was." Gabe sighed. Before he could say more, the payment notification chimed. Gabe ran the check, letting himself smile. Paid in full. No liens against the Double R Ranch of Lakeside, Oregon.

He composed a message to Braun and showed it to Ruby.

Keep your slimy fingers off of my Martiniere Grant candidates, Braun. Or else. GMM.

He exhaled. "And that is that. Obligation discharged."

"Just like that." Ruby shook her head. "I—can't conceive of being able to so casually pay off other people's obligations."

"Money has its uses. It can't buy happiness, but it can sure as hell go a long way toward providing security." He shrugged. "Then again, it creates its own need for security. As you're seeing now, with me and my ex."

Ruby nodded. "And the 'or else' in your message?"

"That will be determined after I talk with Saul. This is the third instance in three years that Braun's done this to one of our Grant candidates. Normally, we don't learn about it until the candidate withdraws and it's too late to prevent the problem. *This* is the first time one of us has been able to intervene. I'm very, *very* happy you told me about your situation."

"Things are that competitive?"

"There's some personal elements above and beyond corporate competition."

Oh, were there ever. Walter Braun was a good friend of Philip's, and hated Saul. Braun would do anything to undermine Saul's control of the Group and the Family.

And then there was his own history with Braun.

"It sounds complicated."

"Anything involving the Family usually is," he said.

JUSTINE WAITED FOR THEM OUTSIDE OF THE BELVEDERE, frowning. No paparazzi here, at least not yet.

"Gabriel. We need to talk," she said. "Privately." A quick smile at Ruby. "Congratulations, Ruby. The others are inside."

Asa Green took Ruby inside while Gabe waited by Justine. He exhaled heavily once they were alone.

"Let me guess," he said. "Our fucking sperm donor."

"He's been arrested and released on bail for assaulting Mindy."

"Aw, crap. There goes the weekend. I'm supposed to go to the Double R on Sunday to brief Ruby and her grandparents."

She shook her head. "I've already talked to Saul. He got your notice about Ruby's selection, just about simultaneously with the shit hitting the fan with Daddy-fucking-dearest's arrest. Saul wants to discuss it with us on Monday. Donna-gran's flying in tomorrow to kick butt."

Gabe winced. He did *not* want to be on their grandmother's wrong side. Not that he had any sympathy for Philip. "Saul wants to see what happens with Donna-gran before talking to us?"

"Apparently, she is pissed off as hell, and may demand that the Board apply sanctions, including freezing accounts for both our father and Joey."

"Oh, this is so going to be a fucking mess." And it involved *his* ex-girlfriend as well. Gabe ran his fingers through his hair. What did this mean for his campaign to become the Martiniere-in-waiting?

"Saul said to tell you not to fret," Justine added. "Though you and I know you will. The Board has already told him that this doesn't impact the selection process for becoming the Martiniere-in-waiting. And as for Mindy—" she shrugged. "It would be one thing if she hadn't been a queen bitch to Cousin Kendra at her wedding last summer. Otherwise, she might have earned some sympathy within the Family factions."

Gabe smirked at that memory. Cousin Kendra was *not* anyone to trifle with. Mindy had picked a fight with Kendra at the reception. Kendra verbally flayed Mindy in response. Mindy ran to Gabe for consolation and support—which he hadn't offered. Then Gabe went out of his way to apologize to Kendra for Mindy's behavior and, well, that was probably another reason why Mindy had ended up in bed with Joey. Hell, it had probably happened that afternoon.

But Kendra was worth twenty Mindys any day. Along with Justine and several other Family women in their twenties and thirties, she should have been among the contenders for the title of Martiniere-in-waiting.

Another thing that you can change if you become the Martiniere, Gabriel. Maybe.

"Well," he said, putting an arm around Justine's shoulders. "That's better news than I expected to hear. And as for tomorrow— well, we can focus on Weeza's horse, and riding. Maybe eat in afterward? I'll be busy on Sunday with Ruby and her family." He paused. "I have to talk to Saul later on tonight, anyway. Zingter tried the loan gambit again, on Ruby's family. She told me, and I took care of it. Then sent fucking Walter a warning to leave the Grant candidates alone, *or else.*"

"Aw, fuck," Justine said. Braun had made passes at her before he had been banned from formal Martiniere functions. Gabe didn't *think* she knew the darker history between him and Braun. "But it's all settled with Ruby?"

"Yep. All settled."

They walked toward the door.

"I'm glad to hear it, Gabie." Justine grinned at him. "What did you think of our Ms. Ruby?"

"She is a very—*interesting*—person."

"Good." A smile twisted Justine's lips and she gave Gabe a sideways glance that heightened his suspicions.

"Tine, she's a Martiniere Grant finalist—"

"I know, I know, hands off," Justine said. "But. Ruby's exactly the sort of woman you should be looking for, not airheads like Mindy."

"I'm aware of that," he sighed. "It's just—finding the time to locate women like her. There's not a lot of Rubys out there."

Another sideways glance from his sister as he dropped his arm from her shoulder and opened the Belvedere's door for her.

"It might not be as hard to find women like Ruby as you think it is, Gabriel."

CHAPTER 4

DINNER AT THE BELVEDERE

RUBY

Ruby's head still spun from—all of this—as Dr. Green guided her into the Belvedere. Gabriel Martiniere had disposed of the threat to the Double R, with little more than a snap of his fingers. Like she had won the lottery. That debt was probably just pennies to a billionaire like him, though it meant financial devastation to her grandparents and herself.

But what price would she pay for *his* intervention? Probably much more palatable than what Zingter and Braun would have exacted from her—but there would be a price. Of that she was certain. This sort of good luck just didn't descend upon any person, especially Ruby Barkley. She had needed to strive for every accomplishment she won. And she had paid a price for each and every victory she achieved.

Unwanted, the memory of Aunt Grace's screeching at her parents' funeral came back to her.

You are a worthless little brat who brought about my brother's death, and you will pay for that. Mark my words, Ruby Marie. I will make you pay for Tony's death.

Ruby shuddered. Grace Barkley was one nightmare that Gabriel Martiniere *couldn't* eliminate from her life. Thank God Grace was not a Ryder but a Barkley, with no claim on the Double R. Thank God Gramps had taken steps to shut the Barkleys out from any claims on the Double R when Ruby's mother Beth married Tony Barkley. And that both Gramps and Granma had gone the extra mile to gain custody of Ruby when her parents' meth habit got out of hand, rather than let Grace take her.

But the consequences of getting free from her parents and Aunt Grace were another price Ruby had paid, over and over again, while growing up in Thunder County. Being the object of harassment from her cousins and their friends. Learning to hold her own in a fistfight rather than let herself be beaten—or worse. Which had happened anyway.

Father-killer. Family betrayer. Red-headed freak. Ruby's germs, no returns.

Ruby shook her head to banish the far-too-familiar taunts. All that was over and done. She was a Martiniere Grant finalist. Might even be on the fast track to becoming part of the Martiniere Group. Her aunt couldn't do anything to hurt her now. And if Gabe lived up to his promise to do well by her grandparents, then Grace couldn't hurt her through them, either.

"Are you all right?" Dr. Green asked as the maître d' led them to the private dining room.

"I'm just overwhelmed," Ruby murmured. "Wondering what I have to do to pay *him* back for taking care of my grandparents' debt."

Dr. Green chuckled softly. "Ruby, you're dealing with the real thing. A genuine philanthropist. You aren't the first person—not even the first of my students—for whom Gabe has done a major financial intervention. No strings attached."

Ruby exhaled shakily. "All right. I guess."

"The other piece? He'll go far if he becomes the Martiniere. Gabe Martiniere already has a reputation in agtech, and if he hadn't decided to compete for the leadership of the Martinieres, he'd be making a name for himself with microbials. You could do a lot worse than affiliating with Gabriel Martiniere and the Martiniere Group. The Group rewards talent and ability."

"That's what he said during the interview."

"Believe it," Dr. Green said as they entered the dining room. Two women and another man already sat around the table.

Louisa Martiniere laughed at something the woman next to her said. Then she looked up and a big grin spread across her face.

"Ruby! Congratulations! Justine and I both put in good words for you."

"So I've heard," Ruby said. "Thank you."

Louisa shrugged. "Eh, when Gabie told us that Cousin Artie and Uncle Gerry were very interested in your work, I figured you would really have to screw up the interview to *not* be chosen."

"Um—" Ruby began as Dr. Green settled her on the right side of the empty chair at the head of the table before taking his seat on the other side, next to Louisa. "Who are they?"

She *thought* she knew, but Martiniere family relationships sounded complicated.

"Oh! Cousin Artie and Uncle Gerry manage the French and European subsidiaries of the Martiniere Group," Louisa said. "Artie handles the labs; Gerry the management. And since the French subsidiaries are cutting edge within the Group, Artie and Gerry's opinions are important. Both serve on the Group's board. With that endorsement—" she shrugged again. "You can't miss."

Yes. *Artie* and *Gerry* were exactly who she had suspected.

Arthur Martiniere. Head of the Group's laboratories in France. Gerard Martiniere, head of the Martiniere Group in Europe, second only to Saul Martiniere, *the* Martiniere, the CEO of the Martiniere Group.

How on earth did I ever attract that level of attention?

She wasn't *that* good, was she?

And yet Walter Braun and Zingter Enterprises also had been interested in her work.

You're better at this than you think, Ruby-girl.

Or so both Gramps and Granma would say whenever Ruby doubted herself.

The man rose and bowed slightly. "I am Donald Atwood. Justine's fiancé. And you must be Ruby Barkley, correct?"

"Correct." She bowed back to Atwood, quickly surveying him. Another attractive, well-dressed man. From what Gabe had said, a philanthropist as well.

"And I'm Virginia Westley," the woman next to Louisa said.

"I'm pleased to meet both of you," Ruby said. Damn. Another heiress.

She was in a room with *multiple* billionaires right now. Granted, she had known that Louisa and Justine were rich, but still—

Life was very different at the barn, and neither Justine nor Louisa acted like affluent, stuck-up heiresses. They both knew how to use a manure fork, and occasionally mucked stalls to help Ruby and Lora. Neither woman was too proud to check stall waterers, stack hay, or groom and tack their own horses. Some of the most difficult boarders and students at the barn were much less wealthy than Louisa and Justine, but put on more airs.

Maybe this won't be so difficult.

Gabe seemed to be a lot like his sisters, after all.

Justine, then Gabe, entered the room. His expression was much less stormy than it had been outside, but lightened even more as he settled in the chair to Ruby's right.

"We're all introduced?" he asked.

"Taken care of," Atwood said, his focus on Justine, smiling slowly. Her eyes met his and her countenance softened, her lips twitching up to mirror his. He leaned over and kissed her, both beaming as they lingered over the kiss, lips parting briefly before they kissed again, several times.

Stop staring, Ruby! she scolded herself, even as a wistful yearning stirred within her. She forced herself to look away, only to be startled by a longing look on Gabe's face as he studied Donald and Justine. Once he became aware of her attention, however, he also changed his focus.

"Get a room, you two," Louisa snickered.

Justine arched her brows. "That will be later."

Gabe rolled his eyes. "Weeza, Tine, knock it off. You'll give Ruby the wrong impression."

Justine snorted. "As if she hasn't seen us having water fights at the barn?"

"We probably *should* show some dignity at dinner," Gabe said. But a smile played at the corners of his mouth. "Especially after certain events that happened this afternoon."

"Nice way to break the mood, Gabie," Louisa said. "Besides, this is Ruby's night—where's that champagne?"

Even as she spoke, a server entered with bottle and ice bucket. She presented the bottle to Louisa. Ruby watched, fascinated, as Louisa examined the label and nodded. The server opened the bottle, without the fanfare Ruby had expected.

"Pour for her first." Louisa gestured toward Ruby. "She's the guest of honor."

A brief panicked moment as Ruby wondered if she was supposed to taste it and issue a verdict. Fortunately, the next pour was Gabe, and he took a quick sip.

"Nice choice, Weeza," he said. "As always. You have excellent taste."

"Give credit to Donald. We had a discussion about which one to choose."

"Still thinking about buying a local winery, Don?" Gabe asked.

"Negotiating on one now," Donald said, smiling again at Justine.

The server finished pouring and Gabe rose, lifting his glass. "A toast to my latest Martiniere Grant finalist. To Ruby Barkley—and may she be the first-place winner for the 2029-2030 Martiniere Grant."

The faint burn of an all-too-telltale blush heated Ruby's cheeks as she sipped along with the others.

The server returned with a single-sheet menu. Ruby studied it, swallowing hard at the prices and the realization that this was one of *those* places, where she had to order everything individually.

Dear God, if she hadn't had the experience that went along with being Miss Rodeo Oregon, she would *really* be in over her head.

Gabe leaned over. "I recommend the petite steak. It's what I usually get here when I'm in town to see my sisters, and it's really good."

"Thank you," she murmured. "Though I've been to places like this before, it always helps to know what's good. How's their produce?"

"Mmm, need to be careful. I've not been seeing good salad lettuce or fresh produce anywhere that I've been traveling. This spring has been too hot and dry."

Ruby nodded. Soup was probably a better choice, along with winter squash (hopefully kept in good storage) and roasted Brussels Sprouts (most likely frozen). Though the beet salad was probably a safe selection as well.

"I apologize for the lack of bread," their server said. "But our bakery is running short on flour this week and—"

"Understandable, given last year's wheat crop," Gabe said.

Nods of agreement around the table.

They ordered. Ruby noticed that Justine and Louisa's orders mirrored hers. She felt better about her choices.

Justine and Donald murmured to each other while Louisa, Virginia, and Dr. Green started a lively conversation about Corvallis and University politics. Gabe rolled his eyes and turned his attention to Ruby.

"I should know better than to seat Asa by Weeza," he sighed. "They'll argue politics from now until forever. Are you doing all right?"

He's on a first name basis with Dr. Green! But why should I find that surprising?

"The champagne is very nice," she said. "And it helps to know Justine and Louisa already—Weeza? How on earth did she get that nickname?"

He smirked. "Self-inflicted. She was very determined as a toddler. I still remember her glaring at our mother and insisting that *I's Weeza!* The Martiniere stubbornness shows up very early, in just about all of us."

"I've wondered. Justine's used the nickname at the barn."

Silence fell between them. Gabe coughed. "You know, you didn't tell me very much about the Double R beyond that one difficult field —Homestead, you called it? Much less why it's called that. How big is the ranch, and what exactly does it produce?"

Ruby took a deep breath, then began to describe the Double R's integrated livestock, hay, and grain production. Once again, she got swept up in talking with Gabe about details. Rotating grain between hayfields to keep the hayfields producing, experimenting with seeding the grains into cover crops such as wild peas and parsnips to reduce tillage.

The cycles of drought that slowly reduced the Double R's cattle herd over the years because they couldn't risk running out of water, and hay crops diminished. Gramps's contract to produce kosher wheat for a New York flour mill. Carbon capture prospects based on the work she had done at the ranch.

They kept up the conversation through the first course, until Justine laughed.

"Looks like Donald and I aren't the only ones who should get a room. Though in this case, it sounds like a lab is more appropriate."

Ruby flushed again.

Gabe scowled. "Tine—"

"Oh, you know, Gabie will talk carbon capture and biologics until the end of forever," Louisa said airily. "Lock the two of them in the labs and who knows what might come out as a result?" She rolled her eyes. "Gabie, it *is* nice to see you with a woman who's your match at scientific discussion. Much more pleasant than listening to Mindy blather about clothing design, and watching you shut down."

That made Gabe flush and take a big gulp of his champagne. "It *is* her business."

"Yeah, *right*, as if Mindy does more than play at design," Justine snorted. "Gabie, I'm sorry, but you're better off without her."

"Not the venue for this talk, Justine," Gabe said, sharpness in his voice.

"I concur with Weeza. But you already know that. It's just nice seeing you happy and smiling at one of these dinners." Justine grinned at Ruby. "I hope we're not embarrassing you, Ruby, but it is nice to see our *favorite* big brother with a smile on his face at a meal. It's been several years."

"Tine—" A sharper, warning note in Gabe's voice.

"Gabriel. I *understand.* Ruby is a Martiniere Grant finalist and not a girlfriend. But she's someone I count as a friendly acquaintance," Justine said. "Tonight's the first time I've been able to hear Ruby talk about her studies and research—not many opportunities at the barn. It's fascinating, Ruby, and quite a change from our usual conversations about horses." A smirk quirked her lips. "It is tempting to consider what the result might be if we *do* lock the two of you in a lab for a week, with instructions to create something useful. I predict that the result would be quite profitable."

Dr. Green broke out laughing, and toasted Justine. "I'll agree with that assessment, Justine. I first began to recruit Ruby for Oregon State when she was in high school because I saw promise in her concepts. Ruby, you've overcome formidable obstacles to make excellent advancement in your studies. I wish I could convince the university administration to grant you more credit for the work you've done when you couldn't formally attend classes, even remotely. By all rights, you should be a junior."

"That might be arranged," Gabe said. "Especially once Arthur and Gerard have had an opportunity to talk to Ruby. They'll wield a bit more influence than I would."

"You can do that?" Ruby gulped.

"Not me, but Arthur and Gerard—most certainly. I'll set it up," Gabe said. "I never completed my Master's study, but Arthur has a doctorate. That carries some weight."

Ruby drained her champagne glass.

Hoo boy. The price needed to pay for all of *this*—might be significant indeed.

And yet it might be well worth the cost.

THEY RETURNED TO CAMPUS AFTER DINNER. AFTER CHECKING with Dr. Green, Gabe sent him home with a security contingent, one of whom drove Green's car.

"Do you need a ride home?" he asked.

"I've probably had more to drink than I should if I'm driving," Ruby said. "But my truck is rather cranky."

"That's all right," Gabe said. "If you give Lance the code and ID, he'll assign someone appropriate to drive it."

Ruby was still reluctant, but—Martiniere security was going to be a part of her future. She needed to adapt. She passed codes and the address to Lance.

Gabe slid to the other side of the SUV's bench seat. He undid his tie and draped it over the seat back, unbuttoning the collar and top two buttons of his shirt, stretching his head and neck.

"Despite my meddling sisters, this was a good dinner, Ruby," he said. "I'll be coaching you for the finalist interviews between now and the Grant banquet. This setting helps me assess what I need to cover with you. It won't be just you—I'm also coaching my other candidate, Jeff Swait."

"Why would you do that?"

He chuckled softly. "It improves your chances of winning the Grant, and reflects well on me. Some of my candidates are a bit—rough, socially. But I've placed at least one finalist in the top five since I started doing these interviews. I hope to repeat that performance with both of you this year."

"That's impressive." As far as Ruby knew, only five of the twenty-or-so finalists actually earned the full Grant.

"Thank you." A brief smile spread his lips before he continued. "One aspect of being a Martiniere Grant recipient is the ability to interact smoothly at corporate and fundraising social functions. Your interviews before the Grant banquet will be conducted by various Family members. Not just Arthur and Gerard, but my grandmother. My mother and Saul. And others."

"I saw that part about corporate and fundraising social responsibilities as a Grant recipient in the application description," she said. "So how much coaching do I need?"

He tapped his lips thoughtfully. "Not much socially. Both you and Jeff are pretty smooth. I want to concentrate on the nuances of Family and Group political interactions, improve your chances of being hired by the Group."

She raised her brows. "All right. Let's start with this. Every time I hear you—and Justine and Louisa, for that matter—say *family*, it's like you're emphasizing an unseen capital letter F. The Family. What's up with that?"

"The Family possesses an old and, if not exactly honorable, *significant* heritage. That's why we refer to it as *the* Family. We're descendants of French and Italian nobility. A bastard branch from the last Valois kings, descent from the Medicis and Borgias." He shrugged. "Therefore, the reason for some of the outdated policies within the Group. Salic Law—inheritance through the male line only

—dominates the governance of Family branches within the Group." He frowned. "I intend to change that. If I can."

"I see."

He studied her. "Because you're a brilliant woman who I want to recruit into the Group, I want you to understand what those structures are. I think you could go far, especially if you know where the land mine issues lie."

She exhaled. "So I should understand both the Family and Group structures?"

Gabe nodded. "One crucial piece is that the Martiniere Group is the legacy of French Revolution-era family associations which provided support for refugees from the Revolution. The Martinieres dispersed into the United States, Canada, Britain, and Russia." He stretched. "That's the foundation for the Group corporate structures. Longer discussion than I want to get into tonight."

"Especially after a few glasses of champagne?"

"Absolutely." He paused. "Justine did bring up an issue to me earlier, and I thought I'd better give you a heads up. I'm coming with them to the barn tomorrow."

"Are you riding?" Ruby calculated. What schoolie could she put Gabe on?

"It's somewhat complicated; tied to Weeza and her bad habit of buying horses that are too much for her."

That.

"She handles the horse well on the ground, and he's not a mean boy. Just young, with more scope than she can handle."

"Pretty much what Tine told me," Gabe sighed. "Weeza has a history of doing this. I don't ride as much as I used to. Not enough time. But when I'm riding regularly, well, Tine and I are close to the same level. Feel free to ask Lora about it. She's taught me. Weeza, on the other hand—" He shook his head. "She falls in love with the most intense horse possible. Sometimes she gets hurt. I'd like to avoid that happening."

"That's pretty much what happened with Midnight," Ruby said.

"Lora wasn't planning to have Louisa trial him, but she saw him move, fell in love, and insisted."

"I'm planning to warm him up for her tomorrow. Tine says you do that regularly."

Ruby scowled at him. "You sure about that?"

The last thing she wanted to be responsible for was getting *this* Martiniere heir injured. Too much depended on him.

"I may not ride daily, but I *am* capable of handling a horse with some scope," Gabe said. "My grandmother had me school one of her green warmbloods two weeks ago. *That* was a rodeo. Talk to Lora about my experience."

"I will," she said as they pulled up at the stable.

Damn right I will.

Louisa and Midnight were under her supervision, after all.

Gabe eyed the barn. "You live here?"

"Caretaker apartment around back," she said.

"I'll walk you to the door. I'll feel better that way."

She didn't argue but slid out, tensing slightly.

Was this going to be the payment, after all? Easy enough for him to insist on a few kisses—or more. And after what he'd done for her grandparents, hell, making her a Grant finalist—she wasn't really in a position to resist any advances Gabe might make.

He hesitated as she started for the graveled driveway that led to her apartment.

"Is there access through the barn? I'd like to see Weeza's folly before tomorrow—if possible. Get a sense of him."

"Sure."

His footsteps were soft and nearly silent despite his boots as he followed her through the door and down the alleyway. The horses roused as she switched on a light. Her horse, Sunshine, came to the front of her stall, nickering through the bars barricading the top section of the wall.

Gabe leaned on the wall as Ruby paused to check Sunshine. "Now you're a pretty girl. Palomino—Quarter Horse?"

"Yes," Ruby said. "She's mine."

He scratched Sunshine's nose. "Very nice-looking girl. What does she do?"

"She's a rehab project. Prone to bucking, and I haven't figured out why yet. When she doesn't buck, she's fast. Half-sister to one of my queen mounts, Beauty."

Gabe patted Sunshine. "Sorry, girl. No treats tonight. Just wait until tomorrow, if that's all right with your human. Now. Where's Louisa's boy?"

Ruby led him down the alleyway to Midnight's stall. The big black gelding whickered, just like Sunshine.

"You're a friendly boy," Gabe said, leaning against the stall wall again, careless of stable grit on his jacket. He squinted. "Gelded?"

"Yes."

"Hard to tell in this light, as thick as his neck is. Nicely put together, from what I can see. Weeza does have an eye for a good horse—except for temperament. I suppose he couldn't be turned into a dressage horse?"

"Oh God no. He *hates* flatwork. Very scopey over fences."

"Typical." Gabe straightened up and shook his head. "Well, he and I will have a little discussion tomorrow—see what he's all about. I'd better let you get some rest—I still have things to do tonight." He patted Midnight's nose. "More tomorrow, handsome boy."

They walked the rest of the way in silence. She clicked off the alleyway lights and secured the door before entering the breezeway that connected her studio apartment and Lora's office to the barn. Gabe waited while she opened the door.

To her surprise, he did nothing more than bow politely.

"I'll see you tomorrow, Ruby. I can just walk around the outside to get back to my vehicle?"

"Yes," she said.

A flash of a grin. "Then tomorrow. Congratulations. Oh, and don't forget to check in with Lora." Another bow, and then he was off, walking in the faint glow from the outside security lights.

Ruby watched him go, wondering at the regret roiling through her.

Had she actually *wanted* him to make an advance?

It didn't make sense.

Oh well. He was respectful, and so far, it didn't appear that he wanted to take advantage of his position of power over her.

So far, she cautioned herself. *Remember, there is a price you will be paying for this good fortune. Eventually.*

CHAPTER 5

INTIMATE BETRAYAL
APRIL, 2029

GABE

GABE SLID OUT OF HIS SUIT JACKET AND TOSSED IT OVER THE back of the SUV's seat to join his tie. Then he sprawled across the bench seat, leaning his elbow on the armrest.

Ruby was tense with him. Had expected him to push some sort of sexual advantage—oh, he had noticed how she tightened up when he suggested walking to her door. It was one reason he had proposed that they look at the horses.

What does it matter, Gabriel? She's a Martiniere Grant finalist, not a potential girlfriend.

It mattered because he wanted to work with her. It mattered because—just because. He *wanted* Ruby to have a good opinion of him.

Gabe sighed. Not something he could fix tonight.

He called Saul. A video call, wanting to see his reactions as well as hear him, get a feel for how bad this mess with Philip and Mindy really was. He could use the excuse of giving Saul a heads up about

Zingter's attempt to move in on Ruby while getting an update about Philip.

Hopefully it wasn't too late in the evening—but if it were, then Saul wouldn't answer. Friday nights were usually private for Saul and Angelica. Family night, when he and his sisters were younger—and now, couple's night for them. Calling only in urgent situations.

Given that Donna-gran was flying in tomorrow to kick Philip's butt, odds were *very* good that couple's night was off the table.

"Gabie!" His mother answered, her formal smile softening to a genuine one. She was informally dressed in a sleeveless lavender silk tunic and leggings, as casual as Angelica Ramirez Martiniere ever got outside of close family.

"Mama." Gabe knew what *that* outfit meant. Saul was working late tonight and Angelica was screening his calls. Not a good sign.

"Is everything all right?" she asked.

"As fine as expected, given the circumstances."

She frowned. "Your father has it under control, Gabriel."

"I know, Mother," he said. "I'm not calling about Philip's antics, at least not tonight. I had another issue come up that Saul needs to hear about. We almost lost a Grant candidate to Braun. *Again.*"

His mother's lips tightened and her eyes narrowed. "I'll see if he can break away from his other call. Your grandmother is furious."

"Not with Papa, I hope."

"No. But with everything that's going on—" Angelica threw up her hands. "It is a mess. Donna is threatening to disinherit Philip and Joey, and in return they're threatening lawsuits and blackmail."

"Oh?"

Blackmail.

His gut tightened, remembering the two years he spent living in the hellhole that was his biofather's house—and God only knew what lies Renate had told Philip about Gabe before her suicide.

Remember, Saul knows all about that fetid horror that is Philip's household. It's why he supported your bringing Justine when you came back home.

"I don't know what the blackmail piece is about, except that it's not about you. Not that it matters. What's left for Philip to try to blackmail you about?" his mother said. She looked away. "Saul? It's Gabie. Braun tried to snatch a Grant candidate."

"That son-of-a-bitch," Saul Martiniere sighed, joining Angelica. He kissed the top of her head and she smiled up at him.

Gabe frowned, studying Saul. Dark circles under his eyes, face gray and lined with fatigue—he appeared *old* tonight. Older than Philip, much older than the hour's difference in age between Saul and Philip.

Gabe's gut clenched.

Damn it.

Saul was in his late fifties. He shouldn't look like he was in his seventies.

"You doing all right, Papa?" he asked softly.

"Well enough," Saul said, running his hands through his thinning, gray-streaked black hair. Angelica got up and Saul settled on the white couch where she had been sitting. "So let me guess. Braun has something on Ruby Barkley."

"*Had* something on Ruby Barkley. Ruby called her grandparents to tell them, in part because of the media swarming us thanks to Philip and Mindy. They had just gotten a notice that Zingter was calling in loans against the ranch, with some pretty nasty interest and conditions for renewal. As soon as she hung up from talking to them, she told me. I took care of it."

"Figured as much." A faint smile quirked Saul's lips. "Braun was yammering at me just an hour ago. Something about you threatening him. Saying he'd go to Philip to agitate against you within the Group unless I reined you in. I told him to go to hell, because he has nothing on you that the Board doesn't already know."

Gabe shrugged. "I paid off the loan. Zingter bought up a group of smaller loans. Fairly recent action. Then I sent a message to dear Walter telling him to keep his slimy fingers off of my Martiniere Grant candidates. Or else. Nothing more than that."

Saul nodded. "Confirms what I suspected. He wouldn't show me the message. I *thought* he was exaggerating. I trained you better than to issue blunt, open threats unless you can immediately follow up on them." He chuckled. "I suspect the bit about *slimy fingers*, if that's the phrasing you used—"

"It was."

"Pricked his pride a bit, then. Good job, son."

To Gabe's relief, the fatigue eased in Saul's expression.

"I learned from the best," he said.

"That you did." Tiredness dropped onto Saul's face again. "But playing with our candidates isn't the only thing Braun is doing, Gabie. He's into this business with Miranda and Philip up to his neck."

"I wouldn't be surprised to hear that he was part of that scene Mindy walked into," Gabe said.

"Don't know that for certain. However, Miranda now wants to drop charges, after making a big deal about filing them, and Braun is backing her."

"Oh God." Gabe shook his head and leaned his face into his right hand. "So just what the hell is going on?" He looked up. "Is it possible that Mindy's been associated with Braun all along? One of his moles?"

"I wish I could say that you are being paranoid, Gabriel. But both Cousin Piotr and your grandmother think it's entirely possible."

"*Shit.*" Cousin Piotr Vygotsky, Serg's father, was involved. Piotr was the head of Martiniere security, and if he thought it was likely that Mindy and Braun were connected, then that made it definite. So just how did this breach happen?

My relationship with Mindy. Has to be.

Gabe groaned and leaned his head against the seat. He thought back to his last days living with Mindy. Just when had he downloaded the 2029-2030 Martiniere Grant application files? When had he started carrying his data chip with him at all times because he had noticed signs of possible intrusion? Cousin Serg hadn't noticed any traces of snooping—wait.

Damn it.

He had downloaded the files at the end of September. Things were already rocky between him and Mindy after the midsummer blowup with Kendra—oh hell, they had been sniping and fighting for a solid six months before then. Two weeks later was when he started tucking that chip into a secured pants pocket whenever he left the apartment. Their breakup happened two days after that.

Two weeks where Joey *could* have accessed those files, because they weren't keyed to Gabe specifically. His damned cousin wasn't bright about a lot of things, but Joey did know his way around computers.

"We'd better go through and check with all the Martiniere Grant applicants for the past year to make sure Zingter isn't bothering them," he sighed. "Not just the finalists but the others. It's entirely possible that Joey hacked the accesses. Maybe not through my computer, but he would be aware of the timeline for candidate selection. And all it would take for him to figure out who was in contention would be one opening to the database. That would give him enough information to reach the rest of it. Especially if he handed the accesses to Philip."

"Joey to Philip to Walter?" Saul's voice sharpened. "That would make sense."

"I *thought* I was being careful. I didn't think Mindy was capable of that level of betrayal; that her involvement with Joey was superficial and only about sex and attention. It looks like I was wrong." He straightened up and bowed as best as he could, given the seat belt and the confines of the SUV. "I am very sorry about this, Martiniere." His voice went formal. "It appears that I was the flawed link in our security. Perhaps I should withdraw from consideration as the Martiniere-in-waiting."

God, that *hurt*. It had been his goal for eleven years, since he was sixteen. To lose his chance at becoming the Martiniere because of a bad relationship choice in Mindy and making the mistake of trusting her—*damn it.*

And yet he didn't really have an option but to offer his resignation to the Martiniere. It was the honorable thing to do, because it was his fucking error.

"Oh, knock it off, Gabriel," Saul snapped. "You do not have to fall on your fucking sword. You are hardly the first candidate for Martiniere-in-waiting who discovered that someone you loved was untrustworthy."

"But to this degree?"

"Yes, and worse." Saul rubbed his face. "More importantly, Gabriel, *you are our best candidate. Our* strongest potential Martiniere. The Family needs *you.* Now stop this dramatic *oh God I'm not perfect and made a mistake so I have to withdraw* bullshit. Mistakes happen. You learn from them." He glowered at Gabe. "You're tired out. I can see it. How many time zones have you crossed in the past week?"

"I've lost track," Gabe admitted. "Enough that the jet has needed to use fuel instead of charging off the solar cells the last two days. And not long enough to fully use any chargers when we've been on the ground."

Saul pointed at Gabe. "There you are. I know I look tired as hell, because I've been scrambling to deal with several messes. But your mother is going to beat me around the head and shoulders if I don't stop very soon—"

"Gabie is the last call I'm letting you take tonight, Saul!" Angelica called from off-screen. She came into view, carrying two glasses of wine. "Gabriel, if *you* don't take some time off, I am going to make your sisters force you into it. We don't need *both* of you working yourselves into exhaustion." She tucked into Saul's side and handed him one of the glasses. He put his arm around her and they snuggled close.

Gabe swallowed hard. If only—if only—

"I'm spending tomorrow with the girls," he said. "Barn tomorrow morning, checking out Weeza's latest folly of a horse purchase. Ruby showed him to me tonight and he seems like a good boy. Just—possibly too strong for Weeza."

Angelica chuckled. "Weeza tells me that you and this new finalist —Ruby Barkley, right?"

"Right."

"Spent most of dinner talking about carbon capture possibilities based on the studies she's done at her family's ranch." She smirked. "That she and Justine were about ready to shove you two into a lab because you clearly needed to get a room. Lab—bedroom—either one seemed to be a possibility."

"Mama!" Gabe shook his head, smiling. "She's a Martiniere Grant finalist. Hands off." He sobered. "But I *do* want to recruit her into the Group. Working with her will be—" he blew a chef's kiss. "Exquisite."

"And that's all?" Saul teased.

"Papa. Power dynamics between us. *If* anything happens, it won't be for quite a while. I don't want to paw the employees, like Joey does!"

"Ah, Gabie, Gabie, Gabie." Saul frowned at him. "Relax a little. If the door opens, don't hesitate. Take the initiative—that's how I beat Philip out with your mama."

"Not likely to be a possibility," Gabe sighed. "Ruby is clearly expecting to pay some sort of price for my paying off her grandparents' loan. I'm not making any moves on her, nor should I."

"I see." Saul raised a brow at Angelica. She smiled and looked down. He kissed her forehead. "Ah well, one can hope that someday you'll find someone worthy of you, son. And Sunday?"

"Flying to the Double R with Ruby to look over the ranch and brief her grandparents on security protocols. Given Zingter's interest, I've assigned Serg to take personal responsibility for protecting Ruby and her family." No need to mention that he'd made the assignment *before* he knew about Zingter.

"Good," Saul said.

The SUV came to a stop. Gabe exhaled. "I'm at the girls' condo."

"We'll talk about Philip next week." Saul grimaced. "I told Justine it would be on Monday, but things could change. It all depends on what Mother does to bring Philip to heel tomorrow and Sunday."

"Maybe I should—"

"*No*," Saul interrupted. "Absolutely not. I can handle this one, including the fallout from whatever your grandmother does. You take care of your candidate."

"Just offering," Gabe said.

"Not needed."

"Go rest," Angelica said. "We love you, son." She switched off the video.

Gabe exhaled. Then he climbed out of the SUV, breathing in deeply of the damp spring night, for the first time letting himself pay attention to his surroundings.

Now, he could admit that he was bone-tired.

Perhaps exhausted enough to sleep, without the nightmares that had been haunting him worse than ever.

CHAPTER 6

HORSING AROUND
APRIL, 2029

RUBY

She stopped by Lora's office in the morning.

"Congratulations." Lora looked away from her ancient iMac's screen to smile at Ruby. "I knew you could nail the Martiniere Grant finalist interview. What do you think of Gabriel Martiniere?"

"He's—interesting."

"*Interesting* is one way to describe Gabe," Lora said.

"Yes. And that's one thing I needed to check with you. He wants to warm up Midnight before Louisa gets on him. I'm worried that he might get hurt."

"Unlikely," Lora said firmly. "If anything, Midnight's better suited to a rider like Gabe than he is for Louisa."

"Are you sure? He said he hasn't ridden much of late—though his grandmother apparently had him ride one of her green warmbloods."

"If Donna Martiniere put him up on one of her greenies and he didn't get hurt, Midnight's not going to be a problem," Lora said. "Just wait and see, Ruby. The man can ride."

"If you say so." She still wasn't sure about that notion.

Lora grinned. "If you're worried, I'll be there too. It's been a while since I've seen Gabe on a horse. Should be a real treat."

GABE AND HIS SISTERS SHOWED UP TEN MINUTES EARLIER THAN Ruby expected. It was all Ruby could do to keep from staring at him as he sauntered in with Louisa and Justine. Properly attired for schooling horses in breeches, half-zip pullover and neatly polished tall boots, carrying his helmet by its harness, except—*damn.*

The man was hot enough in a well-fitted suit. But in breeches and tall boots? Not hard on the eyes, not at all. Add to that the slight tousling of curly black hair that had been neatly groomed yesterday and—well—

Ruby was glad she wore her best schooling tights and her old show boots, polished this morning. Putting on the new show boots would be a bit much, but....

Gabe's dark brown eyes met Ruby's and *something* smoldered in them. The right corner of his mouth twitched up in a mischievous grin.

Oh, he knew the effect his appearance had on her. He *had* to know.

"He's matured quite nicely," Lora said in a low voice. "Surprised the man's still single." She stepped past Ruby as Gabe and Louisa stopped outside of Midnight's stall. "Good to see you again, Gabriel. Ruby said you wanted to warm Midnight up for Louisa?"

"I understand he's scopey," Gabe said, as Louisa led Midnight out of the stall and fastened him in the crossties. Louisa kissed the horse on the white spot on his nose as Gabe continued to speak. "I might be a wee bit rusty. Even though Donna-gran insisted that I do a trial ride on one of her Windraker babies two weeks ago. That was—an interesting ride."

Windraker? He got on a green Windraker even though he's not been riding regularly?

Damn. That was a *tough* Selle Français bloodline. And Midnight's dam was a Windraker daughter....

"Donna does have a fondness for that bloodline," Lora said. "Well, if you didn't get thrown from one of her Windrakers, then you should do just fine with Middy here."

"He's a Windraker too," Louisa said proudly, leaning her head against Midnight's neck. "Selle Français and Trakehner."

The gelding snorted and turned his head toward Louisa as far as the ties allowed. She laughed and slipped him a treat.

Justine led her chestnut Selle Français mare, Glory, out of her stall further down the row. "If you can pull your eyes off of that Windraker, Gabie, look at my Glory girl."

"Maybe later, Tine. I want to get to know this boy before I ride him," Gabe said. "Weeza, where's your grooming caddy?"

As Louisa hurried toward her tack locker, Gabe stepped up to the black horse, scratching around his ears and down the crest of his neck. He chuckled as Midnight stretched his head out and waved his upper lip around to show his appreciation.

"What can you tell me about this horse?" he asked Ruby. "Honest or dirty?"

"Oh, he's honest. Not a dirty stopper. Just strong. He won't refuse, but you have to count strides and make him listen to you, because he's overconfident." Ruby jerked her head toward Justine and Glory. "He's not as powerful as she is yet. Glory will easily turn a two-stride combination into no strides, even from a long takeoff, if you don't set boundaries. He wants to get too close to the fences, and then overjumps."

"She has better haunches muscling."

"He'll be the same after another six months regular work," she said. "Younger and not as well-conditioned. If he spent a summer on the ranch climbing ridges and picking his way through rocky pastures like she did, he'd be pretty damned good."

Gabe raised his brows. "Oh?"

"After I had to drop out sophomore year, Lora started sending me some of her young horses for summer conditioning on the ranch," she said. "Glory spent last summer with me. Wouldn't hurt Midnight to go through the same treatment."

His brows rose even higher. "That's impressive, Ruby. Lora doesn't do that with just anyone."

Ruby shrugged. "It let me keep my hand in with training."

Gabe nodded and turned back to Midnight.

Ruby moved over to Glory.

The big chestnut mare poked her nose out at Ruby and she rubbed it, smiling as she remembered last summer. Galloping Glory up the tractor track to the upper fields to move the wheel lines watering those hayfields. Cutting through the ranch's forested corner to jump over deadfall Ponderosa pines that she had arranged to lay out a rough but solid cross-country course. Popping over the remaining irrigation ditches and splashing through creeks.

Glory had been *fun*.

Gramps had pursed his lips in disapproval when Ruby rode out to move lines wearing half-chaps over her jeans, her good jump saddle on the young horses, but he hadn't said anything about it. Riding Lora's young warmbloods through the Double R fields let Ruby escape the worry and fear over Granma's cancer—and gave her the chance to dream that there could be a life for her beyond the ranch. It kept her sane.

If she couldn't finish her degree, then maybe she could make a little money on the side exposing expensive babies to cross-country rougher than anything they would meet in competition.

At least that had been the theory, pre-Martiniere Grant.

"Since you don't have to warm up Midnight, Ruby, why don't you get Sunshine out?" Lora suggested. "It won't hurt to see how she goes through the gymnastic grid in English tack. And I'm here to supervise."

"All right," Ruby said slowly. And maybe Sunshine wouldn't start bucking in the combination of ground poles and cross poles. All she had to do was canter.

Though if any horse could buck through the gymnastic, it would be Sunshine. Maybe Lora would forget about sending Sunshine through it. That would be the best option.

However, protesting would be a firm guarantee that Ruby and Sunshine would be doing the gymnastic. Best to agree, then hope Lora got distracted.

And maybe Lora was right. A change of tack and some jumping might just fit the golden mare's inclinations.

Game to give it a try, anyway. Done just about everything else to figure this horse out.

Soon enough, the three riders led their horses through the gate into the arena and took turns using the mounting block. Louisa and Lora walked to the center. Justine started Glory in a walk inside of the jumps on the rail, followed by Gabe and then Ruby. Midnight pranced and jigged, pulling against his light restraint. Ruby was about ready to say something when Gabe took up a firmer hold on the reins and sat up taller. Midnight quieted.

Glory picked up a trot. Midnight shook his head and jumped around. Ruby tightened her lips. He needed galloping, lots of galloping, before he would settle and not the usual walk-trot-canter progression, just like Sunshine—

"On your left, Tine," Gabe called out.

Midnight danced sideways and Ruby tensed.

The next move would be an explosive, high leap before a fast gallop that always unseated Louisa, and was one reason why Ruby warmed him up—

Gabe laughed as Midnight bounded into the gallop, sitting with a casual grace, seat never moving from the saddle. He leaned forward to encourage Midnight to run, rising in his stirrups. Sunshine jigged sideways, pulling and antsy, drawing Ruby's attention back to her. Ruby squeezed the reins and sat up even more, until the mare calmed. Only then did she ask for a canter, keeping it slow as they passed Glory and Justine. Then she eased the reins so that Sunshine could extend into a gallop, rising out of the saddle into a half-seat as the golden mare ran.

Thundering hooves on their left as Gabe and Midnight blew past them on their second circuit. They crossed the center and Ruby followed them, asking Sunshine for a flying lead change.

Sunshine bucked a few strides before picking up the change. Normal for her. Midnight's strides started to slow but Gabe moved his hands forward, pushing the big gelding to keep running hard. Another circuit and a cross through the center, changing leads in the other direction. Then Gabe sat down in the saddle, sinking his heels hard, taking a firmer contact. Ruby followed, marveling at how quickly Midnight started to slow, even more responsive to Gabe than he was to her.

Lora's right. Midnight's a better match for a rider like Gabe than he is for Louisa.

"He's a Windraker all right!" Gabe called to Lora as Midnight dropped to a walk. Ruby and Sunshine came up next to them. "I got to ride Windraker himself when I was a kid," he said to Ruby, grinning. "He dumped me, but that was still a thrill."

"Did your grandmother own him?"

"No, but she got me the ride after I'd gone through a rough patch and was struggling with depression." His face tightened momentarily. Then the big grin returned. "A big dark bay, almost black. Powerful. But that first big leap into the gallop shed me the first time. After that, I stayed on." He patted Midnight's neck.

"He goes better for you than for me," Ruby said. "I'm surprised you aren't riding regularly. You're *good.*"

"I don't have a lot of time these days. And Mindy—well, for three years, if I wasn't working, I was doing what she wanted, which was usually something urban and indoors. She actively hated horses or anything that took my attention away from her. Including my work." He frowned. "But let's not talk about that. It feels great to be on a good horse. Since I need to be here once a week to coach you, think I might be able to talk my way back up on this boy?"

"It's up to Louisa."

"I suppose it's time for me to hand him over to her."

"Actually, no. I usually take him through the gymnastic and then a circuit of the fences. By then he has his ya-yas out and will listen to Louisa."

Gabe beamed, as Justine slowed Glory down from her canter circuit. "That's great. Shall I go ahead?"

"Justine's done with her warmups, so yes."

Ruby and Justine rode over to stand by Lora and Louisa as Gabe circled Midnight at a trot before heading down the gymnastic line, a set of low, alternating x-shaped cross rail jumps and ground poles. A motley assemblage of jump standards and rails mixed with plastic blocks meant to hold low jumps fenced the gymnastic away from the rest of the arena, so that unridden horses could be sent through it.

Gabe gently asked Midnight to collect, using his seat, followed by his hands. Then he aimed Midnight for the gymnastic. The big gelding hopped over the first crossbar, then picked up a canter, smoothly striding over the obstacles.

Then it was on to the course. Midnight sped up at the approach to the first fence, but Gabe straightened up, squeezed the reins, and shortened Midnight's stride.

"Look at how your brother uses his upper body with that horse," Lora said to Louisa. "That's what you really need to do to rate him."

"Gabie's taller than I am," Louisa sighed. "He got that from Mama."

"Core strength, my dear, core strength. That makes up for the difference in height."

Gabe and Midnight approached the second fence and cleared it easily. Then it was a loop around to a line of three fences that required a single stride between them.

Ruby tensed. Midnight usually sped up on turns when he faced a line like this, dropping his inside shoulder, and ending up scrabbling to regain his balance, often sending poles flying.

Would he do that with Gabe?

Gabe opted to send Midnight into a tight circle when the black gelding picked up speed. He circled twice, until Midnight slowed, his strides relaxed and rhythmic instead of tense and fast. Then he put Midnight at the line.

"That boy *should* have gone into competition," Lora muttered. "Damn Philip Martiniere and his damn meddling."

"Whew," Gabe exhaled as he rode up to them. "This *is* one scopey horse. Weeza, just what on earth possessed you to buy *this* boy?"

Louisa smirked at him. "Oh, maybe I thought you might need a distraction from breaking up with Mindy as well as the Martiniere-in-waiting madness."

Gabe scowled at her. "Now just what do you mean by that?"

"Well," Louisa said slowly. "The reason I didn't get you anything for your birthday last month, Gabie? This. Midnight's yours."

"What the *hell*?" Gabe's face lightened. "Weeza, you can't be serious."

"I *am* serious," Louisa said. "I sent off the ownership transfer papers shortly after Christmas. They're back at the condo. He's a nice boy, but you're right. I need something that isn't as scopey. Just been waiting until you dropped by for a visit to make the gift. Didn't buy another horse because I wanted to keep it secret."

Gabe looked down at Midnight, shaking his head. Then he straightened up.

"Weeza, thank you so much. Really." Then he grinned at Ruby. "Guess that answers the question about riding Midnight. Might even have to spend more time in Corvallis. We'll have to talk about the summer." The grin widened. "And I'd better get my *own* saddle out of storage, see if it fits Midnight."

Lora exhaled. "Well. I'm glad to see this turn of events. Louisa, let's talk about a potential replacement. Ruby, think you can handle things from here?"

"Certainly."

"Though—" Lora paused. "Let's see you take Sunshine down the gymnastic, first. I want to be here for that."

Ruby heaved a sigh.

Let's hope this works.

She picked up the reins and urged Sunshine into a trot. It took three circles to get Sunshine collected and moving evenly. Then she pointed Sunshine at the gymnastic.

Sunshine's ears flattened as she popped over the first cross pole. She sucked back as she strode over the ground pole, and Ruby booted her with both heels, *hard.*

It didn't work.

Instead of cantering over the next cross pole with barely a break in her stride, Sunshine launched herself into the air, her hind end twisting as she kicked high. She missed the ground pole and crashed into the next set of cross poles, sending them flying. Ruby took a firmer hold and booted Sunshine again, hoping to get her back into a canter and not another buck, especially sideways and into the makeshift fence that separated the grid from the arena.

No such luck.

Sunshine's next leap was to the side and through the rails.

Time slowed as Sunshine scrambled to stay on her feet, poles and jumping blocks scattering around them. For one desperate moment Ruby thought they could make it. But Sunshine's momentum and the tangle of rails made her overbalance to the right, despite Ruby's best efforts to counterbalance and pull her up.

Ruby kicked her feet free from the stirrups as she felt Sunshine's right foreleg give way—they were still moving fast.

This is gonna hurt.

She went flying, seeming to hang in the air as her hands automatically flew up to protect her neck while she went limp.

Then time started again. Ruby hit the dirt hard, mercifully managing to miss one of the rails. She gasped for air.

Anything broken?

Wiggle fingers and toes. Check.

Ankle hurt, but she was sure that was muscle, not bone. All right. Another fall survived. Now if she could just move—damn it, *Sunshine was too close and she was rolling over, would catch her with a hoof—*

Gabe grabbed Ruby, pulling her away from Sunshine's flailing hooves as the golden mare finished rolling and staggered to her feet.

"You all right?" he asked.

"I—think so," she gasped. "Just had the wind knocked out of me."

He helped Ruby up. She turned to Sunshine, steeling herself for the worst.

The golden mare stood spraddled on all fours, eyes wide, breathing hard.

"I'd better check her," Ruby said.

"Not by yourself," Gabe muttered. "God damned crazy horse." He wrapped his right arm around Ruby's waist. She took a step and winced as pain pricked at her ankle. "We'd better have a doctor look at you."

Ruby shook her head. "Just a sprain. That right ankle's bad."

"If you say so." But his voice held a doubting note and he didn't let go of her.

Dare she admit that she liked the feel of his arm? His woodsy, spicy scent?

Sunshine raised her head and started to shy back as they approached, but Gabe let go of Ruby and grabbed her reins.

"Quit!" Ruby snarled to the golden mare. Sunshine quieted and Ruby knelt, running her hands along Sunshine's forelegs, first the right, then the left. She didn't feel anything wrong.

Ruby stood, slowly, favoring her right ankle.

I just have a sprain, thankfully. At least that's what this feels like.

"Gabe, will you walk her?" she asked.

"Sure."

Ruby watched Sunshine. The golden mare moved cautiously, but she didn't miss a step. Ruby heaved a relieved sigh.

Lora joined them. "She'll be feeling that fall soon enough."

Ruby nodded. "I'll put an ice wrap on her legs before putting her up, give her some Bute to take the edge off." She winced.

Twenty minutes of ice wraps. Then put them back in the freezer, to repeat every few hours. And damn it, her ankle *hurt*.

"Keep an eye on that right fore," Lora said.

"I will."

"And then ice pack and aspirin for you?" Gabe asked as he led Sunshine back.

"Definitely." Ruby took a deep breath. She hobbled over and checked the saddle—fortunately the saddle tree still seemed to be sound. But she had to replace this helmet, at least, and further examine the saddle, to make sure. "Would you give me a leg up?" she asked Gabe.

"I shouldn't."

"Hopefully the fall shocked some sense into that horse," Lora muttered.

Gabe boosted Ruby into the saddle. She walked Sunshine around the arena, not bothering to pick up her stirrups. The golden mare was subdued—no more antics from her, not today. Ruby stopped Sunshine by the gate. Gabe and Justine joined her.

"I'll help you," he said.

"*We'll* help," Justine said.

"Maybe I should as well," Louisa added.

"No, no, no," Ruby said. "Louisa, go ahead and talk about other prospects with Lora. Justine, go ahead and ride. Gabe, you too. I can handle Sunshine by myself. I'm not made of porcelain. This isn't our first wreck."

Justine raised her brows but turned Glory away. Not a worry, Justine could handle schooling on her own, without supervision. Louisa and Midnight were the combination that needed watching.

Lora sighed. "All right, Louisa, let's go to my office."

Gabe stubbornly remained, holding Midnight's reins.

"You need help," he said firmly.

Ruby snorted. "Have you ever gone off a horse that's tripped over rocks while chasing cattle? At top speed?"

"No, but—"

"I have. I'll be all right. Enjoy your horse."

"I won't be able to enjoy him for thinking about you dealing with this while limping around," Gabe said. "Let me help. Please."

"All right," she conceded, sliding off of Sunshine.

Hobbling to the crossties was a challenge, and she didn't dare lean on Sunshine for fear of provoking her into another explosion. Ruby managed to get the bridle off, Sunshine haltered, and fastened in the crossties before she needed to sit on her tack trunk and catch her breath.

Damn, this hurts.

But she didn't *think* her ankle was broken.

Gabe left Midnight saddled in the crossties and marched back.

"I'm unsaddling her," he announced, his jaw set firmly. "Then we're doing something about *you.*"

"Thank you," she said, extending her leg to rest it on the trunk. "There's an empty saddle rack by a Western saddle—that's mine. Hang the bridle on the hook in front of the rack. Thanks. The ice wraps are in the tack room fridge. Would you grab them on your way back?"

"What about you?" he asked.

"Gotta wait until she's done icing. I don't dare leave Sunshine unsupervised with those wraps."

"I can get what you need." He glowered at her.

Damn, he was stubborn.

Ruby sighed. "Bring me the ice wraps and I'll tell you how to get into my apartment. Oh, and there's a cabinet in the tack room. You'll find the Bute paste tubes there, one with my name on it. We might as well dose her now."

Gabe nodded curtly. He unsaddled Sunshine and carried saddle and bridle to the tack room. Ruby exhaled. At least Sunshine stood solid on both forelegs.

Wouldn't be the first time this damn horse hurt me worse than she hurt herself.

Was she fooling herself about the possibility of trying to rehabilitate Sunshine? Maybe the golden mare was a lost cause, after all. And she was nowhere near as likely to be as reliable as her half-sister Beauty, who had carried Ruby to several queen titles.

Gabe returned with wraps and the paste tube.

"I checked your saddle. Tree's all right."

"Thanks."

Ruby started to struggle to her feet.

"Stay down," he said. "I've got this."

He approached Sunshine. The golden mare raised her head, snorting. Gabe growled at her, but he scratched her neck and murmured words Ruby couldn't hear. She recognized the tone as reassuring. When Sunshine relaxed, he knelt and put on the wraps.

Ruby dialed the paste tube to the right dose and handed it to Gabe. He deftly inserted the tube in Sunshine's mouth and administered the medication.

He's done this before.

Then Gabe stood in front of Ruby, hands on his hips. "Now. You."

Ruby yielded. "All right. Door code is ninety-one, twenty-eight. If you could bring me my muck boots and an ice pack that would be great. Elastic wraps in the bathroom cabinet. Cane in the closet."

"Got it." He whirled and strode off, pausing to pat Midnight and murmur something to the black gelding.

Ruby exhaled. Now to get the boot off of the offending foot. At least these tall boots had zippers. She unzipped the boot, wincing the entire time. Her ankle had already swollen enough to make it difficult.

Gabe returned. "Let me help."

"Sure."

He eased the boot off and then her sock. "Pretty impressive swelling."

"Old injury. Looks worse than it is. Swells up fast."

Gabe nodded. He placed a towel between her skin and the pack, then deftly secured it with the elastic bandage. Then he produced the aspirin and a bottle of water.

"Now the two of you can just settle back for a little bit while I take care of Midnight."

Ruby leaned against the stall wall, her foot propped up on the trunk, and watched Gabe untack and groom Midnight. He talked to the black gelding in soft murmurs, a wide smile on his face as he worked.

More mysteries about Gabriel Martiniere. A horseman who knew what he was doing, and clearly loved being around them.

But he'd given up horses for a woman he loved.

Miranda Cathcart-Rogers, you're a damned fool to walk away from a man like this.

If only she could find someone like him who was less lofty and out of reach; someone who respected her mind *and* her love of horses. Someone who wasn't as disappointing as dating Ollie and Perry had been. And the other men who had chased Ruby because of her rodeo queen titles, only seeing her as a pretty woman, disparaging her brains.

Maybe she would find someone in the Martiniere Group.

Gabe must not be the only good man there, right?

Though he's starting to be the one I really want. And that is absolutely stupid, Ruby. He's out of your league.

CHAPTER 7

NEGOTATING ACROSS THE GENERATIONS

APRIL, 2029

GABE

Ruby was ready and waiting when Gabe knocked on her door the next morning, opening it after the first rap.

"How are you doing?" he asked as she picked up a bag sitting by her door. She moved stiffly, hobbling, but at least she wasn't using a cane this morning.

That fall yesterday—yeah, he was used to seeing bad falls and tough horses. But the way that damn palomino mare blew up on Ruby bothered him. Something needed to be done, before she got injured worse.

None of your business, Gabriel.

Except that Ruby was his *best* Martiniere Grant finalist. That *should* make it his business, right?

"Oh, muscles just tightened up overnight." She gimped away from the door; jaw set tight. "I'll work out of it. Already better after morning chores. Sunshine's looking good this morning. I got the worst of that fall—like usual."

Gabe bit back a retort about the palomino mare. As far as he was concerned, she either belonged in a rodeo bucking string or in a can.

"Let me carry that," he said instead, taking the handles of the bag before she could protest. Something rattled.

"Be careful, please. It's some things for Granma. Her appetite is still iffy, so I try to bring her some treats when I can, see if that will tempt her to eat more." Her forehead crinkled tighter with worry. "That won't be a problem with airport security, will it? I'm carrying a weapon—is that also a problem? I can leave it here, though I don't want to."

"Not for a private jet."

Hmm. She's armed. Good.

Gabe looked inside the bag, curious. Several tins of smoked oysters. Packages of bacon jerky. A jar of small sweet pickles. Another jar of roasted red peppers. Expensive chocolate bars.

"Savory and sweet things?" Something to consider for future reference.

Ruby nodded. "I'd bring more, but the foods that appeal to her change pretty regularly."

"Yeah. My aunt died from breast cancer, after years of metastasis."

"Then you know the dance. Looks like you're moving a little tight, too."

He chuckled, grateful for the change in subject. "I may be in shape but I'm not exactly in *riding a scopey horse* condition. My abs and thighs are talking to me. Midnight will be good for my conditioning, because I'll need to change my workout."

Ruby laughed.

It was good to see that concern fade from her face.

Ruby's eyes widened as they approached the jet. "Solar cells? I didn't think that was possible with airplanes."

"It's experimental," Gabe said. "Hybrid. That's why it's so small —it can use Jet A fuel, plug in for a charge, and recharge in-flight if we're traveling in daylight. Cost me a pretty penny but it's worth it, given all the travel I do. Most of the time, I don't need to use the Jet A. But—" he sighed. "Not feasible yet for anything larger. And I need to be careful about the number of hours I fly. Otherwise, it turns into a carbon hog."

Serg met them at the top of the stairs, and flashed the hand signal indicating that he had examined the jet, ensuring it hadn't been sabotaged.

"Hey, Gabe," he said. "So this is your latest Martiniere Grant finalist?"

"Yes. Serg, this is Ruby Barkley. Ruby, this is my cousin Serg Vygotsky, second-in-command of Martiniere security. He's in charge of making sure that you and your grandparents are safe."

Serg and Ruby bowed to each other.

"I'll have some questions for you en route," Serg said. He eyed Ruby as she hobbled into the cabin. "Injury?"

"Horse accident," Gabe said. "Sprained ankle. Ruby, why don't you take the couch? Put your foot up."

"It's safe for takeoff?"

"Yes. Seat belts in the couch."

"Then I'll do that."

"Once we're in the air, let me take a look at it," Serg said. "Might be able to help you move around better." When Ruby frowned, he added, "I'm a certified personal trainer and paramedic. Ask Gabe. I've patched him up a few times."

"Serg hits hard in training, but he fixes his damage afterward," Gabe said.

"If I could get more support, that would be a help," Ruby said. "Then I can show you more of the ranch without that ankle giving me trouble."

Serg grinned. "Then we'll definitely do that."

They clustered around the couch once they were in the air and cleared by the pilot. Serg frowned at Ruby's ankle, gently poked and prodded at it while she winced, then opened his bag.

"I'll tape it," he said. "X-rays?"

"No," Ruby said. "Can't afford them. Besides, I know what a break feels like."

"That's going to bite you in the butt one of these days," Serg said.

"If you think we should do it, Serg, we can." Gabe ignored Ruby's scowl. "Your choice, Ruby. Lakeside or Corvallis?"

"Might not hurt," Serg said.

"Damn it." Ruby glowered at Gabe. "Just who the hell do you think you are?"

"You're my top Martiniere Grant candidate and you work at the stable where my horse lives. I have a vested interest in your continued good health. I'll pay for it."

Ruby continued to glare at him, jaw jutting stubbornly. He smirked back at her.

"You are bossy as hell."

"Corvallis or Lakeside?" he persisted.

"Corvallis," she snapped. "It's a fuss over nothing."

Oh, this is so much better than Mindy's whimpering over the tiniest bump and—damn it, Gabriel, what the hell are you thinking?

He exhaled. "Consider it a long-term investment, Ruby."

"Gabe's right." Serg didn't look up from taping her ankle. "Sounds like you've done this before."

"I've *ridden* on a broken ankle," Ruby muttered. "This very one. It's a trick ankle now. Sprains easily."

"And you're how old?" Serg asked.

"Twenty-three."

"Just wait. You'll feel it in later years." Serg finished taping. "Probably nothing, but get it x-rayed tonight to be sure." He packed away tape and scissors. "Thunder County's interesting from a security point of view. Two year-round accesses to the Thunder Valley, several other seasonal routes. Could be isolated easily."

"Easy to catch people with nefarious motives should they try to get out." Ruby's glower softened.

"So it's been blockaded before?" Serg asked.

"Couple of times with armed robbers. Not that the current county sheriff is very good. Been in the job for years, source of controversy." Ruby scowled again. "He's buddy-buddy with my father's shiftless family. The Barkleys will take any chance they can to cause trouble for Gramps and me."

"That's something we'd better watch, Serg." Gabe frowned. Was it tied to her parents' death? He had poked into the court records. He knew that Tony Barkley had killed Beth Ryder-Barkley—but the records on Tony Barkley's death were sealed by juvenile court order. One reference to Ruby being present.

She would have been six at the time.

"Aunt Grace and her daughter Jeannie are all talk and no action, but they're a pain in the ass to deal with. The rest of the family is into petty crime. Low-level thefts and assaults, generally Saturday night drunk fights."

"Exactly the sort that someone wanting to cause trouble would hire to bother your grandparents," Serg said.

"They're more likely to vandalize stuff than hurt someone. Cutting fences, destroying crops, arson. *Most* of them are bullies. They'll back down if you stand up to them." Her lips tightened into a thin line. "As I know, far too damned well."

Now Gabe wanted to put the fear of God into those damn bullies. He could tell that those memories still hurt, from the tension in Ruby's face.

Damn it, Gabriel, back off.

"Perimeter patrols sound like a very good idea," Serg said.

"Not necessarily," Ruby said. "We have good neighbors to each side, Chandler and Reed. The vulnerable portion is the Forest Service boundary at the back of the ranch. The house and outbuildings are set off of the main road."

"Sensors on the fence lines, then," Serg said. "At a minimum. I still like the idea of regular perimeter patrols."

"It's a lot of rugged ground," Ruby cautioned. "Foot or horseback will be required in some spots, and you'll need to bring in your own horses and feed."

"Doable," Serg said. "Any chance we can get out there to look at things today? My staff will have UTVs available."

"We can sure try," Ruby said.

"And while we're at it, let's look at the fields," Gabe said. "From what you said last night, the Double R could pull down a field test facility contract with the Group."

Ruby pursed her lips thoughtfully. "You think so?"

"Given the degree of mapping work you've done already, absolutely," he said. "We've gone into other testing facilities with much less site data than you've gathered."

She cocked her head sideways. "Well, that *would* offset some favors you've already done us."

"Your prompt report about the Zingter loan revealed a major hole in our security," Gabe said. "That's worth quite a bit right there."

And that roused his own questions about how much of a storm Donna-gran was raising with Philip in LA. Asking Serg about it with Ruby present was not a good idea. Things seemed to be quiet. He *hoped* that silence meant nothing was blowing up.

Philip was very damned good at being a pain in the ass, and it was telling that Donna-gran was the one dealing with her wayward son. Not his older twin Saul.

THE DOUBLE R WAS SEVEN MILES EAST OF LAKESIDE, TUCKED into a draw between grassy ridges with rock outcroppings and occasional stringers of trees that probably indicated a spring or seasonal creek. The ranch buildings were out of sight of the main road, accessed by a wide driveway with a battered white and green sign that proclaimed CENTURY FARM—RYDER FAMILY.

The field on the left held Corriente-type cows and calves, multi-colored and lean, the adults with horns. On the right sprouted a healthy field of winter wheat. A long irrigation pipe line on wheels along the fence was still secured for the winter, alternating sections tied to metal T-posts with bright blue plastic baling twine.

"Gramps hasn't started irrigating yet," Ruby mused. "And the wheat looks good. Thunder County must have gotten more rain than I thought since Spring Break."

They rounded the rocky end of a ridge and the buildings appeared—first the big white farmhouse with long-needled Jeffreys pines shading the house. Then several machine sheds that contained tractors, swathers, balers, hay wagons, and trucks, followed by two smallish barns, one with an arena attached to it, along with horse pens. Two smaller houses away from the main house.

Not the newest or fanciest of places; but not decrepit, either.

"Who lives there?" Serg pointed to the smaller houses.

"No one," Ruby said. "One was for a ranch manager; the other is a bunkhouse. Gramps fixed them up before Covid, thinking we might want to do vacation rentals. Didn't go anywhere with that project afterward."

"That could hold security staff."

"Other structures can be fixed up as well." Ruby nodded toward a low-set cement block building with broken-out windows. "Hundred years ago, that used to be a dairy. Back when Thunder County shipped cream to Seattle by the railroad, and fed hogs on the by-products. Everyone had a milking and hog operation." Her voice turned wistful. "I thought it might make the foundation for a lab."

"Hmm." Serg stroked his chin. "I was thinking that we bring in some modular units. I'll have to look at those houses."

Their SUV and the other two security SUVs, all three towing trailers carrying UTV side-by-sides, parked behind the house. Ruby's lips tightened as she eyed the house, the tall, unkempt lawn, and the fenced-off space with bedraggled remnants of plants, torn black plastic, and plastic pipe plant supports on half of it. The other half had been neatly turned over.

"They're not doing much yard work. Aw, crud."

"A problem?" Gabe helped Ruby out of the SUV, steadied her, then grabbed the bag of treats for her grandmother.

"Possibly. Nothing's been done in the garden since I started it during Spring Break. By now the whole thing should be turned over and ready for planting. Lawn sprouted up since I've been here. I don't have time to drive out before the end of the term just to mow. But. That's the outside. They *were* on top of things inside just two weeks ago. I hope this doesn't mean there's more issues that I don't know about."

"Hire help."

"Gabe—"

"I'm serious. Either that, or we fly out over the next few Sundays and do it ourselves. Might not be necessary, though. Security can do yard upkeep as a cover activity for their presence."

She shook her head even as she smiled. "I swear, Gabriel Martiniere, you are one damn bossy son-of-a-bitch."

He shrugged, doing his best to look innocent as they walked up the sidewalk to the farmhouse's back door. "I'll have to be one hell of a lot bossier if I become the Martiniere. Consider this as practice."

Her lips curved up more on the left side, enough to reveal a dimple in her cheek. "So I'm your bossiness test subject?"

He chuckled. "You think this is bad, you should see what my sisters do to me. Or my mother."

Ruby arched a brow at him. "Sounds like I need to talk to Louisa and Justine."

"I'm sure they'd be happy to coach you."

Oh God, what am I letting myself in for?

Ruby's grandparents came out the back door. Ron Ryder lent a hand to steady Ruby's grandmother Ruth as they descended the steps. Which needed painting.

Another task for undercover security.

He glanced at Serg. His cousin looked around, probably thinking the same thing. Lots of cover tasks for a security crew.

Back to the grandparents. Both Ron and Ruth were tall and lanky, like Ruby, but from the way that Ruth's loose-fitting pants and snap-button shirt hung on her, Gabe suspected they hid how skinny she was. Ron looked in decent health, for someone in his mid-seventies who had been working outside all of his life. Lean but appropriately so, long gray hair pulled back in a ponytail.

Ruby hurried toward them, hugging first her grandmother and then her grandfather. She wobbled on her right ankle and flinched. Ron scowled at Ruby.

"What happened to you?"

"Oh, nothing major," Ruby said. "Just a fall with Sunshine."

Ron's lips tightened. Before he could say anything, Ruby took the bag from Gabe.

"Granma, here's some goodies for you."

Ruth peered into the bag. "Oh, honey, you didn't have to." But her wide smile said otherwise as she poked at the items.

Ruby took a deep breath. "Gabriel Martiniere. My grandmother Ruth Ryder and my grandfather Ron Ryder." She gestured to Serg. "Serg Vygotsky, second-in-command for Martiniere security."

Gabe bowed, first and deeper to her grandmother, then to her grandfather. "Call me Gabe," he said. "*Gabriel* is what my mother and sisters call me when I'm in trouble."

Ruby glanced sideways at him, that dimple peeking out again. "Sounds like you're in trouble a lot, then, judging from what I heard at dinner on Friday and when we were riding yesterday."

"Shall we go inside and get down to business?" Ron said, his words edged.

"Sounds good." Gabe stepped up to Ruth and offered his arm, with a slight bow. "May I have the honor of escorting you inside?"

Ruth giggled and slid her arm in his. "Such good manners."

"Both my grandmothers would have my head if I behaved in any other way." He startled at how light and bony she felt.

His reaction must have shown, because Ruth leaned close.

"Don't say anything to Ruby," she murmured. "She's already given up too much for my sake."

"She's pretty observant." He patted Ruth's hand as they climbed the steps, taking it slowly and carefully. "My aunt Moira had cancer —Stage Four, metastasized from breast to lungs, spine and brain. So I have some idea."

"My situation as well," Ruth whispered. Her hand closed on his with surprising strength. "Get her out of here, Gabriel. Help her soar. She deserves the opportunity. She can come back eventually—but help her fly, first."

"I'm doing my best to make it happen." He pushed the door open. They entered an enclosed back porch—orderly, like the brief glimpse he had of Ruby's apartment yesterday. Coats neatly hung on hooks; boots aligned underneath. Hats sat on a shelf above the coats.

"Whatever it takes to get the job done," Ruth said.

"I promise." They went into the kitchen. A wheelchair with a light blanket in it sat in the middle of the room. Gabe guided Ruth to the wheelchair and helped her into it, then tucked the blanket around her legs. He straightened up and looked around, as Ron, Ruby, and Serg entered.

Plain—white sheet vinyl floor and yellow walls with white trim. A bit weathered and worn, but clean. An old green Formica and chrome table sat under the window, with matching chairs. Two cups of coffee were on the table—Ron and Ruth must have been watching for their arrival.

"Help yourselves to the coffee." Ruth wheeled over to the table. "Mugs above the coffeepot, milk in the fridge, sugar in the bowl. We aren't very formal here."

"I'm good with that." Gabe pulled down three cups and arched a brow at Ruby. "Black, cream, or cream and sugar?"

"I like my coffee just as it comes out of the pot," she said.

Gabe filled the cups. Serg grabbed one and Gabe carried the other two to the table, setting one in front of Ruby.

Ron pursed his lips. "Kind of surprising to see someone with your net worth waiting on others."

Gabe shrugged. "Wasn't raised to be a demanding asshole." He kept his tone matter-of-fact. "Not sure how much Ruby has told you, but one part of being a Martiniere Grant finalist is financial and physical security protection for the finalist and their families. Longer if necessary." Before Ron could say more, Gabe raised a hand to stop him. "Past candidates have been targets. What happened to you with Zingter is just one example of financial harassment. Fortunately, Ruby reported it to me immediately, and I took care of it."

"We need to talk about that," Ron growled. "*Privately.*"

"I agree."

Ron rose. "How about now? My office."

Gabe stood. "Certainly." He raised his hand again when Ruby started to get up. "No. Just me and your grandfather."

He ignored Ruby's scowl, following Ron through the swinging kitchen door and down a hallway to a large, darker room with desk, couch, chairs, and computer. Ron dropped into the chair behind the desk, glowering at Gabe.

Gabe sat in the most comfortable-looking chair facing the desk. He stretched out his legs and laced his fingers, waiting.

"What the hell makes you any different from Zingter, Martiniere? I owe you one fucking huge debt."

"No, you don't. Ruby's prompt reporting allowed us to discover a vulnerability in Martiniere Group security. That's worth a good chunk of that payment I made to Zingter." He briefly smiled. "I would have paid much, much more to stick it to Walter Braun. I hate the motherfucker and what he does to people. Ruby was his target."

"*Why?*" Ron's voice quavered, a cry coming from deep within him. "She's had to overcome so many obstacles—why did he pick my granddaughter?"

"Because she's brilliant and her ideas are innovative. And—"

Gabe sighed. "She's an attractive young woman. Braun collects those. Especially if he can force them into compromising positions, by holding their families hostage."

"And you think this was one of those cases."

"I *know* it's one of those cases," Gabe said. "I've seen it before, just too late to do anything about it. Braun's reaction confirmed my suspicions about his motivation."

"Oh?" Ron raised his brows.

Gabe gestured with his right hand. "When I paid off the loan, I chucked in extra money—and told Braun to keep his slimy hands off my Martiniere Grant candidates—or else. He went to the Martiniere to demand that I back off. Braun is also tied to my ex-girlfriend and the entire mess with her filing charges against the man who sired me."

"And you are certain of these connections?"

"Absolutely." Gabe laced his fingers together again and leaned his chin on them. "Just as I am absolutely certain that Philip Martiniere *did* assault Miranda Cathcart-Rogers. It fits who he is—and Walter Braun likes to plays those games right along with Philip. It could easily have been Braun assaulting her instead."

"Pretty significant accusations."

"I spent two years in Philip Martiniere's household. I know what happens there. I encountered Braun enough times in that setting that I had no doubts."

Ron nodded slowly. "So what are *your* intentions toward my granddaughter?"

Oh God. If only I could answer this question the way I'm starting to want to answer it.

"I want to recruit her for the Martiniere Group's cutting-edge research labs in France. Her application is of interest to Arthur Martiniere, who manages those labs, and Gerard Martiniere, who manages our French operations. I think her ideas will revolutionize the development of nanobiobots, and—" he shrugged. "I'd like to see it happen under the auspices of the Martiniere Group."

"But all this? Paying off our debt with no obligation? There has to be more."

"There is. I'm competing to become the Martiniere after my father Saul. Ruby will put me there. Her ideas. Her creativity. And one key to optimizing her ability to help me is relieving her of family worries. Therefore—security here, for an indefinite period. Financial support to cover medical and ranch operational expenses." Gabe exhaled. "Based on the detailed mapping Ruby's done, the Double R would easily qualify for a field test facility contract with the Martiniere Group. When all is said and done—the potential value of that contract exceeds what I paid Walter Braun, plus what I would pay to help with your medical expenses and necessary support."

"I'd have to see that contract."

"Here's a copy." Gabe handed over a chip with the contract and related information on it. "You'll note that ownership of the land is not affected, as long as field test exclusivity remains with the Martiniere Group."

Ron inserted the chip into his computer and scanned through it. Gabe leaned back, waiting.

"This looks interesting," Ron said finally. "But what becomes of Ruby?"

"Whatever she wants," Gabe said, and meant it.

Ron snorted. "Do you offer this degree of compensation to every Martiniere Grant finalist?"

"Only the best."

"And if she decides to leave the Group?"

"Hopefully she doesn't. But if she does—well, we *have* bankrolled former employees establishing their own companies. After five to ten years of experience in the Martiniere Group, Ruby would have the track record needed to finance an independent operation."

Ron squinted at him. "Funny. You don't *look* like the devil asking me to sell my soul. Or trying to buy my granddaughter's soul."

"No. That's my sperm donor. Honestly, Ron, there's no strings attached. Well, maybe one. I have a horse, and I'd like Ruby to work with him when she's back here this summer, like she did with my sister Justine's horse. Which means you'll be seeing me off and on, because I need to ride him too."

"Speaking of horses, do you know what happened to Ruby?"

"The mare started bucking in a gymnastic line—you know what that is?"

Ron nodded.

"Blew out the side, sent rails flying, tripped over them, and went down. Ruby landed wrong on the ankle." He decided to omit the part where Sunshine almost rolled over Ruby. "Ruby is very stubborn. I nearly had to clobber her to get her to accept help—and I intend to take her in for x-rays when we're done here."

"You *sure* your only interest in Ruby is professional?"

Gabe spread his hands. "I am six months out from a nasty breakup. I'm working my ass off to become the Martiniere-in-waiting. One of the reasons for my last relationship falling apart was that I work too hard and too long to give any woman the attention she deserves. I don't foresee that changing very soon."

"I see."

"If circumstances were different, then—yes. I admit it. I would have a personal interest in Ruby, as well as professional. Her brains. Her love of horses. Her beauty. Everything she is." He dropped his hands onto the arms of his chair. "That probably shapes my commitment to financing her. But. The Martiniere Group needs her more than I do."

Why was he saying this to a man he had just met? Especially the part about the Group?

Because he's her grandfather and he has a right to know.

Ron cocked a brow at him. "You'll keep me apprised when the situation changes?"

"Certainly."

He wasn't going to correct Ron by saying *if*, not *when.*

After all, he didn't want the man to be pissed at him.

Gabe *did* have a faint hope that Ron would be right.

CHAPTER 8

SHARED SHADOWS
APRIL, 2029

RUBY

Who the hell does Gabriel Martiniere think he is, anyway?

Ruby glowered, clenching her fists, as Gabe followed Gramps out of the kitchen.

She *should* be part of this discussion. *Needed* to be part of it, to clarify to Gramps that she hadn't lost her head or done anything stupid with Gabe. That she wasn't some fragile glass figurine who needed a man's protection, damn it!

And just what the hell did Gabe think he was to her, anyway? Bossing her around about her ankle, *demanding* that she go for x-rays when she knew damned good and well it wasn't broken?

She started to get up but Granma shook her head. "Ruby. No. You're a distraction. Gabriel and your grandfather have to work it out between themselves, and if you or I go in there, it won't happen like it should."

"I'm not a fragile little woman!" she insisted.

"You know that. I know that. *They* know that. But the men need to posture, just like a couple of pasture bulls in the springtime. Bellow and shove each other around for a while, get things worked out to build trust." Granma exhaled. "Your grandfather feels embarrassed about that loan."

"He shouldn't be ashamed of it," Serg interposed. "Braun is very sneaky. He's fooled a lot of people, including people who know better."

Ruby eyed Gabe's cousin.

Second-in-command of Martiniere security.

Was she really that important to the Martiniere Group—or to Gabriel Martiniere? Right now, she wasn't that certain which was which. Or was it both?

"All right," she conceded, dropping back into her chair.

"Good." Granma grinned at her. She pulled the bag of goodies over to examine it further. "Let's see what you brought me—oh! Ruby! You shouldn't have." She extracted the packages of expensive bacon jerky. "Sriracha. Honey. Teriyaki—oh dear, are you *sure* you should be spending money on me like this?"

"You're worth it, Granma. Especially if you'll eat it."

"Thank you, dear." Granma dug deeper into the bag, exclaiming at each treasure.

Ruby smiled. Each item meant a minor budget sacrifice, though it was worth it to see Granma happy. The Martiniere finalist prize money would let her give Granma more—she wondered how soon those funds would be dispersed. Perhaps she could manage to run a higher balance on her credit cards until she got the payout.

Gabe and Gramps returned to the kitchen sooner than Ruby expected. Gramps's face was no longer tight and worried and Gabe smiled—faintly.

"I'll definitely talk to my cousin Arthur about that test facility contract this week, Ron," he said. "Take some pictures while we're here today, get an idea of how big it's going to become."

Oh. Was *that* all they had discussed?

Gabe sat next to her, and Gramps beside Granma.

"Whatcha got there, Ruth?" Gramps peered at the collection of treats.

"Ruby brought them for me." Granma's smile was huge.

Gramps chuckled. "Some midnight snacks, eh?"

"I've been pining for some of those good smoked oysters." Granma eyed Gramps. "All right. Things settled?" Ruby recognized the tone. Granma taking stock of the situation, calling Gramps to accountability.

"Yes." Gramps leaned back in his chair and rested his arm across the back of her wheelchair. "Among other concerns, Gabe is talking about making the Double R a test facility for the Martiniere Group. It looks like a good deal to me."

"We need to get the security setup in place first, Gabe," Serg said. "You're thinking that a combination of personal and field security, test quality, is required?"

"Test quality covers personal protection levels as well," Gabe said.

"What are we talking about when it comes to the security that you're providing us?" Gramps asked. "People? Drones? Sensors?"

Gabe nodded at Serg. "It's all yours, cuz."

"A combination of all three elements, actually," Serg said. "Personal protection for you and your wife, on site, at a minimum. That would include medical support. Gabe, should I include off-site bodyguards?"

Both Gramps and Granma's eyes widened at the mention of *bodyguards*.

"Let's think about that for a minute," Gabe said. "Ron, Ruth, how likely are you to get harassed by locals away from the ranch? Ruby mentioned problems with her father's family."

"Any problems the Barkleys cause us will be here on the ranch. They aren't going to mess with us in public." A sly smile twitched Gramps's lips. "They've learned. Ruth, wanna start?"

Granma chuckled. She reached under her shirt to pull out her semi-automatic pistol and set it on the table in front of her. Fished out a derringer and the canister of bear spray concealed in her wheelchair.

A slow smile started to spread across Serg's face when it was Gramps's turn and he brought out his concealed pistol, boot knife, derringer, pocket switchblade, and brass knuckles.

"Ruby, you shown them yours yet?" Gramps grinned impishly.

She brought out her own concealed pistol and knives. "Can't carry as much on campus."

Gabe eyed the armaments on the table and laughed. "This almost looks like weapons check at a Martiniere party. Serg, we don't have to advise Ruby and her grandparents about carrying weapons. That's refreshing." He added two pistols and a boot knife to the collection.

Serg shook his head, grinning. "Well, this is a very promising start."

Ron raised his brows. "Ruby, why don't you show them the rest?"

Ruby laughed and headed for the cabinet door that resembled an ordinary broom closet. She opened it and spun the dial on the concealed gun safe.

Both Gabe and Serg got up to peer inside.

"AR-15. Short-barrel shotgun. Regular shotgun," Serg intoned, almost prayerfully. "AK-47. Two of each."

"And all properly licensed," Gramps added.

"Impressive," Gabe said. "Have the Barkleys been that big of a problem?"

Gramps tightened his lips. "You okay with talking about this, Ruby?"

She nodded, biting her lip. It had to be disclosed, but she didn't like it.

"We got custody of Ruby when she was four," Gramps said. "Her parents were heavy into meth and heroin, and we didn't dare let the Barkleys get Ruby because—well—that's reflective of nearly all of them." He sighed. "Tony kidnapped Ruby when she was six. That was a nightmarish three weeks—and ended with both Tony and Beth dead."

"I've seen the records," Gabe said, his voice low and hard. "But who killed Tony Barkley? From the description—"

"I did." Ruby gazed down at her feet, not looking at anyone. Might as well come clean about her role. "They were both strung out after several days on meth. They started arguing. I tried to stop them. He started whaling on Mom with a tire iron when she pulled a gun on him. I—" she gulped. "I knew that whoever survived would turn on me. I just *knew*. When Mom dropped the gun, I grabbed it and hid."

She choked, *the fear* still rising after all these years. The memory of squishy smacking noises. Screams that trailed off. The terror when her blood-splattered father opened that closet door, red-smeared tire iron in hand. Raising that pistol with shaking hands that became steady when she aimed for his nose, just as Gramps had taught her, so she could avoid the bulletproof vest her father usually wore....

"You don't have to say the rest," Gabe murmured. "You really don't." He rested his hands on her shoulders. "Look at me, Ruby. Look at me."

She reluctantly obeyed. Not that she expected Mr. Gabriel Martiniere, *billionaire*, to understand these realities.

"I spent two years in hell with my biological father, from when I was sixteen until I was eighteen," Gabe said, his voice still low and quiet. "His wife tried to seduce me. He beat the crap out of me because I wouldn't participate in orgies, and I didn't dare fight back because he would have hurt Justine instead. When I left his house the day that I turned eighteen, I brought Justine with me, to keep her safe." His hands tightened on her shoulders. "I know what the fuck you're talking about, and I *would* have killed Philip, if the opportunity presented itself."

She sniffled and glanced away, blinking hard to try to keep the tears from escaping. He brushed them away with one quivering finger. Then he cupped her cheek.

"You don't have to say the rest," he repeated.

Ruby dared look at Gabe. No pity in his expression. No condemnation.

Just understanding.

He knew.

That haunted expression on *his* face.

He knew.

She nodded, sharp and curt.

Gabe dropped his hands and turned to face Gramps. "So did the Barkleys come after you once Ruby was cleared?" His voice was hard again.

"For ten years," Gramps said. "Until the most active of them either poisoned themselves with meth and harder stuff, or else went to jail."

At least they didn't tell him—the other.

"Ron and I pulled nighttime guard shifts over Ruby at times," Granma said.

Gabe exhaled. "All right. I'm leaving it to your judgment about whether you need bodyguards or not off-site. But I think an active security detail on the place is an excellent idea. Put them to work doing yard work and repairs around the house, let it be known that you have medical support due to health issues. We can run that cover easily enough. You've received Martiniere money, so you can afford upgrades and help. No one will question that. Add in the field-testing contract and no one is going to be suspicious. That is, if you *want* to be discreet."

"That would be best," Gramps conceded.

"You know," Serg said thoughtfully. "I bet the SPA-2 might be just the tool to leave here."

"SPA-2?" Gramps asked.

"Proprietary semiauto rifle," Serg said. "Current Martiniere standard security weapon. Nice and lightweight. Matching pistol." He waved at the assorted armaments on the table. "Gabe carries the pistol version. Check it out."

Granma reached for Gabe's pistol. She skillfully ejected the clip, checked the barrel for bullets, and worked the action, raising her brows. "Easier for me to handle than what I'm carrying."

"Is there a private range around here that won't have a lot of activity?" Serg asked. "Besides looking at the fields, I'd like to show you a few things with those pistols and the SPA2 rifle. I brought one for each of you."

"We have our own shooting range hidden in a draw," Gramps said. "Don't have to leave the place. Even work it in as part of a tour."

"Fantastic." Serg grinned. "How soon can we head out and who's going with us? My security brought several UTV side-by-sides."

"If we're gonna shoot, then I want to be part of it," Granma said.

Ruby smirked when both Gabe and Serg startled at Granma's words.

Soon enough they had everything organized and loaded into the side-by-sides—Serg in one with Gramps and Granma, Ruby and Gabe in another, and members of Martiniere security in two more rigs. Other security staff stayed behind, one pulling out the lawn mower while the others worked on the garden. A crew started installing sensors around the house and outbuildings.

"Ruby, let's go up through Bridge and Draw fields to Homestead and Lone Pine," Gramps suggested. "Then we can drop down to the lower fields and swing by the shooting range."

"Got it, Gramps." Ruby drove out in the lead, conscious of Gabe's eyes on her.

To her surprise, Gabe automatically climbed out to open the first gate when they stopped at it, without being told.

"Wait for the others or have the last one through close gates?" he asked.

"As long as they know how to close them properly," she said.

All right. He had enough experience to know gate etiquette. Good.

Gabe fished out his phone while he opened the gate. Paused as he talked, then walked back, tucking the phone away. He deftly swung back into the side-by-side.

"No problems. They'll get the gates."

Ruby turned up the track that ran alongside the narrow Bridge field.

"This is the Bridge field?" Gabe leaned forward to study it.

"Yes. Pretty much as Gramps said. Bridge, Draw, then Homestead. Which ones did you want to look at?"

"The first two are pretty straightforward. Homestead can be our first stop."

"All right, then."

Silence fell between them as they drove up the widening draw, until the track took them back over another wooden bridge.

"I'm sorry," Gabe said suddenly.

"For what?" Ruby's hands tightened on the wheel.

He sighed, swatting at something. "Bringing up painful memories."

"Sounds like you have a few of those yourself."

"Yeah. Don't mention this discussion to Justine, please. There are parts tied to her mother's suicide that are—pretty damn touchy."

Ruby swallowed hard.

He protected his little sister. Still is protecting her. But—from what?

"Since you asked about mine—why the hell were you in that situation? If you don't mind *my* asking."

A long pause. "Only fair. You'll need to know most of this eventually. Might as well get this part of the briefing over with, in more depth than I usually do it. You're someone who will understand. Most—won't."

Another pause as he leaned his head against the seat back, staring at the roof. "Saul and Philip are twins; Saul the elder, which means he became the Martiniere by default according to Family tradition, except—they started fighting over control of the Family and the

Group shortly before my grandfather's death. Ugly stuff. Fistfights. Worse. My grandmother—Donna-gran, she's pretty formidable— worried that they would tear the Family and the Group apart in their battles. Part of the fight was also over my mother."

"Oh?"

"She was a ballerina on her way up the ranks. Danced Odile/Odette in *Swan Lake* for the San Francisco Ballet—her goal was New York. Broke her ankle and that finished her career. Both Saul and Philip fell in love with her and courted her."

That might explain some of his fussing about my ankle.

"Anyway," Gabe continued. "Once Saul became engaged to Angelica—my mother—things went nuclear. Attempted assassinations. Donna-gran negotiated a settlement and found Renate for Philip to marry. The next step—she decreed that Saul and Philip's first children would be hostages for their fathers' good behavior. In a rather peculiar and twisted manner. Both men would sire sons on the other's wife—by in-vitro fertilization, to be raised by their brother until both of us—me and Joey—were sixteen."

"That's twisted all right. It sounds like something that would happen in the medieval era, all except for the IVF."

Gabe snorted. "My family *is* descended from the Medicis and the Borgias. As I told you on Friday night. There are *some* Family traditions that go back to that time."

"What happened at sixteen?"

"We were told about our actual parentage. Joey's three months younger than me, so it was on his birthday." Gabe reached for the hand hold, grasping it tight, staring straight ahead, jaw set hard. "Philip immediately demanded that I live with him—and he had lawyers ready to assert his rights. Saul took Joey. He had no choice." Gabe laughed bitterly. "Joey lasted two months before he skittered back to Philip because he wasn't allowed to do as he pleased. Saul had high expectations, and while he was demanding, he was also fair. Or so I thought. Joey didn't. He felt that as Saul's biological son, he was entitled to become the Martiniere-in-waiting." He exhaled. "Joey did *not* care for the second part of Donna-gran's decree—which leads to the current Family situation."

"Which is?"

"Competition between Donna-gran's elder grandsons for the right to become the Martiniere-in-waiting." Another, deep sigh. "In fact, Joey is the only elder grandson explicitly banned from the competition. Leaving Saul's house after two months disqualified him. I went the full two years. Despite Philip's best efforts to force me into quitting so that I would also be disqualified."

"Dear God. That is extremely fucked up." She had gone through a lot but hell—

"You don't know the half of it." Gabe's voice went flat. "I wasn't kidding about Philip's wife Renate trying to seduce me. I don't know if Philip put her up to it, or if she saw me as a potential escape method. She killed herself after the last time I said no to her. I was seventeen and a half." He closed his eyes and shuddered. "I was the one to find her. It was apparently a deliberate choice on her part for that to happen."

"Oh *God*, Gabe."

Should she share the rest of her story? Dear God, he'd gone through hell. Apparently being a billionaire didn't protect one from *everything*.

"An already crappy situation became a fucking nightmare," he said. "I ended up—oh God, Ruby, you don't want to know what I went through in those final six months in Philip's house. Let's just say there was *no consent involved*, except to protect my sister. Justine was turning twelve and the scum lurking around Philip already drooled over her. The minute I became eighteen, I grabbed her and went home. Midnight on my birthday." He gulped. "I appealed to Saul in his role as the Martiniere. Pulled him and Mama out of bed. Begged and pleaded to keep Justine out of that hellhole." He shook his head. "Saul—Papa—looked at me and said *of course, Gabriel*. I don't know what he did to make it happen. But Tine spent her teenage years growing up with Weeza as her sister, free from those fucking shadows. And Philip has no power within the Family and the Group. *My* doing, because I went to the Board and told them what I had experienced. In gory detail."

"Oh God." She gulped and blinked.

This made *so much* clear about Gabriel Martiniere.

"I was a fucking mess for the next two years—Covid lockdowns didn't help. Needed surgery because—" He gulped and shook his head. "Spent most of my time on horseback after I recovered. Ended up telling Lora everything." His mouth quirked. "She gave me the perspective I needed to understand what I had gone through. Talked me down a few times when I became overwhelmed with the memories and didn't see any way out. I owe her one hell of a lot, which is why she has the best damn Martiniere security possible. And if she ever needs money or other help—I'm there for her."

"Fuck." Ruby drew a ragged breath. "I am so damn sorry."

Silence.

"So yeah. I understand what you went through," he said. "But I'm still sorry for bringing it up. My damn curiosity."

"That was only half of my story," Ruby swallowed hard. "Those guns aren't there just because I killed my father. Or low-level harassment from his family."

"Your grandmother said they sat watch over you for several years."

She nodded. "I was assaulted several times before I started carrying a gun, Gabe. Gang-raped by my own damned cousins. Rescued by another cousin who damned near was beaten to death in the process." Oh God. Her throat tightened and she didn't want to continue. This was difficult to share, and only Gramps and Granma knew the full story.

But Gabe trusted her enough to tell her his shadows. She needed to finish sharing hers.

"I ended up—pregnant," she continued. "Had an abortion, just before my tryouts for Thunder County Days Queen. Earning that title was my *fuck you* to my Aunt Grace's damn empty-brained sons."

"They paid?" His voice was colder and harder than ever, and a quick glance sideways showed a dangerous glimmer in his narrowed eyes, mouth tight—

"Yes." She exhaled. "It looked like just another meth deal gone bad. I don't know which one was—" she choked, unable to say the rest of it. "But they all paid. Gramps made sure of it."

"*Good.*" He reached out and rested his hand on her shoulder. "Because if not—Serg and I would be having a *very* private talk about dealing with them. Being a billionaire has some privileges in these fucking circumstances."

That dangerous expression still tightened his face.

"Oh?"

"If someone hadn't tipped off Papa, then he, Mama, and Weeza would have been killed in a plane crash when I was twelve. Sabotage of a chartered jet, and Philip was involved. Couldn't be proven sufficiently to charge him. But that, combined with what I told the Board, stripped Philip of any power within the Group. And the Family."

"And yet they let you go to his house." How the *hell* could they have done that?

Gabe rubbed his face. "They didn't have a choice. And I think Papa—Saul—believed that Philip wouldn't hurt his own biological son, because that behavior was beyond Papa's comprehension. Saul honestly tried to create a relationship with Joey, who just threw it in his face. Now—Papa and Donna-gran know better."

Ruby exhaled a long, shuddering breath.

Gabriel Martiniere understood. Oh hell yes, he *understood.*

Did she *want* to know about those six months of hell he alluded to? From his expression and what he carefully *didn't* say, she could imagine what it was like. Especially when he said *there was no consent involved.*

There had been surgery. Oh God. She could—rape of some sort. That left damage. Oh God. And yet he was sitting next to her, polite and apparently sane.

But it had left him suicidal—no blame there. She had faced that shadow herself.

"You all right?" he asked.

"Yeah. You?"

He nodded.

It was a relief to pull up at the edge of Homestead field. Gabe climbed out, gazing at the Thunder Mountains and the valley below them, the continued rise to the north as the prairie country joined with forest, the canyon country to the east.

"Wow. Just wow. Your data is one thing but actually seeing this—damn. It's beautiful, Ruby." He pulled out his phone and started snapping pictures—including a quick one of her framed against the Thunders, before she could bring her hands up to block her face.

"What do you need that one for?"

"For me," he said, his voice gone quiet as the others pulled up. "To remind me of a beautiful, brave, and brilliant woman in a glorious setting, when the shadows become too much to endure."

That, she could understand. Trauma just didn't go away with the wave of a hand...and she had her own, difficult-to-endure shadows.

Need to find an opening for my own picture of him, because having that reminder of not being alone in trauma might just be useful for those bad nights.

THE REST OF THE DAY PASSED IN A BLUR AS HER ANKLE STARTED throbbing worse than ever. By the time they returned to Corvallis, Ruby was ready to have it examined. Just in case.

As she predicted, however, the x-rays were clear. No break, just a severe sprain, not even enough to be worthy of a boot or cast. The doctor prescribed a painkiller that Ruby would have rejected except for Gabe's glower.

"I won't take them," she said quietly on the way back to the barn.

"I'm the daughter of addicts, Gabe. I don't dare take them. I'd much rather have a stiff drink."

"Understood," he sighed. "But if it gets too bad—please? Just don't mix it with the booze."

"I'll consider it."

He walked her back to her door. Before she unlocked it, she slipped her phone out and took his picture. First real opening without others around.

"What's that for?" he asked.

"To remind me of a noble, generous and bold man who went through hell to rescue his little sister," she said. "Because the shadows become too much for me, too."

He half-smiled. To her surprise, he took her in his arms and kissed her forehead.

"Sleep well, Ruby Barkley."

"Only if the nightmares don't come," she murmured.

His arms tightened around her for a moment, and he kissed her forehead again.

"Let's hope they stay away from both of us." Then he stepped away. "I'll see you on Saturday, all right? I promise you, this is the worst of the Family's secrets."

"Thank you for being honest."

He cupped her cheek for a moment. "Thank you for sharing your shadows." He exhaled. "And now, onward. Saturday morning next week, and Midnight. I'll be looking forward to it."

She watched him walk away.

Maybe, just maybe.

Today's revelations changed things. Big time.

Gabriel Martiniere wasn't as different from her as she had thought.

CHAPTER 9
CONSEQUENCES
APRIL, 2029

GABE

THANKS TO THE HASSLES AND DELAYS AT THE CORVALLIS emergency room with Ruby's x-rays, Gabe got back to the condo late enough that he didn't expect either of his sisters to be awake.

But Louisa lay on the couch, studying. She sat up as he entered.

"Weeza, you didn't have to stay up for me." Gabe dropped onto one of the recliners. It felt good, almost comfortable enough to sleep in as an alternative to his bed.

Have to try it out on one of those restless nights.

Louisa shrugged. "Had a big fight with Ginny and I'm still wound up. Surprised that you're out so late."

"Ruby's x-rays." Damn. He didn't like hearing about Ginny and Louisa fighting—then again, he made nice to Ginny for Weeza's sake. Ginny put on too many airs for his liking.

"Ruby's all right?" Louisa furrowed her brows.

"Serg thought she should have x-rays. She was hurting pretty bad by the end of the day, but at least nothing's broken." Gabe shook his head. "The woman is tough as nails. Talking about riding horses tomorrow. Apparently, she has all sorts of braces and such to support that ankle."

Louisa rolled her eyes. "Not surprised." She sighed. "I have more information to pass on."

"Oh God," he groaned. "About Mindy and Philip?"

He'd deliberately kept away from any news flashes, and their parents hadn't contacted him.

"Philip, at least," Louisa said. "Donna-gran has started the process to disinherit him. The only assets he has left are things personal to him. No more Martiniere Family Trust, no access to anything within the Group. He's not poor, but the money spigot's been shut down."

"What the hell?" Gabe startled up.

"Oh, there's more." Louisa's face tightened, almost a copy of their mother's when she had bad news to deliver. "He attacked Donna-gran. She had him arrested—and that's when she cut him off from the Family. Joey, at least, had the sense to accept her strictures, but she's locked him down so he can't feed any money to Philip."

"So, Philip's back in jail."

"For now. We'll see if he can post a bond."

"He'll probably get help from Walter Braun." Fuck. This was going from bad to worse.

"Probably." Louisa sighed. "Tine's had a really bad day of it. We learned about Donna-gran and Philip when Joey called, begging for her to intervene. She told him to go to hell, but the whole situation brought up a bunch of memories. After he hung up, we talked to Mama and Papa and got the whole story. She took a sleeping pill, and Don's watching her. You're lucky that you were away."

"Oh, my day had its own highlights."

"Ruby's grandparents being difficult?"

"No. Not that at all." He rubbed his face. "She has a history of her own, Weeza, and I ended up telling her my story. My own fucking history. Almost all of it."

"Oh, hell, Gabie."

His sister knew about those memories—some from Justine, some from him. Had sat watch over one or the other of her siblings—sometimes both at the same time—when the shadows got overwhelming.

He leaned on his thighs, shaking his head. "She's had a really fucking rough time of it, Weeza. Worse than I thought. Addict parents, and—*God.*"

"I know she's had an abortion because of rape," Louisa said, her voice low. "My last boyfriend—I thought he'd slipped off the condom. My period was late and I was panicking. Crying into the neck of the schoolie I was riding, after I put him back into his stall. Ruby took me aside. Talked to me about it. Kept me from freaking out, was willing to go to the clinic with me as someone who had gone through the process herself. That was back when we were both freshmen." She shuddered.

Gabe rubbed his face. So Louisa knew some of Ruby's story. It wasn't surprising—*this* little sister seemed to invite confidences from everyone around her, and didn't talk, unless she judged it necessary.

Like our mother.

"Come here," Louisa said. "I spent time holding Tine today before Don got back from his errands and could keep her from freaking out. I can hold you."

He got up. Another thing about this little sister—she was damn good at mothering everyone around her, even though she was adamant that she would never bear children of her own. So much like their mother otherwise. Damn it, he *wanted* her to find the right person.

"Is Donna-gran all right?" He settled in with a sigh against Louisa's side, leaning his head on her shoulder as she put her arm around him.

"She was hurt bad enough to go to the hospital," Louisa said grimly. "They didn't keep her, but Papa was very, very angry. And Mama was fussing over him, which has me worried about Papa as well."

Gabe rubbed his face again. "This whole situation with Philip is a nightmare."

And just how would it reflect on *him?* That Philip was bold enough to physically attack *his own mother*—what did that say about his mental state?

More than that, what did this portend for Philip's biological children?

Maybe he shouldn't try to become the Martiniere. What if Philip was crazy, and passed that down to him and Justine?

Louisa squeezed him. "It'll be all right, Gabie. It'll be all right."

Gabe groaned. He was tired out, damn it, and that last lovely moment when Ruby had taken his picture—that had been enough for him to risk taking her into his arms. She hadn't resisted, either.

But this news wiped out the afterglow from that moment.

"You gonna be all right, Gabie?"

He sat up. "Yeah. Just tired. Maybe all the fresh air at the Double R today—oh God, Weeza, it's a beautiful place—will help me have a good night's sleep, for once."

Not that it was likely, not with this news hanging over him. Even worse, the week ahead of him was just as booked as this past week had been, if not more so. A quick flight to LA tomorrow to meet with Saul, then to Paris to go over things with Gerry and Artie, including the Double R contract and getting Ruby additional college credits. Back to Arkansas to brief Jeff Swait. Calgary. Boise. Then here.

And that was before he took into consideration any fallout from the antics of his fucking useless sperm donor.

Or whatever else that Mindy and/or Walter Braun would do to make his life miserable.

GABE SHOT UP IN BED, GASPING FOR BREATH. THE LAST TRACES of his nightmare still lingered, images of Walter Braun, Ruby, and Philip crammed together. He buried his head in his hands, heart pounding, and tried to steady his breathing. At last, he fumbled for his phone to check the time.

Three in the morning. His thumb activated his *private* lock screen, the one with the picture of Ruby. Not the one he'd taken at Homestead field but one he'd secretly snapped later, during their shooting practice. She was still framed against the traces of snow remaining on the Thunder Mountains, but she looked away from him, smiling as her grandmother shot the SPA2. Pistol in hand at her side. That gorgeous dark red hair coming loose from her braid and scattered in wispy tendrils around her face.

A powerful woman just coming into herself. He could imagine what Ruby would be like in a few years—and if he were lucky, he would be at her side.

Gabe collapsed onto his side, gazing at Ruby's picture.

Maybe he was stupid to keep fighting to become the Martiniere-in-waiting. Maybe he could convince Ruby to flee with him to someplace safe, away from the Family and the Group. Maybe they could start a new life. He could finish his master's degree. She could complete her bachelor's. They could start up a new lab while getting their doctorates.

For one outrageous moment he considered the possibilities of a different life with this woman, working together to design nanobiobots and other devices.

Then he exhaled, groaning.

It couldn't happen.

She had her grandparents.

He had the Family.

Going off on his own would only make him more vulnerable to Braun and his buddies.

But oh. Ruby.

Another random thought occurred, and he almost called her.

No. They didn't have that kind of relationship.

He lay there gazing at her picture, until drowsiness finally overtook him again.

THE WEEK OF ABSURDITY STARTED WITH A BANG WHEN HIS plane diverted from the airport where he usually landed in LA.

"What's going on?" he asked Lance.

"Someone's trying to serve you with a subpoena," Lance said. "We don't know who's involved yet. Saul is sending his own security to meet you."

When they got to Martiniere Group headquarters, security hustled him in through a delivery dock instead of the usual entrances. Which made Gabe's skin prickle. He kept his hand close to his weapon—too easy to be ambushed here, but safer than the main entrance.

They used the freight elevator to reach Saul's office.

"Sorry about the chaos," Saul said when Gabe arrived. "Philip's attorneys want you to testify to his state of mind as part of his bail hearing."

"As if I'd know anything. I've not been around him for eight years. Besides, wouldn't that get him locked up in a psychiatric hospital?"

"If only." Saul scowled. "But my understanding is that the hospital they've specified is more of a country club, and easily escaped."

"We can't have that."

"No. We can't. If Philip has deteriorated to the point that he'll attack Mother, then none of us are safe."

Gabe buried his head in his hands. "Oh God. And what does that mean for me and Tine? We're his biological children, after all. Are we going to become like—him?"

Saul shook his head. "Gabriel, don't beat yourself up, and tell your sister not to worry as well. Neither of you are like your father was at this age. *Neither* of you. Now. You have another problem to deal with. We have a leak within the Board. *Someone* has released portions of your Board testimony from eight years ago to Philip's attorneys. That's why they want you at that bail hearing."

"Oh, *fuck*."

"Exactly."

"Do we have any idea who the source is?" Gabe thought through the prospects. It *had* to be someone who saw him as a threat, who supported another candidate for Martiniere-in-waiting. He wasn't the Board's unanimous candidate—if so, he'd be the Martiniere-in-waiting already.

"No idea, son." Saul scowled. "I can tell you who *is* reliable—Artie and Gerry, of course. Whoever did this is someone with access to Board data."

Gabe sat up and pinched the bridge of his nose, feeling a headache coming on. "Should I keep on with my plans or go to ground? I have candidates to brief, data to share with Artie and Gerry —my talking to them in person has just become more imperative."

"Keep on with your usual schedule," Saul said. "Don't give up the fight yet, son. You've gone through one hell of a lot to get here."

"All right." Gabe dropped his hand.

"What's imperative about this meeting with Artie and Gerry?"

Gabe described the conversations with Dr. Asa Green and Ron Ryder.

"Who's on security for Ruby Barkley and her family?"

"Serg."

For the first time Saul smiled. "Good. Because even though you deny any sort of relationship with the woman other than professional—it's clear to me that striking at her is one way to get to you. And if I can see it, then others, particularly Walter Braun, will figure it out very quickly."

"I know, Papa. But I—" *Should* he tell Saul about the picture exchange? The private conversation with Ruby? Gabe calculated. Pinched his nose again. Decided. "She knows details about my memories."

"That's a risk. Did you do the same with Miranda?"

"Hell, no. She would have run screaming from me. No. Call it a matching exchange. Ruby's also had a rough time. I found answers to things that aren't in her records," Gabe sighed. "Her history is as ugly as what I experienced."

Saul frowned. "How hard do you think it will be for someone with good research tools to discover this information?"

"I didn't find it." Then he remembered. Ruby's aunt Grace and cousin Jeannie. "But she has at least two relatives with the motivation to disclose things. The material could be pretty damn personally devastating if it gets out."

"Pass the necessary data to Piotr. I'll assign him to work with Serg, because Ruby has just become a higher priority. And warn Ruby. Carefully. If you plan to be in regular contact with her beyond the Grant finalist requirements, especially since Louisa gave you that horse, get her a secured phone. I'll approve it."

"Thank you, Papa. Should I hand it to her, or is this something that Serg will handle?"

"Neither. I'm sending Piotr to her." Saul straightened up. "Now. Let's cover what I need you to be doing this week."

He waited to call Ruby until he was safely back in his office.

"Gabe!" She *sounded* happy to hear his voice.

"How are you doing today?"

"Oh, sore, but things are getting better."

"That's good. I—wish I was calling with better news."

"What's wrong?" That guarded tone in her voice again. Damn it.

"Philip's lawyers want me to testify to his mental state as part of his bail hearing. It has to do with—the things I told you. I'm not going to, but some of it has been leaked and may go public."

"That's awful, Gabe." Worry replaced the guarded note. "Will you be all right?"

"I should be. But there's more. Saul thinks you may be identified as one of my weak spots. Someone is coming to brief you—a person that Serg normally reports to."

God, he *hoped* she remembered who that would be from what little he had been able to tell her.

"Your cousin's father, then."

Thank God, *yes.*

"He'll provide you with more secure communications. He will ask you questions—please answer them with as much information as possible."

"I understand, Gabe."

"I'm sorry. As a Grant finalist, you aren't supposed to have these issues. Things blew up bad yesterday. The situation is evolving. The person Papa is sending to you has the authority to explain what you need to know."

"I understand." Hesitation in her voice. "Are *you* all right, Gabe?"

"I've been better." God, he wanted to tell her about the consolation of looking at her picture last night.

Best not to, however. Not until she had a secure phone. Something he should have taken care of himself, before now.

"*Gabriel.*" Her sharp tone made him smile a little, because he now knew her well enough to recognize it as affectionate chiding, like he'd get from his mother or sisters. "If you get too tired, then that damn horse will dump you."

"We can't have that, can we? But *you* need to be careful with *your* damn horse."

"Eh, she's turned up sore. I think she'll have to wait until Saturday."

"That's good." He wanted to be there when she climbed on Sunshine again. He absolutely did not trust that damned palomino mare.

A pause, then, "I need to go. Time for labs."

"Be careful, Ruby."

"You too, Gabe."

Could he help it if he smiled as he hung up?

JET LAG. A NECESSARY CURSE OF GABE'S CURRENT LIFE. Showing that he could cope with it was part of proving his fitness to be the Martiniere-in-waiting, at least in his mind. And while he could sleep on the jet, it wasn't ideal. He left Los Angeles at noon, which was nine in the evening in Paris; due to arrive at almost eight the next morning, Paris time. At least half of the nearly eleven hours in flight needed to be spent working. But he could work the whole damn time and he'd still be behind.

Piotr called him four hours into the flight.

"This woman is a true delight to work with, Gabriel," he said in Russian, his primary language.

"How so?" Gabe switched easily into Russian—the four languages common within the Family were English, French, Spanish and Russian. He wasn't literate in Russian, but the Vygotsky family members could translate if necessary.

"Very pragmatic. Very down-to-earth. If I were a younger man, ah, so tempting."

Gabe chuckled. "Don't fall in love with her, Piotr!"

"As if I would," Piotr said, offense in his tone. "She is a client, after all."

"Everything went well?"

"She provided more than adequate information about how best to deal with her Aunt Grace and cousin Jeannie. As it turns out, those two women are not only easily bribable, but they were more than happy to receive an all-expenses paid, indefinite, Caribbean vacation on Solitaire Island on top of a substantial payment. Donald's mother Barbara will be supervising them."

"Ah."

Oh.

Barbie Knowles Atwood was even more secretive than the

Martinieres, with ties to the British royal family, and she owned a controlling interest in Solitaire. He hadn't known that Barbie worked with Piotr, so perhaps this had been arranged through Justine and Donald? Then again, there were many things he didn't know about the inner workings of Martiniere security, nor how it interfaced with Barbie's Atwood and Knowles structures—though he knew there were multiple connections, had been before Justine and Donald started dating. And those tentacles intertwined even more after their engagement.

In any case, Solitaire Island was a *perfect* if temporary solution to the issue of Grace and Jeannie.

"Ms. Barkley has been briefed on the situation and now possesses a secure phone. You *are* aware that she has a picture of you, Gabriel?"

"Yes."

"Good." Piotr paused. "We have discovered the source of the leakage from the Board. Cousin Fiona. Cousin Kendra caught her sending out more information—their father was careless and Fiona took advantage of it. She is aligned with Philip."

Damn it.

Cousin Mark, the father of Kendra and Fiona, headed the British branch of the Martinieres. While Gabe got on well enough with Mark, there had always been a coolness between them, something connected to Philip. All the same, he had never wished the man ill.

"I'm sorry to hear it," he said.

"Mark has resigned his position as Head of the British Family and his role on the Board. His brother Christopher will replace him."

"What's the status of Philip's bail hearing?"

"Denied."

Gabe exhaled, surprised at the relief washing over him. "Thank you for that news, Piotr."

"You are welcome, Gabriel." Piotr chuckled, a rarity from him. "And may I offer an opinion? Ms. Barkley will definitely be an asset to the Martinieres."

"I plan to recruit her for the Group."

"I am not speaking of the Group, Gabriel. Safe travels."

Piotr hung up before Gabe could say any more. He shook his head. Was his entire family trying to promote this match between him and Ruby? Seemed like it.

Ah well.

Gabe looked at the phone. Calculated the time. In order to function well in Paris, he needed to get some rest, and soon. All he needed was four or five hours, that would get him through the day.

Ruby had a safe phone. Four in the afternoon in Corvallis. She might be working.

He went into the bedroom. Set the alarm on his phone so he would have time to shave, clean up, and dress before landing in Paris. Crawled into the bed after changing into pajama pants, allowing the fatigue he'd been ignoring all day to wash over him.

Then he called Ruby.

"Gabe? What's happening now?"

"Nothing much," he said. "On the jet, six—no, five and a half—hours out from Paris. Getting ready to nap because when I land it'll be nearly eight in the morning there. Trying to unwind, and I thought, why not give you a call to see how things went with Piotr? Need to check on everything, after all."

"Oh Gabe." That deep chuckle of hers. "So just how safe *is* this phone, anyway?"

"As safe as any phone can be—but much more secure than anything commercial."

"All right, then." Another chuckle. "Piotr is very gallant. But I sure wouldn't want to get on his wrong side."

"That is an excellent response to Cousin Piotr," he said. "How are things going?"

"Getting ready to feed horses. I can't talk for long. But if it helps you relax, it's worth it."

"I hope you had a restful time last night."

Hesitation. "Actually—bad dreams. I woke up and looked at your picture for a while."

"The same here," he said. "Did it help you?"

"Yes. And you?"

"Yes."

They chatted a little bit longer. Then Ruby had to go.

Gabe tucked the phone under his pillow, smiling.

Maybe he *should* yield to what he most wanted. After all, if *Piotr* was favorably impressed by Ruby Barkley—Piotr had disliked Mindy from the beginning. He hadn't achieved his position as head of Martiniere security by being easily misled.

Take it slow, Gabriel. You don't want Ruby to lose that chance at the Grant should things go wrong.

But he also remembered what Saul had said.

Take the initiative.

Well, perhaps he should wait and see what the coming week brought.

And bring her some roses. Her reaction might tell him what he needed to know.

CHAPTER 10

THE LANGUAGE OF ROSES
APRIL, 2029

RUBY

RUBY SPOTTED A MASS OF COLOR—*FLOWERS, WHAT IS THAT about?*—outside of Midnight's stall, as she led two horses in from turnout late on Friday afternoon.

What the—

Midnight's door was ajar, just enough for someone to slip inside. Her heart pounding, she put the horses into their stalls as quietly as she could. Then Ruby drew her new pistol and eased down the alleyway. Sure, she should call the sheriff or security, but that took precious time. The worst could happen to Midnight and the culprit be gone, if it wasn't too late already. She needed to be the person to stop it.

Where the fuck is security, that someone can reach Gabe's horse without being caught?

Ruby whipped around the doorframe, raising the pistol—only to freeze as Midnight startled and Gabe whirled from his position at Midnight's withers, hand flying to a shoulder holder, half-drawing his gun.

Nervous chuckles from both of them as they holstered their weapons. Then quick gabbles, each talking over the other.

"I thought someone was messing with the horse—"

"I'm sorry I didn't tell you I was coming—"

They fell silent. Ruby's cheeks burned.

"All right. Let's start all over, shall we?" Gabe patted Midnight, then walked to the door. "See you tomorrow morning, big fellow."

She leaned on the wall, sighing with relief as Gabe slid the door closed, then latched it.

"I thought someone intended to hurt him," she said. "After all, he's another way to get at you."

"I am very glad you are thinking like that." Gabe bent over to pick up the bright collection of flowers she had first noticed. He bowed and presented them to her. "Here you go. I—you're already putting up with a lot more baloney than the usual Martiniere Grant candidate. This is a thank you."

"Gabe, you shouldn't have." But she took them. Roses. Red, white, and lavender roses. At least a dozen. "Thank you."

"It's the least I could do." A slow smile spread across his face. That, and the smoldering *come-hither* gaze of his dark brown eyes, set her heart pounding and warmth pulsing through her. Ruby looked down at the flowers, thoughts whirling wildly.

No. I'm dreaming.

She and Gabe *had* been messaging quite a bit over the past week —several times a day, to be honest. Talking about things she was studying. Updates on Midnight. Little nighttime personal notes, a couple of calls when the shadows became overwhelming for one or the other of them. When Ruby told Linda about it, her friend laughed and suggested that *Gabriel Martiniere has a crush on you.*

Ruby had pooh-poohed the notion, but—flowers? *Roses?*

Gabriel Martiniere is not *giving me roses. Roses! Red, white, and lavender roses. Red roses mean love—I know that much, but does he? What do the other colors mean—if he's even thinking that way? He probably knows—he's the kind of man who would know.*

Now what do I do?

"Thank you," she repeated. "I'd better get them into a vase." The words sounded awkward and tentative, even to her, and she kept staring down at the flowers, her cheeks flaming even more.

He gave me flowers. I've only gotten flowers at the rodeo or from Gramps and Granma. Never from someone I've been dating. And we aren't even dating.

"I have good news," he said. "Artie is talking to the University administration. Unofficially—depends on the credits and what kind of wizardry he can get Asa Green to whip up to document your field work on the ranch—but it appears that you will start next fall as a senior and graduate in the spring."

"Oh. I. Oh." Words. She had to find words somehow. But she couldn't.

One more year and she would graduate. *She would graduate.* And it wouldn't mean working herself into exhaustion, either.

Ruby smiled into the flowers, nervous about what would happen if she looked up at him. Maybe that was what the flowers were really about. Congratulations.

"There's more." That tenor voice. So smooth. Quiet, even as it stirred up tingles all over her body. "Artie will be contacting your grandfather next week—he's finalizing the details on the Double R field test facility contract with the Martiniere Group."

"That's—oh Gabe. That's—" She blinked back unexpected wetness forming in her eyes. How could things suddenly be so easy? Why was this happening to her? It couldn't be happening to her. There had to be a catch somehow.

"It's all right." His hand delicately brushed her face to wipe away a tear, fingers quivering and skittish, then sliding away. "It's okay to be overwhelmed. You've been battling a lot of obstacles for a long time."

She looked up from the flowers and directly into his eyes. Gabe leaned against the stall door, still smiling. But fatigue lines tightened his face and dark circles underscored his eyes. Was his face thinner than it had been last week? Damn it, was Gabe working himself to death, like her cousin Andy had?

Her gut tightened.

Don't go there, Ruby. You don't know him that well yet.

"You look tired," she said, all the same.

"I *am* tired. However, I've been sleeping better, thanks to our messages and calls. But another damn week where I've used too much Jet A and not done enough charging, either solar or a plug-in." He half-closed his eyes, looking more fatigued than before. "I didn't want to wait until tomorrow to see Midnight—and you. Just a quick stop on the way from the airport to the condo."

Riiiight. A quick stop, when she *knew* that the airport was across town from the barn, the condo in between the two locations. And these roses—oh, these weren't supermarket flowers picked up on a whim. Not the sad pathetic specimens she was used to seeing at the store. No. These were *roses*, rarely seen in the market over the past few years. Even more expensive, they were *fresh* roses, possibly a special order.

What was this? She *still* couldn't speak. All she could do was beam back at him.

That provoked an even bigger smile in response that made her heart pound harder.

Then he sighed and pushed himself upright. "I'll see you tomorrow, Ruby. What time is best for your briefing session? I was thinking, perhaps dinner tomorrow night with my sisters at the condo. We can talk about corporate structures. Including the rising young women within the Group. Justine in particular will be very good at identifying potential alliances, more than I will."

"I finish feeding horses at six. And dinner sounds good."

Not a date.

That was probably a good idea. She'd known him all of—one week?

"Then I guess we see each other tomorrow morning."

"Tomorrow morning," she repeated, her voice quavering. "I'll be ready."

Once again, quivering fingertips brushed her cheek. She put her hand over his, to keep him from yanking it away. He twined his fingers with hers—his hand still trembling—and pressed them to his forehead.

Gabe glanced once more at Midnight, smiled again at Ruby, kissed her hand, bowed, then walked down the alleyway.

Ruby watched him go, admiring his smooth, flowing walk.

Then she went to her apartment to take care of these expensive, precious roses.

* * *

Later, after bringing the rest of the horses in and doing nighttime feeding, she looked up the meaning of the rose colors.

Red—intense emotion, usually love or desire.

She already knew that.

White—honorable intentions.

Of *course* Gabe would want to signal that. She had learned *that* much about him.

Lavender—adoration, admiration, possibly love at first sight.

Did he really mean this?

She gulped.

You're dreaming, Ruby. You are not the sort of person who will catch the eye of a billionaire like Gabriel Martiniere for more than a brief flirtation.

But what if she were wrong? What if he *was* conveying—no, no, that couldn't be happening.

Could it?

All the same, perhaps it was time to do more research, before she talked to Linda.

Ruby dedicated most of the evening to scanning the internet. She sipped whisky as she skimmed through as many mentions of *Gabriel Martiniere* as she could find. A second whisky. At last, she rubbed her eyes and called it a night, deciding not to call Linda about this new development yet, pouring herself a third drink.

There wasn't a lot of information online, especially given Gabe's financial and social status.

Gabe didn't have a history of public, casual flirtations. Before and after his relationship with Miranda Cathcart-Rogers, he was just as likely to be at social functions with Justine or Louisa as he was with anyone else. Except Lora, and that was a brief flurry when he was eighteen.

Then she remembered what Gabe had told her about *his* shadows at age eighteen, and Lora's comments. They once had *some* sort of relationship.

Lora might have answers.

Lora showed up early on Saturday morning, as Ruby was doling out the morning grain feed. "I have several prospects for Louisa to try out, so you just have Gabe and Justine to manage this morning."

"That's good," Ruby said. "My ankle's better, so I'm getting back up on Sunshine today. In Western tack this time. I don't think jumping's a good idea until I get her bucking under better control."

"*If* you can get it under control," Lora said.

"I'm not ready to give up just yet." Ruby paused. "Did you know that Gabe stopped by last night?"

"No, that must have been after I left for the day." Lora grinned. "Spending time with his new horse?"

"That, and—he gave me flowers."

Lora's grin softened into a fond smile. "Gabe used to give me yellow and white roses. Tokens of an honorable friendship, he said."

"So rose colors mean something when he gives them to you?"

Lora eyed Ruby. "What colors did you get?"

"Red, white, and lavender."

"Wow." Lora's brows shot up. "You know what that means?"

"I looked it up last night." Ruby slumped against the feed room wall. "Then—it does—it's a deliberate choice?"

"Yes."

Ruby blew hard and buried her face in her hands, then looked up. "Then—wow. Just—wow. He means it."

This changes everything.

"Gabriel Martiniere does not play those kinds of games when it comes to personal attraction," Lora said softly. "If he's giving you that message, he's serious. He's the closest thing you'll find to an honest billionaire—an honest man, period."

"Oh my God." Ruby dropped her hands on her thighs, breathing hard.

"How do *you* feel about him?"

"I—I—oh God, Lora, besides being attractive, he's smart. I can talk programming and carbon capture and biobots without being afraid I'm boring him. He's a horseman. Noble and brave and—" Ruby gulped. "But I'm nobody! He could have anybody! I'm not in his league!"

"If Gabe decides you're in his league, then you *are*." Lora fixed Ruby with a stern glare. "If you're serious about him, Ruby, then go for it. If you're not, then *be honest* with Gabe. Don't hurt the man."

"He told me what happened at his father's house," Ruby whispered. "He's been through enough hell already. He's not taking care of himself and I can see it, even after just a week. I—Lora, I can't believe that I could be this lucky. That—the man of my dreams walks into my life like this. A horseman. Smart."

Lora clasped Ruby's shoulder. "You deserve it. He deserves it. Welcome to life with the Martinieres, Ruby. If you don't betray him or the Family, then you'll be taken care of, even if you break up at some point." Then she scowled. "You have no more excuses. Talk to

Gabe, then call the vet and do a *thorough* workup on that Sunshine mare. Make sure that you're not dealing with kissing spines or some other physical cause for her bucking. You have access to the funds to do that now, through Gabe. Trust me, he'll be happy to pay for it."

Lora left the feed room. Ruby kept leaning against the wall, gulping.

Oh my God.

She wondered what Linda would say.

* * *

AFTER TALKING TO HER FRIEND, RUBY TOOK EXTRA CARE IN dressing before the Martinieres arrived.

Wear your best clothes, Linda suggested.

But that would be her show outfit, which would be far too much. Ruby opted for her new show boots and her best schooling tights as well as her nicest zip-neck pullover fleece.

Then she put Sunshine in the crossties, brushing the golden mare and wondering what she was going to do if the vet identified the complicated spinal impingement known as kissing spines as the cause of her bucking. Sunshine was well-bred, but not enough for value as a broodmare, unless she had a show record. It could be treated—but that might be expensive. Worth it, even with a billionaire's support?

And yet—what Lora had said—

Gabe preceded his sisters into the alleyway, a saddle draped over one arm, still looking tired. He furrowed his brows, a tentative look on his face, studying her reaction to him closely.

She smiled.

He beamed at her, his fatigue vanishing. And dear Lord, if she thought he appeared happy to see her before, *this* expression absolutely melted her.

"I dug out my old saddle." He placed it on the rack by Midnight's stall. "Let's see if it fits Midnight."

"It's gorgeous." Ruby ran her fingers over the soft leather.

"Lora helped me choose it. I hope it fits the boy. I really like riding in it." Gabe placed his hand over hers—still with that slight quiver.

She looked up at him—not that much difference in their heights, perhaps two inches at most. "It's one of the best brands out there." Inhaled quickly, working up her courage. "I looked up the meaning of rose colors last night."

"And?"

Was it her imagination or did his hand tremble a bit more?

"Did you—was it on purpose?"

His hand tightened on hers. "Yes." The questioning expression returned.

"The only times I've been given flowers have either been tied to rodeo queen competitions or from Gramps and Granma." Another deep inhale. "Thank you. I—I don't know what to say, except thank you and—what happens next?"

Again with that big smile. "Let's talk tonight, after the briefing. There will be complications, and I don't know the answer to everything just yet. But rest assured, I intended every single nuance of the traditional meanings when I chose those roses."

She couldn't look away from those dark brown eyes, and *that smile*. "I'm looking forward to our talk. But can I help it if I'm afraid that I'm dreaming about being a princess in a real-life fairy tale, and that sooner or later I'll wake up to a dreary reality?"

Gabe chuckled. "If so, we're both having that dream." He brought her hand to his lips and kissed her palm, closing her fingers over it afterward. "So. Shall we see if the saddle fits my horse?"

"Guess we'd better."

THIS MORNING LACKED THE EXPLOSION OF THE PREVIOUS Saturday. Ruby worked Sunshine carefully, not asking too much of the golden mare, spending most of their time in the center of the arena as she gave instructions to Gabe and Justine. Meanwhile, Lora and Louisa trialed various horses while Justine and Gabe issued opinions.

Louisa seemed to click best with a young Holsteiner mare, Flora, a big dark bay. Ruby considered Flora to be a little lazy, unwilling to move out unless pushed. But she was much more willing for Louisa than she had been for Ruby or Lora.

Gabe insisted on putting Flora through her paces. The big mare made him work harder than Midnight.

"She's perfect for you, Weeza," was his verdict.

Meanwhile, as they untacked and groomed the horses, there were moments when Gabe would talk to her, only to fall silent as they gazed at each other, smiling. Ruby grew bolder and stood closer to him than she would normally. They brushed hands and shoulders, one or the other initiating the contact. When Louisa and Lora went into Lora's office to discuss Flora's purchase, Justine and Gabe sat on tack trunks in the alleyway to wait.

"Do you have anything to do right now?" Gabe asked Ruby.

"No."

He patted the top of the tack trunk he sat on. They sat together, close but not touching, and held hands. Justine raised her brows at them but didn't say anything. Gabe stroked Ruby's palm with his thumb while she kept reminding herself to *breathe*, that this was *real*.

She had a billionaire interested in her. A *smart* billionaire. A *nice* man, who liked her for her brains as well as her looks.

Soon enough, Lora and Louisa returned. Gabe kissed her hand again before leaving with his sisters.

"So," Lora said after they left. "It's happening?"

"I—think it is," Ruby said.

<hr>

LINDA SCREECHED WITH JOY WHEN RUBY TOLD HER. "I KNEW IT! He's definitely your kind of man."

"We still have to talk tonight," Ruby cautioned.

"Ruby. The man gave you roses. It's about damn time something worked for you. Don't forget about me once you're Ruby Barkley Martiniere, okay?"

"Now *that* is jumping the gun."

"Hah! We'll see."

RUBY QUICKLY DEVELOPED A DEEPER UNDERSTANDING OF THE challenges Gabe faced during that night's briefing. The Martiniere Group was *huge*, complex, and growing.

Gabe remained scrupulously polite, keeping physical contact light.

At last, he stretched and sighed. "I think that's enough for tonight."

"You have a big job ahead of you should you become the Martiniere."

"The key is to have the right support people in place," he said. "Papa has been very good at doing that, but we're still just keeping a bare jump ahead of the growing impact of climate change. I intend for the Martiniere Group to be a leader in turning things around. If it isn't already too late." He scowled. "Just so few years left."

"I want to be part of that battle," she said.

He smiled. "And with that—Weeza, Tine, I'm taking Ruby home. I'll be back later."

Gabe put his arm around her shoulder as they left. "Do you want to go someplace for a drink while we talk? Or are you all right with going to the barn?"

"Let's go to the barn. I should do one last check of the horses."

"All right, then."

He had driven them to the condo, but turned the wheel over to Lance. They sat in the second seat, close to each other, Gabe's arm around her shoulder.

"Where do we go from here?" Ruby asked.

He stroked her cheek. "We've only known each other a week. I'd like to take this slow, if you're all right with that. We both have—issues. Pasts to negotiate. I'd like to get to know you better, even be a bit old-fashioned and court you. If you're all right with that?" he repeated.

"Yes. There's an awful lot that I have to learn and get used to," she said. "I—I don't want to embarrass you. Don't want to be a hindrance to your goals within the Group. I don't know much about life at your level. Clothing. Manners. Routines. Things that someone raised to it would know that I have to learn, unspoken things."

"It's not as complicated as it may seem from the outside, and you'll have plenty of help from the girls. Mama as well. You still have another year until you get your degree. We have to figure out how to handle that. Where you're living. I want you to be safe. The barn's all right for now, but next fall? You—*we*—need a different situation."

"I'm not expecting to elope, Gabe. And then there's my grandparents and the responsibilities I have to them. Even with hiring help—I have to be there for some things."

"I understand. And I'm in the final push to become the Martiniere-in-waiting. We both have obligations to consider." Another sigh. "I work too hard. I'll be traveling a lot. I can't always drop everything to see you. That can be a problem."

Ruby snorted. "Gabe, it's part of your job, as long as you don't work yourself into the ground. Besides, it's not as if I'm sitting around pining for you to get back from wherever you are to see me. We both have lives apart from each other. Friends. I'm not expecting us to be attached at the waist, even if—" She paused, unwilling to say the words for fear that they might break the spell. Stop the dream.

"*Good.* Because that's not what I want. I had that sort of relationship for three years with Mindy, and it was godawful." He exhaled. "I —I just want to be in your life, and have you in mine."

The SUV stopped. Gabe helped her out. They slipped into the alleyway and Ruby locked the big sliding doors. Then they walked down the alley, arms around each other, pausing to check on each horse.

At last they reached the end. Went out the door—Ruby locking that one—and walked to her apartment.

Gabe took her hands. "I need to have discussions with a couple of people right away. Saul—to find out how we manage our relationship, given that you're a Grant finalist. It's possible for us to be together without you losing that position, but it has to be done properly, and I don't want you to lose that opportunity. It's not about the money— hell, I can make that up myself. But it's the prestige and the honor you deserve for your hard work." He raised her hands to his lips and kissed them.

"Thank you."

This *was* one reason she was falling in love with this man.

"The other—I promised your grandfather that I would let him know if our relationship shifted to include the personal. I feel oblig- ated to honor that promise. It's not going to give you any problems, is it?"

"I doubt it. So both of our families will know that we are dating?"

"Yes. You don't mind?"

"I'm not going to run out and shout it to the media, because I'd just as soon not be bothered by them," she said tartly. "Though I'll have to get used to their presence as well. But our families—yes. Just —would you let me contact my grandparents first? I'll tell Gramps I asked you to wait."

"Good. Because I would *not* want him angry at me for going back on my promise." That smile again. "I want to build something lasting with you, Ruby. I hope we can do that."

"I do, too."

"May I kiss you?"

"Yes."

Gabe slipped his arms around her, pulling Ruby to him gently. His lips delicately brushed hers, pulled away for a moment. She objected wordlessly to his withdrawal, sliding her arms around him and holding him tight. He chuckled as she sought his lips. They kissed harder, the intensity deepening.

At last they broke apart.

"Much more of this and all of our *go slow* talk will be just that," he said shakily. "Talk. Oh, Ruby. The woman of my dreams. This is so unexpected—and so wonderful." He stroked her cheek.

"I'm still keeping from pinching myself, because if this is a dream, I don't want to wake up."

"It's not always going to be like this," he said solemnly.

"I know. When will I see you again—or do you have any idea what your schedule will be like yet?"

"My parents have always kept Friday nights special. Would you like to do that?"

"Yes."

"I can't guarantee you every Friday night. Might even just be something quiet, depending on how late I get into Corvallis. But some time together on Friday, and then riding on Saturday. Some Sundays."

"That works. I'm waiting on files to do bookwork for a couple of clients. This next week is going to be nuts. That could spill into Friday night."

He laughed. "That *is* one thing you can phase out. Unless you're absolutely tied to the notion of working as a bookkeeper on top of everything else."

"No. Believe me, I'm glad to close out that part of my life. I gave my clients notice that I'm a Grant finalist and ending my book-keeping gig. I'm committed through June for most of them. These two—they're final books that I'm transferring, so that's going to take time. More than I like to dedicate to bookkeeping, but it happens."

"Good." He cupped her cheek. "It's a crazy busy week ahead of me as well. But I'll let you know where I am—and I'll call you every night, when I can. If that works?"

"Yes. Probably best for you to call me since I have no idea what time zone you'll be in, or what obligations you have at what time. At least my schedule is predictable. I'll message it to you."

"If I can't call, I'll message you." He bent forward and quickly kissed her again. "Ruby. My darling. I hope you can stand my crazy life."

"I'll be here."

Another kiss, this time on her forehead. "I'm going to Los Angeles early tomorrow morning and should be there through Monday at noon. I meet with Papa on Monday mornings and that's when my schedule gets decided. At least I know that there's no trips to Paris this week, thank God. Maybe I won't need to burn Jet A— that's what I'm hoping."

"Stay safe, Gabe. And call me if you're having problems."

"I will, my dearest. The same is true for you. I'll take your calls if I can."

Another kiss, this one on her lips. Then, smiling, he turned to walk down the driveway.

Ruby let herself inside her apartment and dropped into a chair, staring at the roses on her table.

Unbelievable. I'm in a relationship with Gabriel Martiniere.

Even in her wildest dreams she had never, ever, anticipated this possibility.

Should she call Linda?

Tomorrow, she decided. Let Gabe make the arrangements he needed to set up first.

Besides, for tonight, she wanted to savor this private, precious joy.

I'm in a relationship with Gabriel Martiniere.

GABE

Gabe was still grinning when he let himself into the condo.

Ruby wants to be in a relationship with me. She really wants to be with me.

The roses had been a gamble that paid off—and how.

Both of his sisters waited for him, arms crossed, almost mirror images of each other as they sat on the couch.

"Spill it, Gabie." Justine fixed him with that stern gaze reminiscent of their shared father, when Philip decided to interrogate them about something. "Are you or are you not dating Ruby? Because your behavior tonight signals that something is going on."

"Oh, look at him, Tine," Louisa said. "That smirk. *Of course* he's dating Ruby. Who else would it be?"

Gabe laughed and dropped into a recliner. "As of tonight, yes. Ruby and I are dating."

"Yes!" Justine pumped her fist and exchanged a big grin with Louisa.

"But." Gabe fixed both of them with a stern look. "I want to talk to Saul about this first, because I have to do it right, so that Ruby doesn't get screwed out of the Martiniere Grant. No blabbing about it to anyone else. Even Mama and Papa. Understood?"

"Got it," Justine said.

"When are you telling them?" Louisa asked.

"I'm flying to LA early tomorrow morning. I'm talking to Saul and Mama then." He laced his hands together. "We're going to take it slow, because there's a lot that has to be worked out. She—*we*—will need your help because she's not born to high society, and you know how snooty some Family members can be. Damn it, I want this relationship to work."

"We'll do what we can, Gabie," Louisa said. "What can I do?"

He spread his hands, shrugging. "I don't know for certain yet. I have to talk to Papa about how this unfolds. Plus all the bullshit with Mindy and Philip. That could come down on Ruby's head as my new girlfriend. Maybe work with her about handling any media blowups?"

"I can do that, and keep track of Mindy," Louisa said.

Justine grimaced. "I'll keep an eye on Joey, make sure that slimeball doesn't get a notion to screw things up. Gabie, once it's cleared, I'll talk to Donna-gran. Get a feel for currents within the Family."

"Thanks, Weeza, Tine." He beamed at his sisters.

Justine rose and kissed his forehead. "This is the best damn news I've had for a while, Gabie. Keep it quiet even from Donald?"

"Yes. Please, until I've talked to Saul. And—Friday night will be date night."

"Does that mean we won't see you except for Saturday mornings and maybe Sunday brunches?" Louisa asked.

Gabe laughed. "Weeza, we're *taking it slow.*"

Justine snickered. "We'll see how soon that changes. The way you two were looking at each other tonight suggests it won't be *that* long."

He sobered. "Tine, we both have issues. Matching histories. That's why I don't want to rush things. Plus, there are a lot of logistics to work out."

"Understood, Gabie. All the same—congratulations."

"And from me as well," Louisa said. "This makes me so happy for you."

Gabe rose. He needed to get to bed soon. "For what it's worth, Piotr told me she would be an asset to the Martinieres after he met with her, and specifically said he wasn't talking about the Group."

Justine's brows raised. She and Louisa exchanged another one of those knowing looks. Then she patted his arm. "If Cousin Piotr's on board, that's huge, Gabie."

"Saul has assigned him to work with Serg on Ruby's security."

"How soon are you announcing the engagement?" Louisa smirked. "If Papa and Piotr can see it, then—"

Gabe raised his hands. "Let's not rush things, all right? I need to get to bed. Too many late nights. I'll tell you what Papa says, after I talk to him tomorrow morning."

"Seriously, Gabie, this is great news," Louisa said.

He left his sisters, certain that they'd be scheming between themselves to storm the Family on Ruby's behalf, once he gave them the clearance.

After he settled in bed, he lay there thinking about Ruby. That occasional sideways glance. The dimple that peeked out of her left cheek when she smiled a certain way. Ruby on horseback. Ruby talking about carbon capture. Ruby.

His Ruby, if he didn't mess things up.

———

Ruby messaged him halfway through the flight to Los Angeles.

—Gramps and Granma know. He wants you to call when you can.

—Thanks. Were they too difficult about it?

—They weren't surprised, especially Gramps.

He grinned at that.

—All right. I'm on the plane. I'll call him right away. Probably call you in the afternoon, if that works?

—That would be fine. I'm free after four.

—Love you. Looking forward to Friday.

—Love you too.

Another smile as he put down his phone for a moment, warmth spreading through him.

She said I love you.

Then he called Ron Ryder.

* * *

As he hoped, Gabe found Angelica and Saul relaxing at home, drinking coffee on the shaded deck that overlooked the Pacific.

"You look tired, Gabie," his mother said, after hugging him.

"I know, Mama. One reason to come here early in the day."

"Wondered what was going on, son," Saul said. "Thought you were having brunch with your sisters."

Gabe grinned. Then he sat, leaning his elbows on his thighs, looking down at clasped hands, then back up before taking a deep breath.

"I needed to talk to you, Papa—well, and Mama too. And I have to do laundry, plus some other things."

"Oh? What's happening?" Saul leaned back in his lounge chair.

"I need to talk to you about dating a Martiniere Grant finalist."

"Ruby Barkley?" Saul smirked. "Piotr's half in love with her already."

"Yes." Gabe grinned back at him. "Do I need to remind Piotr that I'm faster than him?"

"He's sneakier." Saul chuckled, then turned solemn. "Piotr approves of her, and he provided recommendations about what should happen once you declared your interest in Ruby. He has preapproved highest Family clearance for her. However, Gabie, I need to take you through an intimate intention and contact question-naire first."

"All right." Gabe braced himself, scowling.

Has to happen to do right by Ruby.

"Don't look so intense," Saul chided. "It isn't that bad. It really isn't. We need to document that you aren't slipping an unqualified girlfriend into the Grant program, as well as cover potential concerns that HR and the Martiniere Family Trust might have."

"I don't want to make any mistakes. Don't want to screw it up for her."

"Understood." Saul patted Gabe on his knee. "Relax." He pulled out his phone and switched on the recording app. "Saul Martiniere, speaking to Gabriel Martiniere on Sunday, April twenty-ninth, 2029, ten am Pacific time. Gabriel has just informed me that he is dating Martiniere Grant finalist Ruby Barkley. Angelica Ramirez Martiniere is also present as a witness. Initiating intimate intention and contact questionnaire. Gabriel, what are your intentions toward this woman? Is this something casual—"

"Gabie doesn't do casual," his mother interposed.

"I *know* that, Angelica, but this is part of the process. Gabriel, is this something casual, or are you thinking about it being a long-term relationship?"

"Long-term."

Saul nodded. "Is her family aware of the relationship?"

"Ruby told them this morning, and I spoke to her grandfather, Ron Ryder, to assure him of my honorable intentions."

"Good. When did the relationship start?"

"Yesterday. April twenty-eighth."

"There was no existing relationship when you chose her to be a Martiniere Grant finalist?"

"I did not have any spoken, personal, or email contact with Ruby Barkley prior to April twentieth, the day of her finalist interview. All arrangements for the interview were done through her advisor, Dr. Asa Green, of Oregon State University."

He clasped his hands to keep them steady. This had to be done right. It *so* had to be right.

"How was Ruby Barkley chosen for the finalist interview?"

"Her choice was based on her application form, glowing recommendations from Dr. Green and other instructors at Oregon State, and in review with both Arthur Martiniere and Gerard Martiniere."

"You paid a significant amount of money to release Ruby Barkley's grandparents, Ron and Ruth Ryder, from debt on April twentieth."

"Yes."

"Details, please."

Gabe swallowed, thinking it through, choosing his words carefully. The Board would hear his statement at some point—how much should he disclose?

"Ruby was orphaned at age six," he continued. "Ron and Ruth Ryder were her custodial parents and are her closest relatives. Zingter Enterprises had purchased loans from other sources which were taken out to finance medical treatment for her grandmother. Ruby was informed by her grandfather on April twentieth, after our interview, that Zingter was imposing harsh new loan conditions with a short response time. This fit a pattern of past Zingter behavior toward the relatives of Martiniere Grant finalists, particularly attractive young women. They are then coerced into withdrawing their applications and working for Zingter. Ruby reported this information to me promptly upon learning about Zingter's notice. I took action and reported this situation to Saul Martiniere."

Saul smiled and nodded. "Very good, Gabriel. Do either Ruby Barkley, Ron Ryder, or Ruth Ryder owe you any obligations for your payment of this debt?"

"Absolutely not. It is a freely given gift."

"Does Ruby Barkley have any intentions of withdrawing as a Grant candidate?"

"No."

"Do you support her continued participation in the Martiniere Grant program?"

"Yes. It's not just the money. Ruby deserves the honor and recognition. Honestly so. I fully support her future career within the Martiniere Group."

"Should this relationship end and Ruby Barkley be employed by the Martiniere Group, will you swear to treat her honorably and fairly should you be in a professional position of authority over her?"

"Yes. On my honor as a Martiniere."

"Trust-related questions. You intend to engage in a long-term relationship with Ruby Barkley. Do these intentions include marriage?"

"If she'll have me, yes." His voice caught. *Marriage. To Ruby. Could it be?*

"If there are any offspring from this relationship, do you intend to acknowledge and support them?"

"Yes." Children. He didn't know if Ruby wanted kids—he hadn't even thought about *that*.

"Should this relationship end, are you committed to providing long-term financial and security support for Ruby Barkley and any children you should have with her, should it be necessary?"

"Yes."

"Do you swear that you have answered these questions honestly?"

"Yes. I, Gabriel Marcus Martiniere, swear that I have answered these questions honestly and to my best intent, on my honor as a Martiniere."

"Interview completed." Saul flicked off the recording. "There. *That* should take care of any objections."

Angelica rose. "I think this latest development calls for a toast." She bent to kiss Gabe on the forehead before disappearing into the house.

Gabe leaned back in his chair, rubbing his face. "Honestly, Papa, I didn't expect a relationship to happen this fast. But oh God. She's marvelous. A horsewoman. Smart. Weeza and Tine would have my head if I didn't do right by Ruby, because they really like her, too. I—remembered what you said about courting Mama. Took a chance and brought her flowers. We've been messaging and talking all week and—I just felt it was the right time."

"So that's why your sisters have been repeatedly messaging me this morning about whether you've talked to us yet." His mother returned with a bottle of champagne and three glasses. "They must know."

"I told them last night," Gabe said, as Angelica deftly uncorked the bottle. "Came back from taking Ruby home and had *both* girls waiting to quiz me. I asked them to keep this quiet until I talked to you and knew what was happening with Ruby and the Grant."

Angelica smiled and filled their glasses. "Then after we toast, I need to call Weeza and Tine. I'm sure I'll hear all about your Ruby then, Gabie."

"Best of luck in love, Gabriel," Saul said, raising his glass.

Angelica echoed the toast. After she drank, she fixed him with a stern glare. "And just when do *I* get to meet Ruby?"

"It's going to be a few weeks," he said. "Probably not until the end of the term. She's slammed right now between school, working at the barn, and dealing with her bookkeeping clients."

"Hmm. Ambitious young lady." Saul chuckled. "Reminds me of a certain young man. Are you two going to see who can outwork the other?"

Gabe laughed. "Oh, Papa. She's already given notice to her clients—just not going to be able to finish those obligations until June."

"The more I hear about this woman, the happier I am for you, son," Saul said. "Now. *You* look like hell. Take it easy today, no work. Don't rush into the office tomorrow morning. This is an order from me as the Martiniere. Understand?"

"Yes, Papa."

Though that would be *hard*, damn it.

DOING NOTHING MORE THAN HIS LAUNDRY AND ORGANIZING HIS bag for more travel was just as difficult as Gabe thought it would be. He paced his suite, wishing he was in Corvallis with Ruby. Even a session working out and a long swim didn't calm him.

He counted down the minutes until he could call her at four.

"Gabe?" God, she sounded exhausted.

"How are you doing?" He sprawled on his bed, thrilling just to hear her voice.

"Oh, these damn books," she sighed. "I will be so glad to be done with these two clients in particular. I wish I could find something that would let me terminate the contract due to malfeasance so I don't have to spend this week dealing with them. But they're not smart enough to be crooked. Just incompetent. Not that the IRS gives a shit about that."

"I'm sorry. Any chance they could be bought off?"

She laughed and her voice sounded more cheerful. "They're horribly honest, Gabe. Just terrible at keeping records. I have piles of paper to deal with. And they're Thunder County accounts, so—"

"I get it."

"On the other hand, I took Midnight out for a gallop today."

"Did my boy do right by you?"

"Oh yes." The smile in her voice was vivid enough for him to visualize it. "I'm looking forward to taking him over the cross-country course at the ranch this summer."

"Only when I'm not there to ride him. Will you have another horse to keep up with him so we can ride together?" No way in hell would he support her riding Sunshine over *any* sort of cross-country.

"Lora's sending a couple more horses to me. Might even have Justine's Glory—sounds like her wedding preparations and then the honeymoon means she won't have a lot of time to ride." Ruby chuckled. "And both of your sisters dropped in. They not only congratulated me, but admired the roses. Oh. Justine said that if you treated me badly, she knew someone who would make you suffer."

He laughed at that. "That little sister has some *interesting* connections with Mama's family. Not the Ramirezes but mi abuela's family, the Saldivars. I'll have to tell you about them someday. A damn good thing Justine hates Philip's guts. The two of them in alliance would be terrifying."

"I also have Louisa and Justine's personal numbers. They've told me to call if I need anything when you're not around."

"Good."

A pause. "Your mother called me a little bit ago. It was pretty much an echo of your sisters—she sounds very happy."

"She broke out the champagne after we settled the Grant issues."

"She alluded to that. Gabe, did you *really* promise to support me no matter what?"

"Yes." He swallowed. "Our relationship and your finances make you eligible to draw upon the Martiniere Family Trust should some-thing happen to me before—a marriage or prenuptial agreement. Or in case of a breakup. An allowance. Limited to partners of high-level heirs, not the entire Family."

"*Gabe.* This makes me feel like a gold digger. Did you do that with Mindy?"

"No. She has money of her own and—there's differences. God, Ruby, if I could shower you with flowers and jewelry and whisk you off to a life where you had nothing to do but research, ride horses, and be with me—I would. I will. You deserve it."

"Oh, Gabe." She choked. "That—listen. I don't need flowers. These flowers are absolutely gorgeous but if—you really want me drooling, build me a lab."

"You bet. Because that will happen. And I intend to be in it with you as much as possible."

"I was joking."

"I wasn't." He drew a deep breath. "Starting tomorrow, you'll be getting more clearances than the typical Martiniere Grant candidate, because of your relationship to me. Some of the things I'm working on—I want your input."

"That sounds good, but I'm overwhelmed."

"So am I. It's—things are scary, Ruby."

"Climate issues?"

"Yes."

"I said I wanted to be part of the battle," she said, her voice very small. "I didn't realize it would be this soon."

"I'll feed it to you in bits at a time. You have a lot to do already. Oh, Ruby. I didn't mean to get into this stuff during our calls. It gets rough."

"But we're in it together," she said.

"Yes. Together."

May 2029

Not so much traveling this week, but he ended up working longer hours instead.

—*Closing out those two clients tonight,* Ruby messaged on Friday afternoon. —*May keep me working late. I won't be able to do anything big.*

—*That's fine,* he responded. —*It's been a wild week for me as well. Would you like me to bring dinner?*

—*You don't have to.*

—*I want to. Does pasta work?*

—*Yes, but—dinner may just be a break before I go back to work. Are you sure you want to hang out with me?*

—*Absolutely. I can either work or read. I just want to be with you. A quiet evening suits me. Coming in about five. Anything you don't like, allergies, preferences?*

—*No fish. No allergies.*

—Looking forward to seeing my dearest nerd girl. Love, your bestest nerd boy.

She sent him several laughing emojis in return.

GABE BROUGHT THE MAKINGS FOR FETTUCCINE ALFREDO, along with a packet of frozen vegetables, a loaf of *good* artisan bread, his favorite olive oil, and a bottle of decent white wine. He'd know more about what he needed to add to her supplies once he saw what Ruby had on hand.

Ruby looked up with a wan smile as he entered her studio. He set the bag on the counter and crossed the room to kiss her.

"Ah," she sighed. "*Of course,* the damn software is fighting me now."

"I'm sorry."

Her shoulders were visibly tight. He stepped behind her and began to massage them. She leaned back, groaning as she smiled up at him.

"That feels so good."

"There's more when you're done." He bent to kiss her, gently patting her shoulders. "But I need to start cooking."

Her eyes widened. "You *cook?*"

"Mama insisted that we all know basic cookery, and I batched it for four years in college. I've been told I'm not too horrible of a cook."

Ruby grinned. "I am so damn lucky."

Then she turned back to her computer.

AFTER DINNER, AND CLEANING UP, PLUS GIVING RUBY ANOTHER, deeper shoulder rub as she worked, Gabe retreated to the couch with a glass of wine and a book. Much as he should be reviewing another batch of test results, he was just too damned exhausted to focus.

He spared some time to look around the studio. Oh, he'd seen it two weeks ago when getting the first aid supplies for her sprained ankle. But he hadn't taken much time to examine it then. Now, he could.

Ruby had a decent compliment of cooking tools and dishes, as well as spices. Lots of hot stuff. She clearly liked spicy food. But her food supplies—not much. He needed to keep that in mind, bring food so he wasn't gobbling up her stores.

The only furnishings besides the kitchen table she worked at and the couch were two kitchen chairs, the bed and several side tables. Posters of horses adorned the walls—all horses and riders that Lora had worked with over the years, plus one of Lora at the Olympics. Bare bones, probably came with the place. Not much of a clue about what Ruby's personal décor preferences were, except for a neat pile of paperbacks by her bed.

As he'd noticed before, everything was orderly and in place. A necessity in an apartment this size.

Gabe settled into the couch, pulling a pillow close. At some point, about halfway through the wine, he couldn't stay awake any longer.

Fingers caressing his face woke him. Gabe blinked up at Ruby. She sat on the edge of the couch, smiling.

"It's late," she murmured. "Louisa messaged me because you didn't answer her. She wondered if you were coming to the condo tonight. I told her you were out cold on the couch."

He groaned at the thought of getting to his feet, grabbing his bag, and summoning security to drive him. Gabe wrapped his arm around Ruby's waist and curled around her, resting his head on her thigh.

"Gimme moment. Just feels good to be here. With you."

She stroked his forehead, running her fingers through his hair. He gently slid his hand up her side, tugging at her.

"Cuddle? Please?" he asked.

He *hoped* she liked cuddling. Mindy had been all *don't touch me* except for sex. Ruby's willingness to touch him boded well.

Ruby laughed and let him pull her next to him. "Should I tell Louisa you're staying here?"

"Don't wanna go. Too comfy. Let me tell Weeza." He retrieved his phone.

—Wiped out. Too tired to leave. Bring my riding boots tomorrow, please?

—Sure, Gabie. A winking emoji followed.

He dropped his phone back on the side table and snuggled up to Ruby.

"Come on." Ruby shook him awake again. "It's after midnight. Let's move to the bed. More comfortable."

"You sure?" he mumbled. "I can stay here."

"We'll both sleep better in the bed."

As she disappeared into the bathroom to change, he fumbled in his bag for his pajama pants. Then it was his turn.

Ruby sat on the side of the bed when he came out. She wore sensible gray pajamas, with running horses on the t-shirt top.

"I'll sleep on the outside," he offered. "I sleep warm. Unless you'd prefer—?"

She shook her head. "I'm always cold, or so I'm told."

Gabe noticed her pistol on the side table, and added his. Then he slid into bed with her, wrapping himself around Ruby once more.

Early morning. Gabe blinked awake, for a moment uncertain of where he was. Someone spooned behind him, her arm across his waist—*Ruby.*

Had they—no. *Now* he remembered. Coming in late, cooking dinner. Falling asleep on her couch. Being wakened enough to move to the bed at some point, snuggling with Ruby.

She *was* a cuddler, all right. *Perfect.*

Ruby stirred. Gabe turned to face her, moving carefully so he didn't disturb her. Eyes still closed. A strand of that glorious red hair lay across her face. He delicately tucked it behind her ear. She smiled without opening her eyes. He tentatively stroked her cheek with his fingertips, then, daring, cupped it. She turned her head to kiss the base of his palm. That sent prickles of longing through him.

She opened her eyes. "Good morning," Ruby murmured, her alto voice deeper and more intimate than usual. That dimple appeared as she smirked. Her hand tugged gently at him, pulling Gabe closer. "It's not every morning that I wake up with a delightful man in my bed. Especially one without a shirt. Do you always sleep like this?"

"I tend to sleep warm, so yes."

"I noticed. Mmm. A little bit of chest hair but not a lot. I like that." Her hand slipped free from his back to stroke his temple and cheek. Then it slid behind his head, followed by her lips on his.

Mmm.

After several kisses, he had enough presence of mind to whisper. "*Go slow* has just gotten trashed. If you're all right with that."

"You wouldn't be in my bed if I wasn't all right with it."

"Contraception?"

"Implant, expires in a month. STDs?"

"Tested clean, repeatedly, after Mindy. No one since."

"Clean here, too."

"Then I think we're *way* too overdressed for what happens next."

She laughed. "Agreed."

Afterward, Ruby snuggled into Gabe, her arm once again thrown over him.

"I hope I'm not too plain," he murmured. "I like my sex kinda basic."

She arched a brow at him. "Do you hear any complaints?"

"I—just wasn't sure. Been told I'm boring."

"*Gabriel Martiniere.*" Ruby shifted to rest her palm against his cheek. "That's absolute bullshit. Besides, I don't need fancy, either."

He rested his forehead against hers, smiling.

How had he gotten so damned lucky?

CHAPTER 12

SISTERLY DISCLOSURES
MAY, 2029

RUBY

SOMEHOW, THE FAMILY KNEW WITHIN TWENTY-FOUR HOURS that she and Gabe had spent the night together, and that their relationship had progressed to a new level.

Gabe's grandmother sent a small package from Quebec—cooling bandannas Ruby could wear around her neck during the summer.

—*I was told that Gabriel's love is a horsewoman,* the attached note read. —*I've always found these to be useful when schooling during hot weather. Looking forward to meeting you. This is my private and confidential number. Call if you need assistance of any sort. Donna Martiniere.*

An email from his mother.

—*Dearest Ruby—Gabie glows when he talks about you. Justine and Louisa have nothing but praise for you. I am so very happy, and I look forward to meeting you. Please feel free to accompany Gabie to Los Angeles at any time. Saul and I will welcome you with open arms. If you need anything, let us know. This is my private and confidential number. Angelica Ramirez Martiniere.*

Angelica followed up with a video call that included a few stories about young Gabe. Complete with pictures.

Internal emails from the Martiniere Group Labs in France about the state of the Group's study of agricultural carbon capture methods, prefaced with a note from Arthur Martiniere.

—*Welcome to the Group. Gabriel wants you brought up to speed on this research. Ask questions as needed. Feedback is welcome. AM.*

Ruby sent thank-you emails promptly, overwhelmed by a dizzying whirlwind of welcome and acceptance that seemed too good to be true.

Her reception included private visits with Gabe's sisters.

And *those* conversations explained a lot.

ON THE MONDAY AFTER RUBY AND GABE BECAME LOVERS, Louisa dropped by the barn while Ruby did the evening feeding, Chinese take-out and a bottle of wine in hand.

"Gabie asked me to keep an eye on Mindy, in case she decides to stir things up and cause problems." Louisa tossed a flake of hay from the hayloft into the floor opening over Midnight's manger. "I figured you should know their past so you don't get surprised by any of her dramatics." She grinned. "Therefore, the wine. We might need more than one bottle."

"I have whisky on hand. Home brew from Thunder County. As for Mindy, I haven't had a favorable impression of her, from everything I've already heard." Ruby tossed hay to Sunshine. "How on earth did Gabe put up with Mindy for three years? She doesn't seem his type." And that expression on his face in the pictures she had seen —he hadn't been happy, not at all.

Louisa sighed. "You know what happened at Philip's. Next came Covid, and Gabie spent two years hiding from everyone *except* Lora." She dropped a flake to the nickering horse in the stall next to Flora.

"I know they had a relationship. Both Gabe and Lora told me." Ruby fed Glory.

Louisa's lips tightened as she turned to face Ruby. "Mama and Papa were afraid they were going to lose Gabie, because he was just that traumatized, and he resisted counseling after the surgery that fixed—" she sighed.

"I know a little bit about the surgery. Just not what it was."

"All I know is that internal injuries were involved, and Gabie wore an ostomy bag for a few months. I was only thirteen when he returned and brought Tine with him, but I heard our parents talking. He cried on my shoulder many times. Well, him and Tine both. He talked to me, Tine, and Lora, and that was about it."

"That sounds fucking awful."

Ostomy bag. It was bad. God.

Louisa nodded. "And then, when Gabie went to the University of Paris, he was pretty much rattling around the Hôtel Martiniere alone for most of the year—that's the traditional Family mansion in Paris— with only Uncle Gerry and his sons. They had just lost Aunt Moira to cancer. More isolation. That's where he developed the habit of working himself sick."

"He said something about batching it." Ruby grabbed a broom and started sweeping chaff into the assorted stalls. "Nothing about the sick."

Oh God. Is Gabe like Andy was?

Louisa worked on the other side of the hayloft. "Gabie won't admit to working himself into the ground. It takes one of us sitting on him to keep him from overdoing, and that doesn't always work."

"Literally?"

"Just about. Papa has had to order him to stop. Mindy never reined him in. Sometimes Tine and I can influence him, but it usually takes Mama or Papa to get Gabie to rest."

Ruby tightened her lips. *That* would change, unless Gabe was a pain in the ass about taking advice. Too much depended on Gabe *not* working himself sick.

"What about other girlfriends?"

"What other girlfriends? Gabie didn't go out much in college, except for society events. Meanwhile, every high-society Parisian mama wanted their daughters connected to *Gabriel Martiniere*. I think he dated some classmates, but nothing came of that. Short-term girlfriends, nothing more."

They finished cleaning up, then descended to the stable, brushing themselves off. Louisa picked up the food and they went into Ruby's apartment.

"Anyway," Louisa continued, after they had washed, dished up their food, and filled their wineglasses. "How they got together. Gabie met Mindy at a ballet gala sponsored by Mama. Mindy was in the corps de ballet for San Francisco, along with me. Gabie fell hard for Mindy. Mindy pounced."

"I didn't realize she was a dancer."

Louisa rolled her eyes. "She wasn't very good. Mindy only had a contract for one year. She knew a good thing when she saw it, and glommed onto Gabie."

"I thought she had money."

"Oh, she does. Just not Martiniere money and prestige." Louisa topped off their glasses. "And after a year and a half, she insisted that they move in together. I don't think it was Gabie's idea, but he was willing to go along just to keep her." Louisa pursed her lips. "I've talked to Cousin Piotr. *Gabie* thinks that Joey was Mindy's link to Zingter, and it started with this year's Martiniere Grant candidates. *Piotr* is fairly certain she started passing on information to Zingter on her own, no intermediary, after she and Gabie started living together."

"Damn." Ruby swallowed a substantial swig of wine. "Do you think Mindy moved in with Gabe in order to spy for Zingter, or did they approach her after that?"

"I don't know, and neither does Piotr."

"I worry that they'll try to do something like that with me." Ruby looked into her glass. "Zingter tried to get their hands on me once, through my grandparents."

"That's why Piotr's in charge of your security—to keep Zingter at bay."

"Makes sense."

"I maintain a connection with Mindy so I can keep Piotr advised, and even *I* can't decide if she went into the relationship intending to spy on Gabie, or if she truly cared for him at the beginning."

Ruby shook her head. "I can't imagine someone being crass enough to go into a relationship to spy on someone."

"We don't know and probably won't. It was an unexpected relationship from the beginning, and no one thought she was good for Gabie."

"I'm just surprised about the degree to which the Family—" now *she* was talking about the Family in capital letters— "has welcomed me."

"Totally different situation." Louisa pointed an index finger at Ruby. "*You*, unlike Mindy, were thoroughly vetted before you even spoke to Gabie, as part of the Martiniere Grant process. When Gabie showed signs of interest in you, well, we knew what you are about."

"But my grandparents' loan—"

"That was the main hole in your background that was missed, but we knew your finances otherwise. You have many people vouching for you, not just academically but personally." She shook her head. "There is no way in hell that Miranda Cathcart-Rogers can pull down those sorts of recommendations, from *anyone*."

"I'm—flattered."

"Oh, it's more than that." Louisa drained her glass and refilled it. "We all see the difference in Gabie since you came into his life. Even after only two weeks."

"Difference?"

"Ruby, those two years in his father's house crushed my favorite big brother. He wasn't the same person when he came back." Louisa blinked hard, and took a big swallow of her wine. "In the last two weeks I've seen a glimmer of the Gabie that disappeared when he was sixteen." She sniffled. "I know you've gone through rough stuff, just like him. I—I just hope the two of you are good for each other. Hell, maybe you can even shut down his working himself sick. Even if I can't seem to make a relationship work, I dearly want to see Gabie succeed with a love."

Ruby looked down at her hands, then back up. What could she say to that?

Then she knew.

"Do you know how Gabe messages me? He calls me *his dearest nerd girl*, and signs off with *your bestest nerd boy*." Ruby smiled, just thinking about it. "I get a happy tingle every time I see a message from him. He gave me flowers. He's cooked for me. He gets excited about things I want to learn and research. Oh God, I've never been with a man who respects my mind like Gabe does. For whom *nerd* is an endearment, not an attack. He's even—" she gulped. "He's offered to build me a lab. A lab! And he's *nice*. I can't believe it. He's in love with me. *Me*. What have I done to be so lucky?"

"That is exactly why the Family has opened its arms to you, Ruby," Louisa murmured. "You clearly care for *who* he is, not *what* he is. Believe me. We know the difference—especially those of us who are closest to Gabie."

Next was lunch with Justine at the barn on Wednesday, after they galloped Glory and Midnight on the outside track. Both of them had late afternoon classes, so no alcohol. They drank coffee and picked at charcuterie that Justine brought.

"Weeza said you two talked about Gabe and Mindy." Justine scrunched up her face, as if she'd smelled something bad. "That leaves Philip and Joey. And a dose of Donna-gran."

"Donna-gran—that's your Martiniere grandmother, right?" Ruby nibbled at a tiny sweet pickle.

"Correct."

"She sent me a package of cooling bandannas and a nice note about my being a horsewoman." Ruby followed the pickle with a cracker.

Justine smirked. "Oh, trust me, Donna-gran is ecstatic that Gabie's involved with a horsewoman he can science with. In spite of being in a wheelchair—riding accident—she's still breeding warmbloods and sponsoring riders. Complains loudly about being limited to riding quiet horses because of her paraplegia. Take your boots and helmet when you visit her—she'll have you on horseback within an hour. If the two of you don't start sciencing at each other right away." She ate a thin slice of fake cheeze.

"She likes the Windraker bloodline?"

"She invested in him before he went to stud." Justine sipped her coffee. "But that's neither here nor there." Her face tightened. "I'm probably the best person to tell you about Daddy-fucking-dearest and my idiot brother. Not Gabie, the other one."

Ruby snorted. "Your father sounds downright awful." She poked at the fake ham.

"Joey isn't much better. He doesn't take after Saul at all." Justine pressed her lips together, staring into her cup. "But he's easy enough to manage, probably because he's Saul's son and nowhere near as bullheaded as Gabie—Gabie's inheritance from Philip. Our shithead of a father, on the other hand, is downright dangerous to all of us."

"Isn't Philip locked up right now?" Ruby set down a second slice of fake cheeze, her gut tightening.

"There are ways to get around confinement. Especially since he's buddy-buddy with Walter Braun and has political connections and ambitions. Philip's other friends are equally unprincipled and sleazy. If Joey comes after you, he'll at least do it head-on, without guile. Philip? I bet that he's scheming how to hurt any and all of us. Gabie. Me. Saul. Angelica. Louisa. Donald. And you. That's why Piotr is in charge of your security. You're part of the Martiniere's close family circle. Piotr supervises security for all of us."

"Why does Philip do this?" God, Ruby wanted desperately to slop some whisky in her coffee, to hell with remaining sober for this afternoon's class. "Gabe told me some of what happened to him. He glossed over part of it."

"Be glad he didn't go into details. I saw enough, especially after my mother—died." She shuddered. "I've talked it over and over with Donna-gran, Saul, and Angelica, trying to understand my fucking father. Philip has always resented being the younger twin. He accused Donna-gran of lying about which of them was the first born. Donna-gran thinks Philip went over the edge when Angelica chose Saul over him."

Justine shook her head before continuing.

"How can twin brothers be so different? Living with Saul and Angelica was a shock after growing up with my father. It took me a while to realize I wasn't going to be hit for no reason. That I didn't have to put up with old lechers pawing me in dark corners. Just—" she raised her hands. "Night and day."

"Do you know why Philip's like this?"

"It's defined as a disorder." Justine gripped her coffee cup. "Officially, antisocial personality disorder, the psychopathic version. At least that's what Donna-gran told me. Saul and Angelica kept a very close watch on me—and, earlier—Gabie—to ensure we didn't show the first signs of it in our teens. Obviously—not."

Ruby eyed Justine, remembering what Gabe had said about her and Philip.

The two of them in alliance would be terrifying.

If Justine had taken after their father—

"Gabe's the farthest thing from a psychopath that I've ever seen. I —think that's what my father was. A chunk of the Barkley family as well." Ruby shivered as she recalled how Carl, Jim, Randy, and Dave had attacked her.

Especially that one time in the woods. If it hadn't been for Andy—

"Then you know exactly what I'm talking about."

Ruby nodded. A question that had been buzzing in her brain

since she talked to Louisa stirred—anything, *anything* to further banish the creepy-crawling sensation on her skin as she recalled *that night.*

"There's one thing I'm curious about. Louisa told me that Piotr believes that Mindy was spying on Gabe for Zingter from the beginning. What do you think?"

Justine frowned, tapping her lips with her fingertips.

"I don't know," she said, after a long pause. "I despise the woman for the mind games she played on Gabie, but I don't think she's capable of that level of conspiracy. Especially not for three years. Mindy *is* a social climber, however, and it's possible that she unknowingly participated in one of Walter Braun's schemes. *That*, I could see."

Another long pause as Justine stared into the distance.

"I think Mindy jumped from Gabie to Joey because it became clear that even though he cared for her, Gabie wasn't going to marry her," she finally continued. "Yeah, he thought she was *the one*. But honestly? She did him a favor by rubbing Joey in his face and breaking that delusion. Mindy could never be the Martiniere's wife—and sooner or later, Gabie would have had to choose between becoming the Martiniere-in-waiting or Miranda Cathcart-Rogers's husband."

Ruby gulped.

What does this mean for me and Gabe? Am I worthy of becoming the Martiniere's wife?

What happened if the Family judged her as unworthy to be anything more than Gabe's casual love interest?

Is that why there's provisions for Gabe to provide for me? In case it's decided that I have to be put aside for a more expedient relationship? An easy let-down?

Ruby clutched her hands together, staring down at them. She was thinking of Gabe in those terms. Potential spouse. But too soon, after only two weeks—and if this overwork problem was really bad—

"Ruby." Justine's voice softened as she rested her hands on top of

Ruby's. "Don't compare yourself to Mindy. You have me, Weeza, Saul, and Angelica supporting you. That's huge."

Ruby blinked back tears she hadn't realized were forming. "But—"

"Listen." Justine's hands tightened on hers. "Yes, the Family structures are stupid and archaic. But they kept Gabie from making that mistake with Mindy—who might qualify socially, but fails abysmally to be what Gabie needs by every other criterion." Justine shrugged. "Maybe she'll end up with Joey. I could see that happening, appalling though it seems."

"Eww."

"Agreed. However. You are a successful and brilliant woman. More than that, you possess a personal integrity to match Gabie's." Justine frowned. "Saul has done a lot for the Group. But the Group needs a leader to follow him who is capable of extending those reforms and *doing something* about the climate mess falling on our heads in the next few years. That's Gabie. He needs a partner with skills, integrity, and vision to match his, who gives a shit about him as a person and not his social status. That's you."

"The social piece, though—"

Justine waved a hand. "Dealt with easily enough. Weeza, Angelica, and I can guide you through the nuances. And the fact that you have Cousin Artie and Uncle Gerry just *drooling* over bringing you deeper into the Group doesn't hurt, either. The social piece is *nothing* in comparison."

"I hope so," Ruby said. "Because—"

"You love him, and it shows. He adores you." Justine got up, covering the charcuterie plate and sticking it into Ruby's refrigerator. "And I intend to help you in any way that I can."

—Dearest Nerd Girl. Uncertain time coming in today. Will *be there when I can. Your Bestest Nerd Boy.*

Ruby sighed when she read Gabe's message Friday morning. The vet was coming in that afternoon to begin the process of diagnosing—and, hopefully, eventually treating—whether Sunshine might have a form of spinal impingement, and if so, how severe. She had hoped he would be present for the vet visit, in case there was any stickiness about sending the bill to Gabe.

She bit her lip. Hopefully he wasn't running himself ragged.

THE PRELIMINARY EXAMINATION AT THE BARN CONFIRMED Ruby's worst fears. Kissing spines. More detailed examinations needed to follow. Ruby scheduled the next appointment, wincing. Before she could haul the golden mare to the clinic for the—pricey—further imaging that couldn't be done on a mobile call, she needed to check her trailer and her cranky old truck's electrical connections. More money going out—and for what?

Surgery and treatment would sideline the golden mare for a while. More intensive management was probably required. All that most likely meant no barrel racing for Sunshine this summer. *Would she ever be able to turn Sunshine into a decent barrel horse?*

"Girl, at least we know what might be going on with you, but damn. I sure didn't count on this." Ruby shook her head as she brushed the golden mare.

She looked up as she heard the whir of Gabe's roller bag on the concrete of the barn alleyway.

"Hey there." That slow, broad smile spread across his face. He still wore one of his bespoke suits—this one a double-breasted light tan—which suggested he hadn't been in the air long enough to change into more casual clothing. "Sorry I missed the vet. Passed her on the way out. What's the verdict?" He carefully left his bag two stalls behind the crossties so he wouldn't spook Sunshine, before slipping over to kiss Ruby.

"Kissing spines, possibly severe. Appointment next week to start detailed imaging," Ruby sighed. "Which means I'd better make sure my trailer hookup is reliable. It's been cranky."

"Do what's needed to keep the two of you safe." Gabe kept his left arm around her waist while he loosened his tie with his right hand. "Same procedure as the vet bill—have them send the charges to me. If you have to rent a truck and trailer, do so."

Ruby frowned at him, her concerns about overwork coming back. Gabe looked paler than usual and felt heated, warmer than he should be for the day's temperature. "Are you all right?"

"Eh, just a little tired and this suit is hotter than it looks. It happens." His tie loosened, he bent to kiss her again. "I'm gonna go change. Be back out to help you bring in horses and do the evening feeding."

They kissed again, and Ruby turned back to Sunshine.

GABE HADN'T REAPPEARED BY THE TIME RUBY PUT SUNSHINE away and started bringing horses in from turnout.

At first, she wasn't too worried. After all, it was likely that he'd received a work call before switching over to private mode.

But as she finished stalling the last two horses, he still hadn't shown up.

Ruby hesitated in the alleyway, chewing her lip, remembering how pale he had looked and his warmth.

Won't hurt to check.

When she entered her studio, Gabe sprawled face down on the bed, roller bag abandoned in the middle of the room. He still wore his suit, but his tie was in one hand and his shoes lay next to the bed, where he had kicked them off.

Just like Andy had been—

She took a deep breath.

Don't panic, Ruby. He might just be sick.

After all, he had felt warmer than usual earlier.

But Gabe *sprawled like that* triggered memories of breaking into Andy's trailer with his girlfriend Rita, only to find Andy dead on the floor.

Another deep breath. Then she crossed the room, bending over to gently shake Gabe's shoulder. He grunted. She shook harder. He rolled onto his back and threw one arm over his eyes.

Worry twisted through Ruby and tightened her gut. She retreated to the bathroom and pulled out her thermometer. She needed data before freaking out any further.

Gabe roused slightly as she pressed it against his temple. "M'kay."

"You're running a temperature of 100 degrees Fahrenheit and you passed out on the bed after taking off your tie and shoes." Ruby kept her voice steady as she studied him. God. Gabe looked thinner than last week.

Like Andy.

She continued, forcing her voice into calmness. "If you're gonna crash, then let's get you changed into something comfortable and under the covers."

Gabe grumbled, but pushed himself up and slowly pulled off his jacket. Ruby knelt by his bag and took out his usual pajama pants, then moved the bag to its usual place by her closet. When she turned back, Gabe had unloaded his weapons onto the side table, taken off his cuff links and shirt, and sat on the side of the bed, still in t-shirt and slacks, head drooping, eyes half-closed.

Ruby prodded him into exchanging slacks for pajama pants. Once that was done, Gabe crawled under the covers and heaved a heavy sigh.

"Do you want anything for dinner?"

"Broth, if you have it, and crackers. My gut's rebelling, been upset the last few days." He closed his eyes. "Pushed too hard."

Ruby sat next to him and stroked his forehead. "Before or after I feed horses?"

"After. I'm not contagious. Gut stuff. Normal for me, after—"

She kissed his forehead. A faint smile twitched his lips, and he nestled into the pillow with the deepest sigh of all.

Ruby called Louisa while she fed horses, and described Gabe's symptoms.

Louisa groaned. "It sounds like one of Gabie's bad gut flares brought on by stress and not taking care of himself. I'm surprised he came to you—normally he goes directly to Los Angeles when this happens. Take it as meaning he totally trusts you. He doesn't feel comfortable crashing like that around me and Tine. Didn't around Mindy."

"Anything else I can do? How long does it last?"

"I don't know—several days, usually but Mama normally handles it. You should probably call Mama—I don't know if he's contacted them."

"All right. Thanks. See you tomorrow."

"We *can* cancel lessons if Gabie's down," Louisa said. "Just do our usual individual rides. In fact, let's do that. I'll tell Tine. Then you can be with Gabie."

"That sounds like a very good idea," Ruby said.

She finished throwing hay to the horses before contacting Angelica, sitting on a tack trunk in the alleyway rather than going into the apartment for this conversation.

"Oh, *Gabriel,*" Angelica sighed. "No, he hasn't called us, Ruby."

"Is there anything I can do besides feed him broth?"

Saul said something in the background.

"Saul says to tell Gabriel not to worry about doing anything until Wednesday. That's about how long a bad flare lasts. Broth and crackers are good. Water. Acetaminophen. Don't expect him to do much other than sleep until sometime Sunday. If you can keep him there until Tuesday night, that would be best." She sighed again. "He'll want to be up and back to work by Sunday night. If he gives you any backtalk, call me, all right?"

"Just how do we keep this from happening? It has to stop." Ruby bit her lip. "I—I've seen people work themselves to death, Angelica. It *has* to stop."

"If I knew how, Ruby—" Angelica sighed again. "I wish I did. He's been doing this regularly since he left Philip's house. Saul *could* pull Gabriel's online accesses—but there's issues between them about that."

"I'll do what I can."

"Thank you."

Ruby hung up and went back into her studio. Broth. At least she had bullion and crackers for Gabe, the last of the charcuterie for herself. Maybe she could get Louisa or Justine to bring more food tomorrow.

He woke when she brought the cup and a plate with crackers over to the bed.

"Sorry," he mumbled, crumbling the crackers into his cup. "Don't mean to be a bother."

"You're not."

Wasn't the appropriate time to get into his face about taking care of himself. That said, she firmly intended to have a talk with him about *not doing this anymore.*

Once he was better, that was.

She didn't need to lose another good person in her life to overwork, like she had her cousin Andy.

CHAPTER 13
BOUNDARIES
MAY, 2029

GABE

Gabe *still* wasn't exactly sure why he chose to collapse at Ruby's place instead of Los Angeles. He never went to Mindy when he got sick like this. Always home, at least since he graduated from college.

But when fatigue and the ache in his gut became too much this time, he didn't divert the pilot to LA.

Corvallis. Ruby.

It *felt* right.

He fully intended to change and go back out to help her wrap up her late afternoon chores. After all, moving around often helped him feel better. And he didn't want to lose a single precious moment with Ruby.

However, when he got into Ruby's studio apartment and looked around, the bed drew him. Gabe let go of his bag, staggered over to the bed, pulled off his tie, kicked off his shoes, and face-planted.

The next thing he knew, Ruby was shaking him awake. His head pounded and he felt like crap. She bullied him into changing and tucked him into bed. A bit later, after feeding horses, she brought him bouillon and crackers, along with acetaminophen. Then, until she came to bed herself, she woke him periodically to make him drink water.

Just like home—no, actually better, because he could curl up to the comfort of Ruby.

The next day was much the same. At one point Gabe thought he heard Ruby and Louisa talking in hushed voices, along with the rattle of grocery sacks and the distant scent of roasted chicken. But that was a faint rousing between sleeping, drinking water, eating bouillon and crackers, and staggering to the bathroom.

The whole-body aches faded. The headache no longer hounded him. His gut wanted something more substantial than bouillon and crackers, but Gabe knew better. Sleep still sounded good. Curling around Ruby when she came to bed and spooning against her back helped as well. She turned over and held him as he nuzzled into her chest.

"Feeling better?"

"A little bit. Thank you."

She kept stroking his hair. He fell back asleep to that gentle rhythm.

***

Morning, and he was in bed by himself. Gabe rose up on one elbow, blearily blinking.

"Ruby?"

No answer, but he heard horses nickering. Must be morning feeding. Gabe collapsed back on the bed with a sigh. What day was this?

He reached for his phone. Sunday. Morning. Damn it, he'd not just lost a day—he'd lost his weekend with Ruby. He needed to be back on the plane this afternoon.

Gabe groaned and got up. He went to his bag—empty. Ruby must have unpacked it at some point. But where were his dirty clothes—much less clean clothing? Had Ruby washed them for him? He wobbled and sat down hard on the couch, rubbing his face.

Think. Think.

He wanted a shower, but the way his legs trembled, he wasn't sure that was a good idea until Ruby returned to the studio, in case he lost his balance. Food. If he could eat without provoking more cramping in his gut. And he was still so damned tired.

Gabe slowly rose and staggered into the bathroom. His toiletries were in their usual place on the counter, so Ruby had taken care of that. Folded fresh pair of sweats and t-shirt on top of his jeans, including his last pair of clean boxers and socks. He sighed. At least he knew where *some* of his things were.

"Gabe?"

"In here." He finished and made it to the doorframe before he had to lean against it. "Gotta shower and get ready to go, hon. I'm sorry this weekend's a bust."

Ruby scowled at him, placing her hands on her hips. "Buddy, you are *not* going anywhere except *back to bed.*"

He shook his head. "I can't afford—"

"You can't afford to do anything else! Damn it, Gabe, you can't even stand up on your own very well!"

"Food will fix that." But even as he said that, his gut tightened.

She shook her index finger at him. "Listen. Saul said that you are not to go back to work until Wednesday morning."

Gabe shook his head again. "I have too much to do—"

"Bullshit. You're running yourself into the ground, damn it!" She stomped over to him, her jaw set hard. "If you don't get your ass back to bed, I'm calling your mother, and you can argue the point with *her.*"

"Ruby, damn it, this is part of my job."

Was Ruby going to turn out to be like Mindy after all? His gut clenched even more.

"Not to this degree. The traveling, yes. I don't have a problem with that. But working yourself to exhaustion on a regular basis? *Fuck* no. Especially when your father, your mother, and your *sisters* tell me that you do this consistently, have done this since you left Philip's house, and they can't get you to stop it. *No.*"

"Ruby," he groaned, rubbing his face. "You don't understand. There's so much to do."

"You think I don't get it? Too much to do, too few people doing the work, and not enough time to get it all done? *Damn* it all, Gabriel!" She gulped, and her face crumpled. "You scared the *shit* out of me. If I hadn't already heard about this behavior of yours from your sisters—" she choked and buried her head in her hands. Held it there for a moment, then raised it, sniffling.

"Ruby." God. She was *crying*. And her tears jerked at something visceral and deep within him.

"I *know* what working yourself to death looks like," she whispered, looking away from him. "God damn it, I've seen that happen enough times around Thunder County. Been to the funerals. People who had *no fucking financial choice* but to run themselves into the ground like you are *right now*. People who worked themselves into heart attacks and strokes, and couldn't fall back on Martiniere resources to pay for their medical care."

He didn't know what to say to that, especially as tears trickled down her cheeks when she turned to face him. He wanted to kiss them away.

"Damn it, Gabriel. You've lost weight over the last two weeks. That plus how tired you are—" Ruby choked back a sob. "This is *exactly* how I lost a good Barkley cousin. Andy damn near got killed protecting me, and in return he ended up losing his mechanic's job. Had to work several side gigs to make up for it, but no one told me he was in bad shape until his girlfriend Rita didn't hear from him for a couple of days. She called me and we had to break into his trailer. He looked *just like you did* on Friday night. And it was too goddamned late by then." She buried her head in her hands again, tears shaking her body.

Aw fuck.

"I didn't mean to trigger a memory. I'm sorry."

More sobs, and then she raised her head. "Even before Andy lost his job, he was working himself to death, trying to put money aside to get the hell away from the other Barkleys. But he wasn't the only friend I saw knocking themselves out. I can't stand by and watch you do this to yourself, Gabe." Her voice cracked. "I *can't.* Not without saying anything. *I can't lose you too.*"

Shit. This cast a different light on everything. Definitely *not* like Mindy.

Gabe held Ruby as she sobbed into his chest, his mind spinning. He'd been shoving aside everyone else's complaints about his work levels, about how he looked, figuring it was all exaggeration and, in some cases, envy.

And yet—oh *God.* Ruby's tears and words moved him, more than anything anyone else had said or done.

She looked back up. "How are you going to manage things as the Martiniere if you run yourself ragged like this? Especially as cutthroat as I'm realizing the Family and the Group can be? There's a middle ground between fucking off and working yourself to the bone. There *has* to be."

More tears, Ruby shivering and gulping, fighting back sobs.

"Ruby. Rubes." That was all he could say, clinging to her.

"I love you. And I see you killing yourself through overwork and —and everything. Even in the short time we've been together." Her voice quavered. "You're my bestest nerd boy and—and—I don't want to fucking bury you too!"

That struck him hard.

He exhaled. "I'm I—don't know what to say. Don't know what to do. Afraid to step off of the treadmill."

"Go back to bed, Gabe. For me, if not for anyone else." She wiped her eyes. "And then we'll figure it out. But *God,* this has to stop. For your sake. For *our* sake."

"All right." After all, apparently *someone* had talked to his parents if she knew that Saul had ordered him to stay away from work. He could check on that later on today, probably when she took horses to turnout after breakfast.

Breakfast. He wasn't sure if he looked forward to that or not.

"Come on." She tugged at him.

Gabe let Ruby guide him to the bed and tuck him in.

"Just—when you're studying, would you do it in bed? With me? I want to cuddle with you."

"As long as you *rest*," she said. "And don't mind if I occasionally pile stuff on you."

"Not a problem. I'll rest better if you're with me."

"All right. After breakfast and morning turnout. Feel like eating something more than bouillon and crackers?"

"I should eat something but I'm really not sure what."

"Louisa brought your favorite breakfast cereal and some yogurt. Think you could stomach that?"

"I can try," he said.

"I hope to hell this doesn't mean you're on a plane," Saul said when Gabe called, while Ruby was turning horses out.

Gabe laughed weakly. "No. I'm solidly in bed, at Ruby's."

"Will wonders ever cease? I'm glad to hear it, son."

"She—kinda ripped me a new one and then turned on the tears," Gabe said. "I can't fight that."

"*Good.* I don't want us to meet until Wednesday morning at the earliest. Longer if need be."

"I don't think Ruby will let me up until then."

"She has the codes to lock you out of your accesses if you don't listen," Saul said. "I gave them to her last night. Let me check—no, she's not done it. Ruby didn't ask for them. My idea. I gave them to her, when she called your mother to report."

"Seriously?" Gabe didn't know whether to be thankful or angry.

That action was *drastic*. Saul had used that authority once, when Gabe was in college. He had agreed not to yank Gabe's code accesses again unless he was directly observing Gabe—handing the power to Ruby met that requirement, at least.

"Seriously. It's early May, Gabriel. You've collapsed twice since Christmas. This makes three times *this year*. That's too damned much." Saul inhaled. "Look. Your mama had to beat me around the head and shoulders. Do me a favor and listen to *your* woman, all right? Stress from overwork is why my heart is so fucked up, because I kept doing what you are now until I wrecked it. Your genetics are close enough to mine to be problematic. Don't do this to yourself."

"I—guess."

"You have a good woman in your life who gives a shit and isn't afraid to take action, Gabriel. Don't put her through hell, like I've done to your mama. I almost lost her after you were born because she was fed up with me."

"Not to Philip, I hope."

Saul snorted. "He wasn't the only one sniffing around. But no, she was ready to go back to her mother and her Saldivar cousins, and take you with her. By then, I'd put her through several years of working myself into collapses. Don't do that to Ruby. Be smarter than me."

"But how do I make that happen, Papa? And still become the Martiniere-in-waiting?"

"Are you doing this to yourself so you can become the Martiniere-in-waiting, or are you running from something, son?"

"I—" He didn't know how to answer that. "I don't know."

"Rest and think about it," Saul said. "Don't provoke Ruby into shutting down your accesses. Cooperate with her. And remember, she's talking to your mama. I'll know if you're acting up."

"All right, Papa."

Saul's voice softened. "You're a good man, Gabriel. A good son. You take after me in so many positive ways—now find a means to deal with one aspect which isn't. Because it may end up costing you your heart's desire—in more ways than one. Understand?"

"I understand," Gabe said.

Did he *ever* understand the implicit threat in that statement.

GABE DROWSED, RESTING HIS HEAD AGAINST RUBY, A HAND ON her leg, as she studied. Saul's question kept nudging at him, along with that one statement.

Are you doing this to yourself so you can become the Martiniere-in-waiting, or are you running from something?

It may end up costing you your heart's desire—in more ways than one.

Gabe groaned. Ruby's fingers stilled from gentle strokes of his head as she read on her tablet, occasionally stopping when she switched hands to take notes.

"Are you all right?"

"I don't know. Saul said some things and they're—kinda hard to consider."

"Oh?"

He summarized the conversation for her, including the two statements that hit him hard.

"Saul is bringing the hammer down on you," Ruby said when he finished. "For good reason. Third incident since Christmas, and from what your mother says, usually this is only a twice-a-year thing. That's not a good situation, Gabe."

He couldn't say anything in response except to sigh and bury his face in her thigh.

Ruby resumed reading and running her fingers through his hair. Gabe kept thinking.

Why *was* he driving himself like this? The other high-level Martiniere heirs weren't knocking themselves out to the same degree, and there was no question in Gabe's mind about their competence.

David—Chris—Charles—all good men, all with ideas about what the Group could be in the next few years. Not visions that completely matched his, to be certain, but the Group would be in good hands with them.

But the need. Collecting the data. The fieldwork required to document the impending catastrophe, one part of him argued. *Provide the information needed to persuade the Group into shifting a greater emphasis toward fighting climate change, not just profit.*

Gabe's cousins weren't as obsessed as he was about climate change. And the Group could do *so much* about it, if channeled properly.

What *would* happen if he didn't become the Martiniere-in-waiting? Would that be so bad? After all, he could still take action on his own. It just wouldn't be as powerful as it would be if he had the Group behind him.

Would that be so awful?

Then there was Ruby. What would be worse—becoming Martiniere-in-waiting and losing her, or losing Martiniere-in-waiting and keeping her?

His hand tightened on her thigh.

God. No.

He groaned at that thought.

Ruby put aside her tablet. "Gabe. Talk to me. You're moaning and groaning. Stop agonizing. *Talk.*" She slid down in the bed and took him in her arms.

"Still thinking about what Papa said." He shuddered. "As bad as not becoming the Martiniere-in-waiting is, the thought of losing you is worse. And if I lose both—"

She kissed his forehead. "Our relationship is not dependent upon you becoming the Martiniere-in-waiting. I didn't become your lover for the prestige of dating *Gabriel Martiniere.* I did it because of Gabriel the man."

He leaned his forehead against hers. "I know. I know. It's just— coming to grips with things. Your words hit me pretty hard this morning. As did Papa's. *Am* I running from something—and what is it?"

Ruby was silent for a few moments. "How much of this is trying to prove your worthiness because of who your biological father is? That is one thing that keeps coming up. And you started this pattern of working yourself to exhaustion after you left Philip's house."

Could it be that simple?

Granted, it was what counselors had said to him in the past. But he hadn't wanted to listen, figuring that they *just didn't understand* how urgent things were.

"I don't know," he admitted.

"It would match what I saw in Andy," she continued. "He was embarrassed to be a Barkley, especially after what our cousins did to me. Yeah, Andy had to overwork himself to survive—but he was also determined to leave Thunder County on his own two feet, without owing anything to anybody. Even me and my grandparents. And it killed him."

"Aw, shit, Ruby. I'm so sorry."

"I know the pattern. It's one I slide into at times. Understandable. Finding out at sixteen like you did that your father isn't who you thought—and then going through what you did in his house—that's horrific. I don't understand why your family felt you had to go through that experience, and were appalled about it *afterward*. Didn't they know what he was before then?"

"I don't know." God, was that all he could say?

A pause. "It's easier for me. I knew what my parents were at a young age. I grew up knowing what I came from. I can't imagine discovering it at sixteen."

He exhaled hard.

"I don't want to lose you," he said. "I can stand not becoming the Martiniere-in-waiting, as long as it's truly based on merit, and not because I'm Philip's son. I'd like to have both. But if I can't—I choose you."

"If you choose me, then I want you to take care of yourself, damn it!" She drew a deep breath. "Flying commercial like I've had to do, there's one very relevant phrase that the flight attendants say every time, during the safety lecture before takeoff. *Put your own oxygen mask on first before helping others.*" She stroked his brow. "Put your own mask on first. Take care of yourself. Acknowledge that pushing yourself like this isn't just about climate crisis, but about being Philip's biological son."

"And then?"

"Set boundaries. Figure out what *taking care of Gabriel Martiniere* is going to look like. Because the only way you're going to bring about the change you want to see is if you are in good enough health to do it."

"It kinda sounds selfish."

"Selfish? You?" She laughed. "No, Gabe. That is so not you. But you need to think about yourself, so you can be there for others. Your parents. Your sisters. *Me.*"

He kissed her. "Oh God, Ruby. How is it that you're so wise about this?"

"Counseling. Lots and lots of counseling. I'm screwed up in other ways, but when it comes to dealing with wanting to work myself to death? I know that one too well." She gulped. "Andy's death was my wakeup call. It happened just before I headed to college for the first time. And even then, I backslide sometimes."

"I'm sorry that happened."

She shrugged. "I learned. You can, too. Look. You have two more days. Figure out how to step off of that treadmill. Not just for you, but for *us*. Talk to me. Let's work this out *together*."

He nodded.

Ruby slid off the bed. "I'm fixing lunch. Want some?"

"A little bit." He wasn't all that hungry, but he had to eat.

Part of getting off of that treadmill. Part of setting boundaries for himself.

AFTER LUNCH AND ANOTHER NAP, GABE HAD TO ADMIT THAT IT felt as if a huge weight had been lifted from his shoulders when he thought about *not getting on the plane that afternoon.* When had he last taken a break that hadn't been enforced by illness?

Too damn long ago. That needed to change.

Ruby side-eyed him after he showered—pulling on jeans—and moved to the couch, retrieving his computer from his bag.

"Do I *have* to lock up your accesses? I'd just as soon not."

Gabe raised his hands. "No. Just looking at schedules. Thinking about how much of this stuff I'm doing really needs to be *me,* on site, and how much I can delegate or do remotely." He patted the couch next to him. "Work here?"

She laughed, and dragged two chairs over so they could prop up their feet.

<hr>

HIS HEAD STARTED HURTING AFTER HALF AN HOUR, SO GABE switched to something better—Corvallis-area real estate.

Ruby craned her head to look. "What's up?"

Gabe put his arm around her. "Different living situation for us starting next fall. I'm not convinced the condo is an option—security questions, primarily. Tine and Don are buying a winery and will live there once they're married. Weeza can use the space to herself in the condo. Better that the three of us are in separate residences, since I'll be here more often."

She arched a brow at him. "*For us?*"

"If you can tolerate living with me." He hugged her.

"As long as I get some say in the place."

"Oh, absolutely. I'm looking for someplace that I can use as a base, at least until you graduate. That means certain security requirements. Not sure about the horses yet. Would we want to keep them here at Lora's, or have them with us?"

"With us would be more expensive."

"Remember. Expense isn't an issue. Comfort and security are. We can buy or rent. What do you want in a place?"

"It *would* be nice to have a stable on site," she admitted. "But that means more work."

"Mm, we hire help. Prioritize."

"And inside the house?"

He shrugged. "I'm capable of doing my own laundry and cooking. Bring staff in as needed to do big cleaning projects, but honestly, unless you want to entertain or hand off housework to outsiders—"

"Not really." She nuzzled against him.

"Then we can keep the house small, not grandiose. Might take some looking or fixing up."

"Maybe talk to Lora? She might know of some properties."

"That's a good idea."

They spent another half hour looking at places. Then it was time to bring the horses in. Gabe felt good enough to help feed as well.

All the same, he was more than ready to go to bed after dinner.

Gabe spent Monday morning putting together a schedule that would transition him to a Corvallis base by September, whether he was the Martiniere-in-waiting or not, and cut back, if not eliminate, his need to travel.

Doable. Quite doable. He could spend time at the Double R with Ruby this summer.

He drifted over to Lora's office in early afternoon to discuss horse properties for him and Ruby.

"Things are moving pretty fast if you're talking about a place to live together," Lora teased.

"You know me. She's everything I've wanted." Gabe smirked at Lora.

Her expression changed to serious. "You scared her this past weekend. Have to get control of those behaviors, Gabe. They were showing up when you were younger, and you didn't listen when I told you about consequences."

"I know. She yelled at me pretty good. I'm—gonna try to change things."

"I'm glad to hear it." Lora opened her mouth to say more when the high-level security alert tone blared from their phones. He yanked his out.

—Oregon State University campus. Report by JSM. Condition Red.

Justine.

Chilled, Gabe called Lance.

"Justine spotted Joey and Mindy on campus, overheard them asking around about Ruby," Lance said. "And Ruby's not answering her alert."

"She's in class right now, probably has it muted." Gabe shot out of his chair, waving goodbye to Lora as he strode out. She was on the phone to her own security head. "Situation?"

"Ruby's guards have a cordon around her classroom, and Justine with her guards are on their way."

"Class goes for another hour." Gabe stepped out of the barn and switched off the phone as he saw Lance. "Leave her in it or extract her?"

"Extract her," Lance said, face tight. "We don't know for certain what Joey's carrying, but he has some sort of knockout gas on him, possibly from the labs. Incomplete analysis from Justine's scanner. Best if you or Justine, whoever gets there first, extracts Ruby before we have a general evacuation. Less disruption."

Gabe nodded and climbed into the SUV.

Damn it, damn it, damn it.

Ruby's safety. Another reason to stay close, and not go gallivanting around the world.

But if something happened to Ruby, then to hell with it. He *would* work himself to death—

After he made Mindy and Joey pay for what they had done.

CHAPTER 14
MINDY
MAY, 2029

RUBY

Her phone vibrated repeatedly, but Ruby didn't dare pull it out. Dr. Wareham was strict about electronics in class. Sure, she was OSU's Martiniere Grant finalist, but Wareham had made it clear that her status didn't earn her any special privileges. She'd check it at the next break.

The classroom door opened. Dr. Wareham whirled, an annoyed expression furrowing his brows, followed by astonishment.

Then a hand brushed against her shoulder. Someone bent over her as another person, wearing the insignia of Campus Security, went up to Wareham. Her friend Linda, in the next seat, turned to Ruby, her eyes widening.

"Ruby," Justine murmured. "We need to get you out of here, *now*. Condition Red."

Ruby's gut plummeted and her throat tightened even as she gathered up her notes and put them into her bag.

"You all right?" Linda asked.

"Family stuff," Ruby said, hoping it truly wasn't the case. "I'll let you know."

Please don't let this be something wrong with Gramps, Granma, or Gabe. Please.

But she didn't *think* that anything involving Gramps or Granma would trigger a Martiniere Condition Red.

Gabe. Had to be connected to Gabe.

She caught Dr. Wareham's gaze before she followed Justine. He nodded at her as security spoke to him.

"What's going on?" she asked as both her guards and Justine's surrounded them. Right now, with *Condition Red*, four guards didn't feel like enough. Ruby could imagine a number of scenarios, none of them good.

"Mindy and Joey are on campus, asking about you. My scanner picked up traces of a substance containing knockout gas on Joey, right after I saw him," Justine said once they were outside the building, the guards hurrying them along a sidewalk. "Getting you out of the class-room, then evacuating everyone else. Campus is going on lockdown. Gabriel's on his way here to get you."

Ruby inhaled sharply. "Why—?"

"Who the fuck knows right now? It may be a distraction from something that fucking Braun is doing with Daddy-fucking-dearest, or it may be an attack on Gabriel through you."

And then the guards halted, two in front of them, two behind them.

"*Shit*," Justine snarled. "That's Mindy. Where the fuck is Joey?"

Ruby followed her gaze to see Miranda Cathcart-Rogers on an intersecting sidewalk.

Cathcart-Rogers spotted Ruby, and scowled. "*You're* the bitch who took my place with Gabie!"

"*Move*," Justine muttered. "Don't answer her—let's get the fuck out of here! Who knows where Joey is? She could be a distraction."

They wheeled and walked away from Cathcart-Rogers.

"Hey! Don't just walk off like that, you bitch!"

"Oh *God*, she's drunk to boot," Justine said. "She'd never act like this normally."

"You sure she's drunk?" Ruby glanced back quickly, as Cathcart-Rogers followed them, continuing to holler, just like Grace or Jeanie would.

"Justine, you bitch! Are you too chickenshit to give me that beating you promised?"

"She behaved like this after having too much to drink at Cousin Kendra's wedding last summer," Justine said.

"She *does* seem to be rather fond of calling us bitches."

"Definite indicator that she's drunk. Otherwise, Mindy is Miss Priss. You won't hear a profanity pass her lips. Get her drunk, though, and every other word is *bitch*. She doesn't vary at all. All bitch, all the time."

Ruby rolled her eyes. *Very* much like Grace and Jeanie Barkley.

Before she could say anything, faint beeps came from one of Justine's pockets.

"*Run!*" Justine snapped. "That's the knockout gas alert. Damn it, we don't have masks—"

Ruby hustled, feeling very vulnerable. She didn't know if the light-headedness she experienced was genuine or a suggestion effect.

They passed between two buildings, racing along the paved walkway—turned a corner, and—

To her relief, Gabe strode toward them. He wore a heavy-duty mask that covered his eyes as well as his nose and mouth, complete with two huge filters, and carried two other masks just like his. Six masked guards followed him. Gabe handed one of the masks he carried to Justine, then slipped another on Ruby. Justine adjusted her mask skillfully while Gabe checked Ruby's fit.

"Need to train you on this protocol," Gabe muttered. "I hadn't considered this likelihood. *Stupid. Foolish.*"

"Neither did I, Gabie," Justine said. "But who released the gas?"

"If it's Mindy, she just poisoned herself," Gabe said.

Ruby turned and looked. Cathcart-Rogers twitched on the ground, surrounded by several Martiniere guards.

"No sign of Joey," Justine said. "All right, Gabie. You have Ruby. Get her the fuck out of here. I'll handle Mindy."

"I should—"

"*Take care of Ruby.* You may be the target, and this a means to draw you in for something nastier to happen. Get Ruby to the condo. Weeza's safe there already."

"Mindy's not that manipulative. She doesn't have the brains to cook something up like this."

"*Joey* is. *Braun* is, and we know both of them are using her. Get the two of you safe, all right? It's *my* fucking asshole of a scumbag brother who's doing this. *I* am going to take care of it."

"Tine, be careful. Don will have my head if you get hurt."

Justine snorted. "Donald knows better than to blame anyone but me if something happens. Now, *go!*"

Gabe wrapped his arm around Ruby's shoulders as they marched away.

When they reached the SUV, Gabe stopped Ruby from taking her mask off.

"Decontamination protocol first."

"Which is?" How extensive would it be, and what would that do to her bag, tablet, and notes? And was she safe, given her skin exposure?

"Neutralizing spray once we reach the condo. Wash clothing. Take your stuff out and wash the bag. Showers. Scanners are inconclusive about the potency of that gas, but judging by Mindy's reaction, that particular little gem is rather unpleasant."

"What about bare skin?"

"Usually doesn't have an effect; washing will get rid of it. But you can breathe in a dose off the mask if the particles get stirred before the neutralizing spray."

"All right."

They rode in silence the rest of the way, Gabe's arm around her shoulders, his other hand grasping hers.

When they reached the condo, security made them wait while they set up a clear tent with two chambers next to the SUV, entrance into one, exit out of the other. Once they left the SUV, Gabe pulled out his phone and his weapons, handing them to security before he entered the tent. He extended his arms as security in biohazard gear sprayed him down. He stepped into the second chamber, blowers activating, then exited. Ruby copied him, handing her bag to security as well. She trusted that they would return her things promptly.

Gabe didn't take off his mask, but clasped her hand. They took the elevator to the penthouse.

Louisa opened the door for them, pinching her nose. "God, you stink. Your security let me know what's going on. I laid down drip pads to your bathroom, set up containers and liners there for your masks and clothing. Got air purifiers going at highest levels. Sweats and underwear for both of you in the bathroom."

"Thanks, Weeza," Gabe said.

Gabe steered Ruby along a line of plastic rolled across the floor, through a bedroom to the bathroom.

"How concerned should I be about exposures now?"

"The neutralizer should have taken care of it." Gabe wrinkled his nose like Louisa had as he took off his mask and dropped it into one of the containers. "Weeza put the drip pads down to keep things clean. The combination of knockout gas and neutralizer just *reeks*. You want to get it off of you. That's why I didn't take off my mask until now, and why we didn't go through decontam until we were here. It's pure hell to get the stink out of upholstery. Easier to get the knockout residue out."

It was Ruby's turn to grimace as she took off her mask and got the full force of the sharp, sour stench. Gabe finished stripping and turned on the shower—it was the same size of the bathtub/shower combinations she was accustomed to, only shower-only, with a solid

Plexiglas half-wall instead of a curtain, and a floor that slanted toward a steel-covered drain. They entered it and started washing.

She shampooed her hair.

Gabe eyed her. "You'd best use more shampoo. That stuff in long hair can be just nasty. I'll help you rinse it out."

"Thanks."

She stood under the full flow as he gently rinsed her hair.

"God, Ruby, that scared the crap out of me. I was so worried about you."

"It happened so fast," she said. "And I kinda felt light-headed. I suppose that's the power of suggestion—"

"*Shit.*" He pulled back, his hands dropping to her waist. "Do you still feel light-headed?"

"Maybe a little, but—" She swayed slightly.

Gabe swung her back under the spray, soaping her down again. "Sorry. Not doing conditioner on your hair right now. Don't know if this is an emotional reaction or if you got enough of an exposure to feel some of the effects."

Once she was rinsed, Gabe guided her over the low shower step. He used two towels, one to wrap her hair, the other her body, and sat her on the toilet.

"Don't move," he ordered. "May need to put you back in the shower."

Ruby shivered as Gabe finished showering, and dried himself off. He pulled on sweats and stepped out of the bathroom.

"Weeza, I need the counter pills," he yelled. "Ruby's possibly been exposed." Then he knelt in front of her. "Look at me—follow my finger with your eyes." He held up an index finger.

She turned her head slightly to follow his finger and he hissed. "Eyes only. Not your head."

"It's hard." Her voice quavered.

Louisa entered the bathroom and handed Gabe a pill blister pack. "Did she get exposed?"

"Possibly. Having problems tracking my finger without moving her head," Gabe muttered. "Let's try it again—ah. Better. Still should do one of these, for best effect." He popped one of the pills out of the blister pack and stuck it in her mouth. "Chew."

Ruby obeyed. The matching concerned expressions on Gabe and Louisa's faces made her nervous.

"Is this bad?" Chills definitely *not* from sitting in nothing but towels ran down her spine.

"It can be," Louisa said, as Gabe held his index finger up again.

He sighed with relief. "Eyes tracking now. Too quickly for the counter to kick in, so I think it's just nerves."

"All right." Louisa sealed the bags with the masks and their clothing and left.

"I'm sorry," Gabe said, still kneeling. "I didn't mean to scare you, but the aftereffects of exposure to that particular strain of knockout gas can be nasty. Here. Let's get you dressed."

Ruby rose, wobbling slightly. Gabe steadied her, a worried frown furrowing his brows.

"I can do it myself." She recognized this sensation.

Reaction. No more need for adrenaline to be pumping through her system. Ruby looked for a comb, and when she finally spotted one in plain sight, she kept fumbling it.

"Here. Let me get that." Gabe picked up the comb. "Let's go to the living room."

He led her out of the bathroom, through the bedroom—his?—and to the couch. Gabe sat at the end and tucked her between his legs, before gently combing out her hair.

"Is Justine going to be all right?" she asked.

"She carries the counters with her at all times," Gabe said. "Damn it. I didn't think this was a possibility. There's a training that Piotr will put you through—mask protocol, scanner, counters." He set aside the comb and wrapped his arms around her. "That training has just become a priority for you."

A chime sounded. Louisa pulled out her phone. "Hello, Lance. Louisa here. All right, that's good. I'll meet you at the door."

She rose, and returned with a clear bag that contained Ruby's notes and other items, and set it on the coffee table by the couch. Their weapons and phones were also in the bag.

"What now?" Ruby felt better now that she at least had her notes, ID, phone, keys, and weapons within reach.

"We wait until we get the all-clear," Gabe said.

"I'd better call Lora."

"No need," Gabe said. "She got the alert when I did. I was talking to her about properties when it went off. She's being briefed by her own security. The stable is on lockdown."

"Dr. Wareham is going to be *so* pissed at me for disrupting class," Ruby sighed. "He's already given me the lecture about *no break just because you're the Finalist.*"

"All bark, no bite," Louisa said. "We've gone through this with Wareham before. He'll not be a problem." She rose. "However, since I have a test tomorrow, I'm going to study, on the off chance we can leave. The door will chime on my phone, so you two don't have to get it."

"Understood." Gabe eased Ruby onto his lap, holding her tight. "I am so fucking sorry," he murmured into her ear. "I didn't think—*I didn't think.*" He leaned his head against hers.

"Does this happen frequently?" Her voice trembled. "Because you all—seem to know what to do."

"Often enough. High-level Martiniere heirs are trained to deal with various security problems, and we drill regularly." He stroked her cheek. "I didn't think you needed to be introduced to this side of Martiniere life just yet."

"How often is *often enough?* Attacks like this—and others?"

He exhaled. "Several times a year."

"For the entire Family?"

"No. Limited, that I know of. Me. Tine. Weeza. My parents."

"All of you?" Her voice cracked.

He nodded. "Since I was eighteen."

Philip. Has to be his fucking biological father.

Ruby didn't know whether to be afraid or angry, but if she ever had a chance to tell Philip Martiniere what she thought of him—

"Ruby." His voice was flat. "Does this change things between us? Because you can walk away. Still."

His expression didn't match his tone. The tone said *it doesn't matter, I don't care, do whatever you dare to hurt me, it won't penetrate.*

But the stark, despairing way Gabe gazed at her, as if he were saying goodbye, memorizing her features—

"So this is why Piotr is in charge of my security," she said. "Because you—Justine—Louisa—are all targets, and by taking you to my bed, I'm right up there with the rest of you."

He shuddered. "Yes. Do you regret it?" Still in that cold, flat tone.

"Are my grandparents safe?" Endangering Gramps and Granma would be her only regret.

"They just acquired bodyguard escorts when they go off of the Ranch, because of this situation."

"Good." What she hoped. What she expected.

Despair continued to tighten Gabe's face. "Do you regret your choice to be with me?" This time his voice quavered.

Another fucking way he's been broken, damn it.

How many women had looked at the potential of life with Gabriel Martiniere, considered this particular danger, then decided he wasn't worth it?

Gabe might be flawed and broken, but Ruby would be even more of a shit if she let something like the risk of being with him split them up. It was nowhere near as high a concern to her as his tendency to overwork himself into collapse.

Trivial in comparison, even.

Ruby stroked his cheek. "I do *not* regret one thing that *has* happened or *will* happen between us, Gabriel."

His face softened and he held her tight. "I was kicking myself because I haven't shown you how to program your phone to let Family security alerts through, even when you've muted it." He drew a ragged breath. "And when you said you were *light-headed* in the shower—Tine would know what that meant, would have taken her pills. But you wouldn't have known, don't have the counters, and the results—would not have been good."

"It's all good now." Her voice was unsteady again. "We're safe. And you *will* get me that required training as soon as possible, right?"

"Right. And—until we know what is going on, I'm not traveling. So I'll be a good boy, and resting like I should."

"My classes?"

"I'll talk to Asa—have to do that for Tine and Weeza, too. Is there someone you trust to give you good notes?"

"My friend Linda Coates."

Gabe pursed his lips. "A familiar name—oh yes. One of the other Grant finalists. Then again, it's entirely possible we'll get the all-clear quickly and class notes won't be an issue."

Her phone chimed.

"No calls," Gabe said. "Answer those messages but no more; because we're trying to hide, you need to log into the secure network and block direct calls. Damn it. I keep forgetting things. Another reason to listen to you about not overworking, because I'm missing things I shouldn't overlook. Gimme my phone—I need to switch on my blocker, then I'll do yours—show you how."

Ruby fished both phones out of the bag. She had several messages.

One from Linda, asking if she was all right.

One from Dr. Wareham, very similar, suggesting she get notes from Linda for the rest of the week if she couldn't make it to class for security's sake.

One from Lora, asking if she needed clothing and other supplies.

"Lora's asking if I need clothing and other things from my apartment," Ruby said. "What do I tell her?"

"I'd send her a list, just in case," Gabe said. "Security can pick it up, and Lora's not leaving the stable right now. She'll have time to do it. Add my stuff to the list, too. Laundry setup within the condo, so you can wash clothes."

"All right." Ruby chewed on her lip thoughtfully. Most everything she needed for classes was on her tablet, but it *would* be nice to have her computer. Several changes of clothing. Toiletries. Another pair of shoes. Some of her paperbacks.

As she composed the responses to Lora and the others, Gabe pressed feather-light kisses on her temple. When she was done, she handed him her phone and watched as he activated the blocker, memorizing the steps. Then he leaned forward, still holding Ruby tight, to replace the phones in the bag.

"Thank you for not running away screaming from me because of security stuff," Gabe murmured as he settled back on the couch.

"It's happened before?" she asked.

"In college, yes."

"I'm sorry. Foolish women."

"Those relationships probably wouldn't have worked out, anyway," he sighed. "I'm glad they didn't—most of them were high-society, some old nobility, so it wasn't like they didn't know the score about security. No deep emotional involvements—but the rejections still hurt, nonetheless."

"Rejections hurt no matter what. I know that all too well as a nerd girl."

"Even in college?"

Ruby snorted. "Ollie and Perry, those two other Grant candidates? I dated both of them, and got dumped."

"Oliver—I assume that's the one—was a damned pompous ass. But Perrin? He seemed nice."

"His parents didn't like me. I was too smart and independent—and Perry felt the same way, as it turned out. Only he didn't bother to tell me that before he started dating someone else."

"We both wasted too much of our time around fools." Gabe kissed her. "My dearest nerd girl."

"My bestest nerd boy." She kissed him back.

"Let's take this to the bedroom."

Ruby scooped up the bag with their things as Gabe wrapped his arm around her waist.

THERE WAS QUITE A DIFFERENCE BETWEEN MAKING LOVE ON her three-quarter-size mattress at Lora's, and Gabe's king-size bed in the condo. The luxury of having *space* was priceless. Comfortable sheets. Add to that the brightness of Gabe's room, white-walled with shades that let in light even when closed.

So different from her tiny, dark studio.

After they made love, Gabe lay angled to Ruby with his head on her shoulder, slowly running his fingers over her, hip to collarbone and back down. She realized he was tracing the Martiniere trefoil on her wherever he could make it fit.

She chuckled at him. "Staking your claim?"

"Damn right I am." He kissed her. "I'm a possessive son-of-a-bitch."

"Better than being a lying, two-timing, goody-goody asshole."

"Yeah. That's not my thing at all."

"And that's why we're here. Together." She savored his soft kisses on her collarbone. "You realize that the Martiniere trefoil is just like a barrel racing pattern?"

"Even better." More kisses. He rolled onto his back, gently encouraging her to rest her head on his chest.

She nestled in. "I could learn to live like this."

"Making love to me every day?"

"That, absolutely. But the rest of it." She gestured at the room around them before dropping her hand on his chest. "A bright, well-lit room. A big, comfortable bed. Sheets that aren't harsh."

"You'll always have this with me. Even before I went to live with Philip, I wanted living space that was as light as possible. More so afterwards—he prefers dark oak, dark walls, lots of gilt and crystal and mirrors, but always the dark backgrounds. Maroon. Purple."

"Ugh. When Gramps and Granma moved downstairs, I took over their bedroom. Bigger than mine, windows on the west and northern walls. Queen-sized bed. Cottage rose wallpaper with white and gold background. Sometimes it just wasn't light enough—but it was the lightest room in the house."

"I understand that feeling."

"My current cave isn't my usual preference, but it's part of my pay."

"I didn't think it was your choice."

Ruby sighed. "I was really looking forward to that lecture, damn it. Dr. Wareham was talking about microdrones. Not quite the same as what I was contemplating with my biobot, but useful."

"Hmm. Mind sharing your notes? I've done some microdrone studies, and the Group has a project in Calgary that I've been monitoring."

She retrieved her tablet. "Here's the rough outline that Wareham sent out before class," she said after Gabe connected her to the secure network.

Gabe flicked through it. "Oh, that's good. Mm, that's old stuff. Foundational, but not state-of-the-art. Pretty solid, mostly."

Ruby took the tablet back and opened a direct message that Wareham had sent her through the class network.

—In case you can't make it to class for the rest of the week: analyze the strengths and weaknesses of this paper, from the perspective of your nanobiobot proposal submitted for the Martiniere Grant. 2 pages makes up for attendance and participation grade. 5-10 pages on a second paper addressing a possible combined design substitutes for your final. Enjoy.

She tapped open the link, skimming the title and abstract—a study of the use of microdrones to disperse microbial soil treatments to increase plant moisture absorption in hot, dry climates, based on research performed in Southwest Asia and North Africa.

But something more caught her eye. Ruby looked back at the authors. The last name in the list.

G.M. Martiniere.

Gabe chuckled in her ear. "Think Wareham will consider it cheating if we discuss the paper?"

"You didn't *tell* me you were published!"

He smirked at her. "I was the grad student lackey, before I left the Master's program. Contributed enough to get author credit."

"You stinker." But she kissed him before they settled into flipping through the study, lying side-by-side on their stomachs.

"Microdrone nanobiobots," Ruby finally pronounced. "Only ground-based, not flight. That's the solution to the problems your study encountered." She rolled Gabe onto his back and kissed him.

"How do we power them?" he countered. "Disposal afterwards?"

That brainstorming and banter session led to another round of lovemaking.

Ruby managed to secure her tablet so it wouldn't get knocked onto the floor before they became too absorbed in each other.

———

A LIGHT TAPPING AT THE DOOR ROUSED THEM FROM DEEP SLEEP, in darkness.

"Hm? Huh? Who's there?" Gabe challenged, sitting up as Ruby reached for her pistol.

"Me," Justine said. "And Piotr. We have information."

Ruby exhaled, and eased her pistol down.

"Be right there." Gabe rolled over and switched on a light. "How much can you get done on this project over the next week?"

"What are you thinking?"

He waved a hand. "Your microdrone nanobiobot idea for Wareham's class. Create a design proposal to present to Artie and Gerry for Group funding." Gabe grinned. "It would make an excellent summer trial project for you at the Double R. And I'd have to spend more time at the ranch facilitating project management."

"Gabe!" Ruby laughed, then sat up and clasped her knees, thinking. It *was* possible. "What's my timeline?"

"Two weeks?"

"I'll have to have Wareham's project pretty much together by then anyway. End of the term."

"I'll get the specs and a more solid date to you by next week." Gabe kissed her, then rolled out of the bed to pull on his sweats.

Ruby dressed. They held hands as they went to the living room, and snuggled on the couch. Piotr leaned on the back of a straight chair placed under the wall-mounted TV. Louisa sat in one recliner, Donald in the other, Justine curled in his lap. Solemn expressions tightened everyone's faces.

Piotr cleared his throat and straightened up, clasping his hands behind his back.

"Situation report. Joseph used Miranda to trigger several releases of knockout gas on campus, without her knowledge or consent." He grimaced. "The results are not pretty. Miranda is in the custody of her father. I have offered assistance to Erik Rogers, but he believes he has the situation under control. Both he and Miranda's mother are thoroughly appalled by what she has done. It is now a matter of Saul providing compensation for the damage done to Miranda, and capturing Joseph."

Gabe winced. "What was Joey's goal? Harming Ruby?"

"Silencing Miranda—and providing a distraction," Piotr said. "While our primary focus was here in Corvallis—Philip escaped custody."

"*Fuck.*" Gabe rubbed his face. "What's our timeline for continued lockdown?"

"At least through the weekend. Ruby, security has brought the items you requested from your apartment."

"Thank you," Ruby said.

"And before I return to Los Angeles tomorrow, we will have chemical-biological protocol reviews."

"*Good,*" Gabe said, holding Ruby tight.

THE FIVE OF THEM—DONALD WAS APPARENTLY PART OF THIS lockdown—settled in for the week. Justine drew up a chore and area use rotation that included workout times and security trainings. Ruby made arrangements with Lora for Sunshine's scans.

Gabe's bedroom was big enough for them to create separate work spaces. Ruby's professors sent her assignments without any fuss—*just tell them Martiniere protocol,* Justine advised. *They know what that means.* Like Dr. Wareham, they provided term paper options that would cover her finals, even if she never made it to another class. The options for two of those papers included elements she would need for the proposal that Gabe had suggested.

Interesting. Accidental or not?

Nonetheless, it worked—and there was another element.

If she did more classwork related to the design proposal, wouldn't that give Gabe an excuse to linger in Corvallis? Especially if she asked him to advise her?

Yes. More time with Gabe, and further incentive for him to pace his workload better. Win-win, as far as she was concerned.

She told Gabe that.

He raised his brows. "You admit to manipulating me?"

She arched her brows back at him. "Damn right. Honesty works for horses; should work for men as well."

Gabe laughed.

They got the all-clear on Sunday and moved back to the barn apartment. Monday morning, before Gabe left, he took her into his arms.

"Unless something big pops up, I'll be back on Thursday. Hopefully by noon, five at the latest." He leaned his forehead against hers.

"While the reasons that brought about this week together sucked, nonetheless it's been great." He frowned. "Besides the fun of working on the design proposal with you, I'm worried. Another reason to be here more frequently. I don't think this is the last we will hear of my sperm donor and my dumbass cousin."

"Agreed."

"Be careful and watch out, my dearest nerd girl."

"Same for you, my bestest nerd boy."

They kissed, and then he headed down the driveway toward the SUV.

Ruby sighed as he left.

Thursday afternoon was a long way off.

Oh well. She had a design proposal to craft.

CHAPTER 15
THINGS BLOW UP
MAY, 2029

GABE

"Looks like you've done some schedule rearranging while you were locked down in Corvallis," Saul said as Gabe entered his office for their regular Monday morning meeting. "Not so much travel."

Gabe settled into his usual seat across from Saul, leaning back, lacing his fingers and relaxing into the chair. "Ruby's been quite firm about me slowing down. She was kicking my butt all week. But we're also developing a design proposal for her to present to Artie and Gerry next week—it intersects with her coursework, the Calgary labs' research, *and* can be tested at the Double R this summer."

"All under your supervision, of course." Saul's quick smirk faded into tired lines.

"She's proposing ground-based microdrone nanobiobots, dispersing microbials that improve plant moisture absorption and retention. To begin with. The microdrones convey the nanobiobots to tagged locations, release them, then return to their containers for reuse. The nanobiobots then spread appropriately. Dead by the end of the season, degrade into nutrients."

"That can happen this summer?"

"First development round, yes. Ruby's halfway through the design proposal." He couldn't keep a big, proud smile from spreading across his face.

My dearest nerd girl is good *at what she does.*

"Microdrones. Any connection to the research you did?"

"One of her professors assigned the published paper for analysis." Gabe eyed Saul. Dark circles under his eyes. New wrinkles across his forehead. Face sagging into a frown after brief smiles. "Changing the subject. Papa, just how bad is this situation with Philip and Joey? I have the sense that Piotr is holding back information, but haven't wanted to push him."

"It's bad, son. Not enough to justify keeping us under lockdown. That only works for so long, and having all five of you in the Corvallis condo is not as secure as we would like. The house here is only slightly safer for your mother and me, but at some point, I have to put my foot down. I want to enjoy my life. I am not hiding from my fucking brother, and your mother feels the same way. But for now, please—you, your Ruby, and your sisters—focus on staying secure."

I was correct to be concerned about Ruby's safety.

"You need to keep you and Mama safe, too."

"Your mother's been talking to the Saldivar relations for backup. I'm letting her handle that. I haven't authorized any actions involving the Saldivars yet. I don't know what will happen if it becomes a Saldivar vs Zingter shootout. I'm trying to avoid that outcome, if possible."

This could turn *very* bad.

"Another reason for me to readjust my schedule. Ruby has three weeks remaining in her contract with Lora. She, Justine and Louisa have three weeks left of classes. I want to be close by. Am investigating housing options for next fall when Ruby returns to Corvallis. I will certainly breathe easier when she's at the Double R."

"In case of a dire emergency, would the Double R serve as a lock-down location for you and your sisters, possibly your mother as well? Piotr thinks so, but I'd like your feedback, because managing that lockdown will be your responsibility."

Dread cinched Gabe's gut down hard. "It's that bad, Papa?"

The way Saul's mouth and shoulders tightened, that steady, worried gaze? Oh yes. *Bad.*

"Gabriel, should something happen to me—you are the Head for our Family branch, whether you're the Martiniere-in-waiting or not. Guard your sisters. Deal with Joseph and Philip. If you have a secure refuge like the Double R for the three of you, that would be a huge source of relief."

The worst case, then. Preparing for transition of responsibility. Don't react, just process.

"I'll check with Ruby, and talk to Ron. The ranch buildings are out of sight of the main road, in an easily defensible draw. Not much cover, hard for someone to sneak up on us. The house itself—old but sound. Ruby's grandparents had set it up as a bed and breakfast before Covid, added bathrooms and wiring. Three stories and a base-ment. And the Ryders have no problems with weaponry on site."

Another quickly fading smile from Saul. "I read Serg's reports. Both Ron and Ruth regularly practice alongside security at their personal shooting range."

"I'll talk to Ron once we're done." Gabe made a note. "Anything else?"

"Miranda. Criminal charges have been filed against both her and Joseph for the knockout gas releases at the University. She is hospital-ized, and will recover, but—it appears she had been drugged and the drugs interacted poorly with the knockout gas." Saul grimaced. "Erik Rogers refuses offers of assistance because he's honestly appalled by her involvement in this situation, but I have a fund set aside for her expenses, since Joseph is responsible for her condition. Should some-thing happen to me, please honor that commitment."

God, this feels like writing a will.

"Understood."

A long exhale from Saul. "You're a good son, Gabriel. A good man. You're what your biofather should have been. My biggest regret is that I didn't fight Philip and Renate for Joseph. Didn't raise you four together, as siblings." He shook his head. "You, Louisa, and Justine will make a formidable leadership team. The children of Saul and Philip working together, when their fathers couldn't. You—and Justine—are the closest I can come to that solution."

Apprehensive prickles ran down Gabe's neck. "Papa. No need to talk like this."

Saul fixed Gabe with a steady gaze. "Unlike your grandfather, I've been fairly subtle about dealing with threats." His upper lip curled. "I still don't like the idea. But. If something happens to me and/or your mother, then *finish* it, Gabriel. Be ruthless. Use the power of the Family and the Group for vengeance. Because if you don't—"

"Even against Philip?"

"*Especially* Philip," Saul said grimly. "He won't hold back against you. If it were just Philip, I wouldn't be so concerned. But Walter Braun is pulling Philip's strings. I've seen enough evidence to persuade me, but not enough to hold up in court. Yet. You may need to—"

"The Saldivars." His barely-legal cousins. His abuela's birth family.

"Exactly. I'm doing my best to keep things from falling apart, Gabriel. But it may not be good enough." Saul exhaled. "Now. Your plans for the rest of the week?"

GABE DECIDED TO CALL RUBY FIRST AFTER HE RETURNED TO HIS office. He needed to talk to his dearest nerd girl after *this* conversation. Not just for tactical and planning reasons, but—he wanted the reassurance of her voice.

"Gabe!" Surprise, then caution. "Highest security level. Is there a problem?"

"Papa just had the Head of Family transition talk with me." He slumped in his chair, pinching the bridge of his nose. "I'm worried."

"This sounds pretty heavy."

"It means he believes that he's under immediate threat." He paused. "Papa asked about the likelihood of using the Double R as a refuge. Not just for me, but Tine, Weeza, and maybe even Mama."

"It's that bad."

"Yes. I'm calling your grandfather next. Could you discreetly tell Tine and Weeza that Papa had the Head of Family talk with me? Mention the Double R as refuge. Same for Lora. In person, private, would be best. Ask Tine to tell Donald."

His sister's fiancé needed to be included in any refuge planning—the marriage meant that Donald was definitely part of the Family, plus Don had access to Knowles and Atwood resources. That might end up being useful in the long run.

"They'll be out to ride this afternoon."

"Perfect." He fiddled with a pen from his desk. "The other piece? Under these circumstances, I should *not* be spending *any* nights with my parents. Too tempting a target."

"Are you staying here? The condo? Both?"

He took a deep breath.

Big step ahead. Yeah, we'll have our own place this fall, but this is —different. Earlier in the relationship than planned. Can't be helped, though. Necessity.

"Do you have a problem with me staying with you at the Double R? Will I be in the way if I stay there? I'll check with your grandfather, but if you have some office space, even just a closet where I can store things—I'll be coming and going, but it would be my summer home."

"Oh Gabe." A gulp, then a laugh. "No, I don't have a problem, no, you won't be in the way, and absolutely yes, we have room for you. My bedroom is the size of yours in the condo, though the bathroom isn't as nice." She paused. "My old bedroom on the third floor is my office. Big enough for both of us."

"If you aren't concerned about it," he said. "For us. For our relationship."

"We have to do this sooner or later, given the circumstances. We'll have the third floor. As long as you don't have a ton of furniture to move in, it's fine."

"I don't have *any* furniture," he said. "What's in the condo is all Weeza's and Tine's, even my bed. But I'll bring my stuff from here, tonight. Leave it in the condo for now. More space there."

"So how does staying here affect your schedule for this week?"

He flipped his pen. "I'll come in late tonight, probably should go to the condo."

"No. Here."

"You sure? Likely to be midnight or so. Working here until five, packing my things at the house and having dinner with Mama and Papa, and then the flight. It won't be just me; it will be my stuff."

"Gabe. You're coming here. Let's learn to deal with you showing up at late hours starting out, all right? Worst case is that you'll wake me. Not an issue—and that way *I* won't worry. As for the stuff—it's *stuff*. Leave it here."

"All right, my dearest nerd girl." He paused. "Please stay safe. Keep your guards close when you go on campus. Carry your weapons. If things blow up, it will happen very quickly, and we're all targets."

"Should I have my things packed and ready, just in case?"

Oh, he *so* loved this woman. "Yes. The same for Weeza, Tine, and Donald. Probably being extra-cautious, but I'd sooner be overprepared than caught unawares."

"I can certainly live out of suitcases for the next three weeks, just to give us both some peace of mind, my bestest nerd boy."

"I love you," he murmured. "And I will see you tonight. Late, I'm afraid."

"I'll be waiting."

"PIOTR AND I HAVE DISCUSSED THIS OPTION ALREADY," RON SAID when Gabe explained why he had called. "It makes more sense, and from the way Ruby talks, none of you are leeches who would expect us to wait on you. In that case, no problem."

"Hopefully you'll just have me hanging around, not me, my sisters, and my mother. But after the discussion I've just had with Saul—if we all end up at the Ranch, that means things have turned pretty intense. It will also include Justine's fiancé Donald—but he'll pitch in, just like we do." He wondered what had happened with Ginny. She didn't seem to be in the picture with Weeza anymore.

"Like I said, Piotr and I have had discussions." Ron coughed. "I have some idea of what the possibilities are."

"Thank you, Ron. If we can just get through these next three weeks, until Ruby's safe at the Double R—I think if anything's going to happen, it will have by then."

"*Is* Ruby safe right now?"

"Lora Smith has had her own contingent of Martiniere security for nine years now, including sensors. The stable has both Lora and Ruby's security. Mine, too, when I'm staying with Ruby. It's campus that I'm worried about—but Ruby doesn't need to go on campus very much for these last three weeks." Gabe sighed, suddenly very weary at the thought of the work ahead, even *if* nothing happened.

"Heavy sigh, there."

"Considering logistics." He paused. The Double R wouldn't be a big diversion on his way to Calgary tomorrow. Or for the quick flight to Arkansas on Thursday to meet with Jeff Swait. A means to start moving easily, and he could leave his Los Angeles things on the plane tonight, drop them off at the Double R tomorrow. "Actually, I'll start dropping in during my business travels to leave stuff at the Double R, both mine and Ruby's. Tuesday and Thursday this week."

"See you then. And, young man—"

"Yes?"

"Take care of my granddaughter—and yourself."

"I will."

Gabe only left items he didn't use at his parents's house —mostly mementos from his youth. His things at the condo had already started migrating to Ruby's apartment.

Packing brought it starkly home that he hadn't set roots down anywhere since leaving Philip's house. His saddle was already at the stable. When he had lived with Mindy, the furnishings had been hers. Most of what he owned was clothing, some prized hard copy books, workout supplies, electronics, and weapons.

Something like nine years adrift. Eleven, if he counted the two years with Philip.

Would Ruby change that part of his life?

"I have a present for you," he told Ruby on Wednesday night, on his return from Calgary.

"Oh?"

Gabe held the small box out. She frowned, studying the Martiniere security stickers sealing the flaps.

"You're approved."

She deftly cut through the seals, grinning when the security icons flashed APPROVED at her touch.

"It's so damned nice to see that trefoil light up green," she said. "And—oh! Gabe! Is this—" She delicately extracted the fingernail-sized box that held the microdrone.

"It is." He beamed at her. "Sent from the boys in Calgary. Their latest microdrone prototype, complete with documentation. Just in time for you to incorporate it as part of your presentation to Artie and Gerry on Friday."

Ruby set the microdrone container down carefully, back in the larger box. Then she mobbed Gabe with kisses, dragging him toward the bed.

After they made love, she hopped out of bed and buried her nose deep in the Calgary documentation, making little pleased noises, finally pulling out the microdrone to experiment with it.

Gabe stayed in bed, leaning on his elbow, fascinated as he watched his dearest nerd girl at work. Or was it play? Both?

How had he ever gotten so lucky?

RUBY PRESENTED HER MODIFIED DESIGN PROPOSAL IN A VIDEO call to Artie and Gerry early on Friday morning. Gabe lingered in the background, not wanting to hover but ready to answer any questions, if needed.

"This is early in the design process," Ruby cautioned at one point. "We won't know how effective it is until I manage to make the nanobiobots."

"You can field-test the microdrones this summer," Artie said. "And—Gabriel! How soon can you get her access to biobots?"

"It's not going to be until late July at the earliest, and that's if everything goes smoothly with Family politics," Gabe said. "We have to develop the facility from scratch at the Double R, as well as wherever we live in Corvallis next fall."

"If we can develop a working prototype this growing season, I have customers willing to test it," Gerry said. "Gabriel, I'll push for making the Double R lab a development priority at the next Board meeting. At the very least, we can get you a modular setup."

"Thanks, Uncle Gerry."

"Thank *you* for bringing Ruby on board," Artie said. "Now. Ruby. What do you think about—"

NEARLY A WEEK, AND NOTHING NEW HAD HAPPENED WITH Philip or Joey. Gabe let himself relax as the four of them rode in the regular Saturday lessons. Ruby was up on one of Lora's greenies, Trevor, a gangly gelding not ready for anything but flatwork. Lora supervised, alternating between sending Gabe and Justine over fences and monitoring Ruby and Louisa's schooling in the small area separated from the fences by a line of unused jumps. Donald watched, leaning on the arena gate.

Gabe aimed Midnight at a line of three fences set up for one stride between them. The black gelding eased back in response to Gabe's soft tweak of the rein, instead of rushing the jumps. Another pleasant effect of living with Ruby—he was able to sneak in a couple of schooling rides this week. Riding relaxed him.

Midnight's forefeet just touched the ground while landing from the second jump when the alarm sounded—the tone keyed specifically to Gabe. The black gelding startled at the blare, bolting into that third jump and taking it too short, knocking the pole down. Gabe pulled him up quickly, heart pounding.

No. Oh no.

He yanked his phone out of his vest as Midnight pranced uneasily under him.

"Gabriel."

"Bug out," Piotr said. "Saul has been shot."

"Do we know anything?" Gabe turned Midnight to the gate, the others following. Dread washed over him.

Oh God. Oh God.

No. Not the time to react, Gabriel. You have work to do.

"Nothing as of yet. Bug out to the refuge. All of you. Go dark *right now,* until you have arrived." Piotr hung up.

Don opened the gate wide as the four of them slid off their horses, then hurried through, followed by Lora.

"What's happened, Gabriel?" Justine asked.

"Papa's been shot. We have to bug out. Turn your phones dark, now."

"NO!" Louisa screamed, breaking into sobs.

Ruby grabbed Midnight's reins. "Take care of your sister. I'll get our stuff."

"Turn the horses in the stalls, take off the bridles, I'll handle them. Get going!" Lora took Midnight and Trevor's reins from Ruby as Gabe hugged Louisa. His sister sobbed against him.

"Lora! Can I borrow one of the show coolers?" Ruby headed for the tack room.

"Go ahead."

Ruby lugged a big cooler out of the tack room. "Don. Justine. I have a smaller cooler in my apartment. One of you unload the fridge into it, and the other pack the rest of my food off the shelves into this one. Do you have a cooler in the condo?"

"Yes. Two of them," Justine said. She and Don followed Ruby.

Ruby paused, looking at her phone. "Gabe. Gramps just texted me. *We know. Stay safe.*"

"Good."

"What about Mama?" Louisa murmured.

"Piotr didn't say anything about Mama."

Louisa gulped, sobbing more. Gabe held her tight, his thoughts whirling.

Papa shot. Mama—who knew where? Who did it?

And just what the hell is my role in all this?

At the minimum, he was temporary Head of Family for their close kin. That meant seeing to Donna-gran, Mama, Justine, Louisa, Ruby—plus Philip and Joey, damn it.

Check with Donna-gran once we get to the Double R, if Piotr doesn't mention her in the sitrep. Same for Mama.

Send the Saldivars after Philip and Joey.

Those two things he could do for certain as Head of Family.

And as for Martiniere-in-waiting—the Board would select someone *now.* Whether that person would become the Martiniere or not—depended on Saul's situation.

Focus on what you know, Gabriel. Worry about the rest later.

Louisa pulled away from him, sniffling. "Damn it, I need to do something." She hurried off to join Ruby, Justine, and Donald.

As Gabe passed Midnight's stall, Lora came out and handled him his saddle. "Go ahead and take that, Gabe. I'll grab everyone else's tack. I'll bring the horses to the Double R as soon as it's safe. One less thing for you to think about."

"Thanks, Lora."

She didn't have to say *unlikely you'll be back soon.* Lora had been under the Martiniere security umbrella long enough to understand.

"You're Head of Family now?" she asked.

He nodded. "Don't know about the rest of it."

"Good luck," Lora said.

He carried the saddle to one of the SUVs and met Lora in the tack room, enlisting more security to help. Six more saddles, bridles, and then the tack trunk.

Ruby met them. "We're clear."

"Everyone's tack is with you," Lora said. She embraced Ruby, then kissed her cheek. "Soar. And stay safe."

GABE AND RUBY LOADED THE COOLERS AT THE CONDO WHILE Justine and Louisa packed. They cleared the refrigerator and grabbed what other food items they could shove into the coolers and the few boxes at the condo. He hadn't considered the contents of refrigerators and cabinets in his personal evacuation checklist. Supplies were usually a security concern. But it made sense. Why waste the food?

Security wouldn't let them help load the plane when they arrived at the airport, insisting that they board and keep the shades down. Understandable, but that didn't help Gabe's nerves.

He had to keep himself together right now. Not just for the girls, but for any decisions he had to make as Head of Family.

Gabe exhaled. They hadn't even stopped to remove their helmets in the scramble, much change out of breeches and tall boots.

"Tine. Weeza. Ruby. Don't know about you, but I'm ready to shed the helmets. Let's stash them while security finishes loading."

That didn't take long enough. He dropped back into the chair next to Ruby, twining his hand with hers. Down time, extending into eternity.

Justine and Donald tucked Louisa between them on the couch. She stared straight ahead, blinking hard, sniffling.

Now he had time to think. And agonize.

Sixty minutes airtime to the Lakeside airport, once the pilots started rolling—

A roar started outside. Engines powering up. Five more minutes until they would be in the air.

At Lakeside, grab crucial luggage and get in the SUVs—another twenty minutes or so until they were at the Double R.

Eighty minutes until he could know *what had happened.* At the earliest.

And then what?

Head of Family responsibilities at a minimum. Possibly Martiniere-in-waiting—not much change in his responsibilities if the Board didn't make him the temporary Martiniere. It depended on how incapacitated Saul was—or if he were dead.

Gabe shuddered at that thought.

"Gabe." Ruby's voice was quiet. "You all right?"

"Just thinking through possibilities." Gabe rubbed his face with his free hand. "Fretting."

If he became the Martiniere-in-waiting, possibly the Martiniere—that changed a *lot.* Gabe groaned and brought Ruby's hand to his lips.

"Talk to me. Don't agonize, Gabe."

"I may temporarily become the Martiniere. It depends on the Board's decision. And that—is shaped by whatever happens to Papa." His voice caught and he blinked to keep his vision from blurring.

Keep it together, Gabriel. You can't afford to fall apart.

"If you become the Martiniere, how does that affect us?"

Gabe took a deep breath. "It changes the situation entirely."

"If I have to choose between you and the Grant, I choose you," she said, without hesitating.

"Rubes, are you *sure?*"

"Oh hell, yes." Her voice quivered.

He leaned his head against their twined hands. "Thank you. Thank you." He raised his head. "I can't do this without you."

"I'm here."

They sat together silently for the rest of the flight.

Security rushed them off the plane and into the SUVs. Gabe sat with his arm around Ruby, too edgy to pay attention to the landscape except that it was early afternoon and the white and green of the ranch sign looked *so damn good.*

Sanctuary.

More rushing into the kitchen, Ron and Ruth waiting for them. The gun safe was open, the SPA2s leaning against the door.

Ruby performed introductions while Gabe shakily logged into the Double R secure network and called Piotr, leaning against the kitchen counter. He switched the phone onto speaker. No video under this level of security.

"Gabriel." Piotr sounded exhausted. "You are at the refuge?"

"Yes. You're on speaker. Ruby, Justine, Donald, Louisa, Ron, and Ruth are listening. What's the status?"

"Saul is in surgery. We do not know if he will survive it."

Louisa moaned.

"What happened?"

"Philip evaded Saul's guards. One shot to the head, and slipped out. We suspect assistance from Zingter. Your grandmother is secure. Your mother's location is unknown, but we think she is with the Saldivars."

"Piotr—"

"The Board has met."

Four words, pronounced heavily, enough to make his gut tighten. "And?"

A deep inhale. "Gabriel Marcus Martiniere, do you accept the title of Martiniere-in-waiting?"

A matching deep inhale on his part, speaking past a growing knot in his throat. "Yes, Piotr. I do."

But I didn't want it like this!

"Given the uncertainty of the Martiniere's condition, the Board has also decided to temporarily appoint you to the title of Martiniere. Do you accept?"

"I do." The knot in his throat was even huger. Gabe listened dazedly as Piotr swore loyalty to him as the Martiniere.

"Good luck," Piotr said. "I will contact you when I know more."

As Gabe switched off his phone and slipped it into his pocket, his hand trembling, Justine knelt before him, her hands folded. He wrapped his hands around hers and accepted her oath numbly, followed by Louisa.

Then he turned to Ruby. "I need to talk to you. Privately. About —what we discussed on the plane."

She nodded, her lips tightening, and took his hand, leading him to Ron's office.

"This situation changes things?"

"Oh, does it ever." He brought her hands to his lips. "This isn't the way I wanted it to be. None of this is. I was going to watch you soar as the Grant winner. Take you to Family Christmas in Paris, go for a boat cruise on the Seine, propose under the lights of the Eiffel Tower. Straight out of a billionaire romance."

"We can't always have things the way we want." Her voice was soft.

"Yeah. And now—" he swallowed hard. "Ruby, this is really bad. Papa told me to send the Saldivars after Philip if something happened. We are facing the corporate equivalent of a gang war. Under my leadership."

"I told you I wasn't walking away."

"Will you marry me? As soon as possible? Because with—all of this—something could happen to one or both of us. I want us to be married, for however long we survive."

"Yes. Gabriel, yes."

He took her into his arms and kissed her. "We need to marry quickly and discreetly. Probably can't get a license until Monday—how long do we need to wait?"

She chewed her lower lip thoughtfully. "If it's safe to call someone besides Piotr, the Thunder County clerk is an old high school classmate—and a Ryder cousin. Doug Pettigrew. I'll talk to him. He might be able to get us a license sooner."

"You're safe to call out. Use the secure network."

"Do it now?"

"Yes. I have to make a call. Go ahead." Gabe pulled out his phone and brought up his hidden contact list. He thumbed through to Jorge Saldivar.

"Gabriel." His cousin Jorge's voice was smooth and steady, not betraying any emotion. As was always the case with Jorge.

"My mother?"

"Gabie." He almost fainted with relief at the sound of her voice. "You are safe?"

"Yes, Mama. And you?"

"Yes. Hidden, near Saul. Erica is on site."

Erica Ramirez, Mama's older sister. Closely tied to the Saldivar cousins, involved in things he didn't want to know about. Erica would be safer at the hospital than Mama. Not even Philip would dare touch her.

"Good. Mama—" He gulped. "I'm the Martiniere. Temporarily, I hope. I'm marrying Ruby, as quickly as possible." He wanted to keep talking but they had to keep this short, for safety's sake. "I need to talk to Jorge again."

"I understand." She paused. "Congratulations, and stay safe, Gabie."

"You too, Mama."

"Gabriel." Jorge again.

"I am now the Martiniere, Jorge. Running under cover. I have need of your services, as contracted personally by the Martiniere."

Contracted personally. The keywords that targeted Philip. Negotiated years ago by Saul on his wedding night, as the final defense against his brother. Saul had never dared to do it. But he had passed the keywords to Gabe.

So it falls to Philip's son, raised by Saul.

He had Saldivar blood in his veins as well as Martiniere. And both families possessed an equally bloody history.

"Utmost sanctions?"

Death.

He hesitated. A big step.

"Yes," he said. "Utmost, for Philip. Joey, only if he resists."

"I will let you know when it is done."

"Thank you, Jorge." Gabe disconnected.

Ruby exhaled. "Doug Pettigrew will be here in an hour. License paperwork. We'll still have to wait forty-eight hours—don't know how he's swinging it over the weekend. And he can perform the service, here, on Monday afternoon."

He took Ruby into his arms again and held her tight. Soon to be *his* Ruby forever, however long that was.

Now it truly begins.

RUBY

As they separated from that hug in Gramps's office, Gabe was pale, almost shocky-looking.

Ruby couldn't blame him. Was it only three hours ago that they were peacefully riding horses in Lora's arena? And now they were at the Double R with Gabe's close family, Saul in surgery that he might not survive, his mother—safe?—and.

And. The big *and*.

Gabe was the Martiniere. That stricken expression on his face as first Justine, then Louisa, knelt to swear loyalty when they were in the kitchen. The pleading, puppy-dog look in his eyes as he proposed to her, that hardened as he spoke to Jorge Saldivar.

Oh, Ruby knew what the Saldivars were. Tied to one of the big drug cartels. Justine had connections to the Saldivars as well, had dropped small hints here and there about their role in the Family, and how they intersected with the Ramirez family. Ruby had a damned good idea what was intended when Gabe said *Utmost, for Philip. Joey, only if he resists.*

A death sentence.

Ruby didn't need Gabe to tell her that it was now kill or be killed. But oh, how her heart ached for him to have to make that choice.

And now, as his wife-to-be—she had promised Angelica she would take care of Gabe. Ruby took a deep breath. Her job to manage things, especially with *three* shocked and soon-to-be-angry (if not already) Martinieres on her hands. At least she had Gramps and Granma to help her, probably Donald as well.

What was she going to tell Linda? If she could even tell Linda about this rushed marriage to Gabe.

Not the time to think about that.

"Who in security needs to know that Doug Pettigrew is coming here?" she asked.

Gabe jerked, clearly lost in his own thoughts. "Let me do it."

He put his arm around her as he called security. Then he exhaled.

"We'd better tell the others what is going on," he added.

When they re-entered the kitchen, Justine and Louisa sat at the table, staring into cups of coffee. Granma rested her hand on Louisa's back as she sniffled, while Gramps and Donald made sandwiches at the kitchen counter. Ruby eyed the coolers stacked against one wall. Security must be unloading things.

Organization needs to happen.

Normally, that would be Justine's venue. But she seemed to be as stunned as Louisa. Gabe was functioning—because he had a role and a responsibility. All right, she needed to get them moving. Hit them with what she hoped was good news. Then give them a job or two— unpacking and planning sounded good.

She glanced at Gabe. "You want to tell them, or shall I?"

That brought a faint grin to his face. "You."

"Gabe and I are getting married. Monday afternoon. Doug Petti- grew's on the way here with license paperwork."

That brought both Justine and Louisa's heads up, shocked expres- sions changing to smiles, Louisa's sniffles fading.

"What about pre-nuptials?" Justine asked. "Not just for Gabriel. Ruby, you need protection, too."

"I have files you can use," Donald said. "Not just ours but samples of others."

"James Trask provided me with draft pre-nuptial agreements for you, Ruby, when he prepared the family trust to protect the ranch from Grace Barkley," Ron said.

"Then that's covered," Gabe said. "Not worried from my side of things. We dealt with these issues as part of the intention and contact questionnaire in April. Ruby is already enrolled in the Martiniere Family Trust as my girlfriend. She'll have a bigger share as the Martiniere's wife."

The Martiniere's wife.

Ruby caught her breath. So soon. So quickly.

And she hadn't thought about *that* aspect of their marriage.

"There's more news," Gabe continued. "I spoke to Mama. She's safe. Erica is at the hospital." He drew a ragged breath and rubbed his face. "I also talked to Jorge."

"And?" Louisa's voice sharpened.

"Death for Philip. Joey, only if he resists."

Tightened lips, tightened faces on both women. They exchanged glances.

Then Louisa gave Gabe a curt nod. "Thank you for trying, Gabie."

"It's about fucking time." Justine's voice was low and bitter. "When will it be Braun's turn?"

"I promise you, little sister, that time is coming," Gabe said, steadily. "One step at a time."

His arm tightened around Ruby's waist.

Doug Pettigrew arrived right after they finished eating.

"Gabriel Marcus Martiniere, of Los Angeles, California," Doug murmured, eying Gabe's driver's license and passport. His eyes widened. "One of *those* Martinieres?"

Ruby had to stifle a giggle at Doug's reaction, the impulse made worse by Gramps's smirking behind Doug's back.

"Yes," Gabe said. He produced a couple of folded bills. "Please keep this as quiet as possible. We are currently at risk."

Doug pushed his hand back. "You're going to be family."

Gabe pressed the bills into Doug's hand. "That's exactly why. Be very careful over the next few days. Please. This is for the extra work, and for whatever inconvenience being cautious will cause you."

"You seem pretty confident there will be inconvenience."

"The man who raised me has just been shot, by the man who is my biological father." Gabe's voice went even flatter. "Ruby and I are his next likely target. I'd prefer that public knowledge of this marriage be delayed as long as possible. If you want security, I can provide it."

Doug raised his brows. "I see. Following family tradition, Ruby?"

"What?" Gabe looked puzzled.

"There's been—issues in the past," Gramps said. "Ruby's three-greats grandfather Ryder, back in the nineteenth century."

"And a couple of instances with the Pettigrews," Doug added. "Understood, Gabriel." He checked his calendar. "Three pm on Monday?"

"Three pm on Monday should work just fine," Gabe said.

Doug started out the kitchen door, then turned back. "Is it a problem if I bring Julia?"

Another perplexed expression from Gabe.

"Doug's wife," she said to Gabe. "She's good people and will keep quiet. Also a cousin, through the Barkleys. Sure, Doug. Go on ahead."

"See you both on Monday," David said.

Gramps chuckled after Doug left. "Welcome to the old West, Gabe. The Ryders might not be as high-flying as the Martinieres, but this isn't the first wedding of this sort in our family. Ben Ryder, the

Double R's founder, married Mollie Bennett to escape being hung as a rustler, and other problems with the law. The Double R's been a refuge before. You and Ruby are carrying on a fine tradition."

Justine settled in with Granma to craft chore rotations and menu planning, while finding places for the food they brought. Ruby sent Gabe upstairs to contemplate his suitcases and boxes, and figure out where his things could go in their bedroom and office. She, Louisa, and Donald went to the second floor to divide the three bedrooms on that floor between Louisa, Justine, and Donald for personal and office space.

When she made it up to the third floor, Ruby found Gabe, still in his riding clothing and tall boots, sitting on the bed and studying a ring box.

"I think you established your cowboy credentials with Doug."

Gabe chuckled. "I didn't realize you had ancestral history like that."

"Don't get to be a century farm landowner in this part of the world without the possibility of that sort of pioneer background."

Gabe patted the bed next to him. "Come take a look at this. How do you feel about heirloom jewelry?"

"It depends on how valuable it is." Ruby peered into the box, admiring the emerald and pearl gold ring. "I wouldn't be wearing a ring like this daily, just to keep it clean and safe. Especially an heirloom. But I would wear it when possible."

"I guess you could call this an heirloom. Traditional Family engagement ring. Nineteenth century origin. Mama wore it for a while, until Papa bought her another, after Weeza's birth. She prefers more modern designs. They gave it to me, for you, on Monday—" he gulped. "If you like it and it fits—there's a matching wedding band. Eventually earrings and necklace to go with it. Mama has them."

"It's beautiful. Would you—see if it fits?"

Gabe extracted the ring from the box and slid it on her finger. Ruby exhaled as she moved her finger. It fit.

He smiled, no longer looking as if the weight of the world had dropped on his back.

"Perfect." He hugged her.

"There is one thing," she said, pulling back. "I'm due to renew my contraceptive implant next week. I can have it done here, no problem. But. With you. With this. Should I?"

He cupped her cheek. "I can't lie, Ruby. The odds are very high that you will be a widow within the next year. If *you* survive, though your odds are better than mine. It's one reason why I want to get married now. What do you want to do about children?"

"I'm not ready. But if it's a big deal for you as the Martiniere—"

"I don't want to leave hostages to fortune, and that's what our children would be," he said grimly. "Oh God, Ruby. There's too much unsettled. Not just with us, but—everything."

"Then that's decided. I'll renew it." She would have said more, but his phone chimed.

Gabe's face lit up as he saw who was calling. "Mama?" He switched it to speaker. "Ruby's here, too."

"Gabie. Are your sisters with you?"

"They're downstairs," Ruby said.

"All right. Can't talk for long. Saul is out of surgery, appears to be oriented, and recognizes me."

Gabe exhaled and sagged against Ruby. "That's *great* news, Mama."

"He isn't able to speak yet and his left side is paralyzed. But—" a long sigh. "He's alive. I told him that the Board has made you the temporary Martiniere. That you and Ruby are getting married—do you have a date and time yet?"

"Three pm on Monday," Ruby said.

"Good." Her voice caught. "I am so glad—stay safe. All of you. Please."

And then she hung up.

Gabe clutched Ruby, burying his head in her shoulder. "Papa made it through surgery. Oh God." He raised his head, inhaling in deep gulps. "Can't lose it yet. Too much to do. But this is such a relief. Even if—" He shook his head. "He's not going to be able to function as the Martiniere for a while, if at all." He kissed her, then slowly rose. "Let's tell the girls. And I need to talk to all of you, now that I know more about a likely future. Martiniere stuff."

Gabe kept his arm around her as they descended to the next floor.

"Louisa's on the right, Justine and Donald on the left." Ruby tapped on Louisa's door while he rapped on the other.

They gathered in the third bedroom, now designated to be an office, bed against the wall.

Need to bring desks and chairs from the storage shed.

"That ring looks very good on you, Ruby," Justine said. "And the rest of the Martiniere emeralds?"

"Mama still has them," Gabe said. He slipped his arm around Ruby again. "Good news—well, mixed. Mama called. Papa survived surgery. She's seen him. He's oriented and recognized her."

"Oh, thank God," Louisa murmured.

"Mixed news?" Justine raised her brows.

"He isn't able to speak, and his left side is paralyzed."

"That makes you the Martiniere for several months, if not permanently," Justine said.

Gabe nodded. "Which comes to my next step. I need to form my cabinet."

"Cabinet?" Ruby asked.

"Advisors to the Martiniere," Gabe said. "Not the same as the Board. Close, trusted, usually focused on specific areas to monitor and report back to me." He rubbed his face. "The four of you are my first choices. Are you willing?"

"Well—yes," Louisa said. "But are you *certain*, Gabie? Not older advisors?"

"That's what the Board is for, and you four aren't the only ones I plan to have in my cabinet. Are you willing?"

Justine and Donald nodded, followed by Louisa.

"You know I'll be by your side," Ruby said.

"All right." Gabe dropped his arm. "Ruby. I want you to monitor the labs. Have Artie report to you regularly, but that's just Europe. Keith in Calgary, Zeke in LA. I'll introduce you—tomorrow. Pushing things, today."

He turned to Justine and Donald. "Tine. Monitor logistics, security and Family matters. Don. Financials—actually, that's both of you. Not just our personal expenses but how the Group is performing." He shifted focus to Louisa. "Weeza. The media around this whole mess is going to be crazy. Is probably crazy. That's your job. I need a statement about Papa, Philip, and my role as the Martiniere—first, for the Family and the Group, then a public statement for delayed release. After Ruby and I are married, same thing."

"Who else are you recruiting?" Justine frowned.

"Ron and Ruth, for local affairs. Ron as local security consultant. Ruth for logistics. Tine, Don, if the two of you could work with them —building a biobot lab for Ruby on the ranch is a priority. It's already been approved by the Board. Make it happen."

Justine nodded. "We can do that."

"I'm also planning to recruit Serg, Cousin Kendra and her husband Scott, and Cousin Artie's son Charles. Make Uncle Gerry's son David the temporary Martiniere-in-waiting." Gabe sighed. "I am calling an emergency Board meeting for tomorrow morning. Ruby and I need to create pre-nuptial agreements. Figuring all of this out —" he waved a hand. "So much to do, so little time. Including getting ourselves settled in. It's going to be a late night."

"No, it's not," Ruby said firmly. "All of you. Look at us. We haven't changed out of our riding clothes. We're frazzled. Yes, we need to unpack, but—let's give ourselves a break, shall we? A couple of hours? Do what planning needs to happen for tomorrow, but keep it short."

"Rubes—"

"*Gabriel.*" She fixed him with a stern glare. "You promised. We're in a moment where we can catch our collective breath. You'll make better decisions if you have a break. Let's go outside. Take a short walk."

"Outside?" His brows furrowed at her. "You sure that's safe?"

"That's why we're *here*," she said. "Sensors. Drones. Security. We can check with Gramps, but I'm damn certain that the grounds are safe for us to go outside. We can't shut everything down. Ranch won't function otherwise. And once Lora thinks it's safe to ship the horses here, we can ride. Before then, if you don't mind ranch stock."

"Outside?" Louisa's voice suddenly sounded brighter.

"Outside," Ruby confirmed. She turned to Gabe. "And that includes *you*. Let's change, and meet in the kitchen."

Ruby ducked into Gramps's office while sending Gabe to the kitchen to wait for the others.

"How are things going?" Gramps looked up from his computer screen.

"We heard from Gabe's mom. Saul's out of surgery, recognizes her—but he can't speak and is paralyzed on his left side."

Gramps frowned. "That doesn't sound good."

"I suspect it means that Gabe's permanently the Martiniere," she sighed. "I could be wrong."

"Not likely, girl. I'm sorry to hear that. Gabe seems close to his family, and they're decent folks. How are *you* holding up?"

"Other than being dazed by the prospect of a whirlwind wedding —and everything that entails—plus managing Martinieres who are progressing from shock to being pissed off—just fine. We've been through stuff like this before."

"That we have." He smiled at her. "The water rights fight five years ago, for one."

"This is the water rights fight on steroids. We're in the middle of a Zingter vs Martiniere war, or will be shortly."

"We can handle it. And Gabe?"

"Gabe *says* he's holding it together. But this—especially with the shooter being Philip—has him spooked. Which means he defaults to working until he drops. I've already figured that out about Gabe, needed to yell at him—and his sisters—about taking a break. So we're going on a tour of the ranch buildings and nearby, poke into the storage shed for desks. What's our safety perimeter like?"

"Security has a couple of watchers stationed on Ryder Ridge," Gramps said, referring to the northwestern rim that shielded the house from the road. "Sensor fields so tight they can register a mosquito fart, from the road all the way up to Homestead field. Drones—both weaponized and observational. You stay in Ryder Draw, you'll be fine."

Ruby exhaled. "That's great news. Oh. The other piece. Apparently, we're all going to be part of Gabe's advisory cabinet, including you and Granma. You're local security. Granma's site logistics."

"And you?"

"I monitor the Martiniere Group labs for Gabe, worldwide, or so it seems."

Gramps's brows rose. "Climbing high in the world, girl. Congratulations. It's not what I expected for you, not at all, but I'm glad it happened." He craned his head to peer at her hands. "So he gave you a ring?"

"Yes." She held her left hand out for him to examine. "It's a nineteenth century heirloom. His parents gave it to him on Monday —for me."

"*Very* nice." Gramps got up and opened his arms. "Come here, girl. You look like you need a hug."

Ruby buried her nose in his chest, inhaling deep. Gramps always smelled of outdoors and a faint wisp of smoky spice. A different spicy scent from Gabe, but one that always meant *safety. Home.*

"It's a lot," she said finally. "Happening so fast. Like I'm riding a roller coaster without a safety bar or seat belt."

Should she share Gabe's fear that she'd be a widow within a year? *No.*

"You can handle it, girl. You always have." Gramps patted her shoulder as she pulled back. "And your Gabe will do what needs to be done. A bit high-strung, but he's like a fine, high-couraged horse. In your hands, he'll be a high performer."

"Thanks, Gramps."

———

THE TOUR ACHIEVED WHAT RUBY HAD HOPED—A SUBTLE relaxation of all three Martinieres. Getting outside and experiencing that it was safe to be there appeared to make a huge difference in everyone's attitude.

Louisa and Justine peeled off to start dinner, from the assorted leftovers of three refrigerators. Ruby enlisted Gabe's help in carrying a sheet of old plywood and three sawhorses upstairs to their office, to provide a dedicated surface for drone design work. Then she supervised security as they moved tables and desks to her and Gabe's office, then Justine, Donald, and Louisa's office.

Dinner was in the dining room, at the old oak table that had been in the family for years. Gramps sat at one end and Granma the other, both clearly happy to preside over the gathering.

Once they'd finished eating, and before Ruby and Gabe started gathering dishes to clean up, Granma cleared her throat.

"All right. What plans do we have to make Ruby and Gabe's wedding special? Even if it is small, it *should* be memorable. Dressing up. Cake. Nice food. You *do* have dress clothes with you, correct?"

"How formal do we want this to be?" Louisa pursed her lips. "Ruby, what do you have for a gown?"

"I do have several rodeo queen formals—"

"No," Granma said firmly. "You should fit into your great-great grandmother's gown just fine. Your great-grandmother wore it, and so did I."

"Granma, are you sure you want me to wear it? Wouldn't it be too fragile by now?" Ruby had admired the pictures of the gown worn by three ancestresses who had married into the Ryder family—from Brenda to Catherine to Granma—no pictures of her mother, who had eloped with Tony Barkley, and never worn it.

"We can check it."

"Donald and I brought formal wear," Justine said. "Ruby's close enough to me in size that we can make something work if the family heirloom doesn't. Gabie, I think you should wear your black morning coat with the black and gold brocade vest and gold cravat."

"Won't that be a bit formal?" Gabe frowned at Justine.

"Why not?" Justine shrugged. "Ruth, think it'll be a good idea to have a ceremony outside, on the lawn? Won't be big, but it will be nice."

"What's the forecast? Need to make sure there won't be any thunderstorms," Granma said.

"Oh, *that* could make things exciting," Gabe said.

Louisa thumbed through her phone. "Nope, clear weather for Monday."

Granma nodded. "Good. Any of you decent at cake baking? I can supervise, but just don't have it in me to make a nice cake anymore."

"That's me," Louisa said. "I have even taken cake decorating classes."

Gabe rolled his eyes at Ruby as they got up to gather dishes. Once they settled into the routine of putting away leftovers and washing, he chuckled.

"I *was* thinking that this was going to be a very quiet ceremony," he said.

"It'll be small, but—sounds like it will be fun."

"I noticed a very nice bottle of champagne when we packed up Justine and Donald's booze. Think I'll scrounge up something to chill it in on Monday—maybe even appropriate it for just us." He blinked. "I just—I wish my parents could be here."

Ruby wiped her hands and hugged him.

LATER THAT NIGHT, AFTER THEY SHOWERED AND FINALLY FELL into bed, Gabe buried his head in Ruby's chest, trembling, no longer able to hold back his reaction to the day's events. She held him tight as he gulped and choked, fighting back sobs. At last, Ruby rolled Gabe onto his back and kissed him hard, her hands on his face and in his hair, her body on top of his.

That broke everything loose. They made love fiercely, a mixture of passion and terror, sobs mixed with ecstatic screams.

Afterward, he pillowed his head on her chest again. She ran her fingers through his hair.

"I'm sorry," he murmured. "Don't mean to be so weak."

"You're not weak," she said. "You just got hit with one hell of a lot today."

"I've been dreading an attack on Saul. Knowing it could happen —and now that it has—" he swallowed hard. "It's every bit as awful as I feared it would be. Especially since Philip did it. I'm shocked that the Board made me the Martiniere."

"It's probably because you are the only one who would give Jorge Saldivar the sanction to act. No. The only one who *could*, as Philip's biological son."

"And that—in itself—oh *God*—" he shivered. Clutched at her. "My love. My dearest nerd girl. I'm amazed you're still here. That you will be marrying me shortly."

"It's not as if I'm pure as the driven snow, Gabriel."

"That doesn't matter. Oh, my dearest, my beloved." He propped himself up on an elbow, stroking the hair out of her face before cupping her cheek in his hand. "What lies ahead of us—"

She reached up to rest her index finger against his lips. "Stop.

Enough. One breath at a time. Tonight, we're here. We're safe. And that's what matters."

Gabe bent down to kiss her, before settling in, holding her tight in his arms. Drowsiness crept over Ruby, but she didn't succumb until she heard the steady, soft rhythm of sleep breathing from him.

My beloved. Soon to be my husband. My Martiniere.

Dear Lord, what have I gotten myself into?

CHAPTER 17

A VERY MARTINIERE OCCASION

GABE

GABE WAS IN THE UPSTAIRS OFFICE, FINISHING OFF WHAT WORK he could before the ceremony, windows open to allow the faint whisper of a breeze. At least this was going to be a warm but not ragingly hot day. Comfortable for an outdoor wedding with formal wear.

Donald had managed to produce an even better bottle of champagne plus an ice bucket to cool it, and both were stashed in the bedroom, just waiting for the ice. Gabe never failed to be surprised by his soon-to-be brother-in-law's talents—somehow, he hadn't expected Donald to have an ice bucket tucked away *somewhere*, especially in that chaos of an evacuation.

On the other hand, Justine wouldn't have settled for anyone even slightly less resourceful than her Donald.

Ruby had already gone downstairs to prepare for the ceremony, accompanied by his sisters, her grandmother, her friend Remy, and two neighbor women, Vickie Chandler and Carol Reed. After Piotr's reluctant approval, she had called her friend Linda to tell her about the wedding and apologize for not inviting her.

Slamming of multiple vehicle doors. Cacophony of familiar voices outside. *Family* voices, French and British-accented.

Shit.

Gabe scowled and glanced at the clock. Noon. A definite indicator that Family scheming meant this wedding ceremony in three hours would *not* be as quiet as he thought.

Just who was here, anyway? Gabe strained to pick out the voices. Male and female—his cousin David, the new Martiniere-in-waiting. David's wife Therese. Was that Cousin Kendra with her husband Scott? Plus others? How—why—

What the hell?

Piotr hadn't said anything about approving more attendees, and certainly nothing had been mentioned during yesterday's emergency Board meeting.

Gabe went to the window but couldn't see anyone. Oh well. If the Family—even a small portion of it—was descending on the Ranch, he'd better damned well get down there, ensure that Ron and Ruth weren't overwhelmed by the sudden appearance of a swarm of Martinieres. He saved his work and started down the stairs.

David, Scott, Serg, and another cousin, Charles, Arthur's son, intercepted Gabe at the bottom.

"Gabe! Congratulations!" Charles slapped his back.

"How—security—I'm glad but how?"

David smiled. "Careful discussions with Piotr. We couldn't bring everyone who wanted to come, but at least we have a decent representation of the Family. All youngers, not likely to attract much attention, and I'm the most prominent of us—though the announcement has not been made and won't be until I'm back in Paris. Besides, I wanted to swear loyalty to you in person, at your wedding."

"As did I," Charles said.

Soft *shhs* behind him raised Gabe's suspicions. But the cousins were already guiding him toward the front door, saying something about *getting him away from work and in the right frame of mind for a wedding.*

"Ruby will kill me if I get too messed up before the ceremony," he warned his cousins. All of them were notorious hard partiers, at least at Family Christmas.

Laughter answered Gabe, before he was swept up by the horde and onto the front porch.

ONCE THE COUSINS WERE ESTABLISHED ON THE PORCH, THE levity faded. David produced a bottle of good brandy and Charles a set of small glasses. David poured while Charles handed out the glasses.

David raised his glass. "A toast to Gabriel, the new Martiniere. May your leadership of the Family and the Group be fruitful and long."

"Only temporary," Gabe protested, before he drained his glass.

"Not likely," Serg said. "I've looked at my father's reports. A lot depends on Saul's ability to recover—and it's still early. Which is why we're here. Not just for your wedding, as happy an occasion as this is. We have information to share that needs to be disclosed face-to-face. Not over comms."

"We have some big problems developing in the Group as a result of Philip's activities," David said. "Leaks and infiltration by Zingter. High-level Family members being co-opted."

Gabe exhaled. "Above and beyond Cousin Fiona's leaks?"

Fuck. This was not the news he wanted to hear.

"Fiona *and* her father Mark," Serg said. "There are others who, for various reasons—your focus on climate change, your desire to make management within the Group more equitable, even for some the fact that your father is Philip—want to see different leadership. Plus Frank Braun, Walter's son, is active in Europe, recruiting for Zingter."

"Both Frank and Walter are targeting younger sons in the Family with their messages," Charles said.

"Examples include my younger brother Vincent," David said. "Aunt Madeline's son Adrien Durand."

"And others," Scott said. "Many of the British Martinieres."

"I've been hearing rumors," David continued. "I talked with Serg. We decided yesterday that your wedding was sufficient cover for us —" he gestured to include the cousins and Gabe. "—to warn you in person. We've been close friends over the years. No one would be paying particular attention to us—and we're only here for the day."

"What's Zingter's goal in all of this?" Gabe asked. "What do the Brauns intend? Philip's their ally—do they mean to put him in charge of the Martinieres?"

"Yes." Charles leaned back in his chair and twined his fingers. "They'd like to see the Group go public, which would allow the Brauns to swoop in and take over. Frank's estranged wife Vera is escorting Philip around Europe. They are a couple."

Gabe snorted. "Just how estranged is she? Or is this a case where Frank, Vera, and Philip are playing a mutual game?"

Serg shrugged. "We're still figuring it out."

"As for the British Martinieres, while the current Head of Family, Chris, is loyal to you, Gabe, he is also leaning toward taking the Group public," Scott said. "Kendra's pissed about her uncle's choices. Honestly, I think she's the only reliable member of that branch of the Family, and I'm not just saying that because she's my wife. We're both worried about things we've heard Fiona, Mark, and Chris say. And others."

"Noted," Gabe said.

Damn it, that marks Chris as an unreliable Board member. How many more are there?

If he had his druthers, he'd put Kendra on the Board as the repre-sentative for the British Martinieres instead of her uncle, and damn the French Salic tradition of only male leaders.

But—not the wisest move for a new leader to make. Chris was still somewhat one of his allies.

"Braun wants access to our tech," Charles said. "Dad's been dealing with small infiltrations over the past few months."

"Artie hasn't said anything about it," Gabe said.

"He doesn't know as much as I do. I'm running security for the labs, and it's a challenge." Charles raised his hands. "I've not been in the right place at the right time to talk to you in person, Gabe. And until I started comparing notes with David and Kendra, I didn't think much of it. Just thought I was seeing a rise in random hacking attempts. It happens."

"Definitely keep in touch with Ruby. She's your liaison."

Charles nodded. He dropped a fingertip chip in Gabe's hand. "Here's my personal records."

"Thank you, Charles."

David and Scott also produced chips.

"Kendra and Therese are talking to Ruby privately while they do wedding preparation," Scott said. "We're being as careful as possible."

"Thank you for everything." Gabe rubbed his face. "I appreciate it."

"We share your goals," David said. "None of us want to see Zingter dominating the Group. The Brauns are owned by too many people, particularly energy interests."

Gabe eyed them. "All right. I already have part of my cabinet selected. Would all of you be willing to be part of it as well?"

Nods of assent.

David poured another round of brandy.

Gabe raised his glass. "A toast to David, my new Martiniere-in-waiting. May you serve in your role for many years to come."

After they drank, David laughed. "Gabe, as far as I'm concerned, this is as close to becoming the Martiniere as I want to be. And I will do what I can to ensure that you remain in your position for the rest of your natural life, with the hope that someday your son or daughter supplants me."

The group broke up, leaving David and Gabe alone on the porch.

"I wish I had a refuge that looks as easily defensible as this," David said.

Gabe ran his fingers through his hair. "I'm far from the only one who found this to be an easily protected hideout. One of Ruby's ancestors has quite the history."

He'd found a little book in the living room about Ben Ryder and Mollie Bennett, and read it during an insomniac spell. Their story—even if exaggerated, which penciled notes in the margins suggested—could have come right out of a Wild West tale about an outlaw and his lady. Ryder had lived a charmed life, managing to evade accusations of horse thievery, bank robbing, and more, supported by his wife, daughter of a railroad baron. Ben Ryder died at a ripe old age, in his own bed.

Hopefully that boded well for him and Ruby.

"Well, this *is* the Old West," David said.

"As I've been discovering." Gabe grinned.

"It will be *very* interesting to see how the traditions of old French aristocracy and cowboy country mix."

"We'll sure find out."

Before they lined up outside, Gabe pulled Doug Pettigrew aside.

"After the wedding ceremony, there will be a short Martiniere—" he wasn't quite certain how to describe it. Ritual? Oh hell, just call it what it was. "Oath-swearing."

"Do you want to announce it, or shall I?"

"Just set it up for me to talk."

Doug nodded.

Time.

A local acoustic folk and bluegrass group—more friends of Ruby's —showed up to play for the wedding.

Someone had informed the cousins of Ruth Ryder's request for formal attire—Gabe suspected one or both of his sisters, most likely Justine. The men wore morning suits in blue or gray. Kendra and Therese were in form-fitting long dresses, Kendra in light blue, Therese in turquoise. Justine sported an elegant red dress while Louisa was in a silvery sheath.

As the musicians performed an *interesting* bluegrass version of the Wedding March, Donald stood next to Gabe, in a dark blue morning suit. Remy Trask, in a shimmering bronze-shaded dress, processed elegantly down the aisle between the clusters of folding chairs—almost equal numbers of people on both bride and groom's side, how many of them were security pressed into service? And where had the chairs and the carpet runner on the lawn come from?

Not your job to worry about that, Gabriel.

So what was taking Ruby so long? Trask didn't seem concerned, even as the band replayed the Wedding March.

Ruby walked around the corner of the house, holding Ron's arm. Gabe caught his breath.

When he'd heard the talk of *heirloom wedding gown*, he hadn't expected *this*. Even though he'd seen the pictures of other Ryder brides in this gown, commissioned by Mollie Bennett for her future daughter-in-law Brenda from the House of Worth, in Paris.

Soft gold, form-fitting along Ruby's torso, with puffy sleeves tapering to sleek cuffs and lace. Something green glittered at her throat and earlobes—no, *not* the Martiniere emeralds, they couldn't be! Unless the cousins had somehow met up with his mother—

Ruby's red hair was down, lightly curled. The pearl-encrusted cap that held her veil was striking—and he remembered it from another Martiniere wedding—Kendra or Therese?

And then she stood in front of him.

She *was* wearing the Martiniere emeralds. They looked stunning on her—oh, who was he kidding? *Everything* about his bride was stunning.

The ceremony passed in a blur because Gabe couldn't think about anything other than Ruby's utter gorgeousness and how lucky he was that she loved him.

Ring on her finger. Ring on his.

Kiss.

Married.

"And now, I turn this event over to Gabriel Martiniere."

He squeezed Ruby's hand before stepping forward. "Several Family members have expressed their desire to swear loyalty to me as the Martiniere at this ceremony. Now is the time."

Both David and Therese came forward and knelt to swear, David also bowing to Ruby.

Kendra and Scott.

Charles.

Serg.

Instead of returning to their seats after swearing, they stepped to the side. Why?

A woman he hadn't noticed until now glided up the carpet from the last row of chairs. She wore a heavy gray veil that obscured her features, over a teal dress. Something familiar about that graceful dancer's walk—no, it couldn't be, but it would explain how the Martiniere emeralds got here—or was she Aunt Erica?

Angelica lifted her veil, revealing tear-stained cheeks as she smiled at them. And he spotted Jorge Saldivar standing behind the chairs—they must have slipped in after Ruby came down the aisle.

Gabe gulped, a lump hard in his throat.

Mama. Here. For my wedding. In spite of what happened to Papa. Oh, Mama.

"Gabriel. Ruby. I am so happy that I was able to be here." She hugged first Gabe, then Ruby.

Ruby smirked. "I'm glad we could pull this off."

"I—I don't know what to say, Mama."

"It took some planning," Serg said. "And a hard day of organizing for my father and me. Coordinating with David."

"Keeping you from seeing your mother before now was the biggest challenge," Jorge added, joining them.

Gabe gracefully bowed to him. "Jorge. I am extremely grateful to you. Mama, does this mean you're staying?"

Angelica shook her head. "Not as long as Saul is alive." She blinked. "But a quick flight here—I would not miss your wedding if it were at all possible for me to do it safely. Keeping it secret was the hard part."

"Oh, Mama." He pulled both his bride and his mother into an embrace. "How long before you need to leave?"

"Oh, Gabriel. I fully intend to eat and drink and dance before I go."

AND SO THEY ATE AND DRANK AND DANCED.

The cousins had brought in banquet supplies, including more good champagne. Ruby slipped out after they cut the cake to change —*don't want to worry about the heirloom dress, just want to have fun,* she said. But she returned in a stunning, modern version of the heirloom dress that Gabe could have sworn he had seen on Kendra at Family Christmas last year. She still wore the Martiniere emeralds.

His redheaded darling apparently was already making inroads with the Family, if his cousins were loaning her clothing.

Gabe danced with Ruby, and his mother, and delicately guided Ruth Ryder through a short waltz.

Before his mother and Jorge left, Jorge pulled Gabe aside.

"A quick report, Gabriel," he said in Spanish. "We have Joseph, and are discussing surrender to the authorities with him. He is favorable."

"That's good news." Gabe did wonder what *discussion* meant in this case, but he wasn't about to ask. He had his suspicions about what the Saldivars might consider appropriate, but if Joey ended up in a court of law—well, that was his goal, no matter how it happened. "And Philip?"

"He has left the country, possibly is in North Africa."

Gabe winced. "How did he manage that?"

"Private flight with Walter Braun, aided by Braun's daughter-in-law Vera. She has mafiya connections. Rumor has it that she is more involved with her father-in-law than her husband—but who knows?" Jorge shrugged. "Vera has a history of not being loyal to anyone."

"Do you have documentation of the Braun connection to Philip's flight?" *That* would be something to share with the Board, at the minimum, as well as the authorities.

"Nothing that will hold up in a court of law." Jorge's face tightened. "Be very careful in the next few weeks, mi primo. With Vera Braun involved, you are dealing with the Russian mafiya helping Philip."

"Understood." And *that* piece of information, while not surprising given what Gabe knew about the Brauns, was not the best of news. "Please keep my mama safe."

"We will do so, as well as your aunt and your father."

"I'm indebted to you for this, Jorge." Gabe inhaled sharply.

At some point he'd have to pay a price, all right. But it was well worth it.

Gabe casually circulated through the crowd after Jorge and his mother left, relaying the news to David, Kendra, Charles, and Serg.

"Zingter and Braun," David growled. "I'll pass the word on. No avoiding a corporate war with this going on, Gabe."

"I'm afraid so," Gabe said.

Kendra took the news with a sharp nod. "I'll adjust our security and see what I can do to persuade Chris away from the notion of going public. This might be enough."

Charles grimaced. "North Africa. No chance of pinpointing it more directly than that?"

Gabe shrugged. "It was what I was told."

"Already have feelers out," Serg said.

That done, Gabe did his best to dismiss the sense of impending doom that started to creep over him. More dances with Ruby and his sisters helped.

The party lasted into the evening, until only the local attendees remained.

No fleeing the crowd for a honeymoon, and apparently Ruby had threatened mayhem if *anyone* even remotely *considered* a shivaree or the faintest hint of any other newlywed harassment. Before they retreated upstairs, she fixed Justine and Louisa with a glower.

"Remember what I said this morning." Ruby shook her finger at them. Ron started to chuckle and she whirled on him. "That includes you, too, Gramps! *No tricks. No shivaree.* Or I will make you pay—in all the ways I described."

His sisters exchanged glances, and for a moment Gabe worried.

"Got it, Ruby," Justine said.

"Don't worry," Donald said.

"I guess we'll just have to drink," Louisa said, raising a brow at Remy Trask.

"I'm sure we can find something else to keep us busy," Trask said.

Gabe and Ruby left the lawn to whoops and cheers, arms around each other, giggling, drunk more on the occasion than on champagne.

"I think we'll be seeing more of Remy," Ruby said as they climbed the stairs.

"Really?"

"She and Louisa are both coming off of breakups. And I sure worked hard to get them talking to each other today."

He stopped them at the landing, trying and failing to appear stern. "Are you trying to matchmake for my little sister?"

Ruby laughed at him. "As if I could force either of them to do anything! No, Remy's an excellent prospect for Weeza. She just graduated law school, is studying for the Bar exam. Old Thunder County money. Has horses."

They continued up the stairs. "You sure Ginny's out of the picture?"

"She and Weeza broke up shortly after you and I started dating. Just—differences tied to politics and the Real Truthers. Weeza didn't want to bother you with it."

As they reached the third floor, Gabe scooped Ruby up.

"Not about to carry you up those flights of stairs—"

"No reason you should," she interrupted.

"Hush, woman. I'm trying to be romantic here."

She leaned over and kissed him before he could say anything else. It was about all Gabe could do to keep hold of Ruby, open the door, and walk into their bedroom.

Which, to his surprise, had LED candles glimmering, the ice bucket with champagne, flutes on a small table which also held a vase of red roses and a bowl of chocolates, bed turned down—

"Those girls." Ruby shook her head, grinning.

He pressed his forehead to hers. "Think there's any traps?"

"Better not be."

There weren't.

CHAPTER 18
NEW LIFE TOGETHER, NEW CHALLENGES
MAY, 2029

RUBY

Married, was Ruby's first thought when she opened her eyes the next morning. She turned on her side to study Gabe. He slept peacefully, facing her, head resting on his palm—still wearing the silver ring Gramps had produced for his wedding band. Relaxed facial muscles, making him look much younger than twenty-seven, except for the faint black stubble on his chin.

My bestest nerd boy.

She shivered at the wave of possessiveness that swept over her.

Mine.

What did she love about Gabriel Martiniere? His enticing mixture of public competence and private vulnerability. His joy in her work—oh, she noticed when her microdrone or design program work entranced him. Riffing off of each other while brainstorming. Gabe sparked ideas in her—and vice versa. She had never been around someone who so eagerly, so joyfully, wanted to collaborate and create with her. Never.

And he was *hers*.

If anyone besides Linda had told her a month ago that she would be *married* to Gabriel Martiniere, Ruby wouldn't have believed them. Linda would be ecstatic.

Still—here they were.

Meeting some of his cousins yesterday was yet another revelation. They treated Gabe with a mix of respect and familiarity. The uncanny resemblance between Gabe and his cousins. That shared piercing, hawk-like gaze. The high levels of energy.

As Gramps would say, *high-strung, high-couraged.*

Gabe was the handsomest of all the Martiniere men, at least in Ruby's opinion. And watching him during their reception, deftly chatting with his cousins, sharing information while making it look merely social—if she hadn't already been aware that decisions were being shaped and made, she wouldn't have known otherwise. That had been the public Gabriel Martiniere, acting as *the Martiniere*, sliding skillfully into the role that he had been born and trained to fulfill, hiding his fears and self-doubt under a carefully cultivated façade.

Were there any slackers amongst the Martinieres? Perhaps Joey. Possibly Philip.

Gabe blinked and yawned, stretching. That slow smile spread across his face as he gazed at Ruby. She cupped his cheek with her hand and he turned to kiss her palm, trailing more caresses up her arm until he reached her shoulder. He rolled Ruby onto her back and kissed her. Then they made long, slow love.

Afterward, they lay, sated, holding each other, touching their foreheads and exchanging soft kisses.

"My wife," Gabe murmured. "My dearest nerd girl wife. This feels like a dream."

"My bestest nerd boy husband. If you're having this dream, then I am too."

"Folie à deux?" He chuckled, nuzzling her cheek. "I wish we could goof off all day. Breakfast in bed with chocolate-dipped strawberries and champagne—if there were any strawberries to be had these days—go play in some exotic location—that's what you deserve."

"Unfortunately, I have term papers to wrap up and design specs to check. Lab reports to read. Ranch chores."

"I have to deal with my fucking sperm donor somehow, as well as Braun's machinations. Files to review from the cousins. But it could be worse. We're working in the same room. And if we want to take a break together—" he kissed her. "It's a short walk to the bedroom. I promise you. There *will* be a honeymoon, once we can safely travel somewhere besides for business."

"You don't think Philip's presence in North Africa makes things less dangerous?"

"No. It is awfully damned easy to slide into eastern Europe from North Africa. Jorge says the Russians are involved—that means the Russian mafiya. Once Philip's in Europe—from there he can travel to a lot of places. Even here."

Ruby shivered. "How long do you think this lockdown could last?"

"I wish I could give you an estimate, dear one." He kissed her forehead. "However, I plan to talk to Piotr today. It should be safe enough for Lora to bring the horses here. Being able to ride our horses will make a difference in everyone's mood."

"Yeah." Much as she loved the semi-retired geldings that were the only remaining horses on the ranch, Blaze and Cody wouldn't hold up to several people wanting to ride.

"What will be problematic is Justine and Donald's wedding," Gabe sighed. "Scheduled for Los Angeles, and it's a big affair. I've—not dared bring that up to Tine or Mama just yet, hoping things calm down well before the end of July. And then moving Donald and Justine into their new place—same for us."

"So these restrictions could last that long. More than two or three weeks."

"Very possibly several months. I've been told a similar thing happened when Saul and Philip were battling, before Joey and I were conceived. Multiple branches of the Family hunkering down, trying to stay clear of the fray. Grandfather Louis was dying, Donnagran flailing about trying to manage Papa and Philip, and—well—" His voice trailed off and he rubbed his chin before continuing. "Uncle Gerry sent a message to me through David, to not underestimate Philip and his illegal connections. Which is why I'm not relaxing. Gerry's taking precautions, and several other Family branches are as well. With—the *exception* of Chris's family. That's pretty damn telling."

"Kendra was very angry about her uncle's choices yesterday."

Gabe nodded. "Kendra should really be the one in charge of the British Family, not Chris. Damn that fucking Salic Law tradition. I'd change it in a heartbeat—and *will*, once I'm more established." He sighed. "I suppose I should turn on my notifications. I'm certain *somebody* thinks they need my attention, *now*."

"No." She stroked his cheek. "We just got married. Wait until after breakfast."

"I risk Justine jumping me about something," he grumbled.

"She can wait until after breakfast," Ruby insisted. She took his head in her hands and kissed him. "This would normally be our honeymoon, and besides, I've seen you in action, *Gabriel*. If you don't wait until after breakfast to check your notifications and emails, you'll get distracted and not eat. Or not eat much because you're stewing over something you have to manage."

Gabe chuckled. "Is this going to be a new household rule—*no notifications until after breakfast?*"

"Unless we're in a specific crisis situation—yes," Ruby said. "We need to establish a habit, and now's a good time. Breakfast is for *us*. A good start to the day. It's how Gramps and Granma have done things, and, well—fifty-some years of marriage should be a decent example, don't you think?"

"Aw, Rubes. You're going to civilize me?"

"I want you to be around for a good long time," she said.

He smiled at that, and pulled her even closer.

RUBY HAD *SOME* SUSPICION THAT A SPECIAL BREAKFAST WAS planned. The scents wafting up from the kitchen confirmed it—real ham, pancakes, and more of Justine's stash of real coffee. She and Gabe walked downstairs, holding hands. The dining table was set— no breakfast in the kitchen this morning—with an extra setting. Remy?

"Here come the newlyweds," Gramps said from his seat at the kitchen table. "Just about perfect timing. Justine and Donald are almost ready to serve breakfast."

Gabe laughed and kissed Ruby, to hoots and hollers from Granma, Louisa, and Remy. "I'll get you coffee. Go sit."

Ruby flushed and joined the others at the table, taking the last available chair. Gabe set Ruby's coffee in front of her. He took a sip from his own cup, then placed it next to hers and massaged Ruby's shoulders.

"Gabriel, have you looked at your notifications yet?" Justine asked.

"No." Gabe's hands tightened briefly on her shoulders, probably because of Justine's use of *Gabriel*. "Ruby and I decided this morning that unless the world is burning down, I should wait until after breakfast. So is the world burning down?"

Justine laughed. "No. Nothing that dire, Gabie. We can wait until after we eat."

Remy and Louisa exchanged glances.

"*We* should also have a conversation," Louisa said.

Gabe sighed and reached around Ruby to pick up his coffee. "All at once?"

"Nothing big."

"If it's about you and Remy, and whether Remy needs security coverage, set it up with Piotr," Gabe said. "Given current conditions, that's the wisest choice. No further discussion needed. I approve it."

"Thanks, Gabie."

"And that is *all* of the Family business that we are discussing before we eat," Ruby said firmly.

Gabe chuckled. "My love has spoken, and you've all heard her decree." He kissed the top of her head. She leaned back to grin up at him, and he kissed her.

"You two!" Louisa snorted. Then flushed, as Remy planted a kiss on her cheek.

"Newlywed privilege," Gabe said. "But looks like you have new relationship privilege, so—"

"Love's bursting out all over," Granma said. She gave Gramps a sideways glance. "You gonna keep up with the kids, Ron?"

Gramps laughed. "You betcha, Ruthie." Then leaned over and kissed her.

AFTER A FILLING BREAKFAST, LOUISA AND REMY LEFT THE dining room to wash dishes and clean up.

Justine tightened her lips.

"Gabriel. Ruby. Not necessarily urgent news, but you need to know. Ruby's aunt and cousin have disappeared from Solitaire. Barbie called us this morning."

Ruby and Gabe exchanged raised brows, Gabe pursing his lips.

"Did they go willingly?" Ruby asked, dread clutching at her. Now that she was Gabe's wife, the threat from Grace and Jeannie was not as significant as it had been, but all the same—she didn't like them being on the loose.

"From all indications, yes. Barbie consulted with Piotr. It appears to be the same people who may have helped Philip get to North Africa."

"That's problematic," Gabe said. "I suppose Piotr has names of those people?"

Justine nodded. "He forwarded them to you." She took a deep breath. "Donald, Barbie, and I had a big conversation this morning.

I'm calling Angelica right away. We're modifying our wedding plans. We have concluded that going ahead with the big wedding provides too great of a security risk."

"I'm sorry, Tine."

"It's not *your* fault, Gabie. The fucker who sired us is to blame. I just—I know Angelica is going to be disappointed." Justine scowled. "I *was* hoping to come down the aisle on Saul's arm. Now—Gabie, will you do the honors? Just in case Saul can't?"

"Gladly. And I will *happily* step aside if Papa is able to walk you down the aisle. You've been looking forward to that."

"So was Saul." Justine gulped, blinking hard. "Our father. Our goddamned fucking father has to fucking spoil *everything*. I—I would happily shoot him myself if I thought that would change things." She choked back a sob, and Donald wrapped his arm around her. "For that fucker to shoot Saul—*Saul*, damn it, who is four times the man that our damned father can ever be—more of a father to you and me than damned Philip—" She buried her head in her hands.

Aw shit. She's flipping from shock to anger.

Ruby cleared her throat. "You know, this might be a good afternoon to go to the shooting range."

"I'm all for that," Gabe said, a hard tone in his voice.

"Agreed." Justine's voice matched Gabe's.

Lora showed up with a trailerful of horses on Wednesday, the next day. Besides Midnight, Glory, and Flora, she brought Trevor, a bay gelding named Reliant, and a chestnut mare, Stella. Reliant and Stella were more advanced than Trevor, and needed conditioning work.

"Sunshine misses you," Lora said, as they watched the six horses romp in the Double R's small indoor arena, a chance to stretch after the long haul from Corvallis before being penned or stalled for the night. "But she's responding well to the physical therapy. Still will need to do surgery. Prospects look good."

"Glad to hear it."

Lora spent the night. Thursday started out dedicated to riding lessons. Gabe retreated to the office after schooling Midnight, but Ruby worked Reliant and Stella under Lora's supervision. Both were bold jumpers, but would benefit from hacking out at the ranch and going through Ruby's outdoor course.

The warmbloods then joined Blaze and Cody in the big horse pasture behind the house.

"Not a hillside field this year, I'm afraid," Ruby said as she and Lora leaned on the gate, watching while Blaze and Cody met the warmbloods. "With everything going on, it's too risky. Can't set up temporary fencing to keep them out of the danger zone because it's too close to the perimeter."

"That's too bad. Learning to navigate rocky hillsides is good for them—helps with the surefootedness."

"Eh, they'll get it from hacking out. And maybe if things get better, they can go on the hill fields."

After a couple of circuits of the field, the horses started to graze, Blaze and Cody off to the side while the warmbloods—used to being turned out together—settled into their own groups. Midnight and Flora grazed together with Trevor nearby. Ruby watched Glory closely, because the big mare had a history of jumping fences if she didn't care for her companions. But Glory and Stella were good friends, and Reliant often tagged along after them.

"Well, enjoy them for the summer." Lora turned away from the gate. "Do you know what the plans are for the fall?"

Ruby shook her head. "Gabe's been putting out fires connected to the transition of Group authority, and I've either been preparing for a wedding, wrapping up my classes, monitoring the Martiniere labs, or managing Martinieres. A lot depends on what happens with Saul's health—he's showing improvement and can talk now, but it's going to be slow. Uncertain yet if he will be able to walk again."

Lora winced. "Good that he's getting better."

"Yes. You heard that Justine is cancelling the big ceremony, right?"

"Yes, she messaged me. I'm sorry to hear it but not at all surprised. No word on how their plans are unfolding?"

"She and Donald have been looking at a property near Corvallis, Mist Knoll. If they manage to buy it in the next couple of weeks, they'll relocate the wedding to there for an outdoor ceremony. But if they don't get Mist Knoll—it's the most defensible property they're looking at—then it may end up here, just like me and Gabe."

"It's too bad I couldn't make it here for your wedding, but my security didn't think it was a good idea."

"Oh, it was enough of a madhouse." Ruby grinned. "You and Linda both ended up missing the wedding for security reasons."

"I thought you and Gabe would get married." Lora's grin matched Ruby's. "Just not this quickly."

"Gabe—is somewhat worried about how things may turn out with Philip. That fueled his proposal—and also the further strictures that would affect our relationship if we didn't marry."

"I had enough dealings with Philip when Gabe and Justine lived with him. It's a damn shame about Saul. He's a good man. Philip, though, is like one of those sneaky stud horses that you can't turn your back on. Only he has less restraint than that type of horse."

"Yeah, I'm hoping I don't ever meet Philip."

Lora snorted. "You'd kick his butt. Seriously."

"Well, the son-of-a-bitch better not cross my path," Ruby said. "Even indirectly. Not just for what he did to Saul—but also to Gabe and Justine."

REMY REAPPEARED AT THE RANCH ON FRIDAY NIGHT, HORSE trailer in tow. Ruby was weeding the garden when she arrived.

"Hey! You're a billionaire's wife now! Why are you doing manual labor?" Remy smirked at Ruby from outside the fence as she held the lead rope of Beauty, the palomino mare she had bought from Ruby.

Ruby laughed and stood, dusting off her hands. "Several reasons. I don't trust security to know the difference between plants and weeds. If I'm designing a microdrone nanobiobot interface, I need to be aware of the soil conditions I want it to monitor and modify. And gardening grounds me. God only knows I need that."

"Yeah." Remy went solemn. "Martinieres can be overwhelming."

"Tell me about it." Ruby secured the gate—too many deer around to leave the garden unfenced.

"Oh hell, you have it worse than I do." But a secret smile turned up one corner of Remy's mouth. "And for me it's only been a few days. Damn. These Martinieres. Weeza's been sneaking out to spend nights with me and giving security fits. I decided it might be easier if I spent the weekends here. Eventually weeknights."

Hm. Ruby hadn't heard anything about Louisa slipping out to be with Remy.

Should I tell Gabe if he doesn't already know?

"Be nice to Weeza. She's had a rough time with relationships." Ruby patted Beauty.

"Honey, for once I'm with someone richer than me." Remy's grin widened. "That's a huge novelty and removes one roadblock. And she likes horses. I brought Beauty over so we can ride together. Might end up spending the rest of the time here. Dad wants me in the office during the week. Whether I spend weeknights at the Double R depends on how productive my studying for the Bar exam can be."

"We're all either working or studying ourselves, so it shouldn't be too bad. But why did you bring Beauty? There's warmbloods who could use flat work."

"No way. *You* can mess with those critters, Ruby. Not me. Besides, Beauty needs regular work—she got too fat while I was at school. Put her in a pen or the pasture?"

"Pasture. Beauty's always been pretty chill, and the warmbloods are used to turnout. We can watch to be sure."

"You're not worried about quarantine?"

"You've kept Beauty's vax up-to-date? Taken her anywhere?"

"She's been eating her head off at home and yes, her vax are all current."

"Same here. Everyone's vaccinated and been in controlled environments, so no quarantine issues."

"All right then."

They turned Beauty loose. The herd jerked their heads up at the sight of a new horse, then galloped toward Beauty, screeching to a stop around the palomino mare. Glory, who had established herself as herd leader, sniffed noses with Beauty. They squealed. Glory lunged at Beauty. The palomino mare kicked at the other horses that now pressed close to her, then took off running. The herd circled the field, Beauty tossing her head until she made her way to her familiar pasture companions, Blaze and Cody. The herd settled to graze, the three Quarter Horses moving off on their own.

"That's a lot of expensive horseflesh to be running in turnout," Remy said.

"It's how Lora prefers to manage her horses. They're usually stalled at night at her place, but otherwise, unless it's crappy weather, they have turnout in a herd."

"Remy!" Louisa came up beside them. "Where's your Beauty?"

"Out there." Remy jerked her head toward the field, grinning big at the sight of Louisa. They kissed. Ruby slipped away, leaving them to themselves.

Besides, tonight was her and Gabe's turn to fix dinner.

Gabe was already at work in the kitchen, peeling potatoes. "Meatloaf's in the oven. New horse in the herd? I saw you two leading her to the field. Did a double take when I saw the palomino, because I *knew* Sunshine hadn't come over with Lora."

"Beauty's a half-sister of Sunshine. Remy brought her over, so she can ride with Weeza. Add one to meals for the weekend—possibly breakfast and dinner during the week." Ruby rummaged in the refrigerator for the cold cooked vegetables they were using for a salad mix.

Even Martiniere money couldn't locate decent salad veggies, and while she was trying to grow them in the garden, the lettuce was either buggy or bolting.

"That's better than Weeza sneaking out to be with Remy."

"You knew—good."

Gabe shrugged. "Part of the regular morning security report. Weeza's taking security with her—she's not stupid—but I feel better about having her girlfriend *here*. Everyone in the same place. Wish Mama was here as well."

"Remy still has to be at her dad's law office during the day. Space to study for the Bar exam is a factor that will affect her staying here on weeknights."

Gabe started dicing potatoes as Ruby made salad bowls. "Weeza leaving the ranch at night worries me more. We all have things that take us off the ranch during the day. I'd prefer to have us all here at night. That includes Remy." He sighed. "Hope they work out as a couple. I like Remy better than I did Ginny. Oh, Ginny was nice enough—but she had that entitled rich person attitude."

Ruby snorted. "Remy is one of the *last* people who thinks like that."

"Doesn't hurt that she's one of your good friends, either." Gabe grinned at Ruby.

"They'll have to work something out in the fall."

"Mmm, just like the rest of us. Though—there is a possibility—" Gabe frowned. "I'm sorry, Ruby. I had her investigated. I had to do it for our safety."

She arched a brow at him. "Gabe, I understand. Too much discussion of high-level corporate plans around here, insufficient privacy."

He exhaled. "I was worried you'd take an investigation of your friend wrong. She passed with flying colors. No contacts with Zingter, no ties to Philip. Remy's specialty is corporate law, and, well —a lawyer with Family connections is always a good thing to have around."

"You're recruiting Remy? Does this happen to everyone who dates a Family member?"

"Just a select few." Gabe laughed. "Don does financial consulting for the Group. A similar position, only legal, would be possible for Remy. Even if she and Weeza don't work out in the long run. I need to talk to her about it. Remy may already have a job. Someone with her grades and law review background is going to be a prime candidate for top law firms."

"You could outbid them."

"I fully intend to. Not just because she and Weeza are dating, or because she's your friend—all those help—but because I like what I've seen of her law review work. Corporate and environmental law—she'll fit a niche in the Group." He turned solemn. "This fucking business with my damned sperm donor is a distraction from the work we really need to be doing. Sometimes I wonder if it's on purpose."

Ruby finished making salad bowls, and joined Gabe in cutting up potatoes.

"That might be a good assumption to make, given some of the Zingter connections."

"Agreed."

Once they finished dicing the potatoes, set them to cook, and cleaned up, Gabe took Ruby into his arms. They stood together, quiet in each other's presence.

Gabe sighed. "I need to go to Los Angeles next week. I want to see Papa, there's things at corporate that require my presence, and Piotr thinks a quick visit is safe."

"I'm going with you."

"Ruby—" Gabe scowled at her.

"Watching your back. Making sure that you don't overdo. Plus—perhaps Saul should meet your wife, don't you think?"

Gabe continued to frown.

"You're not the only protective one," she added.

"*Things corporate* will include meeting with Joey. It—won't be pretty."

"Then you need me by your side."

Gabe studied her. "You're going to insist, aren't you?"

"Yep." She set her jaw firmly, glaring at him. "Otherwise, I will be fretting and might decide that I need to figure out how to join you. I'm sure Justine or Louisa would help me."

Silence fell between them. She met his glower without flinching.

Gabe rolled his eyes. "All right, then. It may be an overnight or two. I really wasn't looking forward to being away from you and alone in the house, except for security and maybe Mama."

"Another reason for me to travel with you."

"Aw, Rubes." He kissed the top of her head. "So will traveling together be a regular feature of our married life?"

"Maybe not all the time. But right now—" She let her voice trail off.

If her time with Gabe was limited, she intended to make the most of it.

He shivered. "You're putting yourself at risk. If something happens to me—"

"I wouldn't forgive myself if I wasn't at your side."

"Aw, Rubes," he repeated, inhaling sharply. "Hopefully it won't come to that."

"Hopefully."

This time their kiss held an urgency that had nothing to do with desire.

GABE

Preparations for the LA trip took longer than Gabe anticipated. Some of it was security—arranging the meeting with the Saldivars and Joey. Other parts included Ruby wrapping up the last pieces of her schoolwork.

Ruby started rolling out of bed a couple of hours earlier, in order to school horses before breakfast. Gabe joined her, along with Justine, the three of them riding out before the sun rose above the eastern ridges. They didn't jump Ruby's cross-country course yet—Ruby decreed that conditioning needed to be a priority at first—except for one time when she took Glory over the course to demonstrate it for them.

"I want to take Midnight over the full course the first time. Not before we go to LA, however," she said.

"I can handle it."

Ruby shook her head. "Not until we school it jump by jump first, like we would at Lora's. Those tree trunks are solid, and footing's tricky in a couple of places. Midnight won't pay attention to that sort of thing, and he's not ready to power through like Glory. He needs a rider who knows the course."

"Did you do the full course with Glory without schooling jump by jump? By yourself?"

She laughed. "I confess. I took Glory over the whole course first. But given my state of mind at the time, it was a damn good thing I was up on her. She eats up courses like that, as if they were nothing." She fixed Gabe with a stern glower. "And we're all wearing safety vests with neck protection once we start jumping that course."

Gabe grumbled but went along with her edict. After all, Ruby was a professional-level rider, and he needed to respect her judgment.

In the evenings, after dinner, they all rode out—Louisa and Remy, Justine and Donald, him and Ruby. They went along the tractor paths by the hay and grain fields, or followed little trails on the steep ridge walls above the ranch. Ruby never took them to the top of the ridges—mandated by security concerns.

***

But the four days before their departure on Tuesday night weren't all about horses. *Something* kept Ruby up late—probably finishing off the last of her classes as she juggled her various responsibilities.

He had *that* conversation with Remy and Louisa on Saturday. As a result, and as both the Martiniere and the Head of Family, it was his turn to administer the intimate intention and contact questionnaire to his sister. That felt weird, but it was his job now.

"You're recruiting me for the Martiniere Group, based on this short of a relationship with your sister?" Remy asked when they talked privately.

"That's a factor. Others are your field of study, your grades, and your friendship with Ruby."

Gabe laced his fingers and stretched out his legs, slumping in his chair a little bit. His and Ruby's desks were against the wall due to space considerations for Ruby's drone work table, so there was nothing between him and Remy. He liked the setup. Less intimidating.

"Weeza is part of my advisory cabinet," he continued. "You're living here. It's too damn hard to maintain confidential discussions and exclude you in this setting."

"Still—recruiting me into the Group?"

"You've passed a security check with flying colors. I've read your law review articles. I need someone with your mix of environmental and corporate law training on my cabinet—everyone else here is already part of it. You'll be reporting to me directly, as personal counsel, once you pass the Bar. While Ruby and I will be in Corvallis for the school year, after that, we're most likely to be based in Thunder County, until her grandparents die. Whether you continue in a relationship with Weeza or not, it's convenient to have legal representation with local connections."

"I never thought the Thunder County ties would benefit me in corporate law." Remy laughed. "But damn—yes, Gabe. I'll take you up on this offer."

"Good. You can advise me and Ron about land use planning, because we have to get quite a few permits to develop the ranch for our needs."

Remy chewed her lip before speaking. "Let's bring my dad in on that part. He knows the county commissioners, and he has experience with local permitting processes. Some properly placed donations from the Martiniere Group will help."

Gabe beamed at her. "Good. I'll send you the development plans. Let me know what needs to be done."

Tuesday night, they flew out of the Lakeside airport for the three-hour flight to LA, timing tied to security concerns. Gabe put his arm around Ruby as they sat together, holding her tight.

"You all right?" she asked finally, as they reached cruising altitude.

He exhaled. "No. I'm nervous as hell."

"Talk to me."

He rubbed his face with his free hand. "Seeing Joey. Going into headquarters—oh God, I get a headache just thinking about having to sort through Saul's desktop to make sure there's nothing dangling on the local servers that needs my attention. Finalizing my accesses so I'm official and don't have to do workarounds anymore. Has to be done on site." He sighed. "Seeing Papa. Mama's reports—I don't know if he'll be able to come back as the Martiniere. I have to see for myself. And then there's the feeling that there's a target on my back. No drone blockers in LA. Philip confronted Saul in person, but I don't trust him to do that to me. We could come under attack by autonomous drone-carried weapons just going from vehicles to buildings—and I know too damned much about that tech. So does Philip."

"You and I *both* know about that tech," she said, her voice low. "But Gabe, I've rigged up portable jammer microdrones that are more powerful than a dronecam blocker. Not as effective as the permanent versions at the ranch, limited operation life and range, but enough for protection when we go outside in the city."

"We have to go to the labs to build them, and that adds more vulnerabilities—"

"Nope." She grinned at him. "All I need is access to a *good* 3D printer with the right materials. Then I can print microdrones. Been playing with that notion the last couple of days."

Oh *God*, he loved his dearest nerd girl. No wonder she had been working late into the night. Thinking up their protection.

Has she told Piotr about this yet?

Piotr would be drooling if they had that particular tool.

"Have I told you how much I love you?" he murmured, placing featherlight kisses on her shoulders and neck, then her lips.

"Not in the last half hour," she said when their lips parted.

He ran his fingers through her hair, took her face in his hands. "Order the best damn 3D printer and supplies you need for the ranch if you haven't already. Or take one from the office. I don't care. I want you to have the best tools."

My dearest nerd girl might be what keeps us alive.

"We're going to run out of room in the office."

"That's all right. Once we build the lab, we'll have more room at the ranch. Oh, Ruby." He kissed her again, deeper and harder. At last, he raised his head. "There *is* a bedroom in this jet. That's going to be one hell of a lot more comfortable, and we have the time."

Her dimple flashed at him as she smirked. "Are you suggesting we join the Mile-High Club? Granted, I know a spot on the ranch—"

"Absolutely. Now." He unbuckled their seat belts and guided her into the bedroom.

AFTER MAKING LOVE, THEY SPRAWLED ON THE BED. RUBY rolled on her stomach to look out the window and Gabe snuggled next to her, his arm over her back.

"It's beautiful," she murmured. "I never thought...."

He agreed. The last gold and orange glows of sunset hung on the distant horizon, dark blue sky around them with occasional lights shining from the towns and cities below. And he was seeing it next to his beloved nerd girl, after making love to her.

They lay together silently, gazing out the window, until they dressed and prepared for landing.

Then it was time to be tense and nervous again, following security directives, wrapping his arm around Ruby as they sat in the SUV, window filters dialed up so high that they couldn't see out.

The house on the cliff overlooking the ocean looked like a jail and he shuddered. Metal shutters cranked down over the big windows. Glaring blue-white lights. The only shadows cast by security patrolling the perimeter. All that was missing was chain-link fence and razor wire.

The neighbors are going to be unhappy about this chaos.

He needed to talk to his mother about what measures had been taken in the past to soothe complaints. Part of his duties as Head of Family right now—odds were good that between being in hiding and taking care of Saul, she hadn't had time to deal with neighbor concerns.

Details. Multiple details that were up to him to manage.

"It looks like a fortress," Ruby murmured, as they waited for security's go-ahead.

"Only because it's on full lockdown," he said. "Normally it's open and airy and light, with lots of beach vistas. That's why there's all the shutters in a situation like this."

Security opened the SUV door and escorted them to the house.

His mother met them in the foyer. Even though it had only been a week since they last saw each other, she was much more haggard-looking than she had been at their wedding.

"Oh Gabie. Ruby." Angelica burst into tears.

Gabe took her into his arms, and Ruby held her as well. The three of them stood together as she sagged against him. At last, she sniffled and raised her head.

"How bad is he, Mama?"

"He has good days and bad days. Today was bad. But it's so nice to be home, even if it's only for a night or two." Angelica shuddered. "I haven't wanted to be here alone, even if security and Jorge would let me." She exhaled. "Well. Come on in."

As they followed his mother into the main part of the house, Gabe leaned over to Ruby. "Think you can make her some of those portable jammers?"

"Yes."

His suite didn't feel the same with the shutters down. If he was there alone, it would have been unnervingly reminiscent of Philip's house. But Ruby's presence made it bearable.

Though she had to wake him from nightmares.

The next day was dedicated to headquarters work, including that meeting with Joey. Ruby looked exquisitely professional with her hair pinned up, dressed in lightweight dove-gray slacks and a white sleeveless tunic with irregular red, black, and gray slashes. A couture piece from Justine's wardrobe. It looked better on her than on his sister— the coloring worked for Ruby. Her jewelry was a ruby and pearl earring and necklace set that was Louisa's.

Ruby needs nice jewelry of her own. And bespoke outfits that are hers.

Soon enough. Only the best for the queen of his heart.

His dearest nerd girl, who might save them all.

After querying Ruby about the necessary specs for the 3D printer and supplies, Gabe sent an order off to find one in headquarters and move it into his office suite, next to Saul's.

No. *His* office now. And his old office was *Ruby's.*

More tension as the three of them—Angelica intended to spend the morning in her own office before seeing Saul—moved from house to SUVs, then to headquarters. Another entrance through the delivery dock, being hustled to the freight elevator, then up to the office level.

Once there, Gabe heaved a sigh. He went with Ruby to his old office, where tech was finishing the 3D printer setup, complete with extra tables for more work space.

"This was my office. But I'm next door."

"How secure are these windows from autonomous drone attacks?"

"Permanent external jammers around the entire building, like at the ranch."

Ruby nodded. She surveyed the portraits on the wall—all Family members. The big formal portrait from last Family Christmas—Saul, Angelica, and Donna-gran seated; himself, Justine, and Louisa standing behind Saul and Angelica, Philip and Joey on the other side of Donna-gran.

"So that's Philip and Joey." Ruby leaned close to the portrait. "Huh. Except for the expression—oh, I know that glower on Philip's face!—there's not much of a resemblance between you and Philip, at least no more than you share with your cousins. And Joey looks more like the picture of Philip than the picture of Saul. Except for the weight."

"The resemblance is deceiving—parentage was confirmed by DNA tests when we were babies." It made Gabe tense just thinking about it. He *had* hoped all those years ago—until the DNA tests were revealed.

Ruby studied the other portraits—him, Justine, and Louisa. Saul and Angelica. Him and Saul, then him and Angelica.

"Beautiful pictures," she said finally.

"You'll be in the next set, along with Donald and maybe Remy—they're taken every Family Christmas."

If we survive until then.

Ruby gave him a sharp glance. Had he said that thought out loud?

"You're next door?" she asked.

"Let me show you the private access." He demonstrated the tapping code that opened the passage that bypassed the reception areas.

Once she had looked around, then returned to her office, Gabe exhaled. He dropped into the chair, popped his knuckles, and took a deep breath before calling up his screens.

The Martiniere's access transfer protocol, he typed into the primary screen, tensing.

ID scan flashed back to him in red.

Gabe leaned forward and focused on the retina scanner.

Gabriel Marcus Martiniere confirmed. Activating the Martiniere's access transfer protocol.

He expected to see a temporary flag on his role when the interface opened. Saul had walked Gabe through the process a couple of years ago. Just in case.

No. He was clearly marked as the Martiniere.

David was identified as the Martiniere-in-waiting. No temporary label.

That, more than anything else, gave him the chills. Then Gabe pushed his concerns aside and went to work.

Something to think about later.

They met with Joey at four o'clock. Security escorted Gabe and Ruby to a secondary freight elevator that took them to the basement, where security lurked.

Jorge and six other Saldivars met them in the hallway that led to several security holding cells.

"Gabriel." Jorge bowed. "Joseph is ready to be surrendered to the Corvallis authorities. We will take him there after you speak—this was his request."

"Has he been searched?"

"By us, yes."

Gabe signed to Serg. "Then I want another search by my people. Forgive me, but they know Martiniere tricks that you and yours might not."

"But of course."

They waited tensely until Serg stepped out and flashed Gabe the all-clear sign. "He wants to speak to you alone, no security."

"I will be with Gabe," Ruby said. "Does he know that I'm here?"

Serg shook his head and opened the door. Gabe took a deep breath, taking Ruby's hand, before they entered the small room. He snapped a code to activate recording. Just in case.

His cousin looked like hell. Joey sat in a chair turned sideways to a plain table which was bolted to the floor, his wrists and ankles bound in zip cuffs. No marks on his face, or anywhere else that Gabe could see. From the stiff way that Joey held himself instead of his usual slouch, however, he was hurting. Dark circles underlined his bloodshot, widened eyes. If not for the uncharacteristic upright posture, Gabe would have thought Joey had gone on an epic binge of some sort. But he recognized that stance in Joey. Oh, did he ever.

Not the time to remember those circumstances—

Ruby's hand tightened on his. He glanced sideways to see her face go tight and tense. Something spooked her about Joey, but what?

"About fucking time," Joey rasped. "Been asking to see you for—damn, I don't know how long. And who the hell is this?"

"My wife," Gabe said. "The woman that you and Mindy were trying to hurt."

"Huh. Didn't recognize her all cleaned up and looking like a Martiniere instead of a hick hayseed beauty queen."

Ruby jerked forward. Gabe thought she was going to lunge at Joey.

Instead, she stopped herself and exhaled. "At least I don't look like a fucking methhead. And I would fucking know, because enough of my relatives *are*."

Oh. So *that* was the reason for her reaction to Joey.

Joey inhaled sharply. "Well, aren't *you* the delightful little play-toy for Gabie."

Ruby growled something he couldn't hear.

Need to stop this. Now.

"Joey, do you have something to say to me, or are you just going to insult *my wife?*" Gabe drew a deep breath. "I don't have a lot of time to spare. Either spit it out or else we're gone. And while you're at it, apologize to her."

Silence.

Then Joey sighed, shaking his head. "Gabriel, you sanctimonious son-of-a-bitch. You've always put on airs as the Martiniere's son."

"Technically, that's *you*. Remember, I'm *Philip's* biological son, not Saul's."

"As if that mattered. You're the star. The Chosen One. Saul's favorite." An ugly smile twisted his lips. "It did my heart good to see what my *real* father did to humiliate you, *his actual son*, in his house. Knocked you off your pedestal." His eyes darted to Ruby. "Does she know how Walter buggered—"

"*Shut the fuck up!*" Ruby yelled. "You *worthless* piece of shit! If you don't—"

Gabe grabbed Ruby around the waist as she dove at Joey, and pulled her tight against his side. Oh, he recognized this pattern now. Joey trying to provoke a fight as a distraction, avoiding an uncomfortable subject.

"Ruby, *stop it*. Same for you, *Joseph*." He drew a ragged breath, pushing *all those feelings* away. Not the time for them. "And yes. She knows. Maybe not all the details, but *she knows*. Stop playing games."

Damn, this did *not* look like Joey being cooperative. Was it Ruby's presence, or had Joey decided to risk provoking the Martiniere's wrath? Ah. *That* was it.

"If you're just trying to get me mad and beat on you so you can't talk," he added, "that's *not going to work*. We're not boys dancing to Philip's fancies anymore. I'm the fucking Martiniere, thanks to Philip. Who is loose somewhere in North Africa or Europe."

A faint fearful expression crossed Joey's face.

He's afraid of Philip.

"Instead of shipping you to the authorities in Corvallis, maybe I should hand you over to Walter," Gabe continued, his voice turning quiet and malign. "I'm sure he'd appreciate a *special present*."

Joey blanched.

He's even more afraid of Braun. Use that.

"Speak, Joey, or else I tell Jorge to dump you in Walter's lap."

Joey shook his head, looking down at his bound hands. Then he started to collapse into himself, hissing sharply and straightening back up.

"I need the Martiniere's protection." His voice wobbled.

"You haven't sworn loyalty to me."

"All right, all right, damn it!" Joey yelled. He fell to his knees, knocking his chair over, raising his folded hands in supplication. "I swear, Gabie, I'll swear. Please. As Head of Family and the Martiniere. Protect me."

"And just why the hell *should* I protect you?"

Joey gulped. "Because between Walter and Philip, we're all fucked. Oh God, Gabie, *please.* They'll have me killed whether I'm free or in jail. After what they made me do to Mindy—and Philip getting to Saul—I can tell you about that—Gabie, *please.*"

"Do you trust this motherfucker?" Ruby snarled, glowering at Joey. "Because I sure as hell don't."

Joey turned his attention to her. "I'm sorry for what I said about you."

"Tell me why I should accept your apology." Oh, that tone was *sharp.* "Especially since you just tried to insinuate—"

"It's God's own truth what Walter and Philip did to him," Joey groaned. "And me. Gabie got Tine out of there before she became a target, thankfully." Defiance tightened his face. "Besides, you called me a methhead. I've never touched *that* shit."

"Well, that's one point in your favor." Her voice still held that edge. "But you went along with Philip."

"Because I'm not as fucking strong as Gabie!" Joey's face crumpled and he buried his head in his hands. "Because I don't dare resist —I was fucking *grateful* when the Saldivars grabbed me. That got me away from both Walter and Philip. Oh God. How bad is Mindy hurt?"

"Bad enough," Gabe snapped. *Could* he trust Joey? "Significant brain damage because of the interaction between the psychoactive drug and the knockout gas. Don't know yet if it's permanent or temporary. Saul authorized compensation from the Family Trust to her and her family."

"Damn it, he's always so fucking noble and right, *just like you*."

"He raised *me*. He would have done the same for *you*."

Joey shook his head, choking back body-wracking sobs. At last, he raised his head, sniffling. "Gabriel. I will swear loyalty to you, *and fucking mean it*. In return for your protection as both Head of Family and the Martiniere, I'll tell you *everything* I know. Please. For the good of the Family. You're the only one I trust, because you *are* so fucking noble and right. I can trust *your* word, even when I can't trust anyone else's."

Gabe exhaled. "Then swear."

Joey extended shaking hands and Gabe wrapped his around them. After Joey swore loyalty, he rested his forehead on Gabe's hands for a moment. Then, shuddering, he rose.

"All right. You're recording?"

"Yes."

Joey straightened his chair and collapsed into it. Gabe signaled for chairs to be brought in for him and Ruby.

Then Joey began to talk.

Two hours later, Gabe escorted Joey out of the holding cell, Ruby following them.

"Serg. Jorge." He waited until the two men stood in front of him. "Jorge, Joey has information that will help you track down Philip. Serg, Joey has information for Piotr, about how Philip got to Saul, amongst other things." He exhaled. "After Joey shares what he knows with the two of you and Piotr, he disappears. He is under the Martiniere's protection, as long as he does not act against me, Ruby and her close family, or the Family." Another deep breath. "Joey, one step out of line, and you're dead. Understand? I won't fucking hesitate to issue that order."

Joey nodded.

"Jorge, Serg. We need to prepare for corporate war. Braun is coming for us."

Serg's eyes widened. "You're certain?"

"Joey has the details." Gabe put his arm around Ruby, craving her proximity.

Oh God, this is worse than I thought.

RUBY

Oh God. Oh God.

Everything Joey had told them. The schemes between Walter Braun and Philip, aimed at killing not just Saul and Gabe but Donna, Justine, Gerard, David, and a handful of the other high-level Martiniere heirs. Driven by a deal Braun and Philip made to put Philip in charge of the Martiniere Group, turn it public, and give Braun a controlling interest.

Ruby's stomach turned as Joey described Braun and Philip's abusive behavior, at times referring back to experiences shared with Gabe when he had lived in Philip's house. She didn't dare react. Not now. For Gabe's sake. He held her hand under the table and at times clenched it, suppressing tremors.

Dear God, she had thought she'd seen everything growing up. But this—*this* ugliness and mess. The sheer, utter vindictiveness on Philip's part—she repeatedly asked Joey whether Philip was on meth or heroin.

No meth. No heroin or other opiates. Some psychoactives, and lots and lots of roofies, plus alcohol—alcohol was Philip's main drug, and not much of that. But he dosed everyone around him—

Gabe held himself straight and stern as he kept his arm wrapped around her waist while they rode the elevator back up to their offices. Security was around them, so even as he quivered against her, he still maintained that façade of power and control.

The pretense fell the moment they were alone in Saul's—now *his* —office.

Gabe groaned and buried his head in the junction of her neck and shoulder. "Fuck. Oh *fuck*. God, Ruby—I can't take anything more today. I just want to go back to the house and hide. I don't know if I can even stand to be around Mama—no one but you. My head is pounding."

She held him tight, murmuring soothing reassurances.

"I knew this was going to be ugly. Just not how ugly. Damn it, I want to be back at the ranch tonight, but there's no way I'm in any condition to see Papa. And I *have* to see him before we leave."

"Tomorrow will be soon enough."

Gabe shivered and raised his head. "You're all right? With me— with what Joey said—about what happened?"

"You told me."

"Not these details." He gulped. "Not—the—" His voice faltered.

"I had a pretty good idea from what I've already heard. Knowing that you were raped—" She took his head in her hands. "Gabriel. I am *not* going to run away screaming. I've been raped too. I know what it's like. I love you, and I'm pissed off as hell about what happened to you. I'm your wife. I'm your lover. *I'm here.*"

He leaned forward and kissed her. "Thank you. Thank you for being there. For believing in me."

Tapping on the door. "Gabriel? Ruby?" Angelica's voice.

Gabe shuddered. "Come in, Mama."

Angelica entered. Her mouth set in a tight line, her brows furrowing in concern. "You've talked to Joey."

Gabe nodded. "I want to go back to the house right now, Mama. I'm not going to be fit company for anyone. Maybe not even Ruby."

"That bad."

"Yes, Mama. That damned bad. About like—coming back from Philip's house."

Angelica's face paled and her gaze met Ruby's. Ruby nodded.

"All right, then," Angelica said firmly. "I'll order dinner delivery on our way back. Food should be there and checked by the time we reach the house."

"Thank you, Mama."

Ruby swallowed. "I do have good news. My portable microdrone jammer prototypes aren't fully tested yet, but we can run them while going between vehicles and buildings. That's one less thing to worry about."

"Thank *you*, Ruby." Gabe's arm cinched tightly around her.

It stayed there all the way back to the house.

AFTER DINNER, GABE TOOK A SEDATIVE AND WENT TO BED. Ruby cuddled with him for a while.

"You'll be all right if I get up and have a drink?" Ruby asked.

"Just—stay until I'm asleep."

"I will," she promised, stroking his face. His eyes closed and he smiled, for the first time in hours. "I'll leave the door open so I can hear if you start yelling in a nightmare."

"Thank you." He paused. "Rubes?"

"Yes?"

"Don't drink too much. Please. I overwork when I'm under pressure. You—dive into a bottle. I've seen your stress reactions often enough now. Promise?"

"I'll try," she murmured. "But God, Gabe—"

"I get it." He clutched her hand. "Especially after everything we just heard. You're not an alcoholic, but—"

"It's like the painkillers I won't take. I know. Addict parents, and alcohol's a drug." She exhaled. "You may have to remind me. Just like I have to remind you."

He gave her a sleepy smile. "I can live with that."

Once Gabe's breathing steadied into a sleep rhythm, Ruby slipped away. She walked to the kitchen, seeking the whisky they had been drinking last night.

The big kitchen opened onto a dining area and family room. Angelica sat on the couch, legs tucked under her, reading from a tablet, a drink on the side table beside her. She set the tablet down as Ruby entered the kitchen.

"Gabie's all right?" she asked.

"He's asleep, and the door's ajar. I'll hear if he starts having nightmares." A clean shot glass and the bottle of whisky was on the counter.

She had promised Gabe. But—damn it—she needed to dull the memory of Joey's voice reciting *those fucking details*. Including rape. Of Gabe. Of Joey.

Ruby poured herself a full drink and tossed it down all at once, then refilled it before joining Angelica.

Her mother-in-law raised her brows.

"It's been one hell of a day. Two hours talking to Joey—" Ruby shook her head. "I thought my family was fucked up. But Philip takes the cake."

"Yes. The motherfucker certainly does." Angelica exhaled. "Tomorrow is a light physical therapy day, so Gabie can talk to Saul early, if you want to go back to the ranch afterward. I think that might be best for Gabie. Get him away from here. From the memories." She shivered. "I can't stand to stay here alone with the barriers raised. And Gabie's memories of lockdown in this house aren't the best."

"I agree." Ruby studied her drink, thinking through what she wanted to say next. Several things, including the toughest of all, the reason why she was diving into this damned glass. "The other piece—and Gabe hasn't completely accepted this—is that he's still freaking out about all the structures falling into place to make him permanently the Martiniere. Not temporary."

"Saul won't be able to keep up with the position." Angelica's voice was low and troubled. "It's a miracle that he's alive, and rational, and able to talk again. His doctors don't think he will fully recover, so—I *won't* let him take the job back. It was already killing him with heart problems. I'm glad you were able to get Gabie to rest. That's more than I could ever do with Saul, until I threatened to leave him."

Ruby snorted. "I had a horror story to tell Gabe. Lots of those from *my* family. Though his story and Joey's details about life with Philip were worse—how much worse I didn't know until now—"

She downed the second drink, and got up to pour herself a third, aware of Angelica's eyes on her. Instead of joining her mother-in-law on the couch, she leaned against the counter, crossing her arms, cradling her drink. A further distance between them than there would be in the ranch kitchen, and maybe that was a good thing, given that she was bringing up the most difficult subject of all.

"Let me guess. You want to know how Gabie ended up in Philip's household at sixteen."

"That would be good to know, yes." Ruby raised her glass, eying the amber liquid, turning it back and forth to catch the light, relieved that her mother-in-law had brought it up first. But—it was *time* for her to speak up, damn it. "So just why the hell did it happen? Everyone keeps telling me that you and Saul had no fucking choice. I don't believe it. I know better, from my own experience."

"We *didn't* have a choice."

"Bullshit." Ruby took a big swig from her drink. "You could have fought."

"Philip had lawyers."

"So did my Aunt Grace, when she tried to take me away from my grandparents after I killed my fucking father." Angelica winced, and Ruby pressed harder. "*My* damned parents were addicts. They kidnapped me when I was six. My father beat my mother to death with a tire iron. I shot him when he came to kill me."

Angelica started to speak but Ruby raised her free hand to stop her.

"I knew damned good and well what I was doing, because for two years before that, my grandfather taught me how to handle a gun. Where to aim." Another big slug of the whisky. "Grace threatened to make me pay, at my parents' funeral. *Threatened a six-year-old.* Sicced Children's Services on my grandparents, claiming they were unfit because Gramps had been teaching me to shoot—to kill." Her voice caught and she swallowed hard, vision starting to blur.

"Oh God, Ruby."

"I spent six months in foster care before my grandparents got me back. It didn't stop there. I was beaten up at school. Then Grace's sons—my damned cousins—raped me when I was sixteen. One of them knocked me up. No idea which one. The sheriff wouldn't do a damned fucking thing about it. I had an abortion, just before my tryouts for Thunder County Days Queen."

She choked back a sniffle that threatened to escape. If it hadn't been for Granma's willingness to take her to Portland, do what was needed—

"Ruby—"

"Fortunately, the assholes were methheads like my father," Ruby continued. "I don't know how, or who else Gramps enlisted. But he made damned good and sure that they were dead. That it looked like a meth deal gone bad. And then he came home and told me that I didn't need to worry about those fuckers hurting me anymore, and why." She gulped and took another drink. "My grandfather isn't a billionaire. He doesn't have the resources of the Martinieres. *So why the hell couldn't you and Saul do that for Gabe?*"

There. It was out. What she had been aching to say for some time now.

Angelica flinched. Exhaled. Then she rose and picked up her

glass, coming into the kitchen. She filled it, then leaned against another counter.

"I nearly divorced Saul over Philip taking Gabie. I couldn't stand to be around him for several weeks after—Ruby, we were blackmailed." A gulp of whisky. "I couldn't think of anything so bad that Saul would back down from Philip. Philip said something privately to Saul which made him go deadly pale, and he didn't argue any further. When I threatened to divorce him, all Saul would tell me that he couldn't say anything, even if it made me leave. I went on an extended visit to Mama, and took Weeza."

Angelica shook her head. "Things changed. When Philip roared into the house demanding Justine's return two years later, it was like watching the situation in reverse—and that was *before* Gabriel told us everything that had happened to him in Philip's house. All I know is that Philip was in the middle of a rant, claiming that Gabriel was sleeping with Justine, when Saul went up to him and said something none of us could hear. Philip went pale, shut his mouth, and left."

"Gabe should have been told about the blackmail."

Angelica sighed. "*I* don't even know what it was, Ruby. And Saul refused to let me hint anything about it to Gabriel."

"Well, *I'll* tell Gabe. He deserves to know." She glared at Angelica.

A soft rustle alerted Ruby, before Gabe glided into the kitchen barefoot, wearing only his pajama pants—a breathtaking sight, at least for her.

"Tell me what?" He yawned, running his fingers through his hair. "Got up to use the bathroom, overheard a little, mostly tone of voice. What are you two arguing about?" He came over to Ruby and slipped his arm around her.

"Saul was blackmailed into giving you up to Philip," Ruby said, her voice low. "Your mother doesn't know what it was, and Saul wouldn't let her tell you."

"Oh." His voice went dead. "*That.* I found it when I accessed Saul's records today. Just another fucking mess on top of everything else. Saul thought an order he had given was responsible for a lab exploding, resulting in the deaths of ten people. Stupidly, he tried to cover it up. He didn't know that Philip and Braun did it, and forged records implicating Saul. Philip threatened to reveal Saul's coverup. Saul discovered the truth a week later. But he was afraid to say anything, because by then Donna-gran and the Board had decreed that Joey and I needed to stay at our biofathers' houses until we were eighteen, or else forfeit our chances of becoming Martiniere-in-waiting. He feared that revealing his knowledge would result in worse treatment for me."

A puzzled frown tightened Angelica's face. "I knew about *that*."

"You wouldn't have known everything," Gabe sighed. "It was nastier than I described—that's the very much shorter version. What Saul used to keep Justine here was evidence that Philip had ordered the tampering with the airplane six years before, that could have killed you, him, and Weeza. Even though there were—issues with bringing a legal case." He groaned and buried his head in Ruby's shoulder.

"You all right?" she asked.

"Headache. Occasional side effect of this med for me, on top of the headache I already had. Idiosyncratic. Sleepy but it *hurts*. Enough to wake me."

"Acetaminophen?"

"Eh, just working up the energy to get it feels like too much to do. Like I'm bogged down in mud."

"I can handle that." Angelica left, and returned with the container. "One or two, Gabie? This is extra-strength."

"Two." He took the pills from his mother, dry-swallowed them, then accepted the glass of water she gave him. "Just wanna stand here for a little bit."

"We could sit down," Angelica said.

"Then I'd have to get back up. I'm sleepy and I don't think I could do it on my own. Ruby doesn't need to carry me to bed." He wrapped both arms around Ruby, leaning hard. "Mama, is it possible to see Papa in the morning? I'd just as soon return to the Double R as quickly as I can. Wish I could bring you along, because from what Joey told us—this house is a target. And Braun knows too much about the Saldivar safe houses. The Double R is more defendable."

"Saul and I talked, and yes, you can see him tomorrow morning. Which brings up another subject." Angelica tapped her lips with her index fingers. "Not just because this house is a target—though that's part of it. If Saul comes home with the house in lockdown, he'll be depressed. He needs to be able to see and go outside. I was considering taking him to the Saldivar compound in Mazatlán, but if Braun knows about the safe houses, that may not be the best. We need another option."

"I understand how Papa feels." Gabe yawned again. "Ruby, could we find space at the Double R for Mama and Papa—Mama, I'm assuming that we can arrange for a physical therapist or have instructions for one?"

"Instructions are available. I was planning to hire one in Mazatlán," Angelica said. "Approved by the Saldivars."

"There's good PTs in the County. Two of them went to school with me and Remy," Ruby said. "And—let me think. Security hasn't taken over the ranch manager's house. It's small, and I don't know how accessible it is."

"It could be fixed?" Gabe asked.

"Oh yes. It's sound. Security just thought the bunkhouse and then modular housing would work better. There was some talk of using it as a headquarters but they decided against it—layout was wrong for their needs. It's a nice little house with lots of windows, easy to clean, heat, and cool. Two bedrooms."

"Mm. Then let's make it happen. Send pictures to Mama." Gabe raised his head. "How many drinks is that for you, Rubes?"

"Two and—" she studied the glass. "A half."

"That's enough. C'mon. I wanna go back to bed and cuddle." He tugged at her.

Ruby set down her glass, and let Gabe tow her along, back to his suite while Angelica followed them to hers.

THEY DRESSED MORE CASUALLY THE NEXT MORNING, PLANNING to leave for the Double R after talking to Saul.

"Why is it that we can leave here during the day but the ranch only at night?"

"More security at the airport," Gabe said. "Ron and I are planning to put in an airstrip at the Double R, but that doesn't happen right away. Once we have an airstrip and hangars on the ranch, travel will be much simpler."

That made sense.

HOSPITALS BROUGHT BACK MEMORIES OF BEATINGS, THAT horrific time after her parents' death, the surgery after her rape, and Granma's cancer. Granted, Saul was in a nicer room than any she had been in before, but the place still smelled of antiseptic. The low beeps and chirps from the monitoring machines as well as the faint hubbub outside reminded her of where they were.

"Gabie." Saul's voice was thick and slurred with long pauses between words. Yes, there *was* a resemblance to Gabe—probably because Philip was Saul's twin. But Saul's face was fuller. "This. Your. Ruby?"

"Yes. My Ruby." Gabe pulled her close and kissed her temple.

Ruby took Saul's right hand. "I wish we were meeting under better circumstances."

"Me. Too." A distorted smile twitched the right side of Saul's mouth. "Pretty. Good. Taste. Gabie."

"Thank you," she said.

"Care. For. Gabie."

"I am."

"She certainly is." Gabe kissed her temple again. "The best thing that ever happened to me."

Saul continued to beam at them. "Knew. It."

Gabe drew himself up and took on that aspect of himself Ruby was starting to recognize as *The Martiniere*. "Ruby. Mama. I need to talk to Papa alone for a few minutes. Martiniere business. Could you step out?"

"Don't tire him, Gabie," Angelica cautioned.

"I won't. Just a few minutes." He glanced at Ruby. "Rubes, you've heard this. Yesterday."

Shit. Some of what Joey told us.

That was enough to stifle any objections she might have.

They stood awkwardly in the hallway. Ruby wanted to lean against the wall. She was fuzzy from last night's drinks and rising early to work out with Gabe. But something *not right* kept nagging at her.

"I hate this place," Angelica muttered. "And it's going to be several more weeks before Saul can leave. He needs that level of care."

"Don't blame you." Ruby exhaled, looking around. Saldivars and Martiniere security lurked discreetly in both directions. All the same, that *something* sent worried prickles down her neck. What was out of place? What didn't fit, based on her past hospital experiences?

Wait. Someone shambled down the hallway in scrubs, grabbing a cart piled with linens that had been sitting far enough away that security hadn't checked it. Wrong style of cart. Shoulders hunched, glancing around furtively—something familiar about the way that person moved but she couldn't place it—

Gabe's head of security, Lance, alerted, flashing hand sign at two of his staff. The Saldivars clustered around Ruby and Angelica as security staff strode down the hallway toward the person with the cart. The person upended it, revealing—

"*Bomb!*" Lance bellowed.

The Saldivars shoved Ruby and Angelica back into Saul's room, two men coming in with them, the rest joining Martiniere security.

"What the—?" Gabe whirled to meet them.

"Bomb!" Ruby and Angelica both gasped, diving for Gabe and Saul. They flung themselves carefully on Saul's bed, Gabe doing his best to cradle Saul's head.

And waited. Waited. Waited.

Then people burst into the room.

CHAPTER 21

THE DOGS OF CORPORATE WAR

GABE

Bomb. Oh fuck, we're gonna die. All of us. Damn it, Ruby and I didn't get to do even a quarter of what I hoped we would accomplish together.

Gabe cradled Saul's head while Ruby and Angelica did their best to protect the rest of Saul's body, hyperaware of the two Saldivar men standing at the door with pistols drawn. He tensed, waiting for an explosion.

Nothing. Did that mean Lance and his staff had managed to defuse the fucking thing? Or Piotr?

A soft tapping, then the door burst open.

"Moving Saul, *now!*" Piotr snapped.

"What about the bomb?" Gabe eased Saul's head down and straightened up.

"Defused by the Saldivars."

Medical personnel swarmed Saul's bed, a stocky, middle-aged nurse barking orders that even the doctor followed. Gabe, Ruby, and

Angelica were swept up in the chaos, surrounded by security, as the process of moving Saul to another room began.

"We need a more secure location," Piotr growled. "Not just moving around this building. This hospital was *supposed* to be safe. Obviously, it's not."

"Ruby, what about the hospital in Lakeside?" Gabe asked.

"Not set up for intensive care—"

"Lakeside where?" a nurse asked.

"Lakeside, Oregon," Gabe said.

"I know that hospital," another nurse said. "I have a cousin on staff there. Small but one of the top rural hospitals in the country. With a bit of funding—"

"Find out if it'll work," Gabe said. "There'll be money."

They jammed into an elevator. Gabe held Ruby tight with one arm, his mother with the other. Angelica held Saul's good hand.

"Can't relocate him for at least another week without a lot of support," said the doctor with them.

"If it's a matter of throwing money at whatever it takes to provide the necessary level of support to transport him to Lakeside and provide hospital services, *it can be done*," Gabe said. "Including what it takes to bring essential staff on site. The security of my parents is equally as important as my father's recovery, and we've just seen there's a problem! Get him the information for what's necessary." He jerked his head at Piotr. "I'll make it happen."

"It will be expensive—"

"We're talking Martiniere money. Make. It. Happen. I don't give a fuck how much it costs. Network with the Lakeside hospital—Ruby, what's its name?"

"Lakeside Memorial." Her voice quavered a little. He squeezed Ruby, hoping she found it reassuring. She looked up at him, a fleeting smile touching her lips.

The room they ended up in was small, set up for double-occupancy, staff wheeling out two beds before they guided Saul's inside. Gabe slid a chair by Saul's bed for his mother. He and Ruby remained standing. Saul lay with his eyes closed, clearly stressed. Gabe put both arms around Ruby. She trembled against him, but he was quivering too.

So close. So *fucking* damn close. Even though he'd told Ruby the odds of her becoming a widow in the next year were very high—if she survived—he honestly didn't want to face that reality.

But he had to. Now.

Oh fuck. Oh fuck.

Ruby buried her head in his chest. He kissed her.

And they waited. He wasn't going anywhere until this situation was *solved*, damn it.

Gabe had no intention of being in the position to tell his sisters that Saul and Angelica had died due to security problems.

Not if he could prevent it.

It took several hours, a number of financial and security authorizations on his part, calls by Ruby to Remy Trask, Ron, and Justine, but—moving Saul to Lakeside happened.

"I'm traveling with Saul," Angelica said when it was settled, as they conferred in the hallway outside of Saul's temporary room.

"Stay safe, Mama."

"You two as well." She sighed. "Not sure where I'll stay in Lakeside—"

"The ranch," Ruby said firmly. "Justine and Granma are organizing space for you. Do we need to go back to the house to get your things?"

Angelica shook her head. "The Saldivars have my suitcases."

"All right," Ruby said.

Once they were in the jet and in the air, Gabe kicked off his shoes and switched his phone to emergency notifications only.

"I'm going to lie down. Want to join me? Not sex, just—rest. Comfort."

Ruby nodded. "This was scary."

"Honey, it's just the beginning." He tensed. Would this situation be Ruby's breaking point?

"I want to hold you—and be held by you," she murmured.

They lay together quietly on the bed, not bothering to pull down the shades. Gabe nuzzled in close to Ruby. Scenarios raced through his thoughts. He did his best to banish them, but he kept wondering. Who was that bomber? A Braun lackey, or someone tied to Philip?

God. Right now, all he wanted was time with Ruby. The chance to rest and sleep. Go for a ride on Midnight—maybe they might have time this afternoon, maybe not. Stay somewhere that didn't require shutters and blocker tints to keep them safe. Be able to think about carbon capture techniques and the potential for Ruby's bots to make a difference.

That was what he really wished he could do, instead of gearing up for a major battle with Walter Braun and his sperm donor.

Ruby reached up and stroked his face. "I know you said no sex. But. You're fretting. I need the comfort and distraction, and I'm pretty sure you do as well."

That was all the encouragement Gabe needed to make love to his dearest nerd girl.

THEY STAYED WITH SAUL UNTIL HE WAS SETTLED AT LAKESIDE Memorial and Gabe was convinced that all was safe. The hospital CEO herself supervised the process, along with the CFO, the Chief Nursing Officer, and the Chief Medical Officer.

"Thank you," Gabe said to the CEO and her colleagues in the hallway, allowing his parents time to be alone. "Thank all of you."

The CEO flashed him a quick smile. "Mr. Martiniere, given the *sizable* donation in addition to your down payment, you can be assured that Lakeside Memorial plans to do everything we can to provide a secure environment for your father's recovery. You don't realize how much that contribution helps us."

"I appreciate your flexibility to provide service at such short notice, especially since you're accommodating our security needs."

"All things considered, we're grateful."

More words. More thanks and discussions. He was exhausted by the time his mother joined them, and leaned hard on Ruby. She had to be as tired as him. Somehow, she managed to bear up. But oh, the thought of their upstairs bedroom sounded *so good*. The light. No barriers. Being able to *see outside*.

Until now, he hadn't realized how depressed those two nights at the LA house with the barriers had made him.

"How is Papa doing?"

"Tired," Angelica said. "But comfortable. They're doing a good job."

Gabe exhaled. "Let's go."

As they left the hospital, Gabe realized it was late—the sun was setting behind the rolling prairies to the northwest.

What a hell of a day. And it felt awfully damn good when they turned in at the ranch entrance and he saw the CENTURY FARM— RYDER FAMILY sign.

JUSTINE AND LOUISA MET THEM OUTSIDE, FOLLOWED BY Donald and Remy.

"Mama." Louisa hugged Angelica. "Is Papa all right?"

"He's settled in at the hospital," Angelica said.

"We were told there was a bomb threat," Justine said, her voice tight and grim.

"An actual bomb, defused by the Saldivars," Gabe said. "And the bomber committed suicide before we could learn anything."

"Damn it."

He sighed. "Oh, there's more."

Justine nodded. "Serg has told us a little bit. Thank you, Gabie, for sparing Joey." She turned to Angelica. "We can look at the house in the morning, though I'm sure you won't want to stay there until Saul can. For now, we've cleared out a bedroom on the first floor. It can accommodate Saul should we not finish preparing the house by the time he's discharged."

Ruby raised her brows. "Where?"

"Ron's office."

"Oh no, I can't displace him—" his mother said.

"It's *done*, Mama," Louisa said. "Ron offered it."

Gabe and Ruby exchanged glances. "Where is Ron working?" he asked.

"The dining room and their bedroom," Justine said. "Ruth agreed."

Another thing to do—thank Ron and Ruth for their generosity toward his mother. Gabe pulled Ruby close. "We're exhausted. I need to have a cabinet meeting but not right now. Tomorrow morning."

"Dinner's ready for you three," Louisa said.

Gabe realized he was starving. Had they eaten lunch? He couldn't remember. That probably meant that Ruby and his mother were ravenous, too. "Let's go inside."

Dinner was simple—a chicken stir fry. The others left the three of them alone to eat and decompress. Ron joined them as they finished eating.

"Don't worry about cleaning up," he said. "Sounds like you've had one hell of a day."

"Ron, I am so grateful to you for giving your office to Mama," Gabe said. "Thank you. And Ruth as well. Sorry for the imposition."

"Yes, thank you and sorry for the imposition," his mother echoed.

"Given the circumstances, I sure as hell wasn't going to stick you in a house by yourself, Angelica," Ron said gruffly. "I'm just glad that you all didn't get blown up."

"Thanks again," Gabe said.

Ron bowed to Angelica. "Let me show you to your room. You'll be sharing a bathroom with me and Ruth."

"Thank you," Angelica said, her voice low. "I *am* tired."

"Then let's get you settled." Ron glared at Ruby and Gabe. "And you two—don't get any notions about cleaning up. You both look all in. I'd better not see you here when I get back." He and Angelica left, talking softly.

Gabe and Ruby stared at each other across the table. At last, Gabe pushed his chair back. "I'm tired," he said.

"So am I."

"I don't feel like we should leave our things for others to clean up."

"Gramps will have our heads. Come on, Gabe, let's go upstairs."

Even though the curtains were drawn—probably a security precaution, though just as likely meant to keep the sun from heating up the room, especially given how hot the day had been—Gabe didn't feel trapped.

Safe. For tonight.

He nestled into Ruby once they had showered and settled. A faint, cool breeze whispered through the window at the head of their bed—open just a crack, but enough to be soothing.

To his surprise, Gabe slept well.

Gabe was glad for that good night's sleep when he finished talking to Piotr after breakfast, before the cabinet meeting. The options that Piotr offered troubled him. He needed a reality check, *bad*.

Which was the reason why the Martiniere had his advisory cabinet.

But he needed Ruby's feedback *first*. If his dearest nerd girl said *no, don't*—he wouldn't do it. Wouldn't even discuss the options with the others.

Was this why Saul hadn't acted against Philip? Because Angelica said *no, don't?*

Ruby joined him in their office. "Everyone's waiting, Gabe."

He rubbed his face. "Rubes. Several things, before the meeting."

"Oh?"

"Yeah. First, and more personal. The bomber's been IDed. Jeannie Barkley."

Ruby flinched.

"Autopsy shows a high dose of psychotropic medications in her system," Gabe said softly. "The same ones that Philip used on me—"

"Aw, *fuck.*"

"Yeah. Hard to say how much of her actions were under her control. *I know,* too damned well."

Ruby nodded sharply.

"The other personal piece. Your Aunt Grace's body's been found on a Solitaire Island beach. Sedative overdose." He inhaled. "Are there any other close relatives we should notify, or are you it?"

"I'm their closest relative who isn't in prison. If it's up to me— cremate the bodies, donate any inheritance to charity. I don't want a cent of it." Still, she blinked and wiped her eyes.

Now for the most difficult part. "I—Piotr's made some recommendations. I probably need to follow up on them. But—God." He swallowed. "Once I do this, I can't go back. And if authorities discover some of them—my going to prison is a *definite* possibility, at best. You need to know that."

Ruby blanched. "How bad are these options?"

"They include cyberattacks on Zingter Enterprises. Donald's prepared a stock purchase campaign to lay the foundation for a hostile takeover, since Zingter's publicly held. We won't be able to get a majority, but we'll be a big percentage of shareholders, enough to call for a new Board election."

"Are we undergoing cyberattacks?"

"Small ones. Mostly testing our defenses, but Piotr and the tech folks think it's the precursor to larger attacks. We have the capacity to hurt them worse than they can damage us if we act now. If we wait—who knows?"

"All right. That's—reaching a boundary, but still—" Her lips tightened. "What else? Has to be more, if you're talking about the possibility of prison."

He exhaled. "Sending Martiniere forces to assassinate Walter Braun and his son Frank. Not a Saldivar job, like with Philip. Piotr has an elite team who will do it. Discreetly. No obvious ties to us, but—"

"*Fuck.*" Her eyes widened.

"Yeah." Another hard swallow. "If I approve this action, then I've drafted a memo that I will send out to the Board, taking complete responsibility for this decision as the Martiniere, and absolving the Board from any participation in my choice. Killing the Brauns—Saul never could go that far." He rubbed his face. "There may be others in Zingter who come after us even with Walter and Frank dead. I just—damn it, Rubes, am I turning into my biofather by seriously considering this?"

"Can you try the other actions first, saving this one if cyberattacks and the stock purchase campaign don't slow things down?"

"The way Piotr put it to me, it's everything or nothing, because even if we succeed with those measures, it doesn't stop Walter and Frank from acting. There's another piece. The bomb elements are linked to Zingter."

"How stupid could they get?"

"It was sheer luck that we had the Saldivar expert who could defuse the bomb quickly on site. Otherwise, there wouldn't be much left to identify that connection very quickly. Eventually it would have happened—but who knows what would be left of the Group and the Family by then?"

"So we could have been killed."

"Yes."

Her expression hardened, fists clenching at her sides. "How big was that bomb?"

"Powerful enough to take out several floors. It would have killed innocents. Because it was Zingter in origin, it was able to pass security scanners."

"Fuckers." She raised her fists, then dropped them. "And the impacts of all of these actions, if you approve them?"

"All-out corporate war."

"How likely is it that the Brauns will face legal sanctions?"

Gabe snorted. "Piotr has turned the evidence over to LA authorities, and been advised that it's insufficient."

Ruby sighed. "We don't have a fucking choice, then, do we? Either we roll over and live in fear for however long it takes Braun and his lackeys to kill us, or—we kill him and his son first."

"Yes." His dearest nerd girl understood the situation, all right. But what would be her verdict?

"Damn it. Damn it." She pressed her lips together in a narrow line, furrowing her brows, clenching her fists again.

"Rubes—"

"Put me on that memo as also being responsible," she said. "Because if you end up in prison over protecting us—protecting *our Family*—then I should be right in there next to you. I vowed to be your wife in sickness and in health, for better or worse—" she choked, raising her fists to her mouth.

"Ruby." He took her in his arms. She clutched him hard.

He had his answer.

RUBY SPLASHED WATER ON HER FACE BEFORE THEY WENT downstairs to the cabinet meeting in the living room. He and Ruby took turns running through the important parts of Joey's story.

The assassination plots.

Braun and Philip's scheme to take over the Martiniere Group. Their role in destroying Miranda after she filed charges against Philip and kept waffling—while providing a distraction to abet Philip's escape.

And then it was time for more sensitive subjects.

"I have new information from Piotr," he said. "The bomber has been identified. Both the person and the components in the bomb have been conclusively tied to the Zingter-connected syndicate that helped Philip."

"The bomber was my cousin Jeannie, who had already been identified as a threat to me and Gabe," Ruby added.

Shock, then anger flashed across Ruth and Ron's faces.

"What about Grace?" Ruth asked.

"Dead," Ruby said flatly.

"*Good*," Ron muttered. "Good riddance to that witch. Both of them, for the hell they put you through."

"The autopsy shows that Jeannie Barkley was under the influence of a psychotropic medication, one that Philip's been known to use in the past. Including on me. We probably will never know just how much she acted of her own choice." Gabe exhaled.

The same psychotropic discovered in Mindy, that had interacted poorly with the knockout gas. Gabe swallowed hard. He knew *too* damned well what it felt like to not be in control of himself.

"What's our next move, Gabriel?" Justine was first to speak.

"Jorge is working with—allies—to stop Philip in Europe, before he attacks known Family targets there. We assume that this bombing attempt was directed at Saul, Mama, Ruby, and myself. Unfortunately, our flights here in Lakeside can be easily observed. That's our biggest vulnerability in this location."

"Dad's started work on the airstrip permitting process," Remy said.

Gabe acknowledged her with a nod. "That's good, but it won't happen fast enough. Can't be helped." He exhaled. "Piotr is waiting for my approval to start countermeasures, including cyberattacks on Zingter Enterprises. In addition, I want Donald to implement the Zingter stock purchase plan. We won't be able to get a controlling interest, but we'll have a large enough share to call an emergency Board meeting and cause a ruckus."

"What other countermeasures are you assigning to Piotr?" Justine asked.

Ruby raised a hand. "Remy, you'd better not be present for this."

"Why?" Remy asked.

"We're crossing a line that could get you in trouble with the Bar."

Remy inhaled deeply. She exchanged glances with Louisa. Then her lips tightened and she nodded. "I'm staying. So, Gabriel, what are these countermeasures that could threaten my future licensure?"

"Assassinating both Walter Braun and his son Frank," Gabe said grimly. "Not a Saldivar job."

"Gabie—" His mother's face twisted in dismay. "Saul won't—"

"Mama. Braun and Philip have already damned near killed Papa, and tried a second time. We're at war." Gabe drew a deep breath. "I'm taking full personal responsibility for that decision, as the Martiniere, and have dictated a memo to that effect—should there be any issues."

"I'm on that memo along with Gabriel," Ruby said. "I approve of this decision."

"So do I," Justine said.

Gabe looked around the table. "Is there anyone who thinks this is a step too far? Piotr's made it clear to me that we can't do this by half measures. If we *don't* implement *all* of these measures in a timely manner, then sooner or later, Braun and/or Philip will ensure that Ruby and I are dead. Followed by just about everyone else in this room. With the likelihood that Braun will walk away without consequences."

"Are we Martinieres? Or are we afraid of our own shadows?" Louisa said, a grim note in her voice. "Papa was shot. They tried again. Thank God it didn't succeed."

"Innocents would have died along with Gabe, Angelica, Saul, and me, if it hadn't been for the Saldivar who defused that bomb." Ruby said.

"Then *they shall pay*," Louisa said.

His *gentler* sister was supportive. That said a lot.

Gabe looked around. His mother buried her head in her hands. But Ron and Ruth, Justine and Donald, and Louisa and Remy all steadily met his gaze, each nodding as he looked at them.

He exhaled. "All right, then. As Shakespeare said, 'Cry 'Havoc!', and let slip the dogs of war.' Corporate war. Highest security, every-one. Mama, Remy, I'm doubling security for you since you're off the place the most. Ruby's jammer microdrones are mandatory for anyone going off-site. *Be careful.* Everyone. I—want all of us alive to celebrate Family Christmas in Paris this year."

Gabe managed to make it upstairs to their office and bedroom despite his roiling gut. He was able to send the confirmation to Piotr and *that memo* to the Board before he dashed into the bathroom and puked up his breakfast.

Ruby joined him. After they cleaned up, they rocked back on their heels, studying each other.

"I hope decisions like this never get easier," he finally said.

She nodded, and rested her hand on his.

RUBY

To Ruby's surprise, Gabe's pronouncement of corporate war didn't bring about the biggest changes in her life.

The presence of her mother-in-law, and Ruby's growing awareness of what it meant to be *the Martiniere's wife* did that, as they progressed through the last part of June and settled into new routines at the Double R.

The first of these changes started with Justine and Donald's drastically altered wedding ceremony. Angelica's presence at the ranch set planning for the revised event into high gear.

"This is your home," Angelica said to Granma, the second day after settling in. "Is it an imposition to plan a small gathering for Justine and Donald's wedding here? Gabie and Ruby's ceremony was simple, but very sweet and well done. And safe. Saul should be out of the hospital by then. It would certainly ease my mind if he didn't have to travel, even to Mist Knoll. He missed Gabie's wedding. I'd hate to see him miss another one."

Granma tucked her chin into her chest to hide her broad smile.

"It was as much the girls as anyone else that made Ruby and Gabe's wedding what it was, Angelica."

"The girls told me that you said, *what plans do we have to make Ruby and Gabe's wedding special?* And then made it happen. With two days to prepare. We have six weeks to get ready for Justine and Donald's wedding."

"How big do you think it will be?"

Ruby recognized that joyful expression on Granma's face. Granma had always enjoyed planning celebrations. With the exception of Ruby's Miss Rodeo Oregon crowning, the last few years had offered few opportunities for events to happen.

Until the Martinieres came into their lives.

A good thing. Something to keep her grandmother engaged with life and happy.

But then, Granma had always wanted to preside over a house filled with family. Ruby had heard her talk about it many times. The battlefield deaths of the uncles Ruby had never known dashed those hopes. So to have Gabe, his sisters, and his parents, at the Double R, with the need to coordinate schedules and find places for people to stay—that *had* to satisfy Granma's longing to have family around her.

OTHER THINGS KEPT RUBY BUSY FROM THE TIME SHE OPENED her eyes until she fell into bed next to Gabe. Daily conferences with the various Martiniere Group lab leaders. Working with another microdrone designer in Calgary to improve and refine the microdrone portable jammers.

Testing the microdrone jammers' screening ability.

Those tests were *fun*.

During ragingly hot nights, Ruby, Gabe, Donald, Justine, Remy, and Louisa took a picnic dinner, several bottles of wine, the jammers, and attack drones out to the shooting range. Then they activated the jammers to protect themselves before waging all-out laser drone battles, first individually, then in groups. Ruby periodically halted everything to take revision notes.

That is, when they weren't laughing. Gabe and Justine did some of the craziest stunts with the attack drones in attempts to one-up each other, though Remy could sometimes surprise them.

As dark fell, they collapsed onto blankets, eating and drinking, joking and teasing. No fires—the heat dome had dried out foliage not protected by irrigation or Ruby's biobots. A battery lantern provided enough light to eat by. Then someone—usually her—switched off the lantern and the couples settled together, waiting for the night to cool. Sometimes napping. More often, star-gazing and looking for meteors. Gabe or Justine or Louisa told stories from Martiniere family history, old lore that had been passed down through generations.

Soon enough, fatigue took over and they drowsed under the stars, waiting for the temperatures to cool, usually around midnight. Then they cruised back to the main ranch in the UTVs, tiptoeing up the stairs so they wouldn't waken the elders.

"So this is what having siblings is like," she murmured one night.

Gabe chuckled. "The good part. We also fight as hard as we play and tease. Just not as often, thankfully."

Ranch chores. Fighting the heat dome required as many hands as possible for mitigation measures to save the grain and hay crops. Ruby ran the 3D printer ragged, in consultation with the Martiniere Group labs, doing her best to whip up different micro-drone biobots to carry the microbials Gabe created that might help with water uptake and heat resistance.

"Be glad when we have a regular lab to do this in," Gabe muttered at one point, while working in the makeshift basement facility they rigged up. "This setup makes me nervous as hell. The biosecurity sucks."

CLOTHING. ANGELICA ORGANIZED A VISIT FROM A TAILOR, TO prepare outfits for Justine's wedding that would be appropriate for an outside ceremony in hot weather. Then Gabe ducked into one of Ruby's fittings for the dress she was wearing to the wedding. It was an absolutely gorgeous, lightweight, emerald and lapis-shaded fitted sheath dress with a wispy cape of bulletproof sun protective materials that flowed just right, and made her feel ready to step out on a red carpet or fashion show runway.

"Time for you to get some bespoke outfits, Ruby. Not just for formal occasions." He smiled. "I love this dress on you."

"These colors work splendidly for Ruby," Mark the tailor said.

Ruby eyed Gabe. "Professional wear as well?"

"Professional and casual attire. A couple of suits—skirts and slacks both. Casual—think lightweight pieces for business occasions. Everything should be in materials that travel well, in protective fabrics."

Ruby cocked her head while holding the rest of her body still— she remembered fittings for her rodeo queen competition clothing. "What about some of my queen outfits? Updating some pieces? That includes business casual wear."

"Possibilities," Mark said. "We'd have to see them, right Katrina?" he asked the other tailor, who was reviewing designs with Angelica.

"I'll bring some down when we're done here," Ruby said.

To her pleasant surprise, when they saw what Ruby had, Mark and Katrina were excited about the prospect of updating her outfits.

"Unique," Mark said.

"This gives me ideas for designs exclusive to you," Katrina said.

RUBY HAD MARTINIERE RESPONSIBILITIES ABOVE AND BEYOND her role in Gabe's cabinet. They included substituting for Gabe in meetings when he had schedule conflicts. Helping Angelica with coordinating both wedding plans and the remodeling of the manager's house to accommodate Saul's needs. Coordinating media opportunities with Louisa.

Visits to Saul. There was a regular rotation among the siblings to keep from tiring Saul with too many visitors all at once. Angelica spent the afternoons with Saul while Gabe, Louisa, and Justine's visits were much shorter. Ruby covered for Gabe, when he couldn't get away from his duties as the Martiniere.

Gabe decreed that every finalist for the Martiniere Grant would be awarded a Grant this year. He and Ruby called the finalists while Louisa recorded the calls, then sent them to the main Martiniere Group PR division for release.

Ruby worked with Arthur and Gerard to recruit selected finalists for the labs, including Gabe's other candidate, Jeff Swait.

Gabe integrated Ruby more and more into his daily updates—not just the labs, but the day-to-day operation of the Martiniere Group.

"Mama wasn't this active in the Group, because her skills lay in other areas," he said one morning. "But my dearest nerd girl—I need your opinions. You are closest to my heart. You chose to take the risk of being associated with my most dangerous decision—you need to know what is happening. If you tell me to stop, then—I'll stop."

"I appreciate that." Ruby frowned, thinking. "One thing I don't understand—Piotr's not talking about our actions against Zingter and the Brauns. I would have thought that would be settled right away. Or is it just that difficult to implement?"

"It's a matter of timing. For the Brauns, it's a matter of catching them both in the same location, or having teams ready to act simultaneously. And—" a long, studied pause, as Gabe intertwined his fingers, lips tight. "Donald has implemented the purchase program, and is inserting the necessary predecessors for our cyberattacks. Right now, that work has to be stealthy."

"I see." Ruby folded her hands, resting them in her lap.

"These things take time. I'm hoping that it will be settled, one way or another, by August." Gabe ran his fingers through his hair, straightening it out—he had been letting it grow longer, which meant it curled and tangled more easily. "But the security lockdown could go longer. What do you think about joining Justine and Donald at Mist Knoll for the school year?"

"It depends on how they feel about having us around."

"It's a big enough house that we would have more privacy than here, and we could keep the horses on site. There's a small indoor arena." Gabe chewed his lip thoughtfully. "One reason I'm not in a hurry to buy any property is that I'm not certain what Mama and Saul want to do yet. And then there's your grandparents to consider."

"Saul has at least another six months of physical therapy ahead, so that's how long he and Angelica will most likely be at the ranch." She had been part of *that* update yesterday. "And, thanks to your money, Gramps and Granma have support whether I'm here or not—which is huge. It opens up more possibilities."

"We *could* take over the Los Angeles house after you graduate. Or we return to the Double R. Or something else entirely."

Ruby contemplated the possibilities. *Did* she want to relocate to LA?

"I have to think about it, Gabe. I don't know how much longer Granma has—or Gramps, for that matter." Her voice went low and she swallowed hard.

"I understand." His voice softened as well. "Do you think having all of us here is too much for Ruth?"

"She thrives on the company. She's actually perked up since she has all of us to manage and supervise."

His mouth quirked into a quick smile. "And Mama, too. It depends on how well Saul settles at the ranch as to whether they finish his physical therapy sessions here or in LA. I'd really like it if they decided to stay here, but—" He shrugged.

"It might be nice to work in the LA labs," Ruby admitted. "That thought is tempting."

"There's also Calgary—or Paris."

Paris.

Ruby gulped. The Eiffel Tower. The Louvre. And within a decent distance—the old Saumur Cavalry School and the Cadre Noir. One of the foundations of dressage tradition.

Gabe grinned. "I see that light in your eyes, Ruby. I promise that you will spend plenty of time in Paris. In Europe, period, once it's safe." He rolled his chair over and took her hand. "Every December, for certain. Then you'll *really* find out what it means to be a Martiniere and married into the nobility, such as we are these days." He chuckled. "I'll take you by some graves. Palaces. Places of significance to the Martinieres—and oh! That also includes Italy. We mustn't forget the Medici and Borgia ancestors, either. But yes. Europe is in your future. The Winter Gala at the Spanish Riding School in Vienna. Saumur. And more. An equestrienne's dream."

She saw that light in *Gabe's* eyes when he talked about Europe.

Is that where he really wants to be?

For that matter, where *did* she want to be? Getting her degree in ag robotics had been a means to escape Thunder County.

Yet here she was, tied down to the ranch even more than before.

Was that what she *really* wanted?

Ruby had dreamed about leaving the ranch. About traveling. Nothing like Gabe was promising her, however. But would they ever be safe enough to do that?

"Hey." Gabe slid closer and cupped her cheek in his hand. "I made a promise to your grandmother the first time we met. She asked me to help you soar. To give you a future beyond Thunder County." He bent over and kissed her. "It will happen, Ruby. Whether it's here, Los Angeles, Corvallis, or Europe, we'll have our own home. Have faith. *It will happen.* I will move heaven and earth to make it so."

How was it that her bestest nerd boy could read her thoughts?

NEW MODULAR HOUSING FOR SECURITY, OFFICES, AND THE beginnings of a lab arrived on the ranch by the end of June. Louisa yelped with joy and claimed one of the spaces in the office trailer for her PR studio. While Ruby and Gabe kept their office on the third floor, they enlisted help to move the makeshift microbial lab out of the basement and the 3D printer out of their upstairs office.

"It's not much, compared to the regular research and development facilities," Gabe said when they were done moving the lab equipment. He put one arm around Ruby's shoulders, kissing her temple. "But we now have a decent, biosecure, field lab."

"It's a nicer setup than I ever expected to see on the ranch."

"Oh, I intend to spoil you with access to much, much better labs," Gabe crooned. "Only the best for my dearest nerd girl."

***

JULY, 2029

SAUL LEFT THE HOSPITAL THE SECOND WEEK IN JULY, ONE WEEK before the final repairs were finished on the manager's house. Gabe marched around the living room while they waited for him to arrive. Ruby wrapped her arms around herself as she leaned against the hallway entrance, watching Gabe, wanting to hold him but—by now she had learned not to restrict his movement when he paced like this. Justine tapped her fingertips against her chair's arms and Louisa clenched her hands together. Donald held Justine's other hand. Remy wrapped her arms around Louisa.

Why are they so tense? Anticipation—or something else?

"There they are." Gabe halted, peering out the window. Then he bolted for the front door, Louisa and Justine right behind him. Ruby met Remy and Donald's gaze, and shrugged. They followed Gabe and his sisters, remaining at a distance as staff helped Saul out of the medical transport, seating him in a wheelchair.

Gabe moved to take command of the wheelchair, but Angelica shook her head. Mother and son glared at each other before Gabe stepped back. He leaned over to say something to Saul. When he straightened up, first Louisa, then Justine hugged Saul. Angelica then pointedly took control of the chair.

Some dynamic is going on here that I'm not aware of.

Despite hurried work to level the concrete pathway leading around to the front of the house, where a ramp had been erected for Granma, the walk was still rough. When Angelica struggled with the chair as Gabe, Justine, and Louisa hovered—*so why didn't they get a motorized one?*—Ruby bit her lip, until Gabe stepped forward.

"Let me help, Mama. *Please.*"

"Angel. Gabie." Saul's voice was tired. "Both of you. *Stop it.*" He exhaled. "Ruby? Ruth says you give a pretty good ride."

"I *do* know the quirks of this path," Ruby said, wondering *just when* Saul and Granma had talked. She stepped up to the wheelchair. Angelica and Gabe moved aside. "No matter what you do, there's this little slant, and that little jog—the land keeps settling underneath. And other things."

Even though Saul was heavier than Granma, Ruby pushed him along with less effort than Angelica.

"There's a rise you're not aware of," she said to Gabe and Angelica. "It's very subtle but enough to slow you down. And the least wind blows dust into that corner. Just have to learn the feel." They approached the ramp. Ruby took a deep breath, then aligned the wheelchair. "Works good for a motorized chair. I'd recommend that for outside, rather than this one."

Saul grumbled wordlessly. Gabe rolled his eyes.

Aha. There's the catch. Saul objects. Words have been said that I don't know about.

Ruby stifled a sigh. Another Martiniere she needed to manage. "Motorized makes more sense around the ranch," she added. Then she started to shove the wheelchair up the ramp. Gabe came up behind her, and when she slowed, reached around and helped her push.

Once they were on the porch, Ruby stepped in front of Saul, her hands on her hips. Maybe the others would dance around him, but *she* wouldn't.

"So what's your problem with a motorized chair?" she challenged.

"I'm not *that* disabled!"

Saul might not be Gabe's biofather, but Ruby *certainly* recognized that glower. She'd seen it on Louisa and Justine as well as Gabe.

"It's not a question of degree of disability," she said. "It's ease of access. Granma uses a wheelchair inside—" she gestured at Saul's chair. "But outside? A nice little motorized scooter like this when she needs it." Ruby backed up and pulled the cover off of Granma's scooter. "If you ask Granma right, she might let you try it out, Saul. Gives you independence—at least that's what she says."

"I'm *not that disabled.*"

She matched his glare. "I repeat, it's about ease of access. Once you and Angelica are in the little house, a motorized scooter for outside will simplify everything."

Saul growled. "Why is everyone trying to push me into a motorized chair?"

"Independence. You'll also be less of a hindrance in an emergency. If we have to move fast—like say, in case of a fire, which *can* happen, either here or in Los Angeles—your being able to move independently can make a difference." She didn't look away as Saul's scowl deepened. "Ask my grandmother. We have needed to have her independently mobile in the past."

They frowned at each other until Saul looked away. "I'll think about it."

"It's a safety issue."

Gabe rested his hand on her shoulder, his back to Saul. She looked up at him. *Enough,* his lips formed.

Her lips tightened in response, and Gabe bent to kiss her. "Don't push further," he whispered in her ear. "You've made your point. Papa's gotta think about it."

Stubborn men.

Any further comment was forestalled by Gramps opening the door. "Come on in, it's cooler inside."

Ruby and Gabe lingered on the porch.

"Thanks for your input," Gabe said softly. "He's been really grouchy the last few days. Snapping at all of us."

"What's that bit from your mother about you feeling guilty?"

Gabe ran his fingers through his hair. "Well, if it wasn't for my sperm donor—"

"And you have no control over him or responsibility for him."

"True. But maybe if I had handled things better in the past, Philip might not have felt the necessity to align with Braun."

She tapped his nose—one of their recently devised signals that he was falling into a problematic behavior pattern. "*Stop that*, Gabriel. You didn't have a lot of choice, and *you are not responsible for Philip.* Even if you are Head of Family and the Martiniere."

"Ah, Rubes." Gabe wrapped his arms around her. "What would I do—what would *we* do—without you?"

"It looks like *somebody* needs to kick butts in the Family, and that somebody is me." She paused. "Unless you think I'm over-stepping."

"No. I think you said exactly what was needed. Bring it up to him later, but give him time to think first."

"Just like I have to do with you sometimes."

Gabe laughed. "Oh, Ruby. Thank you for being part of my life. For saying what was needed. Mama wasn't in favor of a motorized chair—scooter—whatever, because of what it means for Papa's future mobility. Tine, Weeza, and I have been advocating for it, and—well, there's been some arguments."

"I *thought* everyone was being tense."

"Yeah. Both of them are having difficulties." He sighed. "I wasn't sure if I should bring you into those discussions. Obviously, I should have."

"Should I mention it to Granma? We went through similar agonizing with her. That's where I got the independence and freedom argument."

"If you think it would help." Gabe half-grinned. "Ruth has me twisted around her little finger. Won't take her long to do the same with Papa."

"Then I will."

Granma could be quite persuasive without being confrontational, as Ruby knew, far too well.

A SECOND SCOOTER APPEARED AT THE RANCH TWO DAYS LATER, without anything further being said, to Ruby's knowledge. It wasn't long before Saul was zipping around outside, supervising the final touches on the manager's house along with Angelica, and otherwise enjoying the freedom of being out on his own instead of locked inside or needing help manipulating the wheelchair.

Ruby was in the garden, finishing the harvest of the last of her chard crop before it bolted to seed, when Saul pulled up beside the fence.

"Ruby." His tone was serious, but he smiled at her as she stood.

"Saul."

"Thanks for the advice. You were right." He patted the handlebar of his scooter. "Freedom. Independence. And you had the guts to confront me about it."

"You're welcome."

Her father-in-law smirked. "If you're keeping this tight a rein on Gabriel's behavior—which appears to be the case—thank you for that as well. He's not as obsessed about proving that he's not like Philip as he used to be. And he's pacing himself better."

So this was going to be one of *those* talks? Ruby picked up her harvest basket and left the garden, securing the gate.

"I've seen what happens with people prone to working themselves to death, like I said before." She leaned against the gatepost, waiting for Saul to continue.

"It's not just that. Supporting Gabriel in that decision to assassinate the Brauns—I never could have made that choice, no matter how necessary. Being a part of the interview with Joey." Saul rubbed his chin. He had started to grow out a gray-streaked beard. "I've watched you and Gabie over the last couple of days. What you two have gone through since April would devastate a lot of couples starting a relationship. Instead, it's drawn you together."

Ruby looked down at her hands, then back up. "Despite our different financial backgrounds, we have a lot in common. Gabe has a lot of good ideas, and I want to see them happen. And he thinks that I have good ideas as well."

"I've been worried about Gabie for a long time," Saul said quietly. "Now, I'm not. And talking to your grandmother—you two are good for each other. I think—the two of you will soar high, much higher than the two of you separately would have."

She didn't know what to say to that, but looked down at her hands again.

"Thank you. You and Gabe will fix the problems that I could never solve."

"You're welcome." Ruby pushed herself off of the post. "Shall we head back to the house? It's almost time for dinner."

Saul peered into her basket as she stood next to him. "Will we be eating some of those greens?"

"Yes. Last of this batch, until it cools down."

She and Saul talked gardening the rest of the way to the house. It sounded like Saul wanted to try his hand at it.

That suggested the senior Martinieres might be interested in settling down at the Double R.

Now I just need to decide if I like the Los Angeles house well enough to live there.

Ruby would have to see it without the barriers before she made up her mind. And consider the possibility that she and Gabe might have to *live* behind them.

Not just for his mental health, but for hers.

CHAPTER 23
RAISING THE ANTE
JULY, 2029

GABE

GABE FRETTED ABOUT HIS PARENTS MOVING OUT OF THE MAIN ranch house. What if something went wrong? If someone attacked the houses? How could he ensure that Mama and Papa were safe? Or have help if Saul had a medical problem?

Being foolish, Gabriel. There will be security at that house as well as nurses.

He had to tell himself that over and over. The little house was as safe as the big ranch house—safer than the one in Los Angeles, really.

All the same, he worried, and spent extra time scrutinizing everything. The evening that his parents moved into the house, Gabe stomped up and down the ramp leading to the front porch to make sure it was stable. Measured the doorways to ensure Saul's wheelchair would fit. Checked the door handles—levers instead of knobs. Tested the security screens. Surveyed the heating and cooling systems, even though the AC pumped out cooling air. Then repeated each check.

Ruby leaned against the kitchen counter after his third round, arms crossed, arching one brow.

"Think you've done enough inspecting?"

"Just wanting to confirm it's set up right." He made another circle of the large room that made up the kitchen, dining area, and living room, then paused by the big window that looked toward the Thunder Mountains, large enough for both a rocking chair and Saul's wheelchair. He pulled out his phone to check the connectivity. Again.

"Gabe. It's *fine*. You're fretting."

"I just want them to be comfortable and safe." He put his phone away and ran his fingers through his hair.

"You're as fussy as a cowdog without something to herd." That eyebrow arched higher. "Look. They'll be happy to be here by themselves—or as much as they can be, with security and nurses around. And they aren't that far from us. Less than a five-minute walk!"

"Your grandparents will probably be glad to have their space back," he conceded.

Ron and Ruth had gone above and beyond what was needed. Even so—one reason the Los Angeles house was so big was to give him and his sisters suites of their own. Surprising that no one's temper had erupted at the Double R yet, given the close quarters they were living in. Much as he and his sisters loved Saul and Angelica, having them underfoot could be trying at times now that they were adults and not teens. This little house *was* the best option if he wanted to keep his parents on the Double R.

But that didn't mean he couldn't be worried about them.

"Here they come." Ruby turned to look out the kitchen window toward the main house. "Along with everyone else."

Gabe joined her. Security had helped move Saul and Angelica's things earlier. It looked like more items were being brought over—how could they have missed that much stuff? Then he realized the others carried serving dishes, plates, cups, and utensils.

He and Ruby went out on the new front porch. It was big enough for Saul's scooter, a swing, and space for people to sit. Ruby's idea.

Gabe unfolded the wheelchair while Saul ran his scooter up the porch ramp. He would have helped Saul transfer over, but Saul shook his head.

"I have it, Gabie."

The process was slow, and both Gabe and Angelica bit their lips. Ruby stood guard, ready to assist, as Saul carefully moved from scooter to wheelchair. For some reason, Saul would accept help from Ruby when he wouldn't from anyone else. A father-in-law, daughter-in-law thing, or because Ruby had called Saul out on the scooter issue?

"All right!" Saul rubbed his hands when he was settled in the wheelchair. "Ruth suggested we eat dinner here tonight to celebrate. I can't think of a better thing to do. Come on in, everyone."

Gabe noticed that the serving dishes contained more than enough food for dinner—leftovers for his parents to have?

Ruby hung back as the others settled their dishes and plates on the table.

"Looks like there might be enough for a couple of meals when we're done," she murmured to Gabe. "Pretty typical for what Granma coordinates in a situation like this."

"I'm amazed."

She shrugged. "Normal behavior for Thunder County. Granma used to be known as the person to go to when there was a need. Trust me, she's thrilled, because she hasn't been able to do this for some time."

After dinner, his sisters, Remy, and Ruby bustled about cleaning up and putting things away. Ron and Ruth returned to the main house. Gabe and Donald were shooed away to keep Saul company on the front porch as the sun set, while Angelica helped the night nurse arrange Saul's things in the bedroom.

Saul gazed at the mountains. "A man could get used to this view."

"Think you're staying at the Double R?" Gabe asked.

"Until I'm steadier on my feet," Saul said. "The ranch feels like a pretty good place to hide out and after this—" he gestured to his head. "I'm like a grouchy old bear who wants to retreat to a nice safe cave. Keep my head down, lick my wounds, and recover. As much as I can, anyway."

"You'll be back to yourself soon, Papa." His words sounded like false assurance, even to him.

Saul shook his head, a rueful smile twisting his lips. "You're permanently the Martiniere, Gabriel. While my speech has come back, I can't think fast enough to do the job right now, even if your mother would let me."

And Mama has made it clear that won't happen.

"At least you can advise me," Gabe persisted.

"You have an excellent cabinet of advisors, including your lovely wife." Saul leaned back in the wheelchair. "And, honestly? I think you're better suited to battle Philip and the Brauns than I am." He coughed. "You're younger and you have the strength to deal with the bullshit."

"I appreciate the confidence, Papa."

But Gabe still didn't feel like he was better suited to deal with this situation.

Would that ever change? He didn't know.

Two days later, a message from Walter Braun with a video attached popped up on Gabe's public phone number. He called in Donald and Ruby before he played it, turning the file over to them to search for viruses.

Ruby and Donald conferred, using several tools to check the video.

"It's clear," Ruby finally said.

"Run it." Gabe tensed. What the hell would Braun send to him?

Braun's face was bloody and bruised, and when he opened his mouth, several teeth were missing.

"*Martiniere,*" Braun snarled. "You *God damn motherfucker.* Frank's dead and it's only by the grace of God that I escaped your fucking assassination team." He brandished an index finger. "You think you've been under attack before now? Let me tell you this. You are only making your father stronger, because, by God, I am throwing all of my resources into backing Philip Martiniere, whether I live or die. In particular, you have just incurred the wrath of Frank's wife Vera." He drew a deep, shuddering breath. "My death won't end this. Vera will. *You personally will fucking pay*, and my instrument of vengeance will be *your own God damned biological father*. Damn you to hell. I'll see you there, motherfucker!"

The video ended. Gabe forwarded it to Piotr. Donald pressed his lips together.

Ruby paled, her freckles standing out sharply. "Now what?"

"I'm showing this to Justine." Donald's lips thinned even tighter. "And talking to my mother. It's fucking time that Braun and Philip learn that you and the Martinieres aren't alone, Gabriel. Mother has wanted to move against Philip, but I've held her back until now. And if that motherfucker decides to interfere with our wedding or attack you—well, he'll learn that the Atwoods aren't people to fuck around with."

Gabe startled. Donald *rarely* swore this freely.

Ruby looked from Gabe to Donald and back again. Before she could speak, Gabe's phone chimed again—Piotr. He put it on speaker.

"The team has traced Braun's location in Moldovia, and is moving in," Piotr said curtly. "Waiting for confirmation regarding success or failure of the second attempt."

"How serious is that threat he made?" Ruby asked.

"Vera Braun has ties to the Russian mafiya," Piotr said. "She is a distant Vygotsky cousin. Young, well-trained. She was alleged to be estranged from Frank Braun about the time of Philip's disappearance.

She managed Philip's escape to North Africa and then Europe. She is a very serious threat, indeed."

"Have the Saldivars been informed of this alliance?" Gabe swallowed hard.

Piotr paused. He exchanged some words in swift Russian with someone off-screen—Gabe understood, but it was clear that neither Ruby nor Donald did.

Braun's dead.

He responded in Russian. "Piotr. Is this sufficient cause to unite your Martiniere team with the Saldivars in the pursuit of Philip?"

Ruby raised her brows questioningly.

"I would not recommend direct action by our team against Philip." Piotr continued in Russian. "We will assist the Saldivars, but to act against Philip ourselves will be problematic."

"Understood. Keep me apprised of the situation."

"I will. And be careful, Gabriel!" Piotr signed off.

Another deep breath, as both Donald and Ruby gave Gabe inquisitive looks.

"Braun is dead," Gabe said.

When he didn't say more, Ruby frowned at him. "Those were an awful lot of words just to tell you that Braun is dead, Gabriel. I don't know much about the Russian language, but I don't think death is *that* complicated to explain."

She had him. Gabe sighed.

"I asked Piotr if the Martiniere team should join with the Saldivars. He didn't recommend it."

"I see." Her frown deepened.

"I'll talk to Mother," Donald said. "There will be both Atwood and Martiniere security at Mist Knoll and in Quebec."

"I'll talk to Donna-gran," Gabe said. Given that it was hurricane season at Barbie Atwood's Solitaire Island, Justine and Donald had settled on Donna-gran's Quebec estate for their honeymoon.

Fine for them—but, while Gabe loved his grandmother, her role in enabling Philip's behavior until it was too late to stop him still stirred resentment. Oh, she had tried often enough to make it up to Gabe after he left Philip's household. Her outreach to Ruby suggested that their first in-person meeting at Justine and Donald's wedding would go well.

But he didn't consider Quebec to be a safe location for him and Ruby. Amongst other things, he and Ruby didn't have Barbie Atwood and her extended family as nearby resources.

Donald did—and Barbie Atwood would do anything to avenge her son and his wife if something happened. She was a distant cousin of the British royal family. Gabe suspected that Barbie's connections with the British security establishment went much deeper than he really wanted to know.

On the other hand, those connections could end up being *very* useful.

THE EARLY MORNING SCHOOLING RIDES WERE USUALLY JUST Gabe and Ruby now. Justine was buried in the details of wedding planning and setting up Mist Knoll. Ruby added Glory to her morning ride rotation, and they started spending time on the cross-country course.

Gabe thrilled at the sight of his dearest nerd girl on a horse as advanced as Glory. While the other two advanced horses—Stella and Reliant—were good, compared to Glory they were still novices over the solid jumps.

"Ever thought about competing?" he asked one morning, after she had completed the entire course on Glory, face flushed with happy excitement.

Ruby laughed and rubbed Glory's neck. "Oh Gabe. I don't have the time."

"You're good." Donna-gran would be drooling over Ruby's ability.

She shook her head. "I have to choose because, even with our money, I don't have time to do it all. The labs, school, and the Group come first. Right now, riding is more for fun."

He sidepassed Midnight over and rested his hand on hers. "Rubes. If you really want to do it—"

"I appreciate the thought, Gabe. But dealing with the bots comes first. And, given the state of our current security, neither eventing nor big horse shows are particularly safe."

His dearest nerd girl. Even though he understood her decision, her choice spurred regrets. She could be so stunning in a show ring.

If that ever became her choice, Gabe would do whatever it took to make it happen.

The next threatening video arrived via email, four days before Justine and Donald's wedding. An anonymous sender, and the heading read *ignore this at your own risk, ignorant sprog.*

Philip had sneered *ignorant sprog* at Gabe enough times that he had no doubt about the video's origin. Gabe's gut clenched tight as he stared at the email.

"Rubes." He fought to keep his voice noncommittal.

She looked up from her work. "What's wrong?"

"Philip has sent me a video."

Her lips tightened and she rolled her chair over. "Done the virus check?"

He nodded, but moved back so Ruby could perform her own scans.

"All clear," she said finally. "Hit play?"

"Yeah." He fumbled for her hand and held it tight as the video began.

Philip reclined in a big overstuffed chair. Vera Braun perched on the chair's arm, languidly resting one arm across Philip's shoulders.

"So, my ignorant sprog," Philip taunted.

Ruby tightened her grip on Gabe's hand. He spared a moment to glance over at her. Ruby's face was tight and hard.

"You've managed to kill both Walter and Frank," Philip continued. "Good for you. It makes things easier for me, because when *we* come for you—" he smirked up at Vera. She kissed him. "I will become the Martiniere without having to compromise myself with Zingter Enterprises."

"None of your precautions will keep you safe, *Martiniere,*" Vera sneered. She shifted to Russian. "Ask your dear Piotr Vygotsky about what I can do and who my connections are, if you haven't already. You and your wife *will pay* for the death of my husband and father-in-law."

"If you want to limit damage to the two of you, then this is what you will do." Philip raised one hand and began to count off on his fingers. "First. Resign your position as the Martiniere, and have David resign as Martiniere-in-waiting. No current Martiniere in a position of power—not David, not my useless brother Gerry, not any of the other cowards in the Family—will be allowed to hold a leadership position within the Group. Second. Turn that craven little shit Joseph over to me. Third. You, your wife, and Joseph will meet us at a place we determine. Come willingly, and your deaths will be quick. Refuse, and we will make your dying drawn out and very, very unpleasant. The Family will also pay for your lack of cooperation."

A pause, while Vera bent to kiss Philip again.

"You have twenty-four hours to respond to this email address, my ignorant, feckless sprog. Don't bother tracing the IP address, because you can't. If you say no, or don't respond—then the carnage begins."

The video ended.

"That motherfucker," Ruby growled. "That fucking asshole."

Gabe routed a copy of the video to Piotr.

"Do we tell Justine and Donald?"

"Not until we talk to your parents," Ruby said. "I am not going to let that prick interfere with Justine's wedding unless it is completely necessary."

"Then let's talk to Mama and Papa *now*," Gabe said. "And add Barbie Atwood to the discussion list."

"All right."

He forwarded a copy to Barbie, with a note that he was talking to Saul and Angelica as soon as possible. Then, with a deep sigh, he sent it to his parents as well.

***

"So Philip thinks he has the upper hand," Saul said as they entered the little house. He was in his wheelchair by the window; Angelica next to him in the rocking chair. Gabe and Ruby sat on the couch, his hand clutching his dearest nerd girl's. "What is Piotr's assessment?"

"I haven't heard from Piotr yet. Or Barbie." His phone chimed. Gabe glanced at it. "There's Barbie." He put the phone on speaker. "Barbie. Ruby and I are with Saul and Angelica."

"Well, isn't Philip one arrogant son-of-a-bitch?" Barbie's voice was sharp. "What are the plans for wedding security?"

Gabe took a deep breath. "We have very strong drone jammers at the ranch, including Ruby's new portable designs. I've increased security here as well as at Donna-gran's house. I've spoken to the Saldivars, and they're increasing their efforts." He rubbed his face. "One issue is that Vera Braun is associated with the Russian mafiya. The Saldivars don't possess the same firepower."

"I see." Barbie fell silent for a moment. "Have you talked to Piotr Vygotsky?"

"I'm surprised that I haven't heard from him yet. I sent him a copy of that video."

"Give me some time to talk to my connections," Barbie said. "I've already reached out after speaking to Donald, but had them hold off from doing more than protecting Mist Knoll and Donna's estate. Shall I network with the Saldivars, or with Martiniere security?"

"Martiniere security, please. Piotr is trying to keep Martiniere security separate from the Saldivars."

"Then that will be done." Another pause. "I'll be at your ranch tomorrow. Are we telling Donald and Justine about this latest threat?"

"Not yet," Gabe said quickly. "Let's simply raise security to as high a level as possible, until after I hear from Piotr."

"All right. See you tomorrow. I'll bring a full complement of Atwood security."

"Thank you," Gabe said. He leaned back on the couch, pinching the bridge of his nose again. Damn headache. Again. "Papa. This is one hell of a mess."

"That it is, son. But you can handle it. What are you planning to do?"

Gabe snorted. "I do not intend to dignify that video with a response. My fucking sperm donor is trying to get under my skin. I refuse to let him intimidate me. Nor will I let him screw up Tine's wedding."

"Are you *sure* we shouldn't tell Justine and Donald about this latest threat?" His mother started to stand up.

"*No.*" Ruby's voice was low and firm as she rose. "It's four days until the ceremony. Justine will want to scale things down even more —and damn it, she's already sacrificed a lot."

"Rubes, we were in the same situation—"

"No." Ruby started pacing. "We weren't engaged for a year before the ceremony, with big plans for a celebration, like Justine and Donald have been. Justine's not going to say anything if we have to change plans, *again*. But I've heard her talk. Having a nice ceremony *matters* to her, more than it did for me. I *had* the wedding I wanted, because I married my bestest nerd boy, who has opened up the world for me in ways I could never imagine."

"Ruby—"

She raised her hand to cut him off. "How likely is it that your fucking biofather can pull shit together, enough to attack us here, in four days?"

"With Vera's help, it's entirely possible," Saul said.

"Then we need to put him off his balance."

Gabe stared at Ruby. Was she crazy? "Just how do you propose we do that?"

"*You* may not dignify that video with a response." Ruby drew a deep breath, clenching her fists and raising her chin. "But *I* sure as hell can. And I *will*. The chickenshit bastard wants to threaten you with that bitch and her Russian mafiya connections? He is one God damned fucking coward, and I will call him out on that. If he wants to hurt us, to kill us, then he can at least manage to have the balls to do it himself, looking at our God damned faces, *like my fucking father did to me.*"

Her fists tightened even more, her chin quavered a little, and he saw moisture at the corner of her eyes—but there was no mistaking Ruby's barely contained fury.

"That might just work," Saul said. "Though he'll probably think Gabriel's hiding behind your skirts."

"Oh, I'll deal with that." Ruby's mouth quirked. "I have a plan."

"How are we going to video the response? If we do it in the office or the house, someone's likely to overhear." God. This was just insane enough that it might be effective. Especially if Saul thought so.

"We'll do it here," Ruby said. "Right now." She glanced around the room, then pointed at the rocker. "Move that to the wall, so he can't identify the location easily. Take down the pictures. As few distractions as possible."

She crossed her arms. Gabe grabbed the rocker while his mother removed the pictures. Ruby got a drink of water, inhaled sharply, then exhaled.

"All right, then. Are you ready to film this, Gabe?"

"As soon as you are."

Ruby settled in the rocker. She rested her forearms on the chair's arms, leaving her hands open and relaxed. Another deep, shuddering breath as she looked down at her lap. Then she raised her head, and curtly nodded at Gabe.

He raised the phone and pressed the video button, giving her a thumbs up.

"Hello, Philip. I won't call you father-in-law because despite biology, you aren't my Gabriel's real father. Saul Martiniere is, and he is a *man*, not the *tiny-dicked little boy* you've proven yourself to be." Ruby's tone was artificially sweet and poisonous, matched with an icy porcelain smile that didn't move beyond her lips. It sent a chill through Gabe's guts. "Gabriel is too busy with more important duties to respond to your little video, so your answer is coming from me. Ruby Barkley Martiniere. Gabriel's wife, whose name you don't seem to remember."

She laced her fingers together, resting them in her lap.

"My, my, my." A mocking tone came into her voice. "What an inflated image you have of your power. Expecting us to walk tamely toward our deaths—what do you think we are, idiots? Or are you so self-important that you think we'll quake in our boots at your mafiya babe's threats? I may not have been a Martiniere for very long, but if there's one thing I've learned, we don't scare easily." The mockery faded. "Then again, why should I be surprised that you entertain such fantastic notions, considering what you've done to *your own biological son when he had no ability to resist?*"

Ruby leaned forward, glowering.

"So here's the score." Her voice hardened. "Our answer is *no*, to each one of those ludicrous conditions. And as for carnage, you chickenshit motherfucker—I have stared death in the face before. At the age of six, when *my* damned father beat my mother to death in front of me. Then came for me, bloody tire iron in hand. He may have been a pathetic fucking addict, but he had more integrity in the tip of his little finger than you have, because he had the balls to *do it himself*, and didn't waste time with stupid posturing and expecting me to be passive while he beat me to a pulp. He *knew* I would fight back."

Ruby straightened up.

"And oh. I killed him, *asshole*. I pointed a pistol at his face. Pulled the trigger until the gun was empty and I could see nothing but blood. I survived. So make your cowardly little threats. Hide behind your little Russian babe. Did she betray her husband? I bet she did. You're a fool to trust her."

She pointed an index finger. "But. My ancestors were gunslingers. They did what was needed to keep their families safe. More than that, I have killed in self-defense, and not because I had grandiose illusions of power. Fuck off, you sleazy motherfucker. We will not go down without a fight. And if I get the opportunity—I will put you down like the rabid, arrogant puppy that you are. That's all." She dropped her hand.

After Gabe lowered the phone, Ruby sagged from her upright position.

"I need a drink," she said.

His mother rose and went to the glass-fronted liquor cabinet, pouring Ruby a shot of good whisky.

Saul whistled. "Remind me not to get you really angry at me, Ruby. Your body language and vocal tones are a *lot* like my mother's. You made me wince—which means my brother will, as well."

Ruby took the shot glass. She tossed it back quickly.

"No more," Gabe cautioned. Ruby met his eyes and nodded, before handing the glass back to his mother.

"Thank you, Saul," Ruby said. "Do you think that response will be effective?"

"Oh, it will make Philip very angry. Hopefully, angry enough to react without thinking, so that instead of a calculated strike at Justine and Donald's wedding, he does something stupid." Saul shrugged. "We shall see."

Well, that was better than nothing.

Ruby reached for his phone. "All right. Send it now, or wait until tonight?"

"Tonight," Gabe said. "Let's drag this out as long as possible, to reduce his planning time. For Tine's sake."

Ruby nodded slowly. "For her sake."

CHAPTER 24

COUNTDOWN TO TROUBLE
AUGUST, 2029

RUBY

GABE DIDN'T RIDE ON THE MORNING OF JUSTINE AND DONALD'S wedding.

"I can't do it today, Rubes." He sat up in bed as she rose and pulled on her breeches and a tank top over her new bulletproof safety riding vest. The day already promised to be hot, even though the sun wasn't up yet. "There's too many security things for me to do as the Martiniere before the Family descends upon us. And I don't think you should ride out alone."

"I'll school in the arena." Ruby sat on the bench at the foot of their bed and pulled on her tall boots. "Maybe work Midnight over fences."

"I don't know—"

"Gabe, I have to do *something* besides fretting about what Philip might do. I'm wide awake and it's too early to do wedding prep. And I won't work before breakfast."

He scowled. "Are you going to hold *me* to that stance? Tight schedule today, and there are things happening this morning before the wedding that need my oversight. I may grab coffee and a snack, then come back upstairs."

"Just this once. Don't try it tomorrow!"

"All right," he sighed. "Be careful, will you, my love?"

"Absolutely." She kissed him, stuffed her phone in a pocket, then picked up her bootjack to leave it on the porch, so she could take the boots off before coming back inside.

Justine met her in the kitchen, also dressed in breeches, tank top, and tall boots. "Oh good. You're riding, too."

"Sure you should be riding on your wedding day?"

"Nerves," Justine said. "A nice blowout on Glory will work just fine."

Ruby grinned at her. "I promised Gabe that I'd ride in the arena, but if you're coming with me—let's hit the trail."

Justine laughed. "That sounds perfect."

"Let me tell Gabe."

"I'll tell Donald." Justine pulled out her phone while Ruby did hers.

—*Justine is riding with me,* Ruby texted Gabe. —*We're going out, not in the arena.*

—*You two be careful!!!* he sent back. —*Are you taking the portable jammers?*

—*Yes,* she responded. —*I won't break your sister on her wedding day. Promise.*

Then they replaced phones in their pockets, and went to retrieve Midnight and Glory from the field.

JUSTINE RODE LIKE A MADWOMAN WHEN THEY HAD WARMED UP the horses, sending Glory into a hard gallop along the track which eventually led to the Homestead field. Ruby followed her lead.

What's got Justine riled up? A fight with Donald?

By now, Ruby recognized this Martiniere mood—trying to get

away from personal demons. Something she had seen manifest in Gabe, Louisa, and Justine—as well as Saul.

But what could be haunting Justine on her wedding day, to the degree that the portable jammer microdrones buzzed like angry bees in their efforts to keep up?

"Let's do the course!" Justine yelled.

"You sure you want to?" Ruby called back. "It *is* your wedding day, and I promised Gabe I wouldn't break you!"

Justine didn't answer.

"God *damn* it, Justine," Ruby muttered, and urged Midnight to catch up with Glory, her own complement of jammer drones grumbling after her. "What the hell is eating at you?"

Somehow, they both made it through the course, though much faster than Ruby preferred to ride it. Especially since this was the first time that she had ridden Midnight through the whole course. Justine pulled up at the end, laughing manically.

Fuck. Is she losing it?

"What the hell is going on, Justine?" Ruby demanded as she rode alongside Justine and Glory, half-contemplating the possibility of grabbing one of Glory's reins before Justine took off again.

Justine exhaled with a big huff. "You and Gabriel have heard something from our father, haven't you?"

Ruby tensed. "What makes you say that?"

"Don't bullshit me, Ruby." Justine urged Glory on, but kept the reins long, letting Glory saunter back toward the main ranch. "I know what extreme security looks like, and this is the highest level I've ever seen it—from both Atwood and Martiniere organizations. Donald's talking to Barbie as well because we're both concerned."

"Damn it, we didn't want to fret you," Ruby sighed.

"Then you *have* heard something."

Ruby paused. *Evade?*

No, damn it. This is Justine. She'll be pissed when she finds out, if you don't tell her now.

"Philip demanded that Gabe and David resign their positions, and that Gabe, Joey, and I appear at a selected point so he could kill us. Amongst other things."

Justine flinched. "He did *what?* Good God, what kind of arrogant, motherfucking idiot is he? Don't answer that, I already know."

"Vera Braun is with him, and they claim connections to the Russian mafiya."

"Shit. Obviously, Gabriel didn't comply with his request."

Ruby mulled it over further. Then she stopped Midnight and pulled her phone out of her pocket. "This is the answer I sent him." She cued up the video Gabe had made, and handed the phone to Justine.

Her sister-in-law watched, a smile creeping up the corners of her mouth. By the time the video finished, she was grinning.

"Oh, that will piss off Daddy-fucking-dearest big time." She handed the phone back to Ruby.

"That's what Saul thought as well." Ruby saw a new email from that address. Her throat tightened.

Don't deal with it now.

"So *they* know."

"Saul and Angelica watched Gabe video it."

Justine was silent for a few minutes as they rode back down the path, her expression turning tight and tense again. "What was the intent of your response? I applaud the content of your message, but—"

"Getting Philip so angry that he'll do something stupid."

Justine's expression eased. "Well, if anything will do the job, *that* will."

"Justine—we really didn't want this to mar your wedding day. That's all. Please don't worry. Gabe is taking care of it."

"Oh, I won't be thinking about it once we start preparing for the ceremony." Her lips tightened again. "But I *will* go armed to my wedding, and make sure that Donald is, too."

"I think we're *all* going to be armed," Ruby said ruefully. "And there will be portable drone jammers, as many as we have available."

The knowledge of that unread email nagged at Ruby throughout untacking the horses and breakfast. Gabe came down to eat with the family after all, and gave her concerned looks. Ruby avoided meeting his gaze, hurrying upstairs afterward, ostensibly to shower and start dressing so that she could be part of the group of women helping Justine prepare.

She switched on her computer and opened the message with trembling fingers.

—Watch your step, bitch. We're coming for all of you. PJM.

Ruby drew a deep breath. *—Go to hell,* she typed. *—We'll be waiting with weapons loaded, motherfucker. RBM.*

She yelped as Gabe's hands on her shoulders startled her. Damn, but her husband was *sneaky.* She hadn't heard him at all.

"*Shit,*" Gabe growled as he peered past her. "When did you get this?"

"I saw the notification when I showed the video of my response to Justine." Ruby pressed *send.*

His grip tightened. "God damn him. Did Tine see this message?"

"No. I just opened it now."

"I wondered what the hell was eating at you during breakfast. Thought Tine and Don were just having pre-wedding jitters, but that didn't explain *your* edginess."

"They had figured out that we heard something from Philip. Justine talked to me; Donald to his mother."

"Damn it." Gabe stared out the window for a moment, then whirled to face her. "All right. Let's get through this wedding and send Tine and Don off to Quebec with Donna-gran. Then—fuck it. I am *tired* of sitting around and waiting for my fucking sperm donor to attack us. Weeza's been bugging me about doing high-profile television interviews as the new Martiniere. We had talked about doing them remotely, but to hell with it. Let's go to Los Angeles on Monday and do them in-studio. Should be easy enough to get them set up—much easier than remote, actually. You up for that?"

"Draw Philip away from the ranch?"

"Hopefully. At the very least, piss him off, so he gets reckless."

"I am up for that," Ruby said.

Gabe took her into his arms. "My dearest nerd girl. I bet you didn't think you were getting into a mess like this when we got involved, did you?"

"By the time you asked if that first lockdown changed things between us, I had a pretty good idea about what was going on."

"How did I ever get so damned lucky as to find you, Ruby?"

"That's a question I keep asking myself," she said. "Because—Gabe—you're the man of my dreams."

"Just as you're my perfect woman." He kissed her forehead. "We'd better start getting ready. Once the Family starts showing up in force, we'll both be busy."

Thunder County Airport must be humming.

Justine's wedding brought out more Martinieres than had been present at hers and Gabe's ceremony—and a complement of Barbie's family, the Knowleses, as well as the Atwoods. Some of *those* family members came complete with uniformed security. Ruby didn't recognize the insignia, but one group of the Knowles family arrived at the ranch by military helicopter.

Try it, Philip. Just fucking try it, Ruby thought when the helicopter landed, as she and Gabe waited inside the kitchen for him to take her to her seat. She thought she recognized the woman stepping out—military bristling around her—as a higher-up in the British Government. Barbie Atwood greeted this woman herself, the two of them exchanging air kisses. Clearly intimate. Ruby gulped.

Wow.

Gabe gave her a wry smile. "Barbie called in some family connections."

"I'm surprised we don't have paparazzi and their drones hanging around." There had been a strange lack of them after the first lockdown.

"Excluding them is a feature of high security levels. Especially considering those who shall not be named that are in attendance today—including that person." Gabe jerked his head toward the woman now walking arm-in-arm with Barbie. "No names, even if—*when*—you recognize someone, unless they offer them, okay? Standard procedure with the Knowles and Atwood families." He paused, cocking his head to listen—today he was wearing a very subtle earpiece, due to the greater complexities of *this* wedding. "Got it. Bringing Ruby out now, then Mama and Papa."

He held out his arm and Ruby slipped hers into it. Today, Gabe wore a dove-gray morning suit with a gray and silver waistcoat, identical to the ones that Donald, David, and Donald's best man wore. Ruby hadn't caught the name of Donald's best man, but he was one of the Knowles attendees who came with a gaggle of military uniforms tagging along behind him; hard-eyed men and women who not only were visibly armed but also took up positions around the audience, weapons in hand.

As Gabe guided her down the steps and over to the chairs set up under a big canopy covering the lawn—for security as well as sunshade—Ruby heard the buzz of both jammer drones and the dronecams that Louisa had approved. She took a deep breath, hoping she looked good on video.

The lapis and emerald-shaded dress fit her exquisitely well, and the sunshielding cape was almost like a short train. She had pulled back her hair and secured it with an emerald and pearl-framed barrette that matched the Martiniere emeralds. A gift from Gabe on their one-month anniversary. A quick look in the mirror before joining Gabe in the kitchen had revealed a Ruby that she hadn't expected to see even four months ago—an elegant scion of high society, with a little Western-style embroidery that Mark and Katrina had added to her clothing, after seeing her queen outfits.

Gabe's pistol was holstered under his jacket, and hers in a thigh holster—and she had helped Justine adjust hers. To Ruby's surprise, their dresses had built-in bulletproof vests. Gabe and the other Martiniere men wore bulletproof vests under their suits.

Not that bulletproof clothing would stop a head shot.

Ruby shivered, memory suddenly flashing back hard.

Tony Barkley had been wearing a bulletproof vest *that night*. If she hadn't aimed for her father's head instead of his body...would she be here?

Damn good thing she'd ordered Kevlar helmets with face shields, for all of them to use out riding.

"Are you all right?" Gabe asked softly.

"Just a quick memory that has nothing to do with right now," she murmured. "Old memories. Nothing Martiniere."

He patted her hand before they walked proudly down the aisle. Gabe seated Ruby next to his grandmother Donna. Gerard, David, and David's wife Therese sat by Donna. Two chairs and empty space were on Ruby's opposite side—for Gabe, Angelica and Saul.

"Quite the affair," Donna murmured. "David tells me that your ceremony was much smaller."

"We only had a few days to plan it," Ruby said.

"Ah, my dear, I wish I could stay longer. I've heard about your equestrian ability. I'd love to see you on horseback."

"Maybe when things calm down," Ruby said.

The ceremony went by quickly, almost as fast as her own wedding. Angelica sniffled and Saul set his jaw as Justine came down the aisle on Gabe's arm. Gabe took Ruby's hand after he sat down, raising it to his lips for a kiss. She smiled at him, and for a moment they were lost in each other's gaze.

Oh, she loved this man, more and more each day.

THE RANCH HOUSE WAS QUIETER THAT EVENING, WITH JUSTINE and Donald gone, along with the few house guests they had crammed into spaces around the farmhouse and in Saul and Angelica's house before the wedding.

"Hard to believe that was us only two months ago," Gabe murmured, leaning on his elbow and stroking Ruby's cheek, after they had made love. "I feel like you've been a part of me forever."

"We have gone through a lot already, haven't we?"

"I hope it's just a hectic period and not a situation where we're cramming as much as possible into a short time." He nuzzled her forehead. "I want to grow old together."

"Yeah."

Gabe took Ruby into his arms. She snuggled in close.

Remember his scent. The firmness of his touch. The brush of his cheek stubble. That occasional little purr he makes when happy and holding you.

Storing the memories of being beloved. Just in case.

THEY FLEW TO LOS ANGELES FOR THE INTERVIEWS ON TUESDAY instead of Monday, leaving before dawn, intending it to be a day trip.

"It'll be grueling to do three interviews in a day," Gabe said. "Think you can handle it?"

Ruby laughed. "I've done queen interviews and appearances stacked up like this, Gabe. I can manage it."

Louisa went with them to supervise their support team. Each interview required a change of clothing, but at least they weren't going to the house.

"One of these days, you'll get to see the LA house when it isn't all locked down," Gabe said. "It's a pretty place."

"I'd like that," Ruby said, stifling a shudder at her memories of those two nights in the LA house. Maybe she would feel different once all those steel shutters were rolled up and she could see out.

Three interviews, three different slants. The first interview was business-focused, featuring Gabe as the new leader of the Martiniere Group, talking about his goals and ambitions for the Group. The interviewer was mildly scoffing about Gabe's emphasis on climate change, and ignored Ruby. Gabe and Louisa both seethed after that one.

"I'll schedule a follow up with a different business news-magazine, probably remote," Louisa said. "We'll see how the others turn out. That can give me negotiating leverage."

The second was for a well-regarded and venerable news show. Ruby remembered watching this show as she grew up, and had to pinch herself about being featured on it. While they discussed her research as well as the Group, *this* interviewer was more interested in the dynamics of Gabe and Ruby's relationship, how they got together, and why they were currently located at the Double R.

"They tell me the focus is going to be on Ruby, possibly a segment title of 'From Rodeo Queen to Corporate Royalty,'" Louisa said after this interview. "That was a great session, Ruby. It'll be *easy* to get more interviews with you once people see this one."

Science was the unabashed focus of the third interview. Gabe took a back seat to Ruby as she explained the possibilities of the microdrone-based biobots. They hadn't come up with an easy name for them yet—Gabe liked the idea of calling them the RubyBot, but putting her name on the bots made Ruby uncomfortable.

Still, the biobots *did* come out looking blood-red.

Ruby just wasn't sure she wanted them named after her.

"Another great interview," Louisa gushed once they were back on the plane. "Gabie, it's wonderful to watch your response to Ruby as she talks. You're clearly madly in love with your wife, and proud of her. *Much* better than that first interview."

Gabe loosened his tie, grinning. "I *am* deeply in love with my dearest nerd girl, and proud of what she does."

Louisa tapped her lips. "You need to think about your opposition to naming those bots after you, Ruby. There's a significant positive response to that name. It will be easy to market."

"It's just—it reeks of hubris, I suppose." Ruby slipped her feet out of her high heels, taller than what she usually wore, and flexed her feet. Damn, she hoped to eventually transition back to loafers and low, square heels even for interviews. But these interviews had been Appearances. More importantly, First Appearances as Gabe's wife, and she had to dress appropriately—dressier than she would otherwise choose for business and lab work.

"It's an issue of branding." Louisa frowned. "And with you as the face of the RubyBot—we can take it far."

"I'll think about it," Ruby conceded.

THE REMAINDER OF THE WEEK WAS DECEPTIVELY QUIET. No incidents involving Justine and Donald. No sign of trouble from any other front.

Along with the heat and dryness at the ranch, the calmness made Ruby jumpier than usual.

"I can't explain it," she told Gabe during one of their morning rides along the lower-elevation wheat fields. "Maybe it's just that in spite of the drought, we aren't getting wildfire smoke."

"I could do without that," he said.

"Me too. But there's no rain in the forecast. The heat dome's cooked everything. A good thing the horses are barefoot and not shod because I'd be worried about riding out right now—steel shoe against a rock might cast a spark. The slightest thing could start a fire." She sighed and brushed a trickle of sweat out of her eyes. "If it wasn't that we'd get a thunderstorm with any system that brings rain right now, I'd be thrilled to see one."

"Mm, it's probably the weather getting on your nerves," Gabe said.

Gabe was probably right.

And yet—Ruby couldn't banish that sense of dread clutching at her. Philip had been *too damn quiet,* and she didn't think her last email would have been enough to discourage him.

No. He was up to something.

Question was, what?

"Miranda has been kidnapped," Piotr said during his morning video briefing the following Monday. "And Joseph has gone missing."

Gabe and Ruby exchanged glances. Then Gabe pinched the bridge of his nose. "Is Joey's disappearance a willing or unwilling one?"

"He was not under restraint the last time we saw him, but he was in the company of those associated with Vera Braun's —connections."

"*Shit.*" Gabe exhaled. "We'd better consider this to be connected to Mindy."

After they finished talking to Piotr, Gabe shook his head.

"Damn foolish cousin," he muttered. "I'd be willing to bet that Mindy was used to lure Joey out of hiding."

Ruby clenched her fists. "I knew things were too quiet."

Gabe eyed her. "I know you like getting out to ride. Should we stick to the arena instead of riding the fields for the next week or two?"

"If we don't go out—that means bringing the threat in closer."

"To your grandparents. To Mama and Papa. I know, Rubes." Gabe rose and paced the room. "You can improve our security when we ride?"

"Yes. School the warmbloods in the arena, for one thing. Ride the ranch horses when we leave the main place. They're accustomed to Western saddles with rifle scabbards."

His mouth quirked. "No more cross-country course for a while, then."

"Not over the fences, anyway."

"All right. We'll try that for a while."

RUBY PULLED REMY ASIDE THAT EVENING. "CAN I BORROW Beauty for morning rides? Not for long—just a week or so."

Remy arched a brow. "What's going on, Ruby?"

"More potential threats," she said. "I did cowboy mounted shooting off of Beauty. I want to be on a horse that I can shoot from without worrying about it freaking out and running away, or bucking."

"Beauty's the right one, then. No problem, go on ahead. Are things getting worse, Ruby?"

"Possibly."

Gabe called to her from the top of the stairs. "Ruby. I have to show you something—*now*."

The urgent tone in his voice sent her racing up the stairs. Gabe's face was tight and grim when she reached him. He guided her into their office.

"Jorge and five other Saldivars are dead," he said flatly. "They staged an attack on Philip, in Missouri."

"Oh God." That was close. *Too* close.

"Vera Braun sent these pictures." He guided her to his desk. "Don't look at the pictures, look at the captions. The last one."

Ruby skimmed the pictures anyway, her gut roiling at the gore. She cringed when she recognized Miranda and Joey's bodies.

The last picture was a duplicate of the goriest picture of Miranda and Joey, with YOU'RE NEXT in a maroon, dripping script that emulated blood splatter.

Their gazes met.

"Here we go," Gabe said. "Are you ready, Ruby?"

She nodded. "As ready as I'll ever be."

That night, when they made love, she wondered if it would be for the last time.

Both she and Gabe slept restlessly, rousing each other from nightmares.

GABE

He *almost* wanted to skip riding that morning. Just grab hold of Ruby and hide from the world as long as possible. Then Ruby popped out of bed, standing in the middle of their bedroom with a worried expression, sniffing hard. Something was wrong, and that awareness wiped the desire to hide right out of his thoughts.

She tilted her head, sniffing again.

"Do you smell smoke, Gabe?"

Fire.

They had discussed evacuation procedures with Ron and security. Reviewed them over and over as the summer grew drier. He had hoped they never needed to implement them, because wildfire—

Gabe inhaled, trying to identify what he scented. Maybe the faintest hint of smoke, but no—it drifted away.

"Not really."

Her lips tightened. "Maybe it's just my imagination, or the wind's bringing in some smoke from that new wildfire to the south."

There had been a late-night fire report on Ruby's monitoring app, close enough for her to rouse Ron and have a quick talk with him. They had decided it wasn't of sufficient concern to bother his parents.

"Maybe that's it," he said.

Ruby pulled on her bulletproof, lightweight safety vest—part of a set she had bought several weeks ago, for them to wear in place of their air vests while riding beyond the main ranch buildings. Then she put on jeans. "I'll feel better when I get some eyeballs on what's around us." She added a t-shirt to her outfit, threaded a belt with her holstered pistol through her jean belt loops, then finished with a loose-fitting, long-sleeved shirt.

"Who are we riding today?" Gabe put his vest on, then the rest of his clothing—jeans, a t-shirt, belt with holster and pistol, and an over-shirt, like Ruby.

"I'm borrowing Beauty from Remy. She's been hunted from, doesn't flinch at gunfire. You should take Blaze. He's also an experienced hunting horse. Cody's not so cooperative. And we'll wear the new helmets." Ruby sat at her vanity and twisted her hair into a bun, pinning it in place, low enough not to interfere with helmet fit. Something she did every day, but for some reason Gabe noticed everything she was doing this morning. Foreboding tightened his gut.

"Those helmets aren't going to be much protection if someone shoots at us."

"The new ones are Kevlar. I checked with security before I bought them." Her voice was flat as she slid in the last hairpin and turned to face him. "Less of an exposure. Still have vulnerable parts of the body, but at least we have body mass covered and *some* head protection."

Kevlar helmets. Bulletproof safety vests to replace the air vests they had been using for protection in case of falls. Damn. His dearest nerd girl had been thinking ahead, for certain. He'd known about the vests but not the helmets.

"I wouldn't have thought of these possibilities. Thank you for doing that."

Her expression remained solemn. "My father wore a bulletproof vest but no head protection when he killed my mother. If he had been wearing head protection—I might not be here. After what happened to Saul—"

"Oh God, Rubes." No wonder she had been considering such things.

"I'm not giving up without a fight," she murmured. "Nor am I letting our lives become even more restricted than they already are."

That gave Gabe the shivers, because he remembered Saul saying something very similar, before he was shot.

Please let this turn out differently.

Just because he had warned Ruby of the likelihood that he wouldn't survive a year, didn't mean he wanted it to be true.

———

THEY SLUNG THE SPA2 RIFLES OVER THEIR SHOULDERS BEFORE catching the horses. Midnight came up to Gabe, begging for a treat, clearly confused when Gabe gave him a horse cookie, then bypassed him to halter Blaze.

"Sorry, fella," he said to the big gelding. "Realities. Things are changing."

"We'll ride them in the arena this evening," Ruby said.

There was a stronger scent of smoke in the air as they led the horses to the barn, and the sun just peeking over the horizon glowed eerily red. Ruby squinted to the south.

"Seems heavier over there." She sighed. "In the wilderness. And there's a big fire to the east of us. Hundred miles away so we're safe, but it really mixes things up."

"There wasn't anything yesterday." It felt weird to groom Blaze— the sorrel gelding was much shorter than Midnight, and wasn't as interactive.

"Fires can blow up fast overnight, especially in these conditions."

When they were done tacking, Gabe sheathed his SPA2 in the

scabbard. To his surprise, Ruby slung hers over her shoulder. He started to comment, then shrugged.

She had more experience riding with weaponry. It wouldn't hurt for one of them to be ready to shoot. Just in case.

Ruby snapped her face shield into place before mounting. After a moment's consideration, Gabe did the same.

Even with the jammer drones buzzing around them, this didn't feel safe.

Should he insist they stay in the arena?

No.

He felt constricted and confined when they didn't ride out.

USUALLY, THEY BANTERED AND JOKED THROUGH THE MORNING ride. Not today. Ruby urged Beauty ahead of Blaze, sitting tense and tall in her saddle, one hand on the continuous rein—roping rein, she called it—the other on her rifle's sling. The palomino mare picked up on her nerves, her head high, ears flicking back and forth.

Then Beauty stopped sharply, nostrils flaring wide in a series of deep roller warning snorts. She looked up the steep slope to their right, ears pricked forward. This little rim divided Draw and Homestead from the lower fields, a rocky point that descended from the junction of the two bigger ridges that defined the main canyon which held the ranch.

"I'm going up to look around," Ruby said. "You stay here. Something's moving nearby, and Beauty's been telling me about it. Might just be wildlife, but—

"Are you going to be safe? If someone takes a shot at you—"

"Give them one target instead of two. Beauty's younger than Blaze and more sure-footed. We can move faster." Ruby turned Beauty toward the slope and clucked. The golden mare angled up the slope. Ruby draped the rein over the saddle horn and bent low over the mare's neck, rifle now in both hands.

Not a new thing for her.

Habits gained from hunting, or a remnant from those years of being harassed by her father's family?

Blaze, docile until now, shifted uneasily under Gabe, fussing and refusing to stand still as Beauty climbed away from them.

"Quit!" Gabe snapped softly, taking up the slack in the reins. He used both hands—more familiar to him than neck-reining.

Blaze danced around, whirling to face back toward the ranch.

Wisps of smoke rising, then the flicker of flame—

"*Fire!*" Gabe bellowed at Ruby, as loud as he could. "Between us and the ranch!"

Somehow Ruby managed to turn Beauty on the steep slope. "It's just getting started—but how?"

"I'm checking it!" Blaze bolted forward at Gabe's cue.

"*Gabe! Don't—*"

The sharp crack of rifle fire sounded simultaneously with a hard *whump!* on his left shoulder that knocked the breath out of him. It struck him off-balance as he gasped, shock racing through him and turning everything into a blur. A second shot smacked his helmet. That stunned him enough that he lost grip of Blaze's reins, and his balance went awry.

Gabe fell hard, still struggling for air as even more agony lanced through him, and things went black.

Consciousness returned quickly. He had landed on his side and his right leg hurt, along with his right elbow. Distant voices.

"Where the hell did that bitch go?"

Philip.

Gabe fumbled as best as he could for his pistol, blinking to clear his vision.

Where is he?

"I got a shot off but I can't see her or her horse now."

Vera Braun.

God damn it, how the hell did they get past security?

There. Vision blurry but he saw Philip, carrying a rifle—close enough for his pistol to be effective, or out of range? Damn it, his right hand wouldn't hold steady—

Philip aimed. Gabe aimed. They fired simultaneously. Pain lanced through his forearm and he dropped the pistol, bellowing with pain.

"Got you now, you *ignorant sprog!*" Philip sneered. "You are going to die slowly and painfully, dumbass! And the fire will take out your precious parents!"

Gabe fumbled for the pistol with his left hand as Philip marched toward him, rolling forward to present helmet and protected chest to Philip—another shot from a different angle got his left leg—he yelled.

"Score!" Vera Braun crowed.

Fuck. Braun was in a position to hit his unprotected legs—Gabe screamed as a second shot hit his left knee.

Fuck. Fuck. Fuck. He gasped for breath, feeling light-headed— had those shots severed crucial veins or arteries? Or was this shock from being shot?

Where is Ruby? Oh God, has she been hit?

Philip shot again. It hit Gabe's helmet and careened off. He fired again, hitting Gabe in his left shoulder. The impact rocked Gabe onto his back.

"Save your ammo until you're closer, Philip, he's got protect—" Another shot cut Vera's voice off, followed by two more in quick succession.

Ruby? Oh God, he hoped she was the shooter, and not the target.

Gabe shakily raised his pistol with his left hand, blinking hard to focus on Philip, now gazing off to the side, where Vera's voice had come from, not at him—

He fired. Missed. Philip whirled and raised his rifle. Gabe fired a second shot—missed *again, damn it*—

Philip fired. Gabe bellowed as this shot slammed into his unprotected upper left arm. Fighting for breath, struggling against agony in legs and arms, oh God, he had to be losing a lot of blood—

Hoofbeats of a galloping horse. Gabe blinked through blurry vision as the golden mare bore down on Philip, rider slumped against her neck, red glimmering against her pale blue overshirt—

Philip raised his rifle as Ruby fired her pistol. He yelled. Then Ruby was off the golden mare, tackling Philip—gunshot as his rifle was knocked free—Beauty galloped hard past Gabe, her flank bloody —Ruby and Philip wrestling for her pistol—another shot—Ruby screaming—Philip crowing with jubilation—God, he *had* to find some means to help, even though the world was going gray around him, but he *just couldn't move.*

Succession of shots. Panting as someone staggered toward him.

"Rubes?" he croaked, hoping it was *her* and not *Philip.* Everything was so damn fuzzy and he couldn't keep his eyes open.

We never made it to Paris. Never had our honeymoon. Never—

"Gabe? Oh *God,* Gabe!"

Ruby's voice, thank God. He forced his heavy eyelids up—Ruby pale, blood smeared across her face—*alive.*

"Don't you fucking die on me, Gabriel!" she screamed.

"Rubes," he moaned. So hard to speak. So hard to breathe. "Love."

"*Don't die,* God damn it. *Don't die.* Help is on the way."

He clutched at her as best as he could with the one hand that could still grip, struggled to breathe, wanted to wipe the tears rolling down her cheeks but couldn't move—

The last thing he was aware of before everything went dark was Ruby sobbing, moaning, calling his name over and over again.

FUZZINESS. PAIN. UNABLE TO MOVE ARMS AND LEGS. EYELIDS AS heavy as before.

"Ruby?" His throat hurt.

No answer.

"*Ruby!*" He tried to scream but the agony in his throat made it little more than a scratchy murmur.

Soothing voice suddenly present, familiar hands *but they weren't Ruby's.*

Then warmth spread through him and the world went gray and narrow again.

So tired. So very tired.

SEVERAL OTHER BLURRED, FUZZY AWAKENINGS. GABE SLOWLY became more aware of the world around him. He was in a hospital room, arms and legs bandaged, splints on his legs.

Sometimes his mother was there. Sometimes Louisa.

But no Ruby—had he hallucinated that last faint vision of her taking him into her arms, screaming at him not to die?

THIS TIME EVERYTHING WAS CLEARER AROUND HIM. GABE blinked, surprised as the world fell into focus. Smoke obscured the Thunder Mountains outside the window on his left side, curtains drawn back. No one sitting there.

He turned his head, steeling himself to see Louisa or his mother.

Instead, Ruby sat in a wheelchair next to his bed, her left leg propped up, splints around her knee, gazing at her tablet.

He tried to reach for her but it *hurt.* He moaned.

Ruby startled. She put her tablet on the bed tray in front of her.

"Don't say anything just yet, Gabe."

She let down the bed rail, then reached for a cup with a spoon in it that sat on the bed tray. Scooping up a few crystals, she leaned over and spooned the ice into his mouth.

The cold soothed his throat and he realized this wasn't the first time that someone had been feeding him ice chips. He eyed Ruby. Bandages on one arm, *that leg,* face bruised.

But his dearest nerd girl was *alive.* And so was he.

"Drink." Ruby held the cup to his lips.

He swallowed and coughed. Maybe he could speak.

"I love you," he murmured. Tried again to reach for her face but groaned as the movement sent waves of agony through him.

A pained smile tightened Ruby's face. She rested her hand on his arm. "Don't. Gunshot wounds to both arms, mild fracture of this one —it'll heal all right."

"What else?" At least he could speak, but the scratchiness in his throat suggested he shouldn't say much.

Ruby blinked. A tear trickled down her cheek. "You almost bled out. Braun's shots to your legs—" she sniffled and wiped her eyes with a wrist. "Severed an artery. And—knee's shot to hell, possibly a knee replacement in your immediate future. Ribs broken. Concussion— mild. Smoke inhalation."

"You?"

"Broken ribs. Shot in one arm, thankfully a flesh wound. Knee— still up in the air. May also need replacement. Bruised as hell. Smoke inhalation."

"You were amazing," he whispered. "I was useless."

"Like hell you were useless. They were so focused on hurting you that I was able to take Braun out, then ride down on Philip. After sending an emergency broadcast text."

"Amazing," he repeated.

She shrugged, then winced, hissing sharply through her teeth. He flinched along with her. Ruby exhaled. "Braun stopped shooting at me when you pulled that pistol on Philip. It kept them distracted. That's hardly *useless,* Gabriel."

"In custody?"

"They're dead. We damn near died in the fire they set before help could reach us." She choked, blinking hard. "Three shots to Vera Braun. By then I'd sent the emergency text. I—*hoped* the shots would help pinpoint our location on the other side of the fire from any help. Then I dropped the SPA2, grabbed my pistol, and rode Philip down. Straight at him. Got one shot off. Beauty was wonderful, didn't shy at all, did everything just *perfect*." She gulped.

"Rubes. You don't have to—"

"I *need* to. He got my knee, but I shot him dead. In the face. Just like—" She broke into tears and he groaned, regretting that he couldn't take her into his arms. Ruby smiled at him through sobs and slipped her hand into his, gulping until she could speak again. "I shot him until the pistol was empty. And then dragged myself over to you, barely able to walk. The blood. So damned much blood."

At least he was able to move his thumb, stroke her palm. "Rubes. So fucking sorry. Should never have put you through this."

"*Stop it*, Gabriel." More gulps. "We're *alive*, damn it, and we're *together*." She leaned over as far as she could and rested her cheek on his hand. "And now we have a future. Of sorts."

RUBY

"I promised you Paris, and here we are." Gabe kissed Ruby's temple.

She cuddled with Gabe on the loveseat angled in front of the privacy-shaded big windows that looked out upon the Parisian night sky. They had showered after their flight, donning heavy bathrobes to stay warm before going to bed. Ruby's hand rested on Gabe's bare chest as she watched the lights of the Eiffel Tower. Jet lag even after a nap during today's flight demanded that she should fall asleep soon, but she was mesmerized by the lights.

Paris. We're really in Paris.

"Not too shabby. I didn't realize we rated a separate penthouse, with multiple suites," she finally said.

"Oh, these are the Martiniere's regular quarters in the Hôtel Martiniere." He pushed a loose strand of hair away from her cheek. "Mama and Papa will have their own penthouse junior suite; same for your grandparents when they arrive."

"This is so modern compared to the rest of the—" she waved her hand— "place."

Place? This was a monster mansion. *Huge.* A palace, even. It fit Gabe's tales of the Martiniere descent from old French and Italian nobility.

"Louis and Donna added the penthouse in the early '90s, when the feud between Saul and Philip heated up. The penthouse was supposed to isolate their fights from the rest of the Family. I don't know the whole story behind it. I don't know if any of us ever will. Not unless Donna-gran decides to tell it, and I don't think she wants to. Nor does Saul. Let dead Philips lie."

Ruby exhaled. She was all for *letting dead Philips lie.* He came to life often enough in the nightmares that still plagued both her and Gabe.

Gabe placed little kisses on her temple. Then they sat quietly together.

They had spent nearly four months in Los Angeles after the showdown with Philip. Their injuries—and the support needed for their recoveries—forced the relocation to the Los Angeles house. Knee replacement for her and for Gabe. Mutual, intensive physical therapy, both of them working hard enough to earn discharge to less-intensive rehabilitation just a few weeks ago.

Legal issues tied to the assassinations and her killing of Vera Braun and Philip Martiniere.

She had missed fall term as a result.

Did that matter anymore?

Once she and Gabe resumed their responsibilities in late October, Ruby hadn't been certain about whether she wanted to pick up her studies right away. She *should* get in touch with Linda, but given the atmosphere that had caused her and Gabe to flee the United States, Ruby wasn't certain that was a good idea. Linda's brother-in-law Clyde Newsome was foremost amongst the politicians calling for further prosecution of her and Gabe.

Besides, the RubyBots—oh, she had yielded to Louisa's persuasion and agreed to that name—that survived the ranch fire had performed well. Cousin Arthur wanted her on site to begin the RubyBot Martiniere development program in the French labs after the New Year.

Degree or actual application work?

As if that was really a choice. *Actual application work.* Always.

And after that?

Ruby didn't know—yet. Nor did she know where they would be.

She missed her mountains and her horses, but a panic attack during a ranch visit ruled out staying at the Double R. Midnight and Sunshine now lived at Justine and Donald's Mist Knoll. At some point, she wanted to ride again.

But where would that be?

Gabe squeezed her. "You're awfully quiet."

"Just wondering where to go from here. About the horses. Where we'll live."

"We could return to Corvallis once Artie's happy with the Ruby-Bots. Get you signed up for spring term. Stay with Tine and Don."

She gave him a stern look. "They're expecting a baby. They don't need us underfoot. Even in a separate wing. Barbie and the other Atwoods will be enough for them to deal with."

"We could stay here. You could transfer credits to the University of Paris and probably graduate this fall. I could resume my master's program—"

"And just when would you have time to do that, *Gabriel?*" she scolded. "You'd work yourself to death as the Martiniere if I didn't keep a tight rein on you." She sighed. "Then there's the horses."

"Bring them here." He kissed her temple again. "What do you think about the University of Paris option? It's quite doable, and it *is* close to the work we should be doing next spring."

Ruby contemplated the prospect. "We can bring the horses over?"

"Absolutely. It won't be like having them in the back yard, like at the ranch or Mist Knoll, but it can be done." Gabe chuckled.

"Although, come to think of it, there's a hereditary property near the Bois de Boulogne. We could live there for a while. I'd like that."

"*How* hereditary is it?" She had learned enough about Martiniere history to ask *that* question.

"Oh, it goes back to Aunt Marguerite. Not the entire property she held, alas."

"Aunt Marguerite?"

"De Valois." He smirked at her. "Daughter of Catherine de Medici. Sister to several French kings, wife to another. Not a direct line ancestress, since we're a bastard line from her brother Charles. But when the property came up for sale one hundred and fifty years ago, the Martiniere of that era bought one of the sections. It's a nice horse property—Donna-gran and Louis lived there until he became the Martiniere, and she stabled horses there before relocating to Quebec."

Ruby bit her lip, thinking about it.

"What do you think?" Gabe finally asked.

She smiled up at him. "University of Paris. Living in a French chateau. Am I dreaming?"

"If you are, it's a dream we're sharing." Gabe kissed her again, long and lingering. "We Martinieres no longer have ambitions to rule France, but you—you are definitely the queen of my heart. If this sounds good—"

"Yes," she murmured.

It seemed unbelievable. If anyone had told her last year that she would be married to Gabriel Martiniere, contemplating life in France —she wouldn't have believed it.

But it was true. All of it.

It was a different life from what she had ever anticipated. And oh, the prospects ahead seemed to be so sweet.

"Have you ever thought about how things might have been different? If we had never met—like if that plane had blown up with your family, when you were twelve?"

Gabe shivered. "God forbid that would have happened. Me

spending six years under Philip's thumb, with him as the Martiniere? Oh, that would have been a mess. And ugly." He kissed her forehead. "We would have found a way to get together. Somehow. Even if it meant that I first met you as someone other than Gabriel Martiniere —because I don't think I would have lasted with the Family as myself, in that reality. Sooner or later, I would have taken Philip down. Or tried, at least—and there would have been consequences forcing me out of the Family."

"Do you think we were fated to be together?"

"My dearest nerd girl, I *can't* imagine anyone other than you to be the queen of my heart. In any reality. Temporary substitutes? Possibly. But sooner or later, I would have found my redheaded rodeo queen, and together, we would have brought Philip down. That's what I believe."

Ruby laughed. "You say it strongly enough that I believe it."

"I know just enough quantum and multiverse theory to be dangerous." He kissed her. "Because I think one constant, in any universe you and I are in, is that Ruby Barkley and Gabriel Martiniere are a couple, and unite to defeat Philip Martiniere. And nothing will ever change my mind about that. *Nothing*."

"So we're a constant across universes, hmm?" A yawn escaped her.

"Yes. And now this constant pair needs to get ourselves to bed. Tomorrow is a very busy day."

Arms around each other, they meandered off to bed.

As she snuggled into Gabe, Ruby thought about what he had said.

She found it reassuring.

Even if it was fanciful.

Or was it?

THE END

NEWSLETTER

Like what you've read? Want to follow Joyce either through her monthly newsletter or through an email feed of her irregular blog posts?

Sign up for Joyce's newsletter here:

https://tinyletter.com/JoyceReynolds-Ward

Or follow Joyce's irregular blog posts on her Substack, here:

https://joycereynoldsward.substack.com/

Interested in a different one of Joyce's universes? Check out Martiniere Stories on Substack.

https://joycef1d.substack.com/p/an-introduction-to-martiniere-stories

BOOKS AND PUBLICATIONS

The Martiniere Legacy

First Meetings: A Martiniere Legacy Short Story

Inheritance: The Martiniere Legacy Book One

Ascendant: The Martiniere Legacy Book Two

Realization: The Martiniere Legacy Book Three

A Belated Christmas Honeymoon: A Martiniere Legacy Short Story

The Enduring Legacy: The Martiniere Legacy Book Four

The People of the Martiniere Legacy

The Heritage of Michael Martiniere: An Agripunk Thriller

Broken Angel: The Lost Years of Gabriel Martiniere: An Agripunk Thriller

Justine Fixes Everything: Reflections on Mortality: An Agripunk Thriller

The Martiniere Multiverse Books

A Different Life—What If?

A Different Life—Linda's Story (Release Date—Fall 2022, currently serializing on Vella)

Dreamwalker: Gabriel (to be determined)
The Cost of Power (to be determined)

Goddess's Honor titles currently available (chronological order):

The Goddess's Choice: A Goddess's Honor Short Story
Beyond Honor: A Goddess's Honor Novella
Exile's Honor: A Goddess's Honor Novelette
Birth of Sorrow: A Goddess's Honor Short Story
Pledges of Honor: Goddess's Honor Book One
Return to Wickmasa: A Goddess's Honor Short Story
Crown Anniversary: A Goddess's Honor Short Story
Challenges of Honor: Goddess's Honor Book Two
Cleaning House: A Goddess's Honor Outtake Story
Unexpected Alliances: A Goddess's Honor Rough Draft Outtake Story
Choices of Honor: Goddess's Honor Book Three
Judgment of Honor: Goddess's Honor Book Four

Netwalk Sequence Author Preferred 2022 Editions

Life in the Shadows: Book One
Netwalk: Book Two
Netwalker Uprising: Book Three
Netwalk's Children: Book Four
Learning in Space: Book Five
Netwalking Space: Book Six

Bright Star Fair Witches

Becoming Solo: A Bright Star Fair Witches Novella

Non-Series Titles currently available:

Alien Savvy: A Western SF Novella
Klone's Stronghold
Beating the Apocalypse

Vella Titles:

Falcon of the Martinieres (part of *Justine Fixes Everything*)

Bearing Witness

Beating the Apocalypse

A Different Life—What If? An Alternative Martiniere Legacy Novel

Becoming Solo

A Different Life—Linda's Story: An Alternative Martiniere Legacy Novel

Audiobooks Available:

Alien Savvy: A Western SF Novella

Released from other publishers:

"Queen of the Snows," in *Once Upon A Winter: A Folk and Fairy Tale Anthology*, edited by H. L. Macfarlane

"My Man Left Me, My Dog Hates Me, and There Goes My Truck," in *Black-Eyed Peas on New Year's Day: An Anthology of Hope*, edited by Shannon Page

"Lost Loves," in *All Worlds Wayfarer*

"The Wisdom of Robins," in *Whimsical Beasts: A Campcon Anthology*, edited by Joyce Reynolds-Ward

"The Cow at the End of the World," in *Well...It's Your Cow*, edited by Frog Jones

"To Plant or Pull Up Stakes," in *Pulling Up Stakes: A Campcon Anthology*, edited by Joyce Reynolds-Ward

"The Notice," in *Children of a Different Sky*, edited by Alma Alexander

ABOUT THE AUTHOR

Joyce Reynolds-Ward has been called "the best writer I've never heard of" by one reviewer. Her work includes themes of high-stakes family and political conflict, digital sentience, personal agency and control, realistic strong women, and (whenever possible) horses. She is the author of *The Netwalk Sequence* series, the *Goddess's Honor* series, and the recently released *The Martiniere Legacy* series as well as standalones *Klone's Stronghold, Alien Savvy,* and *Beating the Apocalypse.* Samples of her Martiniere short stories/novel in progress and her nonfiction can be found on Substack at either Speculations from the Wide Open Spaces (general, writing) or Martiniere Stories (fiction). Joyce is a Self-Published Fantasy BlogOff Semifinalist, a Writers of the Future SemiFinalist, and an Anthology Builder Finalist. She is the Secretary of the Northwest Independent Writers Association, a member of the Science Fiction and Fantasy Writers Association, and a member of Soroptimists International.

facebook.com/authorjoycerw

twitter.com/JoyceReynoldsW1

instagram.com/jreynoldsward